Suicide Supper Club

Suicide Supper Club

Rhett DeVane

Writers4Higher
writers hold the key to change

Suicide Supper Club
© 2014 Rhett DeVane
All rights reserved

Date of first publication: February 2014
Published by Writers4Higher
Tallahassee, Florida

Cover photograph by Rhett DeVane
Used by permission from Bella Bella, Tallahassee, Florida

Cover design by Elizabeth Babski, Babski Creative Studios

ISBN: 978-0615863306

Library of Congress Control Number: 2014932949

Printed in the United States of America

Dedication

To the Wild Women Writers critique group, and to all of my writing buddies that spent endless hours helping me sound better on paper. Couldn't be my best without you!

Acknowledgements

Rhett wishes to thank the following people:

My family. For not disowning me. For knowing authors are, at best, a little crazy. To Denise Fletcher and the entire Fletcher gang for their continued love and support.

To Amy and Marc and the gang at Bella Bella! Food good enough to choose for your favorite meal.

The city of Chattahoochee, Florida, for being such a wonderful hometown. Can't think of a better setting for a gathering of novels. My characters are fortunate to "live" there.

The Wild Women Writers Critique authors—Donna Meredith, Peggy Kassees, Susan Womble, and Hannah Mahler.

Tallahassee Writers Association: a group of the most supportive fellow writers on the planet.

Editor Paul Kiger for her careful work. Elizabeth Babski for her graphic design excellence.

Fellow author and friend Roberta Burton, for aiding me with revisions and helping me maintain my sanity.

Law enforcement experts Kathy Kennedy and Kelly Walker.

Medical/nursing information experts Mary Menard, RN, and Dianne Sutherland, RN.

Dr. Bill Cooke, best boss in the world and expert on guns and ammo, and fast cars.

My coworkers for attending book functions and listening to me either whoop or whine. What an amazing group of people!

My network of old and new friends, near and far.

My patients—bless your hearts; you have been there every step of this journey.

And to this universe for allowing me to create. Being a writer is equal parts blessing and curse. But worth it, oh my, worth it.

Chapter One

Nine weeks before suicide
Monday

Sheila Bruner scattered scouring powder liberally around the kitchen faucet and attacked it with a used toothbrush. Mold—the enemy. Given an ounce of opportunity, it grew in every crevice. Like fear.

"Not in my kitchen. Not in this house." She bore down so hard, the skin around her knuckles blanched. The ranch-style brick house wasn't large, less than thirteen hundred square feet. But every inch had to sparkle. Had to. Had to!

The white powder turned to sea green paste. What would happen if someone swallowed it? Just a little. In a tumbler of Jack Daniels. Mixed in the cheese grits. Would the taste scream murder? Or would plunging a butcher knife deep into his heart, twisting it to make sure . . . "Stop it! Stop it!" She pinched the skin on one wrist to break the thought, just like she had read in a self-help book.

Sheila ran through the cleaning schedule, spoken aloud. "Monday. Kitchen. Wipe down the refrigerator, bleach the countertops, organize the drawers, put out fresh towels, sanitize the garbage can, mop the floor, and clean the oven. Vacuum. Make dips and appetizers for Glenn's poker night."

She sprayed diluted bleach on a rag and attacked the countertops.

"Tuesday, Bathrooms. Wednesday, Laundry." The recitation evoked its magic. A sense of calm bathed her.

Bleach vapor stung her nose and eyes. Once, she had ended up at the clinic with a raspy cough and seared throat from the fumes. Glenn had given her a ration of grief, clamped down on her forearm until her fingers tingled and went numb. "Run off to the doctor every g-d time you break a nail, Sheila. Waste my good money."

She overreached to wipe the top of the refrigerator and white-hot pain stabbed her. Grab the door handle to keep from crumbling to the floor. Breathe, Shelia, breathe. Panting came easier; deep inhalations made the throbbing in her side worse. Two short steps and she made it to the kitchen table and lowered herself inch by inch to a chair. Cold sweat chilled her skin and her stomach threatened to eject the dry toast she'd had for breakfast.

Mashed potatoes. Such an easy dish, yet she couldn't quite get them right. Too many lumps and Glenn complained about her carelessness. Too smooth and he accused her of using instant potato flakes. Like his mother's recipe, the end product had to contain a few pea-sized pieces of cooked potato, yet remain creamy. The balance defied her.

"You tried to trick me into eating this fake shit, didn't you darlin'," Glenn had said in a low voice. His words oozed out with a creepy smile.

"I'm sorry. I tried to get them like you wanted." She turned to retrieve the bowl and mashing utensil to prove her innocence. Glenn shoved her—one of his "playful pushes"—and she teetered on one foot. Most of the time, she could regain her balance. This time, her heel had caught on the edge of the rug and she bashed her midsection on the corner of the buffet cabinet on the way down. Clumsy dumb cow.

The wall phone taunted her from its mount only a few feet away. She'd rest, then call for help. Right. Like she could call 911, or even her doctor. Those medical people would take one look at the black bruises coloring her waist and the older purpling abrasion above her eye, and they'd ask prying questions. She could call Loiscell. No. Not her either. Loiscell already looked at her as if she suspected.

Nothing seemed to be broken when she had first assessed the injuries in the bathroom, late last night after Glenn passed out. Had to be a cracked rib, the way it hurt to inhale. No use seeing the doctor. What could a physician do for her that she couldn't do for herself? If only she had been able to go to nursing school, she'd know exactly what to do now.

When the ache subsided to a dull pulse, Sheila rose and shuffled to the bathroom. None of the Ace bandages she found in the cabinet were long or wide enough. Wait . . . sheets! Didn't they once use them to make bandages for soldiers? She cut long strips of an old pastel sheet and wrapped them around her middle, over and over, then popped four aspirins. Time would heal. Always did.

Images perked in her head. A neck artery spurting blood. Foaming poison bubbles between pale lips. Sheila hugged herself and hummed "Jesus Loves Me" to plug the flow. Murder, even imagined murder, was wrong. God wouldn't love her. She would burn in Hell for eternity.

Abrasive cleaner floured the air over the kitchen sink. Muscles flexed in her forearm as she bore down with a stiff brush, reviewing the list for Thursday and Friday.

She clamped her teeth together until one of the molars complained. No! Relax your jaw. What good will a broken filling do? More of Glenn's money down the drain.

Sheila caught her distorted reflection in the microwave's glass door. The bruise around her right eye had faded a little. A spritz of vinegar and ammonia bled her image into long pungent ripples.

"Saturday. Volunteer meetings, Woman's Club, visits to shut-ins. Baking. Sunday. Church. Cook dinner. Bible study."

Sometimes—like today—Sheila visited her one friend Loiscell Pickering. At sixty-two, Loiscell was twenty-three years Sheila's senior. The women had met when Sheila brought chicken soup to Loiscell following her second breast cancer surgery. Sheila arrived, ready in her role of Christian Ladies' outreach to the infirm, only to be rewarded by the older woman's uplifting attitude. For the next three months as Loiscell struggled through rounds of chemotherapy and radiation, Sheila spent as much time as her schedule and Glenn would allow. But then, Glenn approved of her church work, of his wife's compassion toward the community. He might be chosen as a deacon soon!

After she stowed the cleaning supplies, Sheila removed her mummy casing and showered, shaving long careful strips on her legs and armpits, then her forearms. Her side ached with every movement. Did those fine golden hairs really need to go? Like baby fuzz, really. But Glenn hated hairy women.

Wrapped in a fluffy pink chenille robe, she surveyed her side of the master bedroom closet. No bright colors. Only pastels. Women should wear feminine, flowery prints, and always dresses. One black skirt suit for funerals. A few sensible pumps and low-heeled sandals. A pair of sneakers, bright white and barely used.

Sheila pulled out white mule sandals and a pale yellow sleeveless dress. Since she'd lost weight, the dress hung on her frame—perfect, to accommodate the extra padding of the sheet strips. The buttery hue suited her hair when the blonde highlights were fresh. Otherwise, it at least added a little life to her white skin and dirty dishwater locks. What she truly longed for was a yellow print that screamed hello. Or hot pink or pistachio green.

Before leaving the house, she stepped onto the back porch with a clean pottery bowl in hand. "Buttercup! Come on, sugar!"

A small golden tiger-striped cat slipped from beneath the hedge where Sheila had hidden a plastic bin she'd fashioned into a covered bed. It mewed and twirled circles at her feet. Careful to lower herself to a crouch without bending her back, Sheila scooped it up with one hand and cradled the tiny face to hers. Glenn hated animals, except the ones he could kill and eat. No animal would set foot inside *his* house.

Glenn rarely ventured outside. The lawn care was hired. Each day after work, her husband came in, ate, belched, farted, and settled down with the remote. By the time the six o'clock news finished, her husband was on his third or fourth beer. On the bad days, Jack Daniels Black.

But what if Glenn broke that pattern? Sheila held Buttercup close to her heart. What if he stepped outside and the innocent kitty thought it was her? She pictured Glenn's calloused hands around its furry neck. Squeeze and twist. Wouldn't take much.

Buttercup was her secret.

She fed the little cat. It purred and ate at the same time.

If only happiness was as simple for people.

Abby McKenzie scowled at her fogged reflection in the cracked bathroom mirror. "Just do freaking something, for once!" She could stand on her head to blow-dry her hair or use a curling iron until the ends scorched or slather on hair fixative products. No matter, her mousebrown hair would sponge up humidity and straighten like a bird dog's tail.

If her hair didn't do right, how could the day do right? Or heck, how could her life do right?

"Talking to myself does not make me crazy. And if it does, what better place to be than where I live, a town with a state mental institution right on the main drag."

She looked deep into her own eyes—pale green with flecks of gold. What if she didn't wake up, some Monday morning? End of bad hair, end of mind-numbing routines. Just delightful nothingness. Abby stopped herself. Hell awaited people who dismissed life so easily, right?

Maybe her life *was* hell. Maybe that was the ultimate cosmic joke. The big bamboozle secret. You arrived one morning, somewhere in your forties, and nobody rolled out a black welcome carpet. No horns blasted. Abby McKenzie, welcome to your private Hades condo. Grab a pitchfork, dahlin'. Get to work.

She shook her head. Stuck out her tongue. So did her mirror image, the rude thing. Nope. Couldn't be true hell. Not *her* life. If this was hell, she'd at least have some company.

Abby added a third spritz of guaranteed-to-hold gel spray, grabbed her purse, and dashed to the kitchen to add her coffee mug to the unwashed breakfast dishes. She wove her way to the back door through a narrow path, past teetering stacks of twine-bound *National Geographic* and cardboard boxes, mounds of newspapers from God knows how many years back, and baskets of yarn. She made the same promise she'd made every day since her father, then her mother died. Going to clean this crap out. Yep, you just dream on Abby.

A wall of searing air hit her face as soon as she stepped outside. *Cussin' heat*, her daddy had called it. He swore even the hardiest hat-clad church ladies spent hours of prayerful knee-time because of profane words spilled in haste.

Late August. Abby didn't want to think about how much longer she'd have to put up with this summer. The pavement-buckling heat made folks in the small town of Chattahoochee, Florida—folks who normally took life in stride—into snippy, horn-blasting ingrates bent on sharing their dark moods. Sensible people went all stupid: a down payment on disaster.

"And I know about disaster." She scowled at her wilted hairdo in the vanity mirror of the faded-blue Honda Accord. Good thing she had those interesting eyes. Otherwise, she couldn't have been any more plain Jane if she had majored in it in college. Five foot four, a smidge overweight with a small bust and a nice set of birthing hips, thanks to her mother's side of the family. Turned-up nose with a scattering of freckles across the bridge. Good, even teeth. Smooth-faced enough to pass for younger than forty-seven, she assured herself.

Abby turned onto Morgan Avenue and headed into town. Azaleas and dogwood trees lined the sidewalks, their foliage drought-ravaged and drooping from days of unrelenting heat. She parked in her usual space behind a main street building and bustled into the dental office, flipping on lights, turning on the cantankerous computer, autoclave sterilizer, and coffeemaker. While the coffee brewed, she returned to her domain—the front desk—to print the daily schedule, pull charts, and retrieve the voicemail messages from patients begging for attention.

Same shit, felt like same day, same week, same year, same endless summer. Abby the hamster on her exercise wheel.

She sipped the cup of strong black coffee before ferreting out spots to cram patients into the busy schedule. Some days, it came easy, like snapping together Lego blocks. Others, like corralling quicksilver.

Ten 'til eight. Four lines rang at once. People, people, people. Each thinking his problem trumped the others'. She took a breath, slugged coffee and pulled on her happy voice. Give it a half-hour, and the dental lab delivery people would shove case pans on her desk past patients waiting to check in and check out. Lord.

Doggone computer refused to send the schedule file to the printer. Do not start my day this way, Sophie. Abby had named the high-tech piece of equipment after a girl she had known from junior college, an over-the-top brilliant scholar who would often clam up for no reason.

The back door creaked and slammed. Sabrina, the effervescent hygienist, swept into the front office. In the twenty-one years Abby had worked for Dr. Payne, she had never shared the office with a more pleasant woman. The patients adored her.

"Morning, Abby." Sabrina grabbed a stack of charts and flipped through them. "Do you have schedules printed? If not, I can do."

Abby cradled the phone between her shoulder and ear. The familiar cramp throbbed near her neck. "Not yet." She jabbed a finger at the monitor. "Sophie!"

"Let me go set up my room and then I'll see if I can help." Sabrina only had one gear: wide-screaming open. But she wasn't a princess. Thank God.

"Yes?" Abby returned her attention to the man on the phone: cracked front tooth, probable crown prep, two-hour procedure. "Mr. Johns, come and we'll work you in. Bring a book. You might have a bit of a wait."

Abby offered a wry smile to the next employee who walked past. Christine, Dr. Payne's assistant. Not a morning person. Nice enough unless you cornered her before a ration of coffee.

The whoosh of the front glass door alerted Abby to the arrival of the first patient, Caroline "Choo-choo" Ivey. Sore spot under upper denture: ten-minute appointment tops. Except that Choo-choo adored

Dr. Payne, and it would no doubt turn into thirty, or fifty. Abby slid the plate glass reception window open. "Morning, Miz Choo-choo."

For a woman in her eighties, Choo-choo Ivey was well preserved. Silver hair—curly and perfectly coiffed—fair skin with few wrinkles and kind gray eyes that smiled even when her mouth didn't.

"Morning, Abby. Is the good doctor in yet?"

"No Ma'am. Should be here shortly. You're a wee bit early."

Choo-choo pointed to the linen-lined wicker basket hanging from the crook of one arm. "I brought y'all some fresh banana nut muffins to have with your coffee. They were always my Charlie's favorite. I'll pass them over, but make sure you save one for the doctor."

"Wow. Thanks."

"I'll catch up on *People* magazine while I wait." Choo-choo handed the basket through the open reception window.

Choo-choo often brought fresh baked goods. Stopped by some days for no apparent reason other than to say hello. Maybe the sweet elderly woman purposely placed sesame seeds underneath her denture to rub a raw spot. Attention in any form was welcomed when you were lonely. Abby understood that.

A few minutes later, she heard the distinctive snick of the back door once again. Dr. Payne walked up and stood behind her. "Morning. Got a schedule printed, Abby?"

She shook her head and snarled at the computer, one ear still cradled to the phone. Two lines blinked with patients on hold. One less than before. Must've given up or died waiting. The current caller rambled on and on. The doctor grabbed a stack of charts, plucked a muffin from the basket, and disappeared down the hall to his private office.

The next line, a mother canceling three-in-a-row appointments for her children's dental cleanings. Abby endured the gory details of the family's stomach flu, something about flying chunks and green runny bile. Good Lord. Shoot me now. She glanced over the call list. As soon as the phones settled to a dull rumble, she'd fill the blanks in Sabrina's schedule. Bonuses depended on steady production.

Ten after eight. Less than thirty minutes and she was already exhausted. And Sophie still refused to communicate with the printer. Four hours until Ben would drop by with the mail. One thing to look forward to.

Abby reached for her coffee and knocked over the cup. "Crap!" She mopped the desk with a handful of tissues.

The printer beeped twice and spit out a stack of schedules. "Really, Sophie? In red ink no less?"

It was going to be a shoot-fire fine day, a typical cliché of a Monday.

The fast food tuna fish and veggie sub Abby wolfed down in about five minutes threatened to repeat throughout the early afternoon. That's what she got for not picking off the green pepper slivers. She liked them; they did not like her. No one in the office. Good. She bellowed a belch. Give it a while and it'd start from the other end. At the rate she was going, Abby would do more damage to the Earth's ozone layer than a herd of cows and a baker's dozen of over-sized SUVs.

She dug in her purse and found a partial roll of stomach mints. The foil-lined wrapper clung to one side, the other open to God-knows-what. Desperation called for drastic measures, even eating soiled antacid tablets. She popped two into her mouth.

A tap sounded at the glass reception window. What now? Couldn't be the first patient of the afternoon. She speed-chewed the antacids and swallowed. It was only twelve-thirty, still a half-hour of her lunch break left. Abby cupped her hand over her mouth, checked for bad breath. Forgot to order it without onions again too. Sheesh.

She slid the window open slightly, then pushed it back all the way. Postal carrier Ben Calhoun handed a neat pile of envelopes through the window. "Sorry to interrupt your lunch, Abby."

Ben Calhoun had the kind of face most normal women instantly trusted. A big brother kind of face. Blue-gray eyes, a thin nose, and an even, white smile corralled by a thick handlebar mustache. His light brown hair, thin at the temples, was neatly combed.

The rest of Ben's body reminded Abby of the character Ichabod Crane from that old Disney movie, all spindly arms and legs, and so tall he had to stoop forward to enter doorways. Add to the look, the slate-colored postal carrier stripe-down-the-side walking shorts, and Ben approached comical. His browned legs were shapely and not overly hairy, a saving grace.

"Had to pick up my pace a bit. Taking off early for a doctor's appointment over in Tallahassee." He handed over a second stack of magazines and flyers.

"Nothing serious with your health, I hope?" Abby prayed none of the bread had grouted her front teeth.

8

"Nope. Yearly check-up. That and the eye doctor. I try my best to make multiple appointments whenever I have to go to Tallahassee. Traffic's awful right now. The college students are back. They drive like sprayed cockroaches." Ben laughed. Not loud and boisterous like so many Southern men.

Words crowded Abby's throat. Who are you, Ben? What do you think about life, politics, music, art, the world? Maybe we could . . . share lunch one day. Her smile quivered then failed.

Ben adjusted his messenger bag. "You have a good remainder of the day, now." He stepped from the front door, Ichabod navigating a game of Twister. Abby vaguely recalled him having a wife and kid. The wife had died a few years back from some kind of sudden thing. Cancer? Stroke?

Ben seemed to be such a steady man. In an old Western, he would've played the part of the expedition leader, rounding wagons in a circle, protecting the women and children while he took aim at the raiding party. Why in the heck couldn't she have ended up with some-one like him?

Abby couldn't force herself to get past the lump that formed every time she tried to talk to a man, even one as non-threatening as Ben. Only one person to blame for that. William Harvey Hansel. His name growled in her head.

The long hand on the black and white wall clock clicked past the twelve mark. One o'clock. As if some kind of hunting horn had blown, three lines rang at once. She stifled a belch, took a sip of water.

Weary sadness settled over Abby, her private shroud. Alone, alone, alone. And she'd stay that way. Her chest constricted and she forced herself to breathe and jab the first lighted button.

Loiscell Pickering paused in her foyer and looked at the grouping of family photos. There I am, new wife, not a mother yet. The fuchsia cocktail dress, those pumps dyed to match, even the earrings the same shade. Thick wavy auburn hair. Shamrock green eyes. Porcelain skin with dots of rose on high cheekbones. Cupid bow lips painted liquid pink, smiling. Tall, leggy—five foot eight—not an ounce of fat any-where. The next photo—at Panama City Beach. Pin-up posing across a stripped towel like Marilyn Munroe. Mid-thirties. All boobs and cleav-age. Where had that woman gone?

"I ought to go on a TV talk show. A woman's trip down the hill." She pulled a worn pair of gardening gloves from a basket by the door.

Disease had wrecked her body since those pictures. Loiscell had noticed the first lump beneath her right armpit one evening as she showered off the afternoon's sweat and garden grime. About the size of a pea, it rolled a little beneath the skin.

Fifty-two years old at the time, she worked at Florida State Hospital for barely above minimum wage. The kids had grown and moved away, and her husband was deceased from a heart attack. Two rounds of chemotherapy and radiation later, minus her right breast, Loiscell got her wish to shed the pounds childbirth and menopause had gifted. Her appetite vanished. Food tasted like moldy cotton. Pounds melted away.

Some prayers the devil answered.

After the bone-weary tiredness subsided, she had rebounded. Lots of fresh vegetables and fruit. Exercise. Hair growing back in. Face ruddy with sun. She begged vintage rose bush clippings from fellow gardeners, added hardy native plants, and delivered handfuls of cut flowers to neighbors.

Five years passed—victory over the Big C!—before Loiscell noticed the thickened, stippled skin beneath her left nipple. Odd. Back to the oncologist. More x-rays, ultrasound, needle biopsy. "Mrs. Pickering, your cancer has returned." Left breast lopped off like spoiled meat. Follow-up chemo and radiation. The energy to heal her wounds sucked her hair from its follicles. It grew back in nappy dull red patches, crisp-brittle.

Loiscell grabbed a slip of bright cotton from her collection of bandanas and tied it around her head. Wispy hair stuck out around the edges. People associated her with the hair wraps—the bolder the print, the better. Her new signature look.

She stepped outside, where the heavy morning air promised another day of intense heat. Loiscell loved her yard. Two ancient live oak trees cradled the sky, their sweeping arms draped with long strands of Spanish moss. Loiscell moved to the side of the house, to rows of rose bushes—her babies—passion red, dusty pink, coral, yellow. Happy little plants since she'd moved them to the spot beside the rock pathway. Roses needed full sun licking their barbed arms. The fenced-in back yard was less formal, reminiscent of an English country garden. Loiscell had planned it that way, the mix of tamed and random. She started at one end of the rose patch, deadheading the spent blooms. The little darlings did better when some parts were clipped off.

A trickle of perspiration oozed into the space her cleavage had once occupied. Loiscell ran one hand absently across her flat chest, a chest that looked like the pounded, scarred armor of some medieval knight. Should she get tattoos to add a little artsy touch? Reconstruction—a new set of insurance-funded boobs? No. No more surgery.

She spent the next two hours working her way through the flower-beds.

"Hey!" a familiar voice called.

Loiscell stood upright, arched her back to uncramp the muscles, and shielded her eyes with one gloved hand. "What brings you out this morning? I thought this was . . ." She tapped her chin. "What is Monday? Bathroom day, right?"

Sheila grinned. "That's Tuesday. Monday is kitchen day. Done. Got started early. Thought I'd stop by and see if you needed anything."

"Not unless you have a cure for this devil-spawn dollar weed. Wicked stuff grows behind me as I pull it up."

"I brought some fresh cinnamon rolls." Sheila held up a quilted carrier.

Loiscell shucked the garden gloves and wiped her face with a rag. "It's about time for me to go in out of this heat. I got out here so early, I forgot to eat breakfast. One of those rolls sounds perfect. My stomach's beginning to feel like my throat's been cut."

Loiscell led the way into the two-bedroom cottage.

"Bet this bothers you," Loiscell said when she noticed Sheila's gaze taking in the room.

Sheila's hand fluttered to her heart. "Why would you say that?"

"My daughter says this house is over-stuffed. But I love my books and mementos."

"I've always found it welcoming, especially the flowers." Sheila walked around the room, touching first an embroidered pillow, then a chunk of pink quartz. She leaned down to sniff a tea rose blossom. "I wish my house could look like this."

Sheila removed her sunglasses. Loiscell noted the yellow-green and blue smudge beneath one of her friend's eyes. "Mercy, where'd you get that shiner?"

The tips of Sheila's fingers flickered to the tender skin. "Oh that . . . I was scrubbing the baseboards and lost my balance. Fell right into that set of spindle candleholders by the hearth."

"Good thing you didn't put your eye out!" Loiscell noticed how Sheila moved with stiff, mincing steps. "You no more get rid of one scrape, then you have another."

11

Sheila's lips stretched into a tight smile. "Yep. That's me. Silly, clumsy me."

Loiscell studied her for a moment before motioning toward the kitchen. Sheila set the platter of cinnamon rolls on the white wooden table and moved to put on a fresh pot of coffee. Wasn't it wonderful, how true female friends knew each other's kitchen cupboards like their own?

"Heard they're starting a yoga class at the Women's Club," Loiscell said. "Might be good for both of us. Meditation. Flexibility. Could even help your balance."

Sheila's gaze dropped to her feet. "I'll check with Glenn."

Nine weeks before suicide, Saturday

Glenn Bruner's favorite breakfast spread out before him, cooked halfway decent for once: three eggs over easy, two long links of country sausage, grits, two buttermilk biscuits, homemade fig preserves, and strong black coffee thick with cream.

"Glenn, may I ask you something?" Sheila said, her voice soft.

"Humph?"

"They're starting up a yoga class at the Women's Club. Loiscell asked me to come. On Monday nights from six-thirty until about eight."

"Yoga? You?" He laughed then took a loud swill of coffee.

"It's supposed to be good for balance and flexibility."

God, he hated it when her voice went all high and squeaky like that. He chewed a hunk of biscuit heavy with butter. "You *are* damned klutzy, for sure."

Sheila poured more coffee. When he met her gaze, the bruise accused him in ways his wife never would. Leave it to Sheila to ruin his morning.

"Monday's poker night. What do you expect me to feed the boys? Potato chips and dip out of a dadgum can ain't going to cut it."

"It won't be any trouble at all. I can make things ahead and set them out before I leave."

Might be kind of good to have her away from the house. She was always hovering, simpering. Big Glenn's advice popped into his mind: "Women have to be kept in line, son. Otherwise they'll make your life a living hell. Give 'em a little affection time to time. But never, never let them get the upper hand. Key is to keep them off balance."

12

Maybe it was time to throw a dog a bone. "You can go. Long as it doesn't cause any problems. You hear?"

Sheila smiled. Brushed his cheek with one of her cold dry kisses.

"I'm leaving for the day," he said on his way out of the door a few minutes later, not stopping to gauge her reaction. Sheila knew better than to ask why, where, or when he would be home. Woman visited retards and old people for the church on Saturdays, and he wanted no part of that.

Driving—whether in his truck or boat—gave him time to think. Without Sheila's mousy pestering. Without those dipsticks at the prison barking orders. Glenn eased the metallic-fleck, cherry-red F150 pick-up back into the right lane. Good thing CR 269 toward Greensboro had little traffic. This time of day, he was lucky to pass one car going the opposite way. What made a person's mind keep doing something like steering a truck when he was busy thinking? One of them mysteries of life.

"You'd be proud of how my choice for a wife has turned out," he said to his father's ghost. "Way to success is not to go after the purty girls, you told me. No sir! They are trouble with a capital T. Get a plain one, just not butt-ugly. She'll be so happy to have a man, she'll roll over." Need something better, go find it. Like that little whore unit secretary who'd give him a blow job in the supply closet, for a pack of Virginia Slims. Gotta admire a working gal.

"You need a little *change*, go buy yourself a little *strange*."

Good one, boy, he praised himself. You sound more and more like Big Glenn every day. Glenn took a swig of his first cold beer of the day and laughed.

"Sheila lives and breathes for me. She has nothing to complain about. She don't have to work and has a roof overhead and food in her belly. And I ain't got to worry about her slipping out on me." Who would have her? Took booze and a dark room for him to touch her.

Correcting Sheila was like kicking a dog, and always left a scrim of guilt. A few kind words would soothe her. A good roll in bed. All in all, Sheila was easy. But she could made him so damned mad. Like this morning and that bruise around her eye, purple-black. Could've covered that shit up with some make-up.

He pounded the steering wheel. "Why does she have to push me?"

The rage always came over him like an oily black curtain. When it lifted, some part of his wife wasn't the same as before. Small finger-print-sized marks on her upper arm. A blush of ruby on her face or under one of her eyes. Only once had Glenn succeeded in breaking a bone in her hand. Was it his fault that she was so fragile?

What kind of hot babe would've been his if the accident had never happened? His senior year of high school had been his shining time. Glenn Bruner—linebacker, bulked-up big man on campus. Rumor had it, he would be a draft pick for FSU football.

Then life went to hell. One instant, one split second, changed the rest of his life.

Hit below the knee on the right side during one of the final games of the season. Surgery, pins, and hardware put him back together. He would walk, but he could not run. The college and pro football dreams dried up like sunbaked road kill.

So what'd he have now? Work as a guard, minimum-security prison for juvenile boys. Come home to a pain in the ass wife, eat, drink, fish, hunt, and train at the camp. His life: one flaming hot pile of crap. 'Cept maybe for the fishing and hunting and drinking. And weekends at the camp.

Glenn glanced skyward for a moment. "Help me out here, Daddy. Got my eye on a purty little 18-foot bass boat, painted to match this here pick-up. Got a sweet Mercury outboard that will throw a tall fish-tail of water, way out behind. Yes sir, I can see me flying across Lake Seminole!"

On his salary, the vessel loomed so far beyond him as to be a blip on the horizon. But by the time Glenn turned into the chained entrance to the top-secret paramilitary training camp in the deep piney woods, the boat was so fixed in his mind, it might as well have been sitting in a new custom covered garage beside his house.

He'd find a way of getting it, or harelip Hell trying. Man's gotta have something.

Abby McKenzie glanced around the living room and blew out a breath. Clutter infested every corner, every surface. Hers. Her parents'. Mixed into a mish-mash. So organized at the office, why not here?

At one time, she had dreamed of a spacious house, decorated like a *House Beautiful* picture. Glass tabletops and fake plants that never turned brown at the edges. Real framed artwork. A row of gleaming colored art glass in front of a long window. When the morning light hit just right, the room would dance with rainbows.

Today, she would do it. Where to start? She kicked a tall stack of empty cardboard boxes down the hall. Sort and pitch, just like they did on those hoarder reality shows.

Abby opened the door on the nightmarish third bedroom closet. Take a deep breath, start at the top and work down. When she tugged on a plastic storage bin, an eight by ten wooden frame slid forward, teetered for a moment, and fell toward her upturned face. One corner smashed into her upper lip.

"Yowsa!"

She dashed to the bathroom. A line of warm blood snaked to her chin. Face wounds bled like nobody's business, especially the lips and soft tissues inside the mouth. Abby pressed a piece of toilet paper to the cut long enough to slow the hemorrhage. The slice was slight, less than a couple of millimeters. She gently lifted her upper lip and checked the incisors. Everything looked intact.

"This is going to swell."

Minutes later, she returned to the offensive closet with a small ice pack held to her lips, ready to work one-handed. Her family's life history lived on these shelves. Old framed photographs. Cardboard boxes—most without labels—leaned haphazardly. Coats and jackets. A broken telescope. Her father's yard shoes. A cracked mirror. Throw pillows in out-of-date colors and patterns. A flat basketball.

Something had shifted when her parents died—Father, then her mom two years later. Abby had moved from the cramped one-bedroom apartment where she had lived since her ill-fated marriage, into the wooden-framed forest green home of her childhood. The accumulated bits and pieces from her parents' marriage and life curled around her like a glove, or noose.

She shut the door with her free hand. Might as well start in the most important spot, if she was going to do this. She kicked the stack of cardboard boxes in front of her to the master bedroom. Her lip throbbed.

The ghost of her mother's floral cologne stopped her the moment she opened the closet's bi-fold doors. Why hadn't she swallowed the pain and done this years ago?

Abby half-expected her mother to step up behind her. The contents looked the same. Her mother's god-awful canary yellow skirt and matching jacket, the line of carefully-pressed pants, blouses and dresses, sensible shoes in basic tones, a few handbags—pale for spring and summer, dark for fall and winter—wrapped in plastic, belts that had come with the pants, barely-worn navy sneakers, and one pair of elastic-waist jeans. Other than that flick of canary yellow, so much blue!

Overwhelming. Abby couldn't bear to look at her father's side of the closet. She shut the door.

Like this closet, the remainder of the family home remained frozen in time. In the kitchen, she had created space for her meager utensils. Her clothes—the few she owned—hung from a rolling plastic rack in the study.

Even her mother's Lincoln Towncar had sat idle until Abby finally relented and sold it to a man from south Georgia. The battery was dead as a doornail, but after a jumpstart, the car ran fine. Plenty of people from Chattahoochee offered to take the aging gas-hog off her hands, but she couldn't take passing it on a daily basis or seeing it parked by the drugstore uptown.

Abby weaved through the meager path, from room to room, opening doors and bureau drawers. The dust made her sneeze. Maybe she should start somewhere more benign. She left the house and walked a few feet to a block building in the backyard. The key hung above the door on a concealed hook. She wiggled the lock until it complained, then forced open the door. No wonder her mother had considered the shack off-limits after her father died. She closed her eyes and leaned against the door jam.

Always a bit messy even in good times, the out-building had morphed into a sucking black hole of discarded stuff. Her gaze roamed from disintegrating boxes dotted with mouse droppings to piles of gardening utensils and opened sacks of fertilizer. Vintage hard-sided leather suitcases, crates of albums, and rusted tools she couldn't begin to guess the use for. A narrow pathway wide enough for one person wound through the room: the only place she could see the concrete floor. Worse than the house!

Abby slammed and locked the door. Maybe it could be Chattahoochee's time capsule, opened decades later and studied for its relevance to life in a small Southern town.

One word summed up her life: Constipated.

She glanced down at her faded T-shirt and hole-pocked shorts. And when had she turned into such a slob? Somewhere along the line, she had stopped shopping at the mall and favored thrift stores. A Timex was as good as a Rolex. Over-the-counter brands replaced pricey makeup. Why waste fine linen on a card table?

At least she was frugal, not cheap, frugal. She drove an aging Honda. It ran well, got great gas mileage, and best of all had no payment booklet. Credit cards, when used, were paid off each month. Abby could have been the poster child for debt-free living. Terribly un-American, but less stressful.

Her one indulgence—high-speed internet access and a good laptop. A few monthly bills waited. Five minutes online and she would be caught up. No stamps, no fuss. The rest of her life might be for shit, but this she could handle.

She ditched the cleanout project and settled in front of the laptop. When the computer slowed to a crawl, Abby panicked. She picked up the phone and dialed her next-door neighbor. Their stupid mutt of a dog pooped regularly in her front yard—huge, amazing piles she would've sworn came from a mastiff. But their fourteen-year-old son was an accomplished computer geek, complete with dark-rimmed glasses held together with a Band-Aid at the nose. The poor guy's name caused him more than his share of angst.

"Hey, it's Abby. Is Mason busy? My laptop is hacking and spitting. I really need it to work today."

Within moments, the front door swung open and Mason Dixon rushed in, his face flushed. If he could've had lights and a siren, he would have. "Wha'sup?"

"All I did was try to get online and it froze up. I think I killed it."

His brown eyes flickered to meet hers for an instant. "Possibly some old registry files clogging up the works. Have you cleaned out spy ware or run a disk clean-up?"

"I don't know how to do that, and I don't really want to know." Abby shoved away from the desk. "Have at it, Mason. Call me if you need me."

She kicked a stack of hardback novels on her way to the laundry room. A lizard jumped out and dashed to safety. Why did everything in her miserable life need to be cleaned out?

Choo-choo Ivey stood at the stove stirring chicken liver and cooked rice into a mushy paste. "Who would have ever thought I'd be spending my golden years cooking for a dog?" No choice. Charlie's ancient poodle had to eat. Though why did she bother? The dog would turn her nose up at a sirloin.

The one living thing that shared her space looked up with milky eyes: Prissy, a half-blind, half-deaf toy poodle with nappy off-white hair. Most days, Choo-choo wished Charlie's little darling had gone with him. When Choo-choo tried to pet her, Prissy snapped and snarled. Choo-choo understood. If it was socially acceptable, she would snap and snarl too. The two of them were bound together in heartache, each disappointed by who they had been stuck with.

That lovely room-sized oriental carpet? Had to carry it to the land-fill because of the poodle's failing bladder. Then the darn dog shifted affections to the master bathroom throw rug. Better, actually. At least it fit into the washer. As soon as she put it back into place, Prissy peed on it again.

Choo-choo used a mortar and pestle to grind the dog's daily medi-cations—one for arthritis, one for anxiety. Charlie had just tilted Prissy's head back and popped the medication onto the back of her tongue. The times Choo-choo had tried, she practically had to shove her hand to the ankle-biter's stomach. A second later, the dripping pill got yakked to the floor. All Choo-choo had to show for the effort was a saliva-slick hand and elevated blood pressure.

"I should be living in one of those fancy assisted living places where they cook for *me*," she said to the dog.

Prissy lifted her lips and showed a line of yellowed teeth. Charlie had called it a smile. Choo-choo doubted that.

Assisted living facilities. No matter how good, they all had That Smell—a blend of disinfectant and body emissions. Too many memo-ries of Charlie's final days. In spite of volunteering for Hospice and helping Elvina Houston keep up with details of everyone's lives, sad-ness settled into a worn spot and festered. After fifty-five years, two months, and six days of marriage to the same sweet bear of a man, the grief of losing Charlie had carved a hole in her soul.

One morning several months after her husband passed away, Choo-choo had studied her reflection in the mirror. Worry lines be-tween her brows. Deep, comma-shaped crevasses like parentheses around her pale lips. Unkempt hair. No make-up. The saddest expres-sion, like those on the faded art prints hanging in her daughter's old room: ragamuffin moppet children with wide, doe-brown eyes that echoed abandonment, only hers were more downturned.

"If Charlie Ivey could see you now, he'd be displeased with what an old frump you've become," she had said to her reflection.

That same morning, she made an appointment at the Triple C Day Spa and Salon for a cut, perm, and style. No color. Old ladies with dyed boot-black hair flew all over nature's idea of graceful aging.

The next day, Choo-choo took a field trip to Tallahassee for a complete beauty makeover, over two hundred dollars of skin care products and age-appropriate makeup. Then on to Dillards for three pantsuits, two church dresses, a pair of black pumps, and her first ever pair of blue jeans.

The Lincoln was two years old, and barely had the new smell worn off. The house was paid for, and not too big. Other than a few small luxuries, like fine dark chocolate, Choo-choo needed little. No need to go hog-wild.

The sound of Prissy's toenails dancing on the tile snapped her to attention. She frowned at the overcooked mush. Nearly burned! Maybe if she added a little canned gravy . . . "I'll have your breakfast in a moment."

The poodle lifted her head, sniffed, and tap-tapped out of the kitchen. Choo-choo hadn't even put the mush in the dang dog's bowl yet.

"Everyone's a flippin' critic."

The same thing happened every day. Twice. Prissy would sniff her bowl of prepared delicacies, snort, and walk away. Choo-choo found the bowl half-empty later, so she knew the dog ate. Just not in front of her.

At least this morning held a bright spot—the mid-week visit to the Triple C Day Spa and Salon. Good thing. She was beginning to look as nappy as the dog. She could wash her hair, but it hurt to hold her arms above her head for very long, and afterwards, she looked like who-shot-Sam.

Eighty-eight years took a lot out of a person's body. Her favorite nurse practitioner in Tallahassee called it a case of "The Dwindles," a little of this and a little of that. Acid reflux, anxiety, high blood pressure, arthritis, insomnia, nasal allergies, water retention, an occasional bladder infection. A walking medical dictionary.

Choo-choo looked at the marks along the doorframe of the cupboard. Snips of black lines. Her daughter's growth recorded on one side, rising up and up. Hers on the other. One of the few fun things she shared with Jackie. Choo-choo's side stayed at a consistent five-foot five inches, but it had been years since she had backed up and measured against her younger self.

Osteoporosis had curved Choo-choo's spine like a pine sapling bent to strong winds as if her body was attempting to roll into the same

19

fetal position in which it had originally arrived. The nurse at her doctor's office had measured her as five-foot one, last visit.

Choo-choo imagined herself as a wilting Southern Magnolia bloom: fading slowly. A little brown around the edges. Still creamy white in the middle. Dropping one petal at a time.

Choo-choo pulled into the gravel-paved side parking lot and paused for a moment in awe of a restored mansion. Once the home of Colonel Beau and Betsy Witherspoon and only son Jake, the stately Greek revival-style home now served as the heart of Chattahoochee. Nothing within a three-county radius escaped scrutiny and detailed dissection. Choo-choo dared not miss a single installment.

She imagined corseted women in wide-bottomed dresses strolling the grounds with matching parasols to preserve their peaches and cream complexions. Handsome well-appointed men sipping mint juleps on the shaded porch with groomed hunting spaniels sleeping at their feet. She left out the part about the numerous black household and grounds workers. That whole slavery thing was a nasty blight on the South.

The white columned house tucked between towering stands of short-needled pines, dogwoods, mimosas, and ancient Spanish moss-draped live oaks. Cicadas called from the thickets. Birds flitted between the greenery.

The lower level of the mansion housed the business—expansive hair and nail care salon and massage therapy treatment rooms, and a staff kitchen/lounge area. The owner—a New York City transplant—had a private office off the kitchen, and seamstress Evelyn Fletcher's workshop took up a large room adjacent to the reception area.

Instead of passing through the massive front doors, Choo-choo chose the delivery entrance. Company comes through the front door. Friends come in the back. Choo-choo helped herself to coffee.

Elvina Houston glanced up when Choo-choo emerged from the kitchen. From her position behind the antique mahogany reception desk, Elvina kept the appointment books, monitored supplies, and watched *The Young and the Restless*. Elvina ran the town. Knew it all: births, deaths, illnesses, scandals, divorces, engagements, anniversaries. "Morning, Choo-choo. Hope that's still good. Mandy can make it so strong it will take the hair off your chin. If it's too much, I can start another pot."

Choo-choo took a sip. "I like strong coffee. At my age, I need all the lift I can get. Besides, if it cures chin hair, Mandy could bottle it and sell it to women past menopause. I'd buy a case."

"Know what you mean." Elvina motioned to a high-back upholstered chair beside the desk. "Sit for a bit. Mandy's last one was a little late, so it may be a few minutes before she gets to you."

Choo-choo settled in. She spoke with Elvina at least four times a week by phone. Amazing they still could find new things to discuss when they met face to face.

"Heard they're starting a yoga class at the Women's Club on Monday nights," Elvina said.

"Yoga? In this town? I can't imagine it would go over well."

"Lady who's going to lead it is driving all the way over from Tallahassee. She looks to be about fifty or so, and really nice."

"You thinking about signing up, are you?" The mental picture of Elvina Houston sitting cross-legged on a pillow with a blissful expression on her face was almost too much.

"Me? Oh, no. I walk for exercise. But it would be right up your alley. Do you a world of good."

Choo-choo had just taken a large sip of coffee and almost shot it from her nose. "Me?"

"You're always hunting for something new to do. And if you go, it will encourage more ladies to try it. Anything that's helpful for balance has to be a good thing at your age, Choo-choo."

Who was Elvina kidding? She had to be pushing eighty, if not over.

"Only thing you have to do is show up in stretch pants, with a pillow for your behind. Joy Harris—that's the instructor—told Mandy that she'll have plenty of those roll-up floor mats."

"I can barely move now, Elvina. How do you expect me to tie myself up in knots?" Choo-choo stopped, squeezed her lips together before adding, "What are you aiming for me to do, kill myself?"

Stylist Mandy Andrews appeared at the threshold and waved Choo-choo back. She stood and brushed the wrinkles from her skirt. Elvina punched numbers into the phone handset. No doubt, a call to one of her many minions in the little-ole-lady hotline. "It'll take more than yoga to kill you, Choo-choo Ivey. You're tough as a box of ten-penny nails."

Chapter Two

Eight weeks before suicide
Monday

Abby McKenzie sat in her car and took a deep breath. For years, she had avoided the Chattahoochee Women's Club. Each time she drove by the building, the same feelings washed over her like dirty, splashed theme-park water. No matter that her ill-fated storybook garden wedding was years past. Nothing like coming home to a sweet little love nest, only to see your cherished new husband in the arms of . . . someone else.

Not that this building had anything to do with that.

With its dark green shutters, the pristine white structure appeared more genteel family residence than clubhouse. On either side of the entrance, rows of azaleas and dogwood trees lined the cement walkway. In the spring, the fuchsia and white blooms transformed the simple building into a Southern showplace. Now, in the late summer, the heat and extended drought made every living thing appear dusty and droopy, Abby included.

Abby waited for a moment to see if anyone else would show. What was she thinking? She looked ridiculous in stretch pants, and would no doubt be the joke of the group. Heck, she could barely bend over and touch her knees, much less curve herself into some absurd pretzel.

Blame Choo-choo Ivey for this. Her and her mulish civic enthusiasm. Three times in less than two days, Choo-choo had stopped by the office, yakking about the new yoga class and how she was going to be there for sure. And how Abby needed to get out and do something other than work and go home.

Anytime someone suggested a thing might do her a "world of good," Abby worried.

Maybe Choo-choo was right. Lately, Abby found herself waking at odd times of the night, obsessing about some bizarre predicament one of *The Young and the Restless* actors had gotten herself into. Abby spent more time online with the baby boomers women's forum than she did speaking over the hedges to neighbors. Other than the casual banter with the patients who came and went from Dr. Payne's office and the occasional visits to Mandy for haircuts, the only time she ventured out was when there was absolutely nothing left to eat in the house.

Not to mention the lack of physical activity. No small wonder her butt challenged the seams of her scrub pants. All she did was sit, sit, sit. Her body was merely adding padding in the most-used place.

A white Lincoln pulled to the curb behind Abby's Honda. Choo-choo Ivey emerged, resplendent in lime green stretch crop pants and a shirt that read "Om—Where the Heart Is."

Choo-choo walked up to the Honda's window and leaned down. "Well, knock me over with a feather duster. I never believed you'd actually come."

Abby shrugged. "Mondays aren't a big night for television, so I figured what the heck."

"Did you bring a cushion for your rear? If not, I have an extra."

"I grabbed a throw pillow from the couch. Guess it will do."

Choo-choo stuffed a chenille Hello Kitty pillow into a matching carryall and hit the remote lock on her key fob. The Lincoln's lights flashed a coy wink.

Abby got out. She didn't lock the old Honda. Any petty criminal low-down on his luck enough to make off with her piece of crap car deserved pity. It was dependable, but not much to look at, and certainly not flashy enough for a wildcat joy ride with your hoodlum friends.

"I have the key." Choo-choo dangled a skeleton key from one finger. "Let's go on in and open up. Joy should be here soon." Choo-choo led the way to the fern-lined front entrance, then teased the old lock until it clicked open. "Understand she's really good with any kind of ability level, or, in our case, lack of."

"Got that right."

Choo-choo flipped on a bank of light switches. The expansive room stood empty, save for a scattering of ladder-back chairs along the walls. It even smelled the same as Abby remembered: a blend of floor polish, air freshener, and a hint of cinnamon. If buildings held memories, this one hosted the gentle ghosts of time-honored casseroles, laughter, and fellowship. Abby's recollections of her actual wedding event were happy, only the aftermath provided the stain.

"Hello?" a soft voice called out from the doorway behind them. A willowy woman stood at the threshold with an oversized neon blue rolling duffle bag in tow.

"You must be Joy." Choo-choo walked over and grasped the woman's hand. "I'm Caroline Ivey, but folks call me Choo-choo. It's from when I was a toddler and used to love trains. Believe *choo-choo* was one of the first things I learned to say. And goodness, I hope you didn't have any trouble finding this place. Directions often defy me. I can't tell east from west, even when the sun's setting. Lordy. Do you have that problem? Many people do."

Joy blinked. Her smile remained remarkably serene. She took a moment to answer. "Pleased to meet you, and no, I didn't have any problem finding this place. I have a GPS."

Choo-choo motioned in Abby's direction. "This is Abby McKenzie. She's the office manager for the dentist's office uptown. I'll do my best to introduce any others who show up, too. Just remind me if I forget my manners."

Joy tipped her head in Abby's direction, then asked, "Where may I set up? I have a CD player and plenty of yoga mats."

Choo-choo glanced around the room. "Most anywhere you want, I suppose."

"Any idea of how many may come tonight?" Joy said.

"I have no clue, to be honest. Two or three more for sure. Couple of ladies are out of town, but plan on joining us next week. I spread the word and Mary up at the newspaper put in an announcement. Mary's good that way, and she wouldn't take a red cent for the space either." Choo-choo paused long enough to breathe. "Might take a few weeks to catch on. People tend to be a bit shy about new things until they hear enough back to take a chance and come see for themselves."

Joy nodded. "And don't worry about introductions. I like to take a few minutes before I start the meditation, to get to know each of you a little bit." She wheeled the duffle to one end of the hall.

Abby noticed the way the yoga instructor moved, as if she had all the time in the world. When she walked, it was more of a glide with modulated steps, a ballet dancer. Her posture: erect, but not strained. Her straight chin-length hair was the kind for which bottle-blondes aspire—the color of morning sunlight, and obviously natural with no black roots. Her body showed no signs of extra fat. Spandex didn't lie.

If yoga could do all that, Abby was all in.

Choo-choo's gaze roamed to the doorway. Loiscell and Sheila walked in. "So glad you came, Loiscell. I was hoping. And look-ie here! If it isn't Sheila Burns."

Loiscell cast a paisley-printed duffle to the floor. "Why the heck not?" She motioned with a tip of her head. "I dragged Sheila along for support."

Abby remembered Loiscell from the office, though Dr. Payne hadn't seen her for a while. Sheila, she recognized from the events page of the *Twin City News*. Must be nice to have all that extra time to be socially conscious. Abby gave to the United Way and American Cancer Society, and bought fund-raiser chocolate candy and gift wrap from the neighborhood kids, but never had the inclination to head up a committee or charity drive. Tonight was the first time she had seen Sheila sans the prissy clothing, and less than perfect. Might even God have an at-home-in-the-clouds, off-duty robe, slightly worn and faded with use? Maybe there was hope.

Joy unpacked her duffle. A small CD player first, then a four-inch wooden figurine—a kneeling man with prayer hands and bowed head—with a matching incense tray. She lit the long stick, blew on it until a thin stream of woodsy aromatic smoke emerged, and stuck it into the wooden tray. Then she motioned to the restroom sign and excused herself.

"I'm going to have a flashback to college parties," Abby commented. "Of course, the incense then was to cover up the smell of pot." The good old days, when she actually ventured out, tried to meet new people.

Choo-choo's painted eyebrows shot up. "Abby McKenzie. I would've never taken you for a dope fiend!"

"Oh good Lord, Choo-choo. I wasn't. Anybody who went to school during the late seventies and early eighties might say the same thing. Heck, some parties, you could get high just breathing. Doesn't mean *I* smoked. Well . . . that once to see what the big deal was. Didn't like it. Made me feel too wacky and I ate until I got sick afterwards."

"I smoked it when I went through chemo last time," Loiscell said in a low voice.

The three women stared at her. The air conditioner vent above them wheezed.

"Okay, so arrest me." Loiscell adjusted her sunflower-print bandana. "It helped with the nausea. I couldn't eat without wanting to heave my guts up. I had someone—won't tell who so don't bother ask-ing—bring me a couple of marijuana cigarettes. I smoked barely enough to calm my stomach. It was a lifesaver. And Sheila, don't look at me like that, Little Miss Goody Two-shoes."

Sheila glanced from one woman to the next. "She *was* pretty sick. I took her my chicken and rice soup, and she could barely get a spoonful down."

Abby lifted one shoulder, let it fall. "Personally, I don't see why it's against the law. People can drink themselves into a coma. Heaven only knows how many fine upstanding people are hooked on prescription drugs. Pot's a medicine, after all. And it has some good points."

"You're quite a radical, Abby," Choo-choo said.

Abby threw her hands up. "Yep. That's me. Everything about me screams radical."

Eight weeks before suicide, Tuesday

Loiscell Pickering palpated the raised bump to the left of her sternum. "You have got to be kidding me . . . for the love of God!"

Oblong, tender and hard, about the size of a grape. Again with the blasted fruit comparison! Why did the medical profession do that? Now she was doing it. Make it a *dot of evil*, or an *inkblot of wicked*.

What about the dang five-year mark? According to all the hype, at that point a woman could breathe easier. Home safe. Cancer van-quished. Yet for the second time, that milestone had come with a repeat performance of good-cells-gone-bad.

Loiscell closed her eyes and leaned against the shower stall. A wave of dizziness passed over her. Please don't let me faint. Now wouldn't that be a fine how-de-do? Someone—probably Sheila—would knock at the back door. Her friend would hesitate for a few seconds before knocking harder, then let herself in with the key hidden beneath the orange plastic jug of Tide in the washroom.

And there Loiscell would be, her scrawny, naked, no-breasted, scared body sprawled out halfway between the tub and toilet, water still pounding in a steady stream, the curtain jerked askew by her descent.

No, she had to pull it together, at least until she got some under-wear on. When she dried off and stood in front of the full-length mirror, the lump was still there. The skin puckered slightly around it.

"Son of a dog."

A familiar sweet-sick, scorched taste washed over her tongue, the same one that had arrived after chemotherapy and altered everything she tried to eat. Spaghetti, chocolate mousse, cranberry juice, pasta: all flavored like the soiled bottom of a parrot cage. After five years, the stained memory should have vanished, but no, it was right there on her tongue.

Loiscell fumbled for the bottle of alcohol-free mouthwash, took a swig, and tipped her head back for a deep gargle. No use. Even after she spit out the last of the blue-green foam, the foul taste remained.

She would call the oncologist. Make an appointment. Carry her soul-weary self over to Tallahassee.

"Here we go again." Loiscell exhaled a long, slow breath.

How would she tell the kids? Not kids anymore, but she still thought of them as such. Lisa would drop everything and dash from Atlanta, no matter how tough her schedule. Lance would eventually wander through on his way to somewhere: long-distance biking, bungee jumping, surfing. He must've gotten that from Roger's side of the family. Loiscell's idea of high adventure was spraying for aphids without a mask.

"Think positive," said those self-help books cluttering her shelves. Okay. She tried. But deep inside on some cellular, intuitive level, she knew. Cancer had tapped her for a dance, once again. Only this time Loiscell didn't know if she could find the strength to waltz with the dragon.

Friends always prodded her to pray. Thanks to the Internet and Elvina Houston, distant people she didn't know held her in their pleas. Loiscell did talk to God. All the time. But she hated to beg, and many of her petitions to Heaven leaned toward groveling and bargaining.

Loiscell had never been much of a joiner. No garden clubs. No Junior League. No sewing circle. She attended church services a few times, one sect as good as the next. Weren't they all supposed to be heading in the same direction? Only don't tell them that. Each proclaimed they guarded the toll bridge to the Almighty.

A building couldn't hold God. How could you cram something so immense into something so finite? When she pulled weeds, she prayed. When she clipped spent blossoms, she worshiped. When she gathered flowers to share with friends and neighbors, she tithed. When she looked on the garden with awe, she offered up thanks. Not so formal as hours of knee-time, but more comforting.

How could she lose faith when nature didn't? Each season brought change. Spring with its lime green newness. Summer with the afternoon scent of roses, mint and rosemary, and the contented buzz of bees. Fall: rust, yellow, red, and brown. A time to collect, harvest, and ready for sleep. Winter, an opportunity to rest and look ahead. The circle curled into itself and Loiscell followed.

Loiscell plugged in the blow dryer and aimed it at the remnants of her once-thick hair. The appliance whined with a troubling internal rattle. Time for a new one. Since January, the oven, dishwasher, washer, and dryer had been replaced. Then the new roof and gutters. The hot water heater hacked and spit its last breath in May, and the air conditioner compressor crapped out on the hottest day in early July.

"Everything in this house is breaking down," she announced to the silence.

Sheila Bruner paused by her back porch, her ears trained on a faint sound emanating from the shrubs. A mewling noise like the cry of a baby bird, something alive and helpless. She dashed into the kitchen, grabbed a flashlight, and returned. As she neared, a second, familiar cry sounded.

"Buttercup?" The meowing grew insistent. "Where are you, sweet-ie?"

Sheila knelt and brushed aside the foliage. Buttercup peered up at her and blinked in the flashlight's beam. "What do we have here? What have you brought me, you silly old kitty?" Beside the cat, a furry bundle of black and white bobbed its head, its eyes not yet open.

She scooped the newborn into her palm and cradled the kitten into the warmth between her breasts. The tiny feline shivered and poked blindly in search of nourishment. "Where's your mama, little one?"

No way of knowing. The mother could be dead, hit by a car or carried away by a hawk. The rest of the litter might be somewhere starving. Nature could be as cruel as she was bountiful, a fact that often tried Sheila's faith.

"Don't you worry, baby. I'll get you something to eat." She leaned down and gathered Buttercup. "You too. I know you'll worry yourself to death if I take this baby away. You found her . . . him? Let's get you both some supper, shall we?"

Good thing Glenn was passed out in the living room. One cat, now two? How would she keep them from ending up in a sack in the bottom of the river?

Sheila lined a shoebox with a piece of flannel from one of Glenn's old shirts and placed both cats inside. In a few minutes, she set a shallow bowl with canned cat food mixed with a little milk on the floor. "You get the good stuff, Buttercup."

While the older cat lapped the slurry, Sheila cradled the newborn in one hand and fed it warmed milk with an eyedropper. For a few weeks, it would require regular feedings. She'd need to buy goat's milk. Better tolerated, easier for its little digestive system. Somehow, she would find a way to keep it alive.

"What will we call you, hmm? It will be a while before I can take you to the vet to tell if you are a she or he, so it needs to be something that won't embarrass you later."

The kitten nestled deep into her palm, purring. It had taken a few ounces of milk, enough to sustain it. In a couple of hours, she could offer more. Sheila studied the kitten's markings. Midnight black with white paws, a white belly and ruff, and one small lick of white above its upper lip. A tuxedo cat, always dressed formally for any occasion.

"Oreo! How about Oreo?"

Eight weeks before suicide, Friday

Glenn Burner slapped a mosquito and grimaced. Full of blood. What use were they, other than to annoy the beejezus out of a person? And this West Nile virus thing. Yet another worry. Every summer, a few horses keeled over because of it. Snuffed out a few humans, too.

Tents scattered in a nylon rash across a wide clearing deep within the two-hundred acre woodland like one big Boy Scout Jamboree. And Glenn loved every fatigue-clad second: the campfire tales of past military glories; the hearty meat and potato diet; farting and belching; the company of real men. No candy-assed mama's boys allowed; if one dared to show up, he would be strapped to one of the pop-up poster-board people in the three-mile training course. Shot deader than Hell, then buried in a pit so deep in the piney woods, only the devil could claim his sissified soul.

"Sure will be glad when the first freeze kills off the skeeters." Glenn sprayed a coating of bug repellant across the exposed areas of his skin and misted his hair. "Damn things are a pain in my ass."

"Ain't you got enough blood for them to suck, girly-boy?" one of the men said.

Laughter trickled around the circle like pond ripples after a skipped rock. Glenn's face grew hot.

"Yeah, Nancy," another commented. "They can't get enough blood, maybe they can suck your fat off instead."

In the circle of low light cast by the fire pit, Glenn couldn't tell which dude had spoken. His first reaction: show the jackasses a nice view of his gun barrel. "Good beer makes for good love handles," he said. "Guess you assholes wouldn't know about that, since you don't get any." Glenn half-sneered, half-smiled.

"Best tell your wife to cut back on your feedbag, son." This voice came from the head of the group. Retired chief of police. Everyone knew his name, and the small town where he lived and had once reigned as law enforcement king, yet called him by his alias, Big Dog.

Kind of dumb. Wasn't like they were in New York City. Most people within a three-county radius either knew you or your people. The Privacy Rule was one of many "established directives": the secret-code passwords and handshakes, the hazing ceremony designed to weed out the wimps, the suggested firearms and ammo, standardized fatigues and day-glow orange hunter's vests, and the "suggestion" that each "associate" take a different route to the camp every time.

Many times, Glenn had walked past one of the members in a Tallahassee restaurant, acknowledging him with a quick glance. Unless he knew the man outside of the group, he didn't exist.

Anger roiled his stomach. By morning, he would contend with the inevitable case of the runs that came with grease and booze. And that extra weight was all Sheila's fault. She wanted him fat, the ass-end of jokes.

He would deal with her when he got home.

Abby McKenzie didn't recognize the number on the caller ID display.

"Abby?"

"Yes."

Hesitation and the sound of a muffled sniff. "This is Gerald, Sabrina's husband."

"Oh, hi."

"Listen, my wife . . . Sabrina's been in a bad car accident. She's in surgery right now."

"Oh, geez! What happened? She going to be okay?"

Abby heard a long release of breath like the sigh of a nail-pricked tire.

"She was over here—in Tallahassee. Some nut was talking on his cell phone and ran a red light. T-boned the car. It's history, totaled. But that doesn't matter."

Gerald stopped for a moment before continuing. "Her leg's pretty messed up. Some other fractures—pelvis, collarbone. She hit her head."

"What can I do, Gerald? Just tell me."

"I've called the neighbors. They feed our animals when we're out of town, and they have a key, so that's taken care of. I . . . just . . . Sabrina was conscious when I got here. Kept asking me to call you and let you know to cancel patients on Monday." He huffed. "What am I saying . . . she won't be back into work for some time."

"That should be the least of your worries right now. That office will be right there, and I will take care of things." Crap, crap, crap. Add one more pebble to the pile.

"Thanks, Abby. You'll call Dr. Payne?"

"Done. If you think of anything else—and I mean anything—call me. If I can't get it done, I will find someone who can." Abby grabbed the laptop and clicked on her address book icon. Somewhere, she had the names and numbers of a couple of substitute hygienists. Had to get on it.

"Oh, and Abby? Please ask folks to give her a few days before they show up at the hospital, will you? I know her. She'll want to visit and make like everything is peachy. They may have her in Intensive Care for a bit."

"Her patients will want to send cards, no doubt. I'll ask them to mail them to the office, and I'll bring them over later. Which hospital?"

"Tallahassee General. Not sure where they'll send her after the surgery. I'll call you when I find out." Gerald paused. "And Abby? Sabrina hates those big lilies . . . the ones that are kind of white with pinkish in the middle . . . ?"

"Stargazer lilies?"

"They make her sick on her stomach. I remember when she had her hysterectomy. She got two bouquets we had to take out of the room. She said they smelled like cat pee."

Funny, the places a person's mind might go during times of stress. Like her, pissing and moaning about extra work when some surgeon hovered over a coworker. Nice, Abby.

Eight weeks before suicide, Saturday

Sometimes a bad feeling crawled all over Elvina Houston.

A good laxative—what her best friend, the late Piddie Longman, had referred to as "a good cleaning out"—often took care of it. Elvina tried that, twice. If anything stagnant still remained inside her colon after this morning, it would come out bleached-white and begging for mercy.

For the life of her, she couldn't fathom why the twitchy sensation had lodged up under her skin and refused to budge. Sure, if she watched too much news, it could bring on one of her blue spells. But overall, life wasn't so bad.

Elvina rested on a wrought iron bench beside the Piddie Davis Longman Memorial Daisy Garden. Every day since May of 2001, Elvina had come to the spot behind the Witherspoon mansion to talk to her deceased friend. At first, she worried someone would call the authorities and she would be carted off—kicking and spitting in a starched straight jacket—to the nuthouse on West Washington Street. Doomed to be medicated, shocked silly, and God-only-knows what.

Wasn't her idea, this daily gab session. It was the grief counselor's over in Tallahassee.

Hard to fathom. Piddie had been gone for over ten years.

The daisies over Piddie's patch still bloomed, though the relentless summer heat had taken its toll. The stems grew leggier by the day, and Elvina had staked them in thick bundles for support. Soon Jake would pull the faded plants and prepare the bed for the winter with mulch and pine straw.

Elvina smiled. Each time she needed a few words of wisdom, Piddie's voice whispered in her ears—like the brush of a moth's wings against silk. "Spring comes every year, 'Vina. It's all this big circle, going 'round and 'round. You ain't gonna stop it, so you might as well get yourself easy with it."

"Morning, Piddie." She dug into her smock pocket and grabbed a handful of peanuts.

"I got a full day today, and I ain't going to be back out here 'til tomorrow," Elvina called out to the squirrels chattering in the live oak above her. "Got to work, then I'm driving over to Tallahassee to visit Sabrina. So you want some of these nuts, you best roust yourselves out of that cozy nest and get your little fuzzy butts on down here."

Two squirrels clambered down the tree trunk and paused to study her for a moment before launching themselves through the air and onto the bench. Elvina liked to think they were the same squirrels she had made friends with in the first year after Piddie's death, but she knew better. How long did gray squirrels live, anyway?

The smaller one—with the deformed back leg—hopped beside her and sat up on his haunches. "Morning, Gimpy. God might've given you a bad deal of a leg, but you don't fail to be the first one when the feedbag is on, do you?" She held out a nut and the squirrel snatched it.

The second squirrel hunkered down and inched closer.

"No need to be shy. You know I ain't gonna hurt you."

Squirrels tended to be a bit jumpy. Suppose if she was always worrying about being picked off by a red-tailed hawk or shot at by a kid with a B-B gun, she'd be a bit nervous too. Not everyone shared Elvina's high opinion of squirrels. They were bad about chewing wires and wood trim and most everything on a house. Most folks viewed them as rats with better P. R.

She laid a pile of nuts on the bench and brushed the shell dust from her hands, then directed her words toward the flower garden. "Piddie, I'm here early today. The heat takes it out of me. Cool weather can't get here soon enough for me, I'll tell you."

She shifted to alleviate the cramp in her lower back.

"I have got to get Evelyn to fashion me a pillow for this bench. That is, if I can tie her down long enough. That daughter of yours got this big order for some autumn vests and jackets, from a little exclusive boutique in Tallahassee. She's been busy as a bee in a tar bucket. She's here when I come in around six, and doesn't leave until way in the evenings. Joe has gotten to where he brings her supper every day and makes her take a break to eat a bite with him."

Oblivious to her banter, the two squirrels made fast work of the pile of peanuts. A third joined them. Every now and then, one would pause and study her with its head cocked to one side.

"I got this most unsettled feeling, Piddie. You used to call it *a rabbit running over your grave*, though I never did understand what the heck that was supposed to mean. When I found out about Sabrina and that awful wreck, I assumed that was it. You know I am somewhat *psychic-al*. Still, the feeling didn't pass, even after I did my colon purging. What in the world do you reckon it could be?"

Only one thing to do with a crisis of the unknown: visit Lucille Jackson, wife of the esteemed Reverend Thurston Jackson of the

Morningside A.M.E. Church. The little black woman possessed the clearest earthly connection to the Almighty of anyone Elvina had ever known, short of Piddie.

When Elvina first moved to Chattahoochee from Miami following the death of her husband Clyde, she had not been a church-going type. Up until that point, her idea of worship had been sitting hand in hand with Clyde, watching the sunset over the last of the dying surf.

Now she attended church every Sunday, not that she considered herself a religious sort. Piddie prompted that habit, and it stuck. Besides the Triple C, the local churches formed the cornerstones of the communities—black and white—and a person could tune into anything by attending services.

Every other week, Elvina drove her gold Delta 88 down Wire Road to the sanctuary where Lucille greeted her—as she did all comers—at the double wooden doors. Elvina marveled at the simplicity of the building: an elongated room with time-polished pine floors and three rows of pews without benefit of cushions. Reverend Jackson's pulpit stood at one end, centered beneath a crudely carved depiction of Christ on the cross. Three rows of wooden benches held the choir.

Over time, the thick, paned windows had been replaced one-by-one with jewel-toned stained glass, the results of love offerings and hours of bake sales, car washes, and fish fries. Other than a community gathering room and a playground for the children, little had changed at the small church.

On that first Sunday, Elvina noticed the sense of peace that wrapped around her when she sat next to Piddie and Lillian on the first pew. One of the main differences between a white church and a black church, as far as Elvina could fathom: in a white church, a lot of folks came *to be seen*. In a black church, most folks came *to see*.

If Elvina had to pick the one thing she liked most, it would be the singing. All that swaying and clapping and such! Elvina had tried to maintain an air of composure at first, then allowed herself to get drawn in. Before she knew what happened, her hands flew up, and she praised with the best of them.

Some Sundays, a tall, stout young woman led the choir, and Elvina marveled at the fact the roof didn't go spinning into space. When Chiquetta Wilson opened her mouth, a voice larger than a host of angles flew out. Elvina's eyes watered with sheer emotion.

Even now, Elvina could close her eyes and hear Chiquita's voice echoing through the garden as it had the day of Piddie's memorial service. It had been a bold, uplifting song—"Oh Happy Day"—not the usual funeral dirge. The ladies of the Morningside A.M.E., dressed in bright prints, circled the garden as Chiquetta, resplendent in scarlet, belted out the old spiritual. The crowd joined in. If Piddie was hovering nearby—Elvina knew she had been—she was pleased with how everyone had carried out her last wishes for an upbeat and colorful celebration of her earth-time.

The women of the Morningside A.M.E. provided the inspiration that led Elvina to her profitable sideline, designing hats to match Evelyn's custom-made dresses. Elvina wished more white women would embrace the trend. The women of color adored their hats. Before Easter, Christmas, weddings and other special occasions, Evelyn and Elvina worked at a frenzied pace to keep up with orders for seasonal dresses with coordinating headwear.

Elvina sighed. Ten hat orders waited inside—paid in full by ladies anticipating the Christmas holiday rush. Hours of work awaited.

But somewhere in her schedule, Elvina would have to fit in a visit to her dear friend Lucille.

Choo-choo Ivey blinked and allowed her eyes to grow accustomed to the dim green glow of the hall nightlight. She glanced at the digital display on the clock radio by the bed. Three thirty in the morning.

"What is this? Some kind of witching hour or something?"

Prissy shifted slightly, raised her head and growled. The poodle grew even surlier if anything disturbed her beauty sleep. Not that it made much difference. Bless her little shabby heart; age had not been kind to her.

"Oh, hush up. Not like you don't sleep all dang day, anyway. You're lucky I even let you up here."

Blame Charlie for that. He had allowed Prissy to rest at the base of their queen-sized bed from the time she was a pint-sized puppy. Cute and sweet, then. Bad mistake now. Not only did Prissy snore, she gnawed her toenails in the middle of the night. And she farted. Silent, putrid gusts that curled the fine hairs in her owner's nose. Choo-choo should enjoy the company now that Charlie's side of the bed lay empty. It was a scrambled blessing.

Choo-choo stared at the ceiling for a few minutes. Willed herself to fall back to sleep. Fat chance. Once her eyes opened, it was done. Might as well get up. Heaven forbid she should further disturb the princess.

The wee hours had proven to be the worst since Charlie's death. No problem filling the days; someone always needed something. Run errands. Visit the elderly—she thought of this as anyone other than herself. Sit with a Hospice patient. Attend club meetings. Drive to Tallahassee for one of many doctor's appointments or clothing sales. Get the car serviced. Call Elvina Houston.

Somebody should come up with an insomnia network, one where she could pick up the phone and dial in to connect with the other unfortunates whose bodies believed sleep was optional. Choo-choo imagined houses similar to hers with lighted bedrooms: people reading novels, visiting virtual chat rooms, ordering gewgaws off the home shopping network, watching reruns of *Gunsmoke* and infomercials and being ticked-off at their snoozing neighbors. Even prescription sleep aids held no relief. Choo-choo had tried several. She would fall into a deep sleep, only to awaken at chicken-thirty.

What use was her life, anyway? She took up space and breathed air someone younger and more productive needed. And her natural optimism was all but shot. Beaten down, like rock carved by a trickle of water. Day after day. One drip at a time. She hated herself for sinking lower. Fought it with everything she had left. Which wasn't much.

After a stop by the bathroom, she shuffled to the kitchen. Choo-choo heated water for chamomile tea, then flipped through her music selection to find the *Natural Massage* CD, the same one Joy used for background music. The sound of harps and trickling water filled the den.

A hot cup of soothing herbal tea, then meditation. Maybe a few of the yoga stretches. Connect with something higher. Like the floor.

Choo-choo repeated one of her father's favorite sayings: "C'mon, little Choo-choo. Get your engine started."

Her father had always used analogies related to his profession. How he loved those trains. Choo-choo remembered the times she had been allowed to sit in her father's broad lap as he maneuvered the powerful locomotive to switch long lines of boxcars at River Junction Crossing. The engine's vibration rang through her bones and made her giggle.

As a toddler, Choo-choo had been guarded and deliberate. She had waited to walk until she could take more than a few steps. She spoke all at once in full sentences without bothering to try out a few words at a time. Her parents worried she might be a trifle dim-witted. She wasn't.

Choo-choo had been the youngest: the caboose, her daddy's favorite of five—the others, boys. Now deceased. With no engine to pull her along, no still-living sibling boxcars between, and nothing but hills to climb stretching far into the horizon, this caboose rolled slower and slower.

Prissy stumbled into the den, blinked twice, then let out a string of barks and growls.

"Prissy. It's me, you old fool. Hush up! You're ruining my meditation."

The poodle tilted her head, barked twice more, farted, and walked into the kitchen. Sure, the little rat would eat now. No need to give her human caretaker the satisfaction of witnessing it. Choo-choo glanced toward the ceiling and held her palms together.

"Charlie Ivey? If you can hear me . . . Please, please ask God to send me and that dog to different parts of heaven."

Sheila Bruner blamed the lack of rain for Glenn's recent ill humor. The ongoing late summer drought made everybody a little more mean. Fish ponds sucked dry, lawns turned crisp-brown, and the once-wide Apalachicola River narrowed to a shallow muddy strip.

May God forgive Glenn for his anger; the ruddy swelling low on one cheek made Sheila's reverent smile lopsided.

Poor Glenn. If he didn't get out on the water at least once a week, all that edgy pent-up stuff came out. Something about floating alone in his small boat, watching a cork bob beneath the river willows, and drinking a few beers, transformed him into a happier person. That and meetings with his hunting club.

The boat sat idle now, its battery terminals laced to a trickle-charger. Even if Glenn wanted to risk navigating the Apalachicola, a bent propeller from its last encounter with a submerged cypress stump prevented an outing.

Sheila flipped on the Weather Channel. That stubborn low-pressure system trapped the moisture. Clusters of green floated across the radar image, a few minor storms that might spit rain, barely enough to settle the dust. And it would take a monsoon to refuel the river. People prayed for a hurricane, or at least a soaking tropical system, like hoping for an illness to get rest in a hospital bed. Florida's underground aquifer kept North Florida from serious supply worries. Beneath layers of limestone, the submerged reservoir ran clean and clear, less affected by the whims of nature. Even so, Sheila tried to conserve. The washer only ran with a full load. But Glenn hated to see dirty laundry in sorted piles, so Sheila hid it in plastic containers neatly stacked in the garage until she had enough to justify using the water.

If it was up to her husband, the household wouldn't recycle either. Two large plastic bins held rinsed cans, bottles, and plastics. No odor, no mess, no leftover food juices, no stale scent of beer. As long as she kept it spotless, Glenn tolerated her attempts to promote green living.

Sheila stepped from the back door and studied the hedges. The makeshift kitty house wasn't visible unless she moved the lower branches. Good.

"Buttercup? Oreo?"

The leaves parted and the orange tabby peeked out. A second little head appeared. In the past few days, the kitten had grown noticeably and its round blue eyes opened. Soon, she would help it transition to a slurry of chicken or turkey baby food mixed with goat's milk.

She scooped Buttercup in one hand and Oreo in the other and held them to her cheeks. How could anyone dislike animals? Kitty love came without strings, or bruises.

Sheila set them down and watched the two attack a shallow pan of goat's milk. The kitten stepped into the liquid and slurped. Buttercup took breaks between laps to lick milk froth from the kitten's face and head. Though Sheila still used a dropper to make sure it received enough nourishment, she allowed the older cat to help the baby learn about eating from a dish. The sooner Oreo became independent, the better. Already Glenn questioned her frequent nightly bathroom breaks, on the nights he wasn't passed out cold.

When he said, "You have the smallest dadgum bladder," she had countered with "It's a female thing, honey."

The mention of women's issues curtailed further inquiry.

After the cats fed and rested, Sheila took a few minutes to entertain them with a toy fashioned from one of Glenn's broken reed fishing poles, a length of string, and a few feathers culled from a hand-held duster. Buttercup launched through the air in wide arcs, and Oreo followed the bouncing fluff and batted it when Sheila brought it closer to the ground.

She laughed and her breath caught. The ribs were still a little sore, and this last blow had landed in the soft spot over her left kidney. At least she could cover up her midsection for yoga class. Heavy makeup would mask the fresh bruise on her cheek, not such a bad one. Things could be worse. Much worse.

Chapter Three

Seven weeks before suicide
Monday

Abby McKenzie unfurled a purple, jelly-rolled sticky mat into the air and allowed it to land before straightening the edges. Around her, the yoga class members settled in.

"Sheila . . . hon? You need to lay off the blush. Your cheeks look like a Kewpie doll's." Loiscell rested a hand on her friend's shoulder.

Sheila's fingertips touched her camouflaged left cheek. "Is it too much? I'm trying out this new kind. It's a little thicker, and a little redder, than the last one I bought. Guess I should've put it on in better light."

Abby leaned over and took a close look. "You should take advantage of being young enough not to need a lot of cover. When you get closer to fifty, you won't be caught dead without make-up. I don't like to wear it, but I look like death warmed over if I don't."

Choo-choo joined them. The elder's new yoga mat—hot pink to match the trim on her carryall. "Especially when you reach my age. Takes a couple of pounds of spackle to keep the buzzards from circling when I leave the porch."

The women laughed. Since the first yoga class, more ladies had joined. But the core group of four—the self-proclaimed "Yoga Rat Pack"—stuck together, their mats lined up in a tight cluster.

"Anyone heard how Sabrina's getting along?" Loiscell asked.

Choo-choo and Abby exchanged glances, then Abby yielded to Choo-choo's seniority. Choo-choo unwound her yoga mat. "Elvina went over to see her the day after surgery. Sabrina was pretty doped up, but doing okay besides that. Elvina says Sabrina's gotten a lot of visitors, and she's not getting much rest. God knows, it's next to im-possible to sleep when you're in the hospital anyway."

"Her husband Gerald called the office yesterday," Abby added. "More than likely, she won't be back at work for a good while. I know it's eating her alive. It's hard to go wide-open with a cast up to your crotch."

Sheila settled cross-legged onto her yoga pillow. "I'll call and see if I might clean their house before she comes home. It won't do Sabrina any good to come into a mess."

"I can make my ham and scalloped potato casserole," Loiscell said. "Good comfort food, nothing like it. Some fresh roses too. I can do that."

Choo-choo groaned as she eased onto her mat. "I'm too old for this groveling around on the floor." She chuckled. "Good thing I got you all around to help me get up."

Loiscell plopped down. "Give it a rest, Choo-choo. You run circles around all of us."

Abby bent over and touched her toes. Every muscle in her legs protested. "We all could be poster children for the benefits of yoga. I couldn't lean much past my knees when we started. And to get back to Sabrina . . . you know Elvina Houston will jump-start the casserole committee. They'll have so much food, they won't know what to do with it all."

Choo-choo nodded. "That's the good thing about living in the South. No matter what happens to you, you'll always be well-fed."

Joy Harris walked in, her blue duffle trailing behind her like a well-trained dog. "Sorry I'm a little late. There was a tractor-trailer turned over on the Interstate a little west of Midway. I had to get off in Quincy and take the secondary road."

"Highway 90 is so much prettier than the Interstate, anyway," Choo-choo said. "People get to going too blasted fast on those super-highways, you ask me. What ever happened to looking out the window and enjoying the ride?"

Abby huffed. "Maybe, when I retire—if I don't die before that happens—I'll be able to take the slow lane and enjoy the trip too."

The woodsy scent of burning incense filled the room, not over-powering yet intensely present.

"I love that smell, Joy," Abby commented. "What kind is it?"

The blonde instructor doused the match in a piece of foil. "Believe it or not, it's a blend named *Joy*. Sandalwood, musk, maybe a hint of rosewood. I found it in a little gift shop on St. George Island."

Loiscell laughed. "Well now. That's appropriate. How many yoga teachers have an incense named after them? After my second go-round with chemo, I couldn't abide perfumes. Flowers were okay, but definitely nothing unnatural. I couldn't use air fresheners at all. And I had to switch to unscented deodorant, soap, and washing powder." Her expression darkened.

"You okay, dear?" Choo-choo asked. "You looked like the Grim Reaper himself was pointing your way."

Loiscell took a shaky breath. "Fine. I'm fine. Really."

Ben Calhoun stood in front of the Women's Club's double wooden doors. Sure, Elvina had told him the yoga class was open to all, and that everyone was more than welcome, but that didn't mean diddlysquat.

Over the years, his job had nudged him from his innate shyness. He couldn't dump off mail and packages without so much as a how-do-you-do, not in a town the size of Chattahoochee. A repertoire of questions and comments for any situation stood ready. "How's your mama and 'em?" "Did you have a nice vacation?" "Are you feeling better since you had that terrible flu?" "Looks like you got another package from your daughter out West. How's she doing? And the grandkids?" "How's your husband's case of the gout?"

Some folks didn't cotton to chatting with their postal carrier; those he left alone. Most of the elderly and shut-ins welcomed Ben's regular visits. As many times as he had been offered homemade baked goods, especially around the holidays, Ben marveled at how his body had not added more than an inch-to-pinch around the midsection. The walking helped, and the occasional times he forced himself to go for an evening jog. Still he longed for physical activity and, on a deeper level since his wife passed away, company.

Ben braced himself and pulled his shoulders back. What was so scary about walking into a roomful of females? Wasn't like they were going to circle the pack, kill him, and pick his bones. The same uneasy feeling clobbered him whenever he had stepped into a gathering of his wife's friends. Laughter and conversation would stop dead, all eyes trained on the masculine invader.

41

His late wife's gentle way of asking *have you lost your mind? And what could possibly be so important that it couldn't wait*—"Yes, dear?"

There he would stand, muttering something unintelligible and bobbing his head like it perched on a spring. Mumble, nod, slink from the room, and be darn glad you escaped with your manhood intact.

Ben hated Monday night television. Couldn't possibly take one more rerun episode of *Mayberry, RFD*. He entered the class quietly and hesitated at the back of the room.

Joy Harris opened her eyes and smiled when she sensed his presence. "Come on in. We've barely started the meditation." She motioned to a spot at the rear of the group between two ladies. "So glad you joined us."

Ben seated himself on his thin foam camping mat, trying his best to blend into the background. "Um . . . it is okay? I mean, I heard this wasn't just for women."

"Of course it's okay. I have had a few men in my classes, from time to time. It evens out the energy—all about balance, you see."

Choo-choo swiveled back around after learning the identity of the newcomer. "Elvina will pitch a fit and fall in it. If Ben Calhoun proves to be less tight-lipped than most males, think of the inside scoop he might offer," she whispered to Loiscell. "I'll have to invite him to unroll his mat next to me next class."

Abby glanced back, though she knew the voice. Her hand automatically lifted for a slight finger wave, then stopped. Even that small gesture brought on the sputtering hesitation, like an engine in need of a tune-up.

Without the official U.S. Post Office garb, Ben didn't look half bad. Kind of cute, actually. He wore tight knee-length black biking shorts and a long, loose FSU T-shirt with the sleeves and neck opening cut. His Spandex was a good idea for yoga class; no use running the risk of Big Jim and the Twins waving hello during one of the upside-down postures.

"Remind me next time, and I'll bring my digital camera for you," Loiscell leaned over and said in a low voice.

Abby jerked her attention back to the front of the room. A slight flush stung her cheeks. Other body parts warmed too. Betrayed by her own body.

Emotions collided inside Abby: annoyance mixed with desire. She wiped them both from her mind and forced a tight smile.

Seven weeks before suicide, Tuesday

"Where is that recipe, now?" Elvina Houston asked aloud.

Buster, nearing the same mark in feline years as his human counterpart, lifted his head, trilled once, and studied her with round butterscotch eyes. Since the snipping of his manhood several years back, the old Tom had become a homebody. He rarely left the house, content to follow Elvina from room to room and comment when it seemed necessary, or when his food bowl lay empty.

"I had it just last month. You know the one, cat. That cheesy chicken and rice bake with the crunchy topping. Has those little green sweet peas and shredded carrots in it. It was Sissy Pridgeon's grandma's recipe."

To hell with this old age business. She couldn't recall things like she used to, couldn't see, and couldn't hear. Piddie used to say, "I'll swannee, 'Vina. You're getting to where you can't hear a fart in a jug!" Not such a bad thing, experiencing the world with the volume turned down a notch. Young people played their rappity-tap-tap music loud enough to wake the dead, and most folks only talked to hear themselves blather.

On a few occasions since she had taken over Piddie's front desk position, patrons had ended up in the wrong appointment column. Elvina picked up enough clues when one called for a service—or kidded herself she did—and plugged them into the schedule. Even after she went to the color-coded organizational system, mistakes still occurred.

"Elvina? It's high time you admitted your problem." Mandy Andrews, head stylist, had to broach the subject. "Makes us look plumb foolish when we get someone in the chair and start doing one thing, when they asked for another."

Elvina had called the audiologist in Tallahassee the next day. The twin hearing aids fit snuggly, and if she remembered to pull a little fringe of hair down from her bun, were barely detectible. A whole new world opened up. Conversations bloomed around her, and she burned up the phone lines passing them on. Now she needed new glasses, it seemed.

"A person has to be dang near dead or blind as Choo-choo Ivey's poodle for insurance to pay for anything," Elvina groused to Buster as she dug through her recipe box. "Small wonder they have the tallest, fanciest buildings in any city."

If something on her body wasn't receding, it was being pulled by gravity. Her small breasts sagged like two baseballs suspended in plastic grocery bags. A church key—like the kind on the top of a sardine can—might prove more effective than a bra; she could roll them up and tighten the skin at the same time.

Elvina frowned at the jumbled recipe box, then caught her distorted reflection on one of the shiny pot lids. Jowls instead of firm cheeks! If she wasn't in the active state of smiling, she looked ticked off, all because her face was busy sliding toward the floor. Elvina had never been the sugary old lady who whipped up Tollhouse cookies for the kids on the block. Her disapproving expression scared children off before she even had a chance to offer them a Fig Newton. The only time they flocked to her house was at Halloween. Costumed in one of her mid-calf black funeral dresses and a painted mole on her chin, Elvina made a passable witch.

"You have to work with what the Good Lord gives you," Elvina said to the cat. "Knowledge is a Southern woman's power. Once you paint over beauty with a few age spots, it will be only a dim memory in some scrapbook picture."

Buster yawned and regarded her with a bored expression. "I don't know why I put up with the likes of you," Elvina said. "You have a way of looking at me like I'm dumb as a stick. Guess the reason you tolerate me at all is because I can operate a can opener."

The Tomcat trilled. Enough of a reaction to continue the one-sided conversation.

"I got a visitation for that Johnson fellow over across the river tomorrow, and I'm counting on taking that casserole to his next of kin. There's a boatload of 'em, and they'll start pouring in. People got to eat."

True, Elvina lived for a good funeral. She had more black in her closet than most undertakers. But she never arrived to witness a family's low point without a vat of comfort food in tow. Food was the tie that bound people to her and her to them.

"Grief isn't fed by spice, Buster. No one in the depths of despair longs for enchiladas or sushi. Suffering calls for thick stews, dishes oozing with cheese, or maybe a triple-layered coconut cake. Substantial food. Stick-to-your-ribs food. Remind-you-of-your-grandma's food."

Elvina stopped the scavenger hunt long enough to make a glass of iced green tea. The heirloom recipe box gaped open. Piddie's recipe box—Elvina's most valued possession besides her smartphone—should've, by rights, gone to Piddie's daughter Evelyn. But bless her heart, Evelyn was as much a cook as Mother Teresa was a fallen woman. Evelyn's kitchen boasted every culinary gadget known to The Food Network, yet the woman couldn't boil an egg without exploding it. Good thing her husband Joe knew his way around a stove.

"Ah-hah! Here it is!" Elvina plucked a dog-eared card from the cramped box and held it aloft. "What the blue blazes is this doing up in the appetizers?"

Buster stretched and repositioned.

"I'm proud to see you are so riveted to my problems. Maybe I should let you out to fend for yourself." She huffed and reached down to ruffle the cat's fur. "Who am I kidding? You wouldn't slap a mouse if it walked up and bit you on the behind."

As she bustled around the galley-style kitchen, Elvina chewed on the latest bit of gossip to come through the doors of the Triple C. Ben Calhoun had joined up with the ladies taking the yoga class. Even Jake Witherspoon had taken to going when he wasn't swamped with wedding or funeral flower orders. Elvina thought of Jake as one of the girls anyway. Heck, Jake did too, for that matter. She wasn't trying to be mean about it. Elvina loved Jake and his partner as if they were her sons. Who cared really, which way your weenie wiggled?

"Always figured Ben Calhoun might be gay too. Nah, he's not flashy enough," Elvina said. "Nice, but plain as white bread spread with cheap margarine." Ben didn't seem the type for sports, though she'd seen him jogging on occasion. Didn't appear to be the artsy-crafty type either.

On top of it all, Choo-choo Ivey had told Elvina that she caught Abby McKenzie admiring Ben's butt. Abby, who hacked up a hairball any time an interested man was within two feet. Imagine.

"Too much gray anymore, Buster." She measured a teaspoon of salt into her cupped palm and added to a pot of boiling water. "Used to be, a thing was either black or white."

Loiscell Pickering entered the oncology office and signed in. The receptionist nodded from behind a sliding window, not someone she recognized from the check-up the previous year.

The room had been redecorated in lemon yellow and Wedgwood blue—a country French theme. White shelves near the ceiling held an array of ceramics, dried herbs and flowers, and tasteful trinkets, enough to keep her eyes busy if she didn't want to read one of a variety of magazines. Loiscell appreciated the effort, anything to take her mind somewhere else.

Last time, the décor had reminded Loiscell of a rental beach house, complete with lush tropical plants, tranquil seaside paintings, and whitewashed rattan chairs with cabana-print cushions. She could recall the room's many incarnations. The underlying message, as far as she could tell: we change for the better, and so will you.

Cancer. The very word made Loiscell nauseated. The same thoughts popped to mind. Get your affairs in order. How many months do I have left? Is this the final battle?

Cancer: a caged dragon she lived with and periodically battled with all she had. Clip its scaly wings, Loiscell. Cut off its lifeblood. Jab it with a spear until it retreats far back into the cave.

But did the dragon ever die? Or did it hunker down, hibernating with its heartbeat slowed to an undetectable crawl until its keeper let down her guard?

Loiscell grabbed a recent copy of *People Magazine*. Nothing like reading about all those movie stars in rehab, or marrying each other, or divorcing each other, or not eating enough to keep a flea alive. She flipped to a section featuring female actors in awards-show regalia. A few had shucked the current hole-pocked, streetwalker designs for classic, tailored gowns. Others tried for the shock effect and succeeded.

The door between the reception area and back office opened. "Loiscell! It's so good to see you," Dr. Johnson's nurse said.

"Hey, Brenda. I'd say it's nice to see you too, but I'd much rather bump into you at the mall." She gave the nurse a warm hug.

"Good thing I have a strong ego, or that comment would hit me hard." The nurse ushered Loiscell into an exam room, reviewed the health history, and jotted notes about Loiscell's recent concerns.

"Why don't you go ahead and undress. Slip into the gown." The nurse motioned to a neat stack of plastic-lined paper on the exam table. "I'll let Dr. Johnson know you're waiting."

When the door closed, Loiscell donned the flimsy paper gown. Oh, for the days when they were soft cotton. Suppose the disposable ones were easier. No laundry bills. She heard a knock.

"Well, Loiscell Pickering." Dr. Johnson entered and grasped her hand. His hands were warm and his grip firm. Loiscell despised a limp, fishy handshake.

"You never change, Doc. How's that possible?"

"Good genes? That and *Just for Men*." When he smiled, genuine concern colored his features. It didn't hurt to have a handsome oncologist. He glanced over the chart. "So you've found a little problem?"

"I think it's back, Doc."

"Let me call Brenda back in, and we'll take a look."

The best thing about Dr. Johnson—besides the fact he was George-Clooney gorgeous—was that he never sugarcoated anything. Third time wasn't always the charm, no matter the old saying. Especially with cancer. He knew it. She knew it.

When she left the office a half-hour later, Loiscell held the paperwork for the inevitable series of scans and a biopsy. She folded it a few times and crammed it in the bottom of her purse with the used tissues and breath mints.

Chapter Four

Six weeks before suicide
Tuesday

Abby McKenzie closed her eyes and inhaled through her nostrils, held it, then exhaled through her mouth at the same measured rate: a centering technique from yoga class. Different day, same drama. "Kimberly's a very good dental hygienist, Mrs. Warren. She's subbed for us before. I haven't had a single person say anything bad about her."

She pinched her nose at the bridge. That headache she'd put off with two aspirins was back. The woman yammered on and on.

"It may be several weeks before Sabrina's well enough to come back to work. Even then, it might be part-time for a while."

The woman on the other end wheezed, hacked twice, and said, "Put me down, end of January. My teeth ain't going to fall out before then."

Three more months to layer on the nicotine stain. Sabrina would be thrilled. In a way, Abby could understand the patient's reticence. Professionals who provided good personal care were as valuable as dark chocolate. A doctor who actually listened, a hair stylist who didn't leave you looking like a startled squirrel, a nurse who gave a flu shot without charging across the room with the needle in hand like a dagger, a hygienist who didn't lecture you to dang death.

Abby tapped the computer keys to access the next year's schedule. "I'm afraid it will be the second week in February. I can put you on her cancellation list."

The woman huffed. "If that's when it is, so be it. Ten in the morning. Doesn't matter what day. Could you send me a card in the mail? If you tell me now I won't remember it, and I don't get my free calendar from the insurance company until sometime in December."

"Will do, Mrs. Warren. You have a good day, now."

Abby picked a time slot and entered the name. The computer program automatically supplied the rest: contact numbers, medical and drug alerts, and type of appointment. Though Sophie the Manic Computer often made life a living hell, Abby appreciated the ease of managing the practice. She tried her best to remember that fact when the computer refused to cooperate.

Some days, she wouldn't be surprised if patients asked her most anything. *Could you pick up my dry-cleaning and drop it by on your way home? I need a gallon of milk, too. And my tires need rotating. Do you think you could ask around and find out who my husband is sleeping with?*

The strangest question Abby had ever had: How often should a cat urinate? It took every speck of professionalism not to laugh or offer a sarcastic reply. *First of all, I don't own a cat. Second, if I did, I wouldn't follow it around counting bathroom breaks. Third, I work in a dental office...ma'am.*

She didn't envy Elvina Houston her position in the community. How exhausting. Abby could barely keep up with her own life, much less monitor everyone else's.

A tap sounded on the reception room window and she slid it open. Ben Calhoun handed over a tall stack of mail. She knew without looking, most of it would be junk flyers and magazines.

"Afternoon, fellow yoga person." Ben's mustache curled up with his lips.

Every cell inside her went all goofy schoolgirl. Easy there, gal. Abby tossed the mail onto the desk. "Ever have one of those days where you wish you could snap your fingers and end up on the moon?"

"Oh no. Not at all."

"Wouldn't have taken you for the Pollyanna type, Ben."

"I hide my grave dissatisfaction behind a veil of well-being."

She laughed, amazed at how easy conversation had become with him. "Very profound. So are you enjoying Monday nights?"

"Very much. My back doesn't bother me nearly as much as it did. You?"

"Uh-huh. I use the breathing thing all the time. Can't believe the class is so popular. Who would've ever thunk it? You're responsible in part."

His light brown eyebrows shot up. "Me?"

"Because you're male and you started taking classes. I notice a few more husbands and boyfriends there now." Abby wanted to add: and the best part, I can say more than two words to you without my throat closing up. Her heartbeat thrummed. Her headache eased up too.

"We men folk have such a hard time doing anything that doesn't involve heavy padding, bloodshed and bruising, or a power tool." Ben checked his watch. "Guess I'd better quit yakking and get back to work."

Abby looked at the stack of mail. "Me too." There it was again, the niggling pain in her temples.

Ben held up his index finger. "I almost forgot." He rummaged in the black messenger bag and handed her a small paper sack.

"Special delivery? What?"

"I searched for this after we talked about old childhood toys, last night in class."

Abby opened the bag and gasped. "Oh my gosh! I haven't seen one of these in years." She pulled a three-inch tall rubber doll from the bag. Its bright orange acrylic hair stood straight up. When she turned it around, the distinctive logo etched on its mid-back attested to its authenticity. "A troll doll! This has to be over forty years old."

"I found quite a collection. Forgot I still had so many. All different sizes. Used to make my mom crazy, me calling it a *DAM* doll, though it wasn't cussing really since that was stamped across the back." Ben gestured toward Sophie. "Thought you'd like one to keep by that ornery computer of yours."

She'd rather keep *him* by her computer. What would it feel like to have his slender fingers twine through her hair? That mustache tickling her neck, then her throat as he kissed lower and lower . . . Her insides froze. Sex. She'd only done *it* six, maybe seven times, if she didn't count the sweaty moments she had pleasured herself. Good girls didn't admit to that. Shame, shame.

Abby rubbed the troll's coarse hair, a ritual that was supposed to make wishes come true and ward off bad things. Help me with Ben. I can do this.

Prissy whined and danced in front of Choo-choo Ivey's front screened door, wiggling and stepping from one leg to the next.

"What in the blue blazes has crawled up your shaggy butt and lodged sideways?"

The poodle looked up through milky eyes and yelped twice. Choo-choo peered through the screen. "There's nothing out there, you little lunatic. Just the breeze blowing the flag."

A cool front had pushed the early morning temperatures down into the mid-seventies. Not chilly by any measure, but a welcomed change from the high eighties. Might as well enjoy; the forecast called for upper nineties by next week. More stifling heat. Like a cat tormenting a wounded lizard, letting up and pouncing, letting up and pouncing.

The dog's urgent keening escalated, a sound that could've been used to torture sensitive information from a captured spy.

"Oh, all right. Walk out with me to get the paper. What's up with you anyway? Do you have to pee-pee? Can hardly fathom that. I can't remember the last time you asked to go out to do your business."

Choo-choo tightened the sash on her robe, looked again to make sure none of her neighbors watched, and opened the door. Prissy sailed out, banging the side of the wooden screened door against the house.

"Don't you go far! I refuse to look for you this time of morning! You hear me?"

The poodle spooled from one side of the yard to the other, her nose to the ground. Maybe the cooler weather had spurred her on. Choo-choo rescued the *Tallahassee Democrat* from the middle of the yard. When she stood up, she froze. The largest pit bull dog she had ever seen barreled toward her from the right. A flash of fur passed by from her left.

Prissy went straight for the pit bull's throat, missing twice before gaining purchase on the loose skin beneath its chin. In one blazing movement, the large dog flipped the smaller one into the air and pinned her down, its massive jaws wrapped around Prissy's upper body. Choo-choo reacted before she had time to consider, yanking the massive dog off Charlie's pet and shoving it away. Prissy shook, struggled to her feet, snarled, and jumped in the direction of the prostrate pit bull.

"Have you lost your mind?" Choo-choo snatched the poodle into her arms. She shuffled as quickly as possible to the house. The pit bull followed, wagging its nubby tail. Once they were safely inside, Choo-choo ruffled her hands through Prissy's hair. No visible gashes or blood, only ropes of slobber.

"What to do? What to do?"

Prissy, now locked in the spare bedroom, yelped and keened. On the porch, the pit bull sat down and cocked its head, tongue hanging out. Choo-choo could swear it was smiling.

"I can't leave you to run loose, now can I?" she asked from behind the screen. Choo-choo swallowed hard and opened the door a crack.

When she stepped onto the porch, the canine came to her. The nub of a tail wagged the dog, and its tongue slathered her knees with liquid love.

"You're not so bad, are you gal?" She noticed the undeniable evidence to the contrary hanging beneath the muscular hindquarters. "Um . . . excuse me, fella."

Choo-choo lowered herself to a squat with a moan. Why was it, since she had moved into advanced age, each movement out of the ordinary came with vocal accompaniment?

The pit bull's jaws reminded Choo-choo of one of those huge earthmovers with the vise-trap maw. She shivered. What had she been thinking? Proof positive that adrenaline made a person strong. And stupid. The pit bull could've not only eaten Charlie's dog like a chew-toy, but killed her too.

"Let's see your collar, big boy."

The green bell-shaped metal rabies tag showed a recent date, vaccination number, and the name of a Tallahassee veterinary clinic.

"Only problem here, the vet's office won't be open yet. You don't have any other ID tag, so what am I to do with you? Can't let you run free."

Choo-choo stood and moved to sit in a porch rocker. The pit bull followed and rested his bowling ball-sized head on her lap.

Who could she call? Elvina? No. She was a died-in-the-wool cat person, and would fall out if she saw the size of the pit bull. Besides, Choo-choo wasn't in the mood for a lecture about how foolish she had been for intervening in a dog fight.

"You stay right here, boy. I have to make a call."

Loiscell's Volvo screeched to a halt at the curb in a matter of minutes. She dashed through the front yard and stopped cold when she spotted Choo-choo petting the pit bull. "Good Lord! You didn't tell me it was the size of a Shetland pony!"

"It's okay, Loiscell. He wouldn't hurt a fly. Only I don't quite know what to do with him. I can't keep him here. Prissy won't tolerate it."

"Where is Prissy? Is she hurt?"

Choo-choo motioned toward the house. "She's still whining, so I know she's alive. It didn't look like he actually bit her."

"You can't blame her, Choo-choo. Prissy was protecting you and her territory."

Choo-choo tilted her head. "Hadn't thought of that. Up until this point, the only thing Charlie's dog has ever protected was that mangy bed of hers."

"We'll have to call the police. Animal control won't pick up this early."

"You know everything, Loiscell. I swannee. And I thought Elvina Houston held that title."

Loiscell flipped open her cell phone and hit the speed-dial number assigned to the Chattahoochee Police Department. "I had a stray at my house a couple of months back. Not like I'm a whiz kid or anything. And things like this always happen at odd times. Must be some kind of Murphy's Law or something."

Within ten minutes, a police cruiser pulled up behind Loiscell's Volvo.

"Morning, Miz Choo-choo. Miz Loiscell. What have y'all gotten yourselves into, this early in the day?" Officer J.T. Smathers adjusted his gun belt and grinned. He picked up the rolled newspaper, forgotten in the fray, and walked toward them.

Choo-choo returned the smile. She was a sucker for a man in a uniform. It was all she could do not to speed just to get pulled over and talk the officer out of giving her a ticket. Old enough to know better. Female enough not to give a care.

"We hated to call you," Loiscell said. "But we don't have a clue what to do with this stray dog."

Choo-choo rubbed the velvety hair on the dog's muzzle. "He's not mean. I have to make that clear. Prissy went after him, not the other way around."

J.T. chuckled, handed over the paper. "Your little poodle went after this huge dog?"

Choo-choo nodded and stuffed the newspaper underneath one arm.

J.T. leaned down and let the dog sniff his hand. After the brief introduction, he examined the animal's head and neck, then ran his hands along the dog's flanks. "No healed cuts or signs he's been used for fighting. Judging from how healthy he is, I'll bet he's someone's pet. No doubt, somebody paid a lot of money for this dog."

The officer pulled a nylon leash from his belt and snapped it onto the dog's collar. "I'll ask around at the station. See if anyone recognizes him. We'll call the vet's office in a little while. If nothing else, I can always take him home with me. Melody loves animals."

Choo-choo reached out and grasped the officer's hand. "I thank you kindly, J.T. You're a good man."

The young officer winked. "Some days. Depends. You might ask Melody about that."

If Choo-choo was ten years younger, she'd give that Melody some heavy competition.

After the cruiser pulled away, the women went inside and double-checked Prissy for injuries. Other than a case of the shivers, the little dog appeared unharmed.

"She reminds me of that Looney Tunes cartoon, the one where Wiley Coyote takes those earthquake pills. Then, he takes to shaking every step or so . . . " Choo-choo petted the poodle. To her surprise, Prissy licked her hand.

"She's working off the adrenaline dump," Loiscell said. "You got any coffee on?"

"What Southern woman worth her salt wouldn't?" Choo-choo positioned a soft pillow on the couch and lowered Prissy down. The dog twirled three times in a circle before curling into a tight ball and falling asleep.

"After this, we might need to add a shot of that Jim Beam you keep for medicinal purposes."

Choo-choo patted her friend on the back. "I have something better. Homemade Kahlua."

"You made Kahlua?" Loiscell's eyebrows arched.

"No, not me. Elvina. She gave it to me last year for Christmas. It's G-double-O-D, good!" Choo-choo grabbed two pottery mugs from the kitchen cabinet. "Elvina's not as lily-white as she lets on. But don't you dare breathe a word that I told you about her making spirits. She'd throw a clot."

Six weeks before suicide, Saturday

In the minutes before full sunrise when faint light filtered through the plantation blinds, Sheila Bruner watched her husband sleeping. The lines around his mouth relaxed from the usual pursed disapproval. Long, brown lashes curled against the tanned skin beneath his closed eyes. His breathing, deep and even. Innocent. Sweet.

She struggled to recall the times early in their relationship when he had been less angry, less in need of her total submission.

But that was before that football game dashed his dreams, and before his daddy's sudden death dashed his heart.

Sheila closed her eyes and feigned sleep until she heard him rise and go into the bathroom. Then she changed into a cotton housedress and slipped into the kitchen to start the coffee.

Glenn approached the new day like nothing had happened the night before, wolfed down a tall stack of blueberry pancakes with maple syrup and bacon, showered, dressed in bark-printed camouflage, and left for his weekend at the hunting camp.

Glenn Bruner started at the sound of a deep voice.

"This cherry boat you keep going on and on about, why isn't it sitting at your house?" Julius Herndon—*Clay* to his club associates—regarded Glenn with an indifferent gaze.

Other than a handful of men Glenn knew personally, few of the others—particularly the older ones—gave him the time of day. This fellow stood out for his lack of redneck-flavored southernisms. If Glenn had to guess where Clay was from, he couldn't. The guy had that flat of an accent. And he hardly ever cussed; the sound of his voice alone was enough to rivet attention.

"You kidding me? You *are* kidding me, right?" Glenn ejected the spent magazine from a Glock .45 caliber semiautomatic. No use for more target practice today. Though still far from setting, the sun threw scant light through the thick pines. The two men were the last diehards left on the firing range.

Glenn's gaze took in the weapon Clay used—a .308 assault rifle with all kinds of fancy scopes and optics that marked him as one of the standoffish elite. Who were they all kidding anyway, with their weapons of choice? Oh, they'd say they were planning an elk-hunting trip to Colorado, or maybe something vague about Canada. Right. That, and monkeys would fly out their butts. Glenn was no fool. The assault weapons should've been in the hands of a tactical team member or a professional assassin, not some Joes planning a hunting expedition.

Glenn listened to the others as they cussed, spit, and farted around the campfire. About how they longed for weapons beyond the long-range rifles. Something fully automatic. "Spray and Pray": the phrase some of the men used in jest. Spray the area with fire and pray it hit something. Why worry so much about proper aim? No matter how hard they tried to pitch the All-American, right-to-bear-arms thing, the only reason to carry such a piece was to kill a man, or several. Death in the fast lane.

"I look like the kidding type to you?" In the dim light, the shadowy hollows beneath Clay's cheeks added to the skeletal likeness.

Glenn shrugged to cover an involuntary shiver. "Hell no."

Clay regarded him with bored, lifeless eyes. Glenn had seen the same lack of expression in a few of the incarcerated juvies at the correctional institution, the ones he knew wouldn't be fazed by the good-intentioned work training and anger management counseling. The ones who had a body part or two in zipper-sealed bags in their freezers or buried beneath their mama's prize rose bush.

In the short time he had known Clay, Glenn had seldom seen any emotion from the man. The only time his rough features registered a flicker of humanity was when he fired a weapon. Clay seemed to have a different gun every morning, like those lacy girl-panties Sheila had with a day of the week stitched across the ass.

"So why don't you already have that boat?" Clay said.

"I can think of several thousand dollars' worth of why." Glenn used a soft lint-free cloth to wipe down his gun. Only one true color for a handgun: flat black. No chrome to reflect light. Prettier than a high-end whore and a lot more dependable, not to mention less trouble.

Clay returned his rifle to a hard foam-lined case. He chewed on the end of a splayed toothpick, rolling it from one side of his down-turned mouth to the other. "Money should never stand in the way of a man and what he requires."

"Yeah. What do you suggest I do, rob a bank?"

When Clay laughed, Glenn steadied himself to hide the shock. The sound didn't come out joyful; rather, it erupted like the rasp of a dying engine. "No! You wreck me." Clay winked: another out-of-character gesture. It was like watching that Jack Nicholson's ax-wielding character in *The Shining* turn into the cuddly fabric-softener-commercial bear.

Glenn joined with his version of good-ole-boy bluster, hoping he might gain entrance into the coveted inner circle. "You holding out on me, man? You really some long-lost Donald Trump love-child, or something?"

Clay nodded once, a decision made. "The real money, my friend, is in contract work."

"Like . . . for the government?"

The two walked toward the main encampment. The scent of ignited charcoal and lighter fluid made Glenn's mouth water. No beans and stew tonight. No sir-ee. The word had been handed down at the last meeting: bring your own steak to throw on the grill. The thicker and bloodier, the better. The Committee of Seven would supply all the fixings: baked potatoes, bread, maybe a couple of salads, and fat slabs of homemade cake—compliments of someone's wife or girlfriend.

Clay narrowed his eyes. "Privately-funded contract work. Only for those with the keenest eye and best marksmanship. And someone man enough to do what is necessary."

Glenn stopped dead. "You're talking about shootin' somebody, ain't cha?"

Clay grabbed Glenn's elbow and dug his fingertips into the tender flesh close to the joint. "Lower your voice, you imbecile. Let me tell you something, you want the kind of money to buy that boat with all the bells and whistles, you have to do whatever it takes to get it. And you're not going to do that on your chicken-feed, state kiddy-prison guard salary."

Glenn shrugged off the now-loosened grip and squared his shoulders. "I don't think—"

"That's your problem, girly-boy. You're trying to think." Clay slapped Glenn on the back so hard, it nearly knocked out his breath. "One is merely providing a fee for a service. An honest few minutes of work that pay huge."

Glenn stood, rooted to the ground. From anyone else, that "girly-boy" crap might earn them a bloody nose or black eye, or at least a smart-ass comeback. Clay wasn't the type he could sass. Around them, the peace of the deep woods settled in for the early evening. The melancholy call of a whippoorwill echoed in the distance. Glenn forced his bubbling irritation to a simmer.

Clay looked Glenn up and down. "Maybe I had you figured all wrong. Thought you were different from the rest of these weekend commando-wannabes with their adolescent secret codes. Like any of them could actually get it up if a group of real terrorists hit within ten miles of this place."

Glenn swallowed to wet his throat before trusting his voice. "You think it's such a bunch of losers, why do you come out here?"

Clay's shoulders lifted and fell. "Only decent practice range within easy driving distance. Sure don't come for the fireside ambience, or for the scintillating conversation."

The two men stood side by side for a moment. Anyone watching from a distance might think them good hunting buddies sharing one last raunchy joke before rejoining the group.

"You mention a word of our little talk . . ." The older man shifted his gaze from the camp's evening activities to Glenn, his intentions clear. "You decide you really want that fancy new boat, you come find me."

Sheila Bruner stared at the knob on the hall closet a few minutes before opening the door. It wasn't a sin, really. Not if it didn't hurt anyone. Besides she needed something—anything—to lift her up after Glenn's behavior the previous evening. She couldn't recall a time when she had prayed so hard or for so long. The night seemed to last forever. Glenn's brutal, forced affections had left her sore and raw, ripped up inside. Nothing new, until he pulled out the gun he kept beside the bed and held it to her temple. The act seemed to excite and enrage him at the same time.

Sheila moved two pastel-printed hat boxes full of old photographs to access a third thin coat box. No plain cardboard containers were allowed inside the house. Glenn hated the sight of them, so Sheila watched the Dollar Store and garage sales for attractive storage containers.

Maria Bruner had taught her daughter-in-law well, about cleaning, about cooking, about pleasing the Bruner men. During the three years Glenn's mother had lived with them after Big Glenn's fatal heart attack, Maria had been a lukewarm ally. Then Maria's heart had given out too, though Sheila suspected it had been shattered for many years.

Glenn would never see the contents of this particular box: Sheila's most prized possession. She untied the pink grosgrain ribbon, lifted the lid, and parted a layer of white tissue paper.

Her other little secret—besides the forbidden pets—lay folded inside, a thrift store find. A garish popsicle-purple women's basketball jersey with the number 40 in large yellow letters and some other woman's last name on the back. Not exactly a color combination she would've chosen. Better, the garnet and gold of the Florida State University women's basketball team.

Glenn wouldn't return until late Sunday evening. The postal carrier wouldn't be around until mid-afternoon, and no one ever dropped by the Bruner's unannounced. Perfect.

Sheila took one last peek out the front window. Other than one woman power walking, the street was deserted. She slipped the flowery house dress off and stood in her bra and panties in front of the hall mirror. Fresh bruises and patches of reddened skin dotted her thighs. Otherwise her body was as firm and unmarred as the day she graduated from high school. So what if she hadn't been able to successfully carry a fetus to maturity?

From what she overheard in the grocery store line or at the hair stylist's, pregnancy and childbirth altered a woman's body beyond repair—the stretch marks, extra weight, spider veins. Sheila loved babies, but pushed that aspect of her spirit aside. Better to love a stray animal than bring an innocent child into a home where fear reined. She shuddered, imagining her husband's reaction to the insistent cries of a hungry infant, the questions of a developing mind, or the blatant rebellion of a teenager. God knew what He was doing when He allowed Sheila to miscarry three times. The hysterectomy had prevented future conception.

Sheila shook her head to clear the unpleasant thoughts. This time was hers. No sense wasting it on regrets.

The uniform hung from her frame, the baggy shorts reaching the bottom of her kneecaps. The original owner had been more substantial and a good six or seven inches taller.

The welcomed, timeworn fantasy unfolded in her mind's eye.

Florida State University. She is a freshman nursing major. The class burdens are tremendous, but not impossible. She looks down at the white uniform trimmed in Garnet and Gold, with the number 14 printed in black block lettering: *Florida State* above, and *University* below. Her last name printed across the upper back. She glances across the polished wooden floors to where Sue Semrau stands (small matter that the coach wouldn't have been there so many years back. Sheila admires the woman, so Sue *is* her fantasy coach).

Her boyfriend is the star center of the Florida State Men's Basketball team. He towers above her. Strong, but sweet. Shy. Handsome in a boyish way. They make love every opportunity they get, the sex delightful and unhurried.

When they graduate, they marry and have a house filled with children. She earns her master's degree, then on to nurse practitioner training. They live in a sprawling country-styled house with a wraparound porch, and sip iced tea while the children play in the grassy front lawn.

Her two daughters are strong women, unafraid of the future. Athletic. Her three sons, though different from each other in temperament, respect others and go on to successful careers.

She and her handsome husband grow into their nineties, still in love. Still holding hands in public and kissing at unexpected moments.

The doorbell sounded. Sheila snapped back to the present. "Oh!"

She shucked the uniform and pulled the housedress on, stopping to check her hair in the mirror before answering the door. The walking lady she noted earlier stood on the stoop.

"Hi, I'm Melissa Strand. We just moved in a couple of houses down . . ." The twenty-something woman motioned with one hand to a vague point somewhere to her right. "I'm asking around . . . found this little black and white cat—actually, a kitten—next to your curb. It's still alive, but . . . Do you know who it belongs to? It looks like it might have been hit by a car, or something."

A wash of icy dread dripped from Sheila's shoulders and lodged in her heart. Sometimes punishment for foolish fantasies came quickly. When, oh when, would she learn the lesson about God's vengeance? She vowed to burn the uniform as soon as possible.

"Let me slip on some shoes."

Sheila used a wadded tissue to dab a fresh crop of tears from the corners of her eyes. "I appreciate you so much for riding over here with me, Loiscell. I don't know how I could've driven and held Oreo at the same time." Wrapped in an old soft blanket, the kitten purred, crying out only if Sheila shifted positions.

"No problem at all, hon. I didn't even know you had a cat, much less two!"

The veterinary emergency hospital in Tallahassee held two other pet owners and their animals: one wiggly Dalmatian puppy with a cut on its muzzle and a yowling Persian in a cat carrier. Good thing they were open on Saturday mornings. The vet servicing Chattahoochee came to his satellite office three days a week, and never on weekends. Only one technician stayed on the grounds to care for the boarded and sick animals. If they were too ill, the doctor transferred them to the larger facility in Marianna.

"Technically, I don't own the cats. They kind of wandered up and I started taking care of them. First, the little yellow tabby. Then she brought me this half-starved newborn kitten a few weeks back. Glenn doesn't care for cats. He likes dogs okay, as long as they're hunting dogs." She shrugged. "Even then, he wouldn't stand for an animal in the house."

"I used to have both. When they 'crossed over the rainbow bridge,' as my daughter puts it, I swore I'd never get another," Loiscell said. "Sometimes I miss the company, but my life is uncertain, and I wouldn't want the responsibility of a pet. Besides, the dander makes my allergies kick in. My body changed in that way after all the chemo."

After they turned Oreo over to a vet tech, Sheila paced the roomy waiting area and Loiscell tried to calm her down. After some time passed, a young woman in dark green scrubs stepped from behind a hinged door. "Mrs. Bruner? Doctor Greeley would like to speak with you in exam room two."

"Want me to go in with you?" Loiscell asked.

Sheila's hands trembled. "Please."

They stood in a small tile-lined room furnished with a cabinet and a stainless steel elevated exam table. In a few moments, the rattle of a chart on the door behind them announced the arrival of the doctor.

"Good morning. Ben Greeley." A sixty-ish man with silver-tipped hair held out his hand.

"I'm Sheila Bruner, Oreo's mama . . . and this is my friend Loiscell."

"I've examined Oreo. From the x-rays, I can see that one of his back legs has multiple fractures, and the hip socket is crushed."

Sheila held her hand to her lips to suppress a sob.

"Will you be able to save the little thing?" Loiscell rested a hand on Sheila's shoulder.

"It will mean amputating the rear left leg, I'm afraid. And he'll require hospitalization for a few days so we can monitor him. After that, he'll need special attention at home." The veterinarian paused. "It will be quite expensive, Mrs. Bruner. I can have the office manager provide an estimate."

Sheila's thoughts roamed to the thick roll of cash she had grabbed from her bra drawer. The emergency escape fund. "Do whatever it takes to save him. I will pay."

Dr. Greeley nodded. "Okay, then. If you'll fill out some paperwork at the front desk, I'll get started. Surgery will take a while, if you two would like to go grab a bite to eat. I can have one of the ladies call if you'll leave a cell number."

"Where to?" Loiscell asked when they pulled out of the parking lot a few minutes later.

"Starbucks? I'd love one of those mocha lattes." Sheila dabbed moisture from her cheeks. Hard to fathom she could still produce tears.

"Good enough. There's one right down from the mall." Loiscell thought a moment before she asked, "not to pry, but how are you going to squeeze the money out of that tight-wad husband of yours?"

"I have money."

Loiscell smiled. "You been hookin' on the side, hon?"

"Right. Like someone would pay me for sex." Sheila's face flushed. "If a person saves a dollar or three here and there and tucks it aside, it adds up in a few years."

"Grandma's cookie jar." Loiscell pulled the car into a tight space in front of the popular coffee shop.

"I don't follow," Sheila said.

"Hiding money in a cookie jar so the man of the house, or the kids for that matter, don't know it's there. Old farm women called it their 'butter and egg money'—the little spare change they'd get from selling a few eggs or churned butter."

They stepped into line behind a college-aged young woman with multiple piercings and a blue streak in her short brown hair. In contrast, Loiscell's rainbow-striped bandana seemed tame.

"This has to be one of my favorite things in the whole wide world." Sheila paid, and carried the tall latte as if she supported the crown jewels on a flocked velvet pillow.

"You're not hard to please," Loiscell said. "We should come over here more often, catch a movie or shop . . . Maybe next time." She spotted a two-seater near the front window and led the way. Sheila trailed behind.

"Yeah. Next time."

"Something else eating at you, Sheila? I mean, besides the kitten thing?" Loiscell asked after they took seats.

For a flicker of a second, Sheila considered confiding in her best friend. If the words started, would she be able to stop them? And what if someone overheard? Never tug on a loose thread in a tight-knit sweater. The whole thing might unravel.

"I . . . I don't know what to do with Oreo once he's released. I have a little house set up in the bushes for the two kitties, but with him recovering and needing special care . . ."

Loiscell consulted her cell phone. Those tech-savvy folks made fun of the older clam-style device, but it still worked. "I know exactly who we can call on. Abby. She's one of those caretaker sorts. Always has been. Once I tell her about Oreo, she'll pitch in. I'm sure of it."

Chapter Five

Five weeks before suicide
Monday

Abby McKenzie did her best to perform the "tree," one of the *asanas*—yoga poses—that required her to stand on one leg, palms held together at chest level, with the sole of the other foot planted on the thigh of her weight-bearing leg.

"Ducks and seagulls do this and sleep at the same time." Loiscell wobbled and flailed her arms to regain balance. "All that with a brain the size of a field pea."

Abby stifled a giggle. Silent concentration was encouraged, but the class wasn't so structured that a well-placed comment felt intrusive. "Oreo seems to manage with one less leg. I can too."

Sheila nodded and glanced toward Abby. The two women had grown closer since the kitten's release from the animal hospital. Every day after Glenn left for work, Sheila walked the two blocks to Abby's, helped her with the kitten's wound care, then rushed home to finish the day's cleaning chores before cooking dinner. Oreo—imprinted to Sheila as his first adoptive mother—now clung to Abby. Buttercup came and went from his usual home beneath the shrubbery, and managed to stay out of sight.

"Focus on a point in front of you, right at eye level," Joy said. "Allow your breathing to become even and calm."

Loiscell maintained the one-legged pose for a minute before tottering. Choo-choo gave up with an exasperated sigh.

"You will become better at using the breath to help you lift the body and hold each *asana* as you progress with your practice." Joy's smile radiated serenity. "Come back into stillness, now."

The group returned to the standing pose: torso erect, weight distributed evenly between both legs, arms at the sides with palms facing forward, and head level. They joined Joy in two sets of cleansing breaths—deep inhalations followed by long exhalations. "Let's go down on the mats and into *savasana.*"

"This is my absolute favorite yoga thing," Choo-choo whispered.

Loiscell stretched out supine on the yoga mat, arms at her side with palms facing up. Around her, the twenty members of the class positioned themselves in the classic reclining pose.

"Remember, when you practice at home—which, I hope you all do at least once or twice between classes—make sure not to short yourself time in the relaxation poses. They are as important as the active poses."

"What's not to love about any form of exercise where relaxing's as important as work?" Abby said in a low tone.

Joy's voice, calm and even, floated between the yoga students, providing guidance. "*Savasana* is also called the *corpse* pose, for obvious reasons."

Ben's deep voice sounded behind them from the second row. "I like *savasana* better."

"Sounds like some kind of pasta dish. *Savasana* with pesto," Loiscell said.

Joy chuckled. The class grew silent for a few minutes, until the teacher spoke again. She led them in a series of asanas, followed by another rest period. Then they rolled onto their bellies for an equal number of poses before Joy asked them to turn supine.

Joy switched the CD. The sound of ocean waves brushing the shore filled the room. For the next twenty minutes, she led them in a guided meditation.

"Allow yourself to return to the present. Feel the changes in your body," Joy said. "When you are ready, open your eyes and sit up into the lotus position." The closing poses completed, Joy bowed to the class—palms held together as if in prayer—acknowledging a third of the group at a time. "*Namaste,*" she intoned. The class echoed the word and bow.

"Wow." Loiscell rolled her yoga mat and fastened it with a Velcro strap. "I don't know what I did before this class. Really. I am so calm after this, I love everyone and everything."

Choo-choo stored her mat in its matching carrier. "Me, too. But I've been meaning to ask, Joy, what does that last word mean?"

Joy extinguished the incense. "Namaste means *peace to you. I bow to the divine in you.*"

Choo-choo rolled up her small blanket. "That's a nice sentiment." She turned to Loiscell, Abby, and Sheila. "I need a cheeseburger. Let's take this show up to Bill's Homeplace and bow to one of those."

When Abby led the Yoga Rat Pack into the Homeplace Restaurant, the faint blended scents of cooked sweet onions and brewed coffee greeted them. An intimate *at-home* ambiance echoed in every furnishing: rows of shiny red vinyl-seated booths, Formica tables circled with wooden ladder-back chairs, country-themed memorabilia, and printed cloth gingham valances in the signature sunflower print. Everything shouted personal pride from the spotless windows to the shiny linoleum floors.

"Those folks in Tallahassee have nothing on us," Choo-choo said, sliding into a booth. "I've eaten many a cheeseburger, but Bill's burgers put them all to shame."

Loiscell plopped down beside her. "Add a pile of home fries and you have what folks around here call *heart attack on a plate.*"

"Got to die of something." Abby grabbed a laminated menu. "It's my belief that one day they'll find out that grease makes you live longer. Won't that be a slap in the face for all the folks who've been eating nuts and berries and choking down cholesterol drugs by the handfuls?"

Choo-choo flipped the menu over and studied it. "Look at the pretty little sunflowers around the edges."

Julie Nix, veteran head waitress, stood beside the booth. "Evening, ladies. Yoga class must be over."

Choo-choo nodded. "About five minutes ago. Hey, when did y'all get these fancy new menus?"

"The cook's granddaughter is at FSU in some kind of design classes or the other," Julie said. "She did those as part of one of her assignments. Mr. Bill liked them so much, he decided to use them. They pick up our sunflower motif." She motioned to her printed cotton apron. "Though, I'll have to admit, by the time I get out of here at the end of the day, I'd run screaming naked to Georgia if I had to look at one more sunflower."

"You don't usually work the evening shift, do you?" Abby turned to the others. "My office orders lunch from here a lot. I like the French dip sandwich, Christine eats the BLT, Dr. Payne loves the fish sandwich, and Sabrina—she's our health nut—sticks to a chef salad."

Julie grabbed the pen from behind her left ear. "My other server took a week off to drive up to North Carolina with her husband. Those two nuts are going white-water rafting. Can you fathom such?"

Sheila spoke for the first time. "I think it sounds like fun."

"Tell you what's fun, a dentist named Dr. Payne. Anyone ever comment on that?" Loiscell looked to Abby.

"Every day." Abby's lips drew into a wry line. "And he's so gentle with patients."

"I can attest to that." Julie flipped an order pad open. "What'll it be tonight, ladies?"

Choo-choo spoke first. "I want a super-sized cheeseburger, all the way, with home fries. Tell the cook not to scrimp on the mayo. I hate a dry burger."

Abby added, "I'd like the same, except no fries. I'll take fried onion rings instead."

Julie's gaze shifted to the opposite side of the table.

"You have any pie left?" Loiscell asked. "The hell with *demon sugar.* Short of Sheila's cinnamon rolls on occasion, I've starved my cells of anything remotely connected to sinful for so long, I can't recall the last time I've eaten even a bite of pie."

"I still have a couple of slices of my deep-dish apple. Made it early this morning. Used Granny Smiths. Makes it a little twangy, but the brown sugar and cinnamon evens it out."

Loiscell smiled. "I'll take a big slice of that, then. And vanilla ice cream on top."

Julie scribbled. "And you, Miz Sheila?"

"A cup of decaf coffee with cream, please."

Her three tablemates stared Sheila down.

Choo-choo snorted. "Live a little, for heaven's sake. You're skinny as a snake's shadow."

"I'll have a fried egg sandwich with mayo on toasted bread. And cheddar cheese . . . two slices, please." Sheila slapped the menu shut.

Choo-choo patted Sheila's hand. "There you go!"

After the waitress walked away, Loiscell leaned over to Sheila. "You call home?"

"Yes."

"Glenn okay with you staying out this late?"

Sheila shifted in her seat. "He's fine."

After Julie returned with their drinks, the conversation flowed around the booth.

"I had an amusing, little chat with one of my Hospice patients yesterday," Choo-choo said. "You know me. I like to kid around, and I find humor often comforts the dying. Depends on the person of course. Some folks lose any semblance of levity when they are so ill."

She took a long swill of cola. "This lady's nearly a hundred, and funny as the day is long. She has memory issues—fades in and out like a bad light bulb—so I don't think she even realizes how cute some of her sayings are. We were talking about old age, and all the trials and tribulations that seem to come with it. I commented, 'I don't know how I feel about getting near the one hundred mark. From all I've seen, I think I might just hire a hit man to take me out one afternoon as I'm rounding the corner somewhere.' "

Choo-choo smiled. "Know what she said? 'Honey, you might want to check with some of your friends. Y'all might be able to get a good group rate!' "

The women cackled, a sound like a flock of disturbed chickens. A few fellow diners directed attention to the group for a second.

Abby took a giggly breath and added, "I can see it now. This group gets together and goes out for a really nice meal. Right after some rich, gooey dessert, Uncle Guido comes in and mows them all down." She held her hands out, mimicking the rapid fire of an Uzi. "Dat-dat-dat-dat!"

Loiscell jumped. "Oh, I got it! The perfect name for that group—The Suicide Supper Club."

Five weeks before suicide, Tuesday

Loiscell Pickering's kitchen phone rang at six a.m. Unusual, since her friends knew to wait until at least nine to call. She was awake by five-thirty—a leftover from workday habits—and generally in the garden by sunrise. Her pulse accelerated. Phone calls at odd times generally brought unwelcome news.

Her daughter's voice: "Mom?"

Loiscell set her filled coffee mug down so hard, it sloshed onto the kitchen counter. "Lisa? Honey, what's wrong? Are you okay? Rachel? Rick?"

The sound of Lisa's laughter eased the tension gathering in Loiscell's throat. "Rach is fine. So is Rick. I'm good too. Overworked as usual, but fine."

Loiscell released a long breath. "You scared me." She sopped up the spilled coffee with a rag.

"Sorry. I had some fantastic news and I couldn't wait until the weekend to share."

Every Friday night, as dependable as the evening train whistles sounding from River Junction, her daughter phoned and the two talked for at least an hour. Thank God for cell phones and unlimited minutes.

That aside, Loiscell worried about her daughter's finances. The twins attended college—Rachel at Emory and Rick at Georgia Tech. Kids, no matter what age, required a steady influx of funds. Lisa had a good career as an attorney for a small law firm, but still. And that lousy ex-husband, who the heck knew where he was? Handsome man. Between his and Lisa's good looks, Rachel and Rick were amazing representatives of the human race. Beyond that contribution, the man had failed miserably, skipping out on responsibility when the twins were five years old. Still, Lisa had made it through college and law school. Loiscell's daughter—tenacious and independent—provided more reason for prideful boasting than any of her rosebushes.

"Now that I've gotten my heart out of my throat, tell me!" Loiscell said.

"You know I've always messed around a little with writing . . ."

Loiscell tasted her coffee, frowned, added more cream. She liked coffee with muscle, but this batch could bench press her Volvo. "It's important to have at least one creative outlet. 'All work' is not good for you, Lisa."

Her daughter chuckled on the other end. "I know, Mom. You've only told me that for over thirty years."

"Guilty as charged."

"You remember how Daddy used to tell me little stories at night, ones he made up?"

Loiscell's heart warmed. "Yes."

"I sat down a while back and started writing down some of them. He had this one funny character—"

"Big Joe the Big Toe," Loiscell supplied.

"Yes! Big Joe!" Lisa laughed again.

Loiscell couldn't remember a recent time when she had heard her daughter express so much mirth.

"I've written a series of picture book stories featuring Big Joe the Big Toe. And the best part . . . I'm going to be published!"

Loiscell transported her coffee to the front porch and settled into a rocking chair. "Details, I need details!"

"Short version: I had lunch with one of my friends who works for a small publishing house here in Atlanta. She kept urging me to submit one, so I did. And they accepted it! Plus they want more! Can you believe it?"

"I've seen some of those picture books they have out now. If a farting dog can be a hit, then I don't see why Big Joe can't make you rich. When will you have a copy for your old mama?"

"One, you're not old, Mom. Two, it will be about a year. I just signed the contract yesterday."

"This news will keep me going for at least a week. I can't wait to tell the Yoga Rat Pack."

"Listen, I need to hang up and pay attention to my driving. Even with this Bluetooth, I can't talk and watch out for idiots at the same time. I'll phone you Friday night, 'kay?"

"One quick thing before you go—your brother. Has he called you?"

"You know Lance, Mom. I think this might be the time of year when he and his nutso buddies bike Moab. Why, do you need him? I can see if I can leave a message with one of his friends. Most of the places he goes don't have very good reception." She hesitated. "You . . . all right?"

Her daughter had a drama antenna. The slightest hint of distress from her mother, and up it shot. "Just wondering about my other child."

Eventually she would have to tell Lisa. Maybe not. Could she put her daughter through yet another of her mother's battles?

"Nice move, butthole." Lisa growled. "Gotta go, Mom, before you hear me lose my religion for real."

Loiscell sat for a few minutes, enjoying the fuzzy aftermath of the conversation. Her daughter, a published children's author. Who could ask for better news at sunrise?

Songbirds trilled. Loiscell cocked her head to pick out the separate calls. A few of the migratory crooners from up north had filtered into the area on their way to warmer climates, a sure sign of upcoming changes.

Chapter Six

Glenn Bruner took a swig of Jack Daniels to help him think straight. If killing was a job, how could it be considered a sin? If so, every soldier defending the good old U. S. of A. would be in danger of damnation. Besides, as he had heard in a movie once, "some folks needed killing." Not that he cared, really. All that religious fretting had belonged to his mother, not to him or Big Glenn.

The boating supply catalog next to his recliner was more dog-eared than any girlie magazine Glenn had ever owned. He flipped through its glossy colored pages, mentally marking digital GPSs and fish locators, depth guides, marine radios, and tackle. Who would need to worry about cost? If he had the boat he wanted, he wouldn't want to scrimp on the extras. Nor would he need to get a two-day shoulder cramp trying to install the equipment. Hell no. He'd pay some boat shop peon. And clothing—not to ignore that! He perused the section with special waterproof pants and jackets, and one of those fancy vests with all the mesh pockets. No more T-shirts and jeans. He'd put all those high-falutin' bass fishermen to shame.

Glenn took another swill of whiskey. The familiar burn slid down his throat and warmed him like a campfire.

How would it feel to watch a man—for surely, it would be a male—crumple and hit the ground? On the network crime scene shows, the blood always spread out in a large, dark pool.

Glenn thought back to his first deer kill. He was ten and barely able to hold the gun steady when he spotted the ten-point buck. His arms and legs ached in the early-morning cold. He would never live it down if he let this one pass and Big Glenn found out.

His heart beat so wildly, he feared the big buck would hear. Glenn squeezed the trigger. For a moment, the blast rang in his ears. He heard the sound of a loud thump. His eyes, pinched shut by reflex, opened wide. The massive animal lay on a bed of brown leaves, quivering with the final rattles of death.

His father appeared a few moments later, puffed with pride. "Damn, Boy! Lookit what you went and done!"

The rest of the memory, a dim blur. Glenn watched his father and hunting buddy gut and clean the buck. They saved a bucket of animal entrails and poured it over Glenn's head: a sticky rite of passage.

His mother prepared some of the venison when it came wrapped from the processing shack—a tender choice cut called the back-strap—soaked in buttermilk, then floured and fried. He ate a tall tower of home fries with catsup. When he tried to chew a small chunk of the back-strap, the meat rolled around in his mouth. Though the deer had been killed while it was calm and still, the meat tasted strange and wild. The more he chewed, the larger it seemed. He spit it out in a napkin when his father wasn't looking, then forked the remaining piece and hid it beneath a glob of catsup. His mother caught the furtive movement and smiled slightly. Each time he thought of the buck and the bucket of blood and entrails, his stomach roiled.

The mounted head of his first proud kill hung in his parents' den beside the menagerie of his father's mounted deer and fish. Its ebony glass eyes mocked him every time he passed by.

By the time the next hunting season came and Glenn killed again, the shock had worn thin. His father and a couple of his cronies lifted his kill to a hook on a two-by-four braced between two trees. Glenn grabbed a skinning knife, and his father stepped back with a nod. Glenn sliced the buck's throat and the blood poured, red molasses sweet with the scent of death. His father cut off the testicles, then ran a deep gash lengthwise of the belly. Glenn watched, fascinated, as the steaming intestines curled into a large trough beneath the suspended carcass.

Would human blood have the same ripe odor? Glenn shuddered involuntarily. How would it all unfold? How would he go about planning the event? Who would he whack?

Whack. Like a gangster. Glenn chuckled and swigged his whiskey.

Abby McKenzie unrolled a newly-purchased, on-sale yoga mat. Unlike her older friend's, Abby's mat matched neither her outfit nor carry bag. "How is your killer guard dog?"

Choo-choo huffed. "Prissy's fine. That little dickens has had me waiting on her hand and foot. She was in a state for a few days after her little run-in with the pit bull—which, we found out, belonged to a young man almost to Greensboro fifteen miles away. How that dog made it into town and kept from getting run over is anyone's guess."

"I'd be in more than a state if I'd taken on something ten times my size," Loiscell commented. She winced, then loosened the sweat-drenched orange and blue tie-dyed bandana wrapped around her head.

"Don't I know it," Choo-choo said. "Prissy and I seem to have reached some kind of truce. I suppose this little incident has been a good gift in a plain paper bag."

Sheila plopped down and crossed her legs lotus style. Other than Loiscell, she was the only Yoga Rat Pack member who could accomplish the pose. "You mean, she's stopped urinating on the bathroom mat?"

Choo-choo's lips drew into a thin line. "Said it was a truce, not a miracle."

Sheila smiled. "Animals can sense when we like them. They need approval too."

"The only approval Prissy ever accepted came from Charlie. Since he passed, that dog has been downright surly. Only here lately, has she stopped growling at me for living and breathing."

"That's a little harsh, don't you think?" Abby asked.

"Everyone has to have a fair share of aggravation. Prissy has seen to it that I've had mine." Choo-choo stretched to one side, then to the other before lowering herself to the mat with a grunt. "Her hips have been bothering her a lot. I've had to start lifting her onto the bed."

"This, from the woman who said she'd rather drop-kick the poodle in the middle of the night. When was that...?" Abby tapped her chin with a finger. "Just a couple of weeks ago?"

"I have a heart, Abby McKenzie. I can't help it if I've been sharing space with a she-devil of a dog, up until she decided it was a good notion to lose her mind completely and go after a dog the size of a bulldozer."

Loiscell reached over and patted Choo-choo on the back. "You're getting yourself all fired up, hon. Take a deep breath and chill, or you won't get a thing out of Joy's class."

Behind them, Ben Calhoun settled onto his mat. "Good evening, ladies."

Choo-choo rotated to return the greeting. Her eyebrows arched. "Well, I swear, Ben. You've gotten your hair styled! And something else . . . the mustache is missing. I've never minded facial hair on a man, but you look a good ten years younger without yours."

Abby stared at him for a moment. "It does look . . . um . . . nice."

When Ben smiled at Abby, the corners of his lips curled up and pushed twin dimples into place. Heat rose to her face.

"Look there, all the more reason you're better off without that lip fur," Choo-choo added. "I don't think I've ever noticed how nice your smile is."

Four weeks before suicide, Tuesday

Choo-choo Ivey noticed Prissy's total lack of appetite. Most small dogs had a reputation for acting finicky, but not the poodle, at least not while Charlie was alive. One of the first snapshots Charlie had taken of Prissy showed a puffball of fur asleep with her head resting on a shallow bowl of kibble. Prissy had never met a food bowl she didn't like, until her dotage, when she ate in secret to protest her beloved owner's demise.

When Choo-choo folded back the comforter, the little dog shifted and whined. Too far out to be an aftermath of the scuffle.

"Mama will fix you some nice chicken and rice. I'll bet that will whet your appetite. You stay in bed, sleepy-head."

Choo-choo hesitated at the door to the kitchen. How many years had it been since she used that old saying? Not since Jacqueline was small. Could it be, her daughter would be . . . what? She counted the years. Sixty? No, that couldn't be right.

She placed a frozen chicken breast cutlet into the microwave and took a container of leftover white rice from the refrigerator.

Jacqueline. *Jack* to her closest friends. Her daughter's given first name had been Choo-choo and Charlie's idea of an inside pun based on a female member of the famous First Family—Jacqueline Kennedy; they now had their own "Little First Lady." Choo-choo's daughter refused to answer to the name, preferring first *Jackie*, then *Jack*. Heck, she might even have had it legally changed by this point, for all Choo-choo knew. When Jacqueline moved to Portland, Oregon, she had positioned herself as far away as possible, short of Hawaii or Alaska, or Europe.

Jacqueline had been a daddy's girl. Charlie adored his daughter from the first time she held his index finger in her tiny grasp. Maybe Choo-choo should have nursed the infant the old-fashioned way. But at that point, bottle-feeding was in vogue. None of her friends embraced the natural way. Not like current days, when a woman might pop out a plump breast anywhere and nurse. Choo-choo admired them, how they fought gallantly for the most basic of mother's rights.

The most likely cause of their problems: their similar personalities. Both liked to be in the thick of the action, to see and be seen. As a teenager, Jacqueline had constantly pushed the limits to fit in with her peers. At one point, Charlie had nailed the window shut in his fifteen-year-old daughter's room. That, and a scattering of creaky boards near the front and back doors, kept Jacqueline from slipping out past the witching hour.

Once Jacqueline turned twenty and moved from home, the chasm widened. Charlie's death removed Jacqueline's basic desire to return home. No matter how hard Choo-choo tried, their infrequent meetings—at one of the end-of-the-year holidays—were strained and exhausting.

Choo-choo anticipated Thanksgiving and Christmas with a miasma of emotions: joy at seeing Jackie (she refused to call her Jack), sadness over the estrangement, and apprehension about making the holiday perfect. The house would be spotless, dust and dog-hair free. The linens on Jackie's bed cleaned and ironed. The second bathroom, gleaming. The refrigerator and pantry, stocked with anything her daughter might enjoy. Not that it would matter. Each year brought some new preferred style of eating and never what Choo-choo had on hand. Strict vegan? Middle-Eastern? California Fusion? French? What would it be this year?

"I simply refuse to make a soy turkey," Choo-choo said aloud. "I've yet to see a bean I could stuff and serve with mashed potatoes."

She reduced the chicken and broth to a simmer, then poured a tall mug of coffee and sat down at the kitchen table. The original dining set had contained four ladder-back chairs. When it was clear there would be only one child, Charlie had put the spare chair into storage. After Jackie left, Choo-choo insisted on two chairs, and another joined its mate in the workshop/shed. The cramped kitchen needed all the space it could beg, borrow, or steal. She could remove Charlie's chair, but a table with a solitary chair seemed so bleak.

After it cooled, Choo-choo shredded the boiled chicken into the rice and forked the mixture into Prissy's clean bowl. When the little dog refused to move from bed, Choo-choo gently lifted her and carried her into the kitchen.

Prissy looked at the food, then up at Choo-choo, her cloudy eyes thick with mucus. Choo-choo knelt down and picked up a small portion. "Try to eat a little bit for mama."

The dog licked the moisture from her fingers, then ate a couple of small bites.

"Is that all you want? You must really feel bad." Prissy wobbled and whined. "Your daddy wouldn't like you feeling this way."

Choo-choo ruffled the dog's hair, then picked her up and carried her back to bed.

While she showered, Choo-choo's thoughts wandered from worrying about Prissy to the previous night's dream. Charlie—dressed in his old khaki coveralls—waited at the back fence. His hair was dark and thick like it had been when they first married. Poor man, he had succumbed to male-pattern baldness in his mid-thirties.

Charlie's face wore an impatient expression, the one he used when she wasn't moving quite fast enough. She tried, she truly did. Choo-choo attempted to cram too much into too little time, and it never worked.

The same dream had occurred—or some variance of it—the past four nights. What did it mean? Was her time finally coming? Would she see him soon?

Choo-choo pitched the disposable razor and opened a fresh one. Since her circulation had become so poor, very few hairs grew below her knees. Still, she wouldn't take any chances. The funeral director would paint up her face and make her look good from the waist up, but Choo-choo would be hanged before she'd go to her eternal rest with prickly legs.

Loiscell reclined on the exam table.

"The biopsy was positive for cancer. I'm sorry." The oncologist's words circled like vultures riding the thermals. Twice before, Dr. Johnson had been in the position of handing her the news. Poor man. How many times a day, a week, a month, did he have to say those same words? His voice remained professional; the fine worry lines around his eyes and mouth told the real story.

The air sucked from the room, as if oxygen had suddenly dropped from the periodic chart. She heard the snick of the inexpensive wrist-watch strapped to the arm she had tucked behind her head; smelled the faint aura of germicidal cleaners overlaid with a pleasant clean-linen scent; noticed the dust motes suspended in the light rays coming from a series of narrow, high-set windows. The downy hairs on the nape of her neck prickled.

No. No. No!

Loiscell slipped chunks of raw chicken into boiling water, added a generous amount of salt, and stirred. Through both regimens of chemotherapy, she had stocked containers of chicken and rice in the refrigerator. The Southern staple was one of the few dishes Loiscell's ravaged stomach tolerated. When she picked up the black pepper mill, memories stunned her. Memories of chicken pileau cooked in deep iron pots.

The chicken pileau dinner on the last night of a long summer weekend was as well-planned as any gourmet meal. Pots suspended over hot coals held gallons of broth. Chicken, cooled and plucked from the bones, stood ready in heaping bowls.

Loiscell's father loved pepper, and added the spice to anything and everything.

"Why do you put so much pepper in there, Daddy?" she asked.

"It adds the right amount of punch, little gal. It's hard to cook out-doors. Too many gnats flying around. Pepper helps disguise the few that dive in."

Being such a girl, Loiscell squealed. "Eww! Daddy! You mean . . . we *eat* them?"

Her father—always the jokester—answered, "Gnats are good protein."

Loiscell ground more pepper into her pot. No matter how hard she tried, her pileau never tasted as rich as her father's. Must be the lack of gnats.

A few minutes later, Loiscell dipped the cooked chicken into a bowl to cool. She thought about fear. Before that first go-around with cancer, the notion of "tasting fear" seemed preposterous. Just some author's dramatic attempt to portray the body's reaction to a threat.

Now she understood. Fear had a distinct flavor: a blend of brine and acid. Metallic, like the twang of chewing down on an errant piece of aluminum foil sugar-glued to the bottom of a hot pastry.

When she spoke, her voice seemed to come from somewhere outside of herself. "I can't do this again. I simply cannot."

Loiscell glanced down. The chicken carcass steamed in a pool of fat and broth. Shreds of meat hung from the brown/gray bones like tattered sails. After a fashion, when so much of a thing was cut away, what remained?

She picked up the bowl and cast it, bones and all, into the garbage.

Four weeks before suicide, Saturday

Glenn Bruner drove the hilly county highway leading to the private entrance of the camp. The land around Chattahoochee stood out in sharp contrast to central and south Florida; it wasn't one big flat parking lot overrun with mouse-crazed tourists. The area signaled the foothills of the Appalachian Mountains, though not as impressive as its counterpart above Atlanta.

The truck seemed to steer itself, and with no traffic on the back road, Glenn's mind was free to wander to a time before his father's lust for alcohol trumped his need for anything else. Glenn had long since memorized every detail. Played it over and over in his mind until it seemed more a favorite movie than his actual past.

Over his mother's feeble protests, his father had packed the Ford sedan with a few meager supplies, and the two left for a week in the Smoky Mountains. His first camping trip. And with his daddy.

Glenn knew to keep his mouth shut and not whine about the endless miles of peanut and cotton fields of southern Georgia. He whittled the time by counting the handful of automobiles they passed, mentally burying them when they went by a cemetery.

The road game kept him occupied until they reached the outskirts of Macon and left the narrow two-lane highways for Interstate 75. Cars and trucks whooshed past. When they hit Atlanta, Glenn's mouth hung open at the traffic and tall buildings. Everyone seemed to be in a big fat hurry, changing lanes and speeding past as if they were hell-bound. The topography morphed into gentle rolling hills as they moved north, where the deciduous trees painted spring lime-green against the deeper hues of the short-needled pines.

Hours later, they pulled into a small family-owned campground. By the time the sun set and the evening chill sent shivers down his back, Glenn sat beside his father in a folding aluminum-framed chair, warming his hands over the low flames of a small campfire.

At home, Big Glenn cooked on a charcoal grill, but avoided the kitchen. That was his mother's realm, and Big Glenn couldn't find the salt and pepper shakers without asking for directions. Now, Glenn watched in amazement as his father prepared simple meals over an open pit fire.

"Ever heard of S'mores?" Big Glenn asked.

Glenn shook his head.

Big Glenn handed him a butter knife and a package of graham crackers. "Slap some peanut butter on a couple of these. I'll get the marshmallows and Hershey bars out of the car."

His father sandwiched hunks of marshmallow and milk chocolate between the peanut-butter-slathered graham crackers and wrapped them in a sheet of aluminum foil. "Now, we just pop this right into the fire . . . over here where the coals are nice and red-hot."

In a few minutes, his father used a fork to move the soot-blackened bundle to one of the smooth river rocks lining the fire pit. Glenn wiggled in his chair. No use to act impatient and make Big Glenn angry. For the first time in as long as he could recall, his father seemed happy. He hadn't hollered once since they had left the traffic in Atlanta.

"Most folks don't add in the peanut butter." His father opened the foil and handed over a gooey cracker. "Came up with that on my own."

Glenn bit into the warm cookie sandwich. The blended flavors oozed over his tongue and marshmallow goo roped down his chin. Big Glenn took a long swig of cola, then handed the bottle to his son. "Shore good, ain't it?"

If Glenn concentrated hard, he could still feel Big Glenn's rough fingertips brush his temples.

Glenn spit a wad of tobacco out the lowered window and reached into a small cooler for a beer. Sometimes, the smell of wet, rich country dirt could evoke that memory. He passed a low, hand-lettered sign for a primitive Baptist church and took the second unpaved road to the right. Oak saplings reached their skinny arms to rake the sides of the truck.

"You'd think as much as we pay in dues, they'd widen this pig trail of a road!"

Each time he visited the camp, Glenn spent a good couple of hours afterwards with a container of rubbing compound, trying to erase the dashes and dots in the top coat. If he had that extra loot, he could buy the fancy bass boat and have enough left over to pick up a used truck, one with faded paint that he could drive to Hell and back if need be.

The noise of his passing disturbed a covey of quail. They rose into the sky in a fluttering mass of sound and beating wings. Glenn pointed his trigger finger at the birds, certain he could bring one or two down, easy. Shooting for a living, it was a job custom made for him.

What would his father think of this latest business opportunity? Big Glenn believed in an eye for an eye, and thought they ought to put a rush-to-the-devil delivery stamp on anyone sitting on death row, or put in electric bleachers so a bunch of them could be fried at once. The heck with years of appeals, delays, and free room and board at the taxpayers' expense. "Torch 'em all and let God sort it out," Big Glenn often said.

Some living things—human and animal—were better off dead. Glenn shot deer, squirrels, rabbits, quail, dove, and anything else in season, or not. If he could skin it and eat it, or mount it on his wood-paneled den wall, its death served a higher purpose. The Good Book said animals were put on earth for men to lord over. Plain and simple. Even his Bible-thumping mother had agreed with that. And people were basically animals, after all.

"What would you do, Daddy?" Glenn's question joined the slurry of dust and morning air rushing between the pick-up's lowered windows.

Glenn could swear he heard Big Glenn's boozy reply: "If you stand by a money tree and expect it to drop dollar bills, you're stupider than you look, boy. But if you shake that trunk, you deserve whatever falls your way."

Choo-choo Ivey took a few moments to soak in the ambiance of the Hospice patient's country kitchen. White windowpane-styled cabinets stacked with heirloom pottery dishes and glassware hung above white tile countertops. A set of ruffled chintz curtains defined the single window over a deep double sink. Crock canisters stood in a cluster beside a white pitcher filled with wire whisks and wooden spoons. Overhead, a wrought-iron rack held suspended pots and pans.

All of the trinkets told a story, Choo-choo was certain. This was no showplace without substance; it was a cook's kitchen. The woman who owned this kitchen had no doubt poured love into every dish. The coffee, flavorful and rich. The confections, gooey and satisfying. The conversations, confidential and reassuring. Choo-choo wished she had known *that* woman.

Johanna, the second of three daughters, walked into the room. The faint circles beneath her blue-gray eyes spoke of hours of worried concern, but her lips held the remnants of a smile.

"I heard you and your mama laughing a few minutes ago," Choo-choo said.

Johanna opened a cabinet, pulled out a mug, and poured herself a cup of coffee. "You must think us weird, Miz Caroline. I mean, who laughs at a time like this?"

"Not at all, Johanna. And please, call me by my nickname Choo-choo. Caroline is a fine name, but I use it only for legal dealings."

The young woman drew a hand through her long brown hair. She was the middle child of the Hospice patient down the hallway. The other two, Choo-choo had met once in passing. They lived out of state and managed infrequent visits to relieve their sister. As with many of the families she visited, one person shouldered the majority of care.

"Sorry, Miz Choo-choo. You'd think I'd remember that by now. Mama always taught us to be a bit formal. Respect, you know."

"And I appreciate it. So many young people these days don't respect anyone, much less themselves." Choo-choo took a sip of coffee.

"I try to teach my boys respect. It's hard. Especially when all of their friends don't do the same." Johanna's shoulders lifted and fell. "We all do the best we can, I suppose." Her lips curled up, though her eyes remained sad. "Mama fades in and out, with the morphine. Most of the time, she's asleep. That's not a bad thing. She's too good of a person to hurt."

"From what little I know of your mother, I agree. If I'm not prying, what were you and Miz Anna in such a stitch about?"

"We had this cat when I was little." Johanna's features appeared to shift slightly, revealing the girl behind the woman. "Daddy named her *D.B.* That stood for *Damn Bitch*, excuse my language. That cat hated my father and took any opportunity to let him know it. But she adored Mom. It was kind of funny."

"I know all about animals bonding to one person over another." Boy did she.

"Every Christmas, Daddy went to the woods behind a friend's house near Grand Ridge and cut a short-needled pine. Problem was, they were often bare on one side, so he'd cut two and wire them together."

"Good thinking."

"They weren't bad little trees. Not as picture perfect as the Frasier firs they ship down here now. Every Christmas, D.B. would crawl behind the tree and pee."

They laughed, then Johanna continued, "It made my daddy spitting mad! He tried everything. All kinds of repellant sprays that stunk up the house to high heaven and did no good, little bells tied to the bottom branches so he could catch her in the act. He even rigged up this mat that would alarm if it was touched. Nothing worked."

"Cat urine is so much stronger than a dog's," Choo-choo added. "If Prissy—my old poodle—was a cat, I'd have to burn the house down to rid myself of the smell."

"Mom learned to wait until D.B. did her thing before she put the quilted tree skirt around the base, and definitely before she put any presents down. One year, she had to rewrap everything after that cat wet. I know people could still catch a whiff when they got their gifts that year."

Choo-choo stood and refreshed both of their coffees. "Did you have to get rid of that cat?"

Johanna slapped the air with one hand. "Are you kidding? D.B. slept on Mom's side of the bed and followed her around like a puppy. Other than hating my daddy and the Christmas peeing, D.B. wasn't such a bad little animal."

"So you and your mother are able to share those memories. That's good. Not everyone gets that chance."

Johanna tucked a long curl behind one ear and propped her chin on her hand. "Mom's pretty open about things. And me being the one close-by, I suppose I'm the one she's leaned on since my daddy died five years back."

"She's lucky to have you, and your sisters."

Johanna reached in her jeans pocket and extracted a folded tissue. "Sorry." She dabbed the moisture from her eyes. "I cry if someone looks at me sideways."

Choo-choo reached across the table and patted Johanna's hand. "Grief comes bubbling up when it's supposed to. Best to let it out, or it will harm you."

For the second time in less than two weeks, Loiscell Pickering screeched her car to a stop in front of Choo-choo's house. She flung open the door and scrambled up the walkway. Choo-choo opened the door before Loiscell had a chance to knock. "Thank you, thank you, for coming."

Loiscell stepped inside, noticing her friend's red-rimmed eyes and nose. "What's happened? I couldn't make out a single word you said over the phone. Good thing I recognized your voice and have caller I.D., or I would've thought it some kind of crank call."

"It's Prissy . . . I . . . I think she might have passed away."

Loiscell took a deep breath and pulled her shoulders back. "Where is she?"

Choo-choo led the way to the master bedroom and motioned toward the bed. A small hot pink dog pillow rested on one end. At first glance, the poodle seemed to be asleep, until Loiscell looked closer and noticed the absence of movement.

"I stayed over at my Hospice patient's house a little longer than I planned to," Choo-choo said through muffled sobs. "I planned to take Prissy by the vet's first thing in the morning."

Loiscell sat on the bed beside the pillow and reached a hand over to touch Prissy. The little animal's skin was cold. She held a couple of fingers in front of the dog's nose to test for breath signs. Nothing. "Oh, honey. I'm so sorry."

Choo-choo folded onto the edge of the bed. "She acted better this morning. I even got her to eat a few bites of soft scrambled eggs. We walked outside for her to do her business—imagine that—then she came and sat down beside me on the steps and we enjoyed the cool morning air."

Loiscell hugged her.

"All these years since Charlie left us, and Prissy and I didn't get along worth a toot. It's like we lived to aggravate each other. We finally got past it and now, this."

Loiscell soothed, "I know. I know."

"I can't just leave her here. What shall I do?"

Loiscell kicked into fix-it mode, a familiar role. "I have to ask some hard questions, Choo-choo. So please don't be angry with me."

Choo-choo sniffed and moved her head up and down once.

"Do you wish to bury her, or would you prefer cremation?"

"Never given it much thought. Suppose I could bury her in the back yard." Choo-choo's white brows knit together. "But once I'm gone and the house is sold to someone else, she'll be left alone."

"True."

"How do I go about the other?"

Loiscell held Choo-choo's hand as she spoke. "It's too late in the day to do anything, dear. Monday morning first thing, I can ride over to Tallahassee with the two of you. There's a veterinary clinic over there with a crematorium. They usually get the ashes back to the owner in a couple of days."

"Do I let her be until then?"

Loiscell shook her head. "No. That wouldn't be good, honey. What we'll do is this: we'll wrap her in a soft sheet and put her in a plastic bag. I have room in my deep freezer. That way, she'll be protected until we can take her over to Tallahassee."

"I don't think I have the heart to do this, Loiscell."

"That's why you have me, Choo-choo. Now if you have a sheet or towel you don't mind giving up, I'll get her fixed up."

Choo-choo rose and walked to the linen closet off the master bedroom. She handed Loiscell a plush throw in a pale shade of pink.

"You sure you want to part with this, Choo-choo? You won't get it back."

"Charlie gave me that before he died. It doesn't match my furniture. I think he would like Prissy sent off in it. Very fitting for his little princess."

"All right, then. Now, bring me a clean white garbage bag."

Choo-choo started to leave the room, then turned around and walked back to the bedside. She reached down and stroked the poodle's head. "It was you Charlie was coming for, wasn't it? Leave it to you to beat me out of the next spot in heaven."

Loiscell waited until her friend left the bedroom to lift the dog. She rested the body in the middle of the throw and folded the edges envelope-style.

Choo-choo returned. "This seems so . . . ordinary. To be put in a trash bag."

"One thing about death: there is little dignified about it. But we can make it special, for Prissy. We'll have a little ceremony and sprinkle her ashes, if you'd like. I know Abby and Sheila will want to be there."

"I'll put her over our family plot. Charlie can keep her company, and soon I will be there too." Choo-choo reached into her pocket and withdrew a lacy handkerchief to dab her eyes.

Loiscell lifted the wrapped parcel and worked the bag around it. She wasn't particularly happy about having a dead poodle in her freezer, but what could she do? It was only for overnight. She needed to clean out the deep freezer anyway. Most of the meat was frost-burned, and who knows how long those bags of peas and beans had been in there?

"I don't think I can stay here alone tonight." Choo-choo's gaze darted around the room.

Loiscell draped an arm around Choo-choo's shoulders and gave her a gentle squeeze. "I'll take Prissy over to my house and get her settled in. Then I'll grab some pajamas and maybe a couple of funny movies. We'll sit up all night long if you'd like. I can either crash on your couch or in your spare bedroom." Loiscell let go of Choo-choo and picked up the plastic-wrapped bundle, cradling it as if it was an infant.

Choo-choo Ivey walked through her house with a cardboard box, collecting dog paraphernalia: a water bowl, a half-chewed beef bone sticky with Prissy's dried saliva, a leash, a squeak toy, a grooming brush. Dogs died. Every day. They farted and peed on rugs and chewed their toenails until one day they didn't.

She carried the box outside to the rolling trash bin, threw it inside, slammed the lid. Back into the house to strip the sheets and covers from the bed. No way would she or anyone sleep on them. In the laundry room, she pulled the detergent bottle from its perch above the washer. A battered tin of Yip-Yap Doggie Breath Fresheners grazed the washer lid and clattered to the floor.

Choo-choo crumbled to her hands and knees and sobbed.

Chapter Seven

Three weeks before suicide
Monday

Glenn checked his watch for the third time in less than thirty minutes. The daytime hours when he wasn't distracted by work dragged as if he walked through cane syrup. It had been a long, agonizing three weeks since his discussion with Clay.

Glenn Bruner hadn't experienced such itchy eagerness since he was a kid awaiting Santa. Big Glenn used to call the state a "high rolling boil," as if his son's moods compared to a hot, churning pot of grits right before they burped over onto the burner. In the early years, Big Glenn had snuck presents under the tree long after he tucked his son into bed, and even ate the cookies left out by the hearth, always leaving one half-eaten on the plate. One year, his father had dipped his work boots into the fireplace soot and walked to the tree, leaving telltale prints. Magic had come easy back then.

Glenn thought about Sheila. Why does she keep on nag, nag, nagging me?

The dumb bitch could do no right. If a legal way existed to be rid of his wife with no mess, fuss, or prison time, he gladly would embrace it. But without Sheila around, Glenn faced the disgusting tasks of washing dishes, sorting laundry, and cleaning the bathroom. He couldn't eat fast food every meal.

Sheila appeared, a fresh beer in one hand. He snatched it and popped the top, then gave her the wicked eye. As she turned to leave, Glenn reared back and gave her a shove with one of his bare feet. She lurched, teetered a moment before catching her balance, then looked back at him with a pained expression.

"Dadgum, Sheila." He guffawed and took a swig of the cold brew. "You looked like you was doing that stupid yoga for a minute there."

Sheila joined in with a forced laugh.

Glenn belched. "You're just plain-out crazy sometimes, woman."

She lowered her gaze and shuffled off toward the kitchen. If he slipped up and punched her in the kidneys again, that soft vulnerable unprotected spot, would the itchy feeling go away?

Big Glenn had often used that same sucker-sneak trick on him. When his father was around, Glenn remained ever vigilant. It didn't help. One night, Glenn had tiptoed across the dark hallway on the way to the bathroom, safe because his father slept on the couch after swilling a bottle of that brown stuff he called "my medicine." Glenn's small bladder burned. Most of the time, he was good at holding it until the coast was clear.

A shuffle sounded behind him. A heavy foot shoved him and he lurched forward, his head snapping back like a test crash dummy. Glenn managed to catch himself with the edge of the lavatory. A trickle of hot urine flowed down one leg. He jiggled in place and prayed his father wouldn't see the wet patch spreading across the front of his pajama pants.

His father's deep-throated laughter boiled at his back. "Walk much, boy?"

Glenn blinked in the low green night-light illumination. His mother, where was she? Cowering behind the master bedroom door? Sleeping soundly with the knowledge her husband had passed out on the couch and wouldn't bother her for a few hours?

The key was to not react in a way to send Big Glenn's black humor into a spitting rage. Go along. Make fun of himself for his father's benefit. He pushed out a giggle. "No sir. I never learned that walking thing too good."

His father grunted. "You're a kick in the pants, kid." Satiated and chortling at his own twisted play on words, Big Glenn had shoved past him into the bathroom and pissed a long stream before staggering back to the couch and free-falling into the cushions.

Glenn doubted his father recalled the many times he had humiliated his son. Funny how he had strived to make Big Glenn look at him with some sense of pride. Too bad the old man wasn't alive to witness what his son planned now. Big Glenn would be stunned by his son's conviction and courage.

Glenn added his father into the ever-evolving daydream. He imagined hitching that new bass boat to its matching pick-up truck, launching it below the Jim Woodruff Dam, then sending the boat onto a skimming plane inches above the river's glassine surface. Big Glenn smiled back at the towering rooster-tail of water kicked up by the powerful Mercury outboard. The cooler, packed to capacity with ice-cold beer and sandwiches, awaited. Fish cowered in their shallow beds. The two masters of the river were loose, and no one would be safe.

Three weeks before suicide, Saturday

Glenn Bruner and Clay stood side-by-side on the firing range. The older man had toyed with him since Glenn arrived at the camp: ducking into groups of hunters, avoiding eye contact, making himself conspicuously unavailable. Many members had packed up for the day and left the grounds. A few still worked their way through the newly-constructed obstacle course. In the distance, Glenn heard an occasional shouted curse and pop of gunfire. The course was a real ball-buster, and would be wicked hard on his bad knee. Walls, ropes, and low barbed wire, plus rutted running trails, workout stations, and a fake town with pop-up targets. Glenn had yet to tackle it, and a few of the inner circle members had commented on his lack of enthusiasm. He would. He would. Just, later.

"Looks like you got you another new rifle," Glenn said.

Clay grunted.

"I don't know how you find room for 'em all. Don't think I've ever seen you out here with the same one twice. Must be nice, being able to afford all those fancy guns. I would have to build on a room, if I had 'em."

The older man lowered the assault rifle and turned his head. Those dead eyes bored right through Glenn, and the muscles around Clay's jaws flinched and relaxed. For a moment, Glenn wished he was anywhere but here. Odd since he had dreamed of the chance to talk to Clay, every second since their last encounter.

"Ever notice how some people run off at the mouth, but don't have jack to say?" Clay raised the rifle, took careful aim and fired. Dead heart-center of the human-shaped outline.

Glenn's face flushed. Anyone else who spoke to him in such a manner would live to regret it. "I've thought about your offer."

This time, when Clay's eyes rested on him, a flicker of interest lurked behind them. "That so?"

"I'd like to try it."

Clay studied him. How Glenn would like to master the ability to make someone wither beneath such a steely-eyed stare.

"It's not guard duty at Disney, what you're signing on for."

"I realize that."

Clay's face morphed into a stained mask of pleasure, the same expression a predator wore anticipating a bloody takedown. "A few things you and I have to get straight." Clay fished a toothpick from his jacket pocket and stuck it between his lips. He rolled it from side to side before docking it in one corner. "You have to keep your stupid mouth shut. You don't, and I'll have to contend with your lack of discretion. Got it?"

Glenn nodded. Clay's version of *contend* had to mean a whole lot of not breathing.

"Keep your nose clean. That means doing nothing to draw attention to yourself. Nothing. You don't get so much as a speeding ticket. You play pretty with the neighbors. You resist that burning urge to pound your wife to a bloody pulp."

"Hey, man. I don't hit . . ."

Clay huffed. "Who you think you're kidding, girly-boy?"

Glenn swallowed hard. His mouth felt drier than it did after a hard weekend of whiskey.

"I've met plenty like you. Men who think they get some kind of sick power by beating women." Clay extracted the toothpick long enough to hurl a wad of spit to an inch in front of Glenn's boots. "What you do at home is none of my business, unless it interferes with mine. You work with me; you follow my rules. I don't care if you feel she needs it to keep in line, or whatever reason you've made up to make it right, you don't put a mark on her. You make nice. The last thing one of my hires needs is to get hauled in on domestic abuse charges. Am I clear?"

"Sheila would never—"

"Shut up. I said you don't so much as put a finger on her. Are. We. Clear?"

Glenn's head bobbed up and down.

"*I'll* find the job. *I'll* work out the details. You will do everything *I* say. If you go off half-cocked, I never heard of you." The toothpick slid to the opposite side in one practiced motion. "I can disappear into thin air so fast, you'll believe you imagined me."

"I get it. I get it. So when do we start? Do I get one of your fancy rifles? Do I—"

Clay held up a hand to plug the diarrhea of questions. "In time. First, the job. Then, the weapon. You will be provided with what you need."

Glenn's heart rate picked up its pace.

Clay took out a small leather-clad notepad and scribbled a phone number. "If you have to reach me, leave a message on voicemail. Don't go into details. Don't say my name. I'll contact you and arrange a meeting."

"You'll call me soon though?"

"No time frame." Clay tore off the page and handed it to Glenn. "This isn't a nine-to-five. When the job becomes available, you will know."

Glenn glanced at the block-printed note as if it was the winning lotto ticket, then stuffed it into his pants pocket.

Clay picked up his rifle. "In the meantime, practice, girly-boy. Practice." His cold stare fixed on Glenn. "One thing you have to know: I hate loose ends. You work with me, you best not leave any behind."

Three weeks before suicide, Sunday

Sheila Bruner retrieved the "special box" from the hall closet. God forgive her, she hadn't destroyed it like she promised after Oreo's accident.

Late Sunday: God's day. A day of rest.

Glenn would be home soon. Such a chance to take, but she needed it. Had to feel the material next to her misused body. She peeled the housedress off, hesitated, and removed her bra and panties.

The silken material clung to her bare skin. The elastic waist hung on her hip bones like a dust cover draped over a chair. She should take the uniform to the sewing machine and alter it. Soon the baggy shorts wouldn't be able to grip enough to stay up.

Scales didn't lie. The last time she weighed, the indicator line had rested barely above the ninety mark. But she had always been naturally thin. And who could eat? Nothing appealed to her. She nibbled and drank enough to stay alive, though why? Surely one of these nights, her husband would take care of that.

Could she pack up a few things and escape to that refuge house somewhere in Tallahassee? Sure. What then? No family. No money. No formal training in anything. No means to scrape out a meager living. No faith in being able to make her way alone.

No hope.

Sheila touched the cover of her Bible. She read it, every day. The tissue-thin pages she dog-eared—where she had read the parables and promises over and over—failed to buoy her as they once had.

When she prayed, she asked for the same things again and again: To be able to relax and take a deep breath without fear. To be safe in her own home. To have a reason to want to live.

Sheila closed her eyes and melted into the worn sports fantasy. So deeply. So thoroughly. She didn't hear the sound of the back door opening until Glenn stood in front of the couch where she sat, dreaming.

"What the hell do you have on?"

Sheila opened her eyes and mouth at the same time, but no sound came out. The certainty settled on her shoulders. This was it. Did doomed people all share this one moment of clarity before the end?

"I . . ."

Her husband's features shifted. The neutral expression frightened Sheila more than all of his past rages rolled together.

"I'm going to walk out to the truck. When I get back in this house, I want you to be out of whatever that is you're wearing and throw it in the garbage, and have my supper on the table." He turned to leave the room, then spun around. "No, on second thought, don't throw it out. Everyone has a little secret, huh?" He winked and flashed a toothy smile on his way out.

Sheila fought a wave of dizziness. The back door slammed. She took several deep breaths, stood, stripped off the uniform, and redressed. In less than eight minutes, Sheila set a plate heaping with homemade beef stew and crusty bread in front of her husband.

Glenn reached out and grabbed her hand in a painful grasp that morphed into a sexual caress. "Now that's more like my good little girl. Isn't it?"

Abby knew he moment her sneaker slipped, she had stepped in a fresh pile of dog poop. "Crap, crap, crap! Literally . . . crap!"

She released the throttle bar on the push lawn mower and the aging engine sputtered and died. Wiping the odoriferous goop across the

91

trimmed grass didn't help. The base and sides of her sneaker looked like a sprouted Chia Pet. The problem with athletic shoes: too much tread. Every wavy indentation overflowed with feces and the odor wafted upward.

"Mason Dixon," she muttered, "I adore you. Love the fact you can fix my computer in less time than it takes me to sneeze. But I hate your dang dog!" The last two words, she spoke with extra emphasis and volume.

"Don't care for dogs, then?" a voice asked from behind.

Abby jerked upright. The offensive shoe dangled from her fingertips. Ben Calhoun, sweaty in running attire, stood beside the curb wearing dark sunglasses and a bemused smile. Abby's pulse skipped. "Actually I like animals, though I prefer cats to dogs most of the time. I despise it when a dog leaves a huge tower of crap in my yard."

"Murphy's law says you'll always find it, too. And you know the chances go up exponentially if you're bare-footed."

Abby's upper lip curled and her nostrils flared. "Eww . . ."

Ben motioned toward the mower. "May I help you finish up?"

"You're in the middle of exercising."

Ben tilted his head slightly when he chuckled, a mannerism Abby liked. "And mowing isn't? Since when? C'mon. Go grab a hose and clean your shoe before that poop hardens into mortar, and I'll finish the last few rows."

"What the heck. Knock yourself out. I don't particularly like yard work. Who am I to argue? Besides I feel kind of guilty when I have to do this on a Sunday afternoon. That whole *day of rest* rule. It's just, I'm tired during the week when I get home, and I like to goof off on Saturdays." What had happened to poor, conversation-challenged Abby? The new version babbled like a freak. "So that leaves Sunday afternoons to catch up. Plus, with fall coming, the days are getting shorter. I run out of light before I get everything done around here."

Ben grabbed the start-rope and yanked. The engine fired up on the first try. The dang contraption took her three or four shoulder-wrenching pulls, sometimes more. Abby hobbled off with the soiled shoe in one hand.

She unwound a sun-faded garden hose from its rusty mount on the side of the house, doused her face and arms, and took a long swill before attacking the shoe. Recently she read somewhere that drinking from an outside hose wasn't such a great idea—carcinogens in the plastic or whatever. If that was true, her generation was doomed, especially the ones from the South. In her youth, Abby had ridden in the back of pick-up trucks, played kick-ball in the street, ate food swimming in animal fat, ingested sugar in every form and shape, and swigged gallons of cool water straight from the hose.

She rinsed the shoe and recalled one particular childhood game. Did it even have a proper name? She and her cohorts had called it *Ain't No Boogers*. Darkness was required. One person, tagged *the booger*— Southern-speak for the bad guy, ax-murdering nemesis of children— lurked outside the small pool of front porch light and waited for an unaware victim to pass by. When the booger called out "ready or not, here I come!" the other players walked, skipped, and ran around the yard singing a little ditty. "Ain't no boogers out tonight! Grandpa killed 'em all last night!"

Good old Grandpa. The poor man must've kidded himself that he'd vanquished evil, but wait! One last booger jumped out from the shadows, chased down the nearest child, and squealed, "Tag! You're it!" The rest dashed to the safety of home base: a designated spot in the round ring of light. The former booger returned to the victim pool and the newly-tapped booger scurried into the darkness to start the next round.

How innocent that time had been. Predators had existed. Only, not in her small town world.

She snapped to attention with the sudden cessation of the lawnmower motor. A car whooshed by, sending dry leaves skipping across the asphalt. Two cardinals bickered over the wild birdseed in the feeder. The ordinary sounds reminded her how much she disliked the intrusive drone of a gas-powered lawn mower. Before next year, she would research electric alternatives. Better yet, a push mower with nothing but human power behind the whirling blades. No fumes, only the watermelon scent of cut grass.

"Want me to rinse this down before I store it?" Ben asked.

"You're kidding right? That thing is ancient. Look at it. It has dried grass from the Garden of Eden."

Ben did the head-tilt/chuckle thing again. "Still works, doesn't it? No use to cast a thing aside because it's slightly used."

Abby stood, the dripping shoe held at arm's length. "Suppose not."

They made eye contact and held it a little too long for Abby's comfort. She cleared her throat. The signs of a friendship budding out of control loomed. How many times had she pulled her little red wagon down the same path, only to stand on her ear trying to apply the brakes? Too many.

Abby's aversion to even a hint of commitment attracted more hits than a website for cheap prescription painkillers. Men gravitated her way in unlikely places: the grocery store line, the waiting room at her ophthalmologist, the self-serve gas lane. The universe plotted to hook her up with a man, any man.

Ben's gaze fell to his feet. "So, you going to yoga tomorrow night?"

"Wouldn't miss it. You?"

He bumped the toe of his running shoe against the curb, watching it as if it held the key to love. "We should, maybe . . . catch a cup of coffee afterwards."

Abby's trapdoor slammed shut so fast, it surprised even her. "No. Can't."

His expression withered. "Oh okay . . . all right, then." He stretched each leg once. "See you later."

Ben jogged away before Abby could respond.

"Way to circle the wagons, Calamity Jane." Abby shoved the mower toward the tool shed. Hot tears stung her eyes. Her insides curled and snapped like old, rotten elastic.

Chapter Eight

Two weeks before suicide
Monday

Abby McKenzie breathed in the Homeplace's blend of cooking scents and brewed coffee. For once, the smell of food didn't entice her. The late afternoon light filtered through the room in a surreal jaundiced shade of yellow. Abby thought about movies and how changes in the light meant some kind of shift. She took a deep breath and forced down a ripple of nausea as the Yoga Rat Pack members sat down at their usual booth.

"Y'all sure are a quiet group this evening." Julie flipped open her order pad. "Maybe I should substitute the high-octane coffee for you, eh?"

Loiscell's shoulders lifted and fell.

Abby waited for someone to speak, then filled in the awkward gap. "You seem to be working a lot more night shifts, Julie. What's up with that?"

"I-Pods and laptops on my boys' Christmas wish lists. That's what's up. It's a ways off, but I have to stockpile funds, or Santa will be bringing nothing but rocks and coal. I long for the days when I could buy them something from the Dollar Store, and they'd be content. Not anymore. Nothing comes cheap." The waitress pushed a stray sprig of hair behind one ear with the end of her pencil. "So here I am. What'll it be, tonight?"

"Cup of decaf for me," Choo-choo said.

"Make that two," Abby said.

Loiscell blew out a breath and returned the laminated menu to its clip. "One for me, too."

"I'll take a cup of hot water, please," Sheila said. "I have my own tea bag."

The server shoved her order pad into an apron pocket. "No pie? No fries? I think I may need to sit down. I feel faint."

The four women exchanged glances. The weight of shared *something*, beyond the weary sadness, threatened to swallow Abby.

Julie nodded. "If y'all change your minds, I have cobbler. It's really good, even if I do say so myself. I used those North Carolina Alberta peaches I put in the freezer last month."

Abby waited until the server left the table to speak. "I didn't want to say anything before class and get you all upset, Choo-choo. Loiscell told us about Prissy. I sure am sorry."

Sheila reached over and rested a hand over Choo-choo's. "I know how much little animals steal your heart away. Is there anything we can do?"

"It wasn't like the two of us were the best of buddies. Well, not until the last few weeks." Choo-choo's red-rimmed eyes watered.

Loiscell put her arm around her elderly friend's shoulder. "You got us, sugar."

Choo-choo offered a weak smile that didn't make it to her eyes. "I do, at that."

Loiscell turned her attention to Abby. "What's up with you? You've been walking around tonight with your lower lip dragging the dirt."

"And I couldn't help but notice that Ben took a spot so far back, he practically sat outside." Choo-choo dabbed her eyes with a tissue. "Did you two have a little lovers' spat?"

Abby stuffed the urge to blurt it all out. How she was so flawed, no man would ever want her. How she cringed at the thought of loving a man. How she lay in bed every night feeling so depleted and alone, even her anonymous online chat friends couldn't boost her. "First of all, Ben Calhoun and I are *not* involved. Second, what do I care where he chooses to sit in yoga class."

Loiscell whistled low. "Whoo, hit a raw nerve."

Sheila rummaged in her clutch and extracted a zipper-lock plastic bag of assorted tea bags. "Y'all leave her alone. If she doesn't like the man, she doesn't *like* the man."

"Gosh, Sheila." Choo-choo tilted her head to one side. "That's the most fire I've ever seen come out of you."

Julie appeared with their drink order. "Wave me down when you need refills. From the looks on your faces, you're going to be here a while."

"What do you suppose she meant by that?" Sheila asked after the server walked away.

Abby added extra cream and sweetener to her cup. "We look like someone stomped on us—all down and out."

Choo-choo took a deep breath and exhaled. "I *am* down and out. Not only did Charlie's dog die, but my favorite Hospice lady passed this morning. It hasn't been a stellar week. Sometimes, living is such a chore." She threw down her crumpled tissue. "That suicide supper club thing is sounding better and better every day."

Sheila dipped a chamomile tea bag into the steaming water. She didn't lift her gaze when she said, "I've heard worse ideas."

Loiscell grabbed a napkin to swipe a ring of spilled coffee. "What if we *could* choose to leave this earth instead of having to go through all this crap?"

"Life *is* about choices," Abby added. Her stomach lurched again and a sour taste coated her tongue.

Choo-choo tapped one coral-painted nail on her chin. "Wonder how one would go about it? Say a person wished to hire someone to take her out of circulation."

"Not like you could look up *Hit Men R Us* in the yellow pages," Abby said.

The comment elicited half-hearted laughter.

"It would cost big money, for one thing," Sheila said. "More than I could come up with."

"I could sell my car." Abby tilted her head toward the window. In an illuminated pool of a streetlight, her Honda leaned into the curb like it had been ridden hard and left to suffer. The others tittered again.

"You'd be better off torching it for the insurance money, hon. Not meaning to offend." Loiscell leaned forward and lowered her voice. "Sheila's right. It's not the kind of cash you get from hosting a bake sale."

Choo-choo's voice came out in a near-whisper. "I have the money."

The friends sat for a moment before Abby found her voice. "Wait. You're talking like you're seriously considering this." The taste of bile bit her tongue again and she took a shaky breath.

As if she had received some kind of cosmic nudge, Sheila jumped. "Why not? It's a free country."

"What would be so wrong about taking control, for once?" Loiscell's lips set in a thin line.

Choo-choo's expression brightened. "We could find a spot out of town. Some place with great food. Eat until we can't choke down another bite. Right after some really sinful dessert, boom!"

"Get real, y'all." Abby leaned forward and whispered, "How would we even know where to contact—" she glanced around to make sure no one was listening "—a hit man?"

A shimmer of fear crossed Sheila's face, then her features hardened into something Abby had never seen there before—resolve. Sheila dabbed a trickle of tea from her lips. "I could make some inquiries."

Her tablemates openly stared. Abby pushed her jaw back in place, because surely it had dropped.

"Since when do you have connections to the underworld, dear?" Choo-choo asked.

"Glenn works in law enforcement."

"A prison guard is going to help us find a sniper?" Loiscell huffed. "That's a bit of a stretch, don't you think?"

Choo-choo held up one hand. "Does anyone else have a better idea?" She glanced around the group. "No? I say if our resident Martha-Stewart-wannabe thinks she can finagle a name for us, then let her. What the heck?"

Loiscell pointed at Sheila. "Okay. Do it and report back to us."

"I will." Color brushed Sheila's cheeks.

Choo-choo looked from one woman to the next. She enunciated slowly, as if each word carried an equal weight. "If we decide to go ahead with this, none of us asks the others why they want to leave here. That is between each woman and her conscience. Clear?"

The other women cast fleeting looks around the group, then nodded.

"Good. That's settled. I'll get busy moving some funds around." Choo-choo's features brightened so abruptly, Abby looked at the others with her eyebrows lifted.

The butterscotch incandescent light bathed her friends' faces and Abby compared it to watching an ethereal scene in some 3-D theatre. Her stomach roiled. Then, a separate sensation floated through. A tinge of excitement mixed with what, relief? *Am I really considering this?*

"You know what," Loiscell said. "Suddenly I have a taste for a giant bowl of hot peach cobbler á la mode."

Two weeks before suicide, Tuesday

Sheila Bruner hugged Buttercup to her chest and enjoyed the deep rumble of the cat's contented purr. Surely God would allow pets in Heaven.

Risky, bold business, stepping outside to love the cat with her husband home. But the odds of Glenn looking for her—at least for the moment—were slim. He was on his fourth Jack Daniels and an ESPN college football round-up blared on the flat screen. If there was a Hell, Sheila was certain it would have a monolithic flat screen television tuned to the sports network with an endless monologue by retired players and eons of "the big game" highlights. The only sport worth watching—women's basketball—never entered Glenn's radar.

"I'll be damned if I will sit here and watch a bunch of dykes run up and down the court!" He had made that comment so often, Sheila could hear it echo in her head. In Glenn's estimation, an athletic, strong woman had to be gay. One of the first things he had required of Sheila when they started dating: quit the high school women's basketball team. No way any girl of his would play sports.

Thinking about versions of Heaven and Hell made Sheila's spirit slide even lower. If she took an active part in leaving this life behind, would she still be worthy of a golden afterlife? Or would the one final act of desperation cancel all the selfless mercies, the mounds of charitable giving, and the hours of prayer and Bible study? Couldn't He look down in all of His boundless wisdom and see how she had no viable options?

Sheila lowered herself to sit on the top step; the cat curled in her folded arms. Leaving Buttercup behind, that she would regret. She'd find a good home for the young feline, one with a nice furry rug in front of the hearth, in time for the cold weather.

Seek and ye shall find. Ask and it shall be given unto you. So many times in her life, she had read that promise. She had pleaded repeatedly to be rid of bearing Glenn's rages. Prayed as much for him as for herself. Divorce wasn't an option. And if she screwed up the courage to flee, Glenn would find her. He often reminded her: "You ever do that to me—just up and run off—I'll track you down and make you sorry you ever drew a breath."

Glenn Bruner never made idle threats. The only way she could leave her husband was death. He would take that decision away from her at some point. It was only a matter of time.

Buttercup nuzzled her hand and she rubbed the downy fuzz around his ears.

Glenn's recent even temper frightened Sheila more than any well-aimed sucker punch. Over the years, she had grown to understand the cycle. Relative good humor followed by a mounting edginess that bloomed into anger and physical acting out. Like a macabre waltz, Glenn led and Sheila followed. Hurt. Heal. Hurt. Heal. The intervals grew smaller. Soon, Sheila feared no space would exist between the extremes.

A dog, often beaten, belly-crawled with anticipation of abuse. Even if the hand above its head held no threat, the animal reacted as if it did. Sheila empathized. Better to exhibit the groveling posture of the Omega than risk the wrath of the Alpha.

"Go on back to your little house, baby." Sheila kissed the yellow kitty on the head and lowered it to the ground in front of the shrubs. The cat looked at her with sleepy eyes, meowed softly, and disappeared behind the leaf cover.

Sheila stood and shook off her fear before opening the back door. What could possibly happen if she asked Glenn *the question*? Slap, punch, rape? Nothing she hadn't experienced before. Worst case, he would beat her to death. Then the answer would be pointless.

Glenn reclined in the den. Either his hearing was failing, or he kept the volume loud because he could. Sheila waited until a commercial break and handed him a fresh glass of whiskey. "Would you like some chips and dip? I have some of that horseradish and bacon stuff mixed up." She faked a smile.

Glenn released a resinous belch. "Yeah. Sure. When's dinner?"

"About fifteen minutes or so. I'm just waiting until the rolls are done." Sheila picked up the empty highball glass.

"Smells like spaghetti."

"Actually, I made lasagna."

Glenn's eyes narrowed. "Some special occasion? What do you want now?"

"Can't I make my husband's favorite dish without a reason?"

The sportscaster's voice blared. Glenn turned his attention back to the television. "Whatever. Shut up. You'll make me miss my show. And bring my plate in here."

Sheila glanced at the flat screen, the only recent furnishing in the house. The couch and recliner—hand-me-downs from Glenn's parents—showed so many wear facets, they appeared moth-eaten. Throw pillows disguised the worst spots. The kitchen appliances clicked and moaned. But by golly, Glenn Bruner had a high-definition LED television. "I do need to ask you one question, Glenn."

"Can't it wait until the next commercial?"

"Sure." Sheila returned to the kitchen. A few minutes later, she heard Glenn bellow her name and she scurried back into the den, a basket of chips in one hand and a bowl of dip in the other.

"So what's this burning question of yours?" He scooped a tablespoon-sized dollop of dip onto a tortilla chip, crammed it into his mouth, then chased it with a swig of booze.

"I was wondering, if a person wanted to hire . . . umm . . . a hit man. How would she, or he, go about it?"

Glenn sputtered a mouthful of whiskey onto his shirt. A milky sheen of dip shone on his lips. "The hell? What kind of a lame-ass question is that?" He swiped his mouth with the back of one hand.

Sheila took a slow breath. Steeled herself. She would finish this. "Just curious."

"You have someone in mind needs killing?" His rheumy gaze caught and held hers. "Huh Sheila?"

"Don't be silly, Glenn. I'd never. Taking the life of another is against God's commandments. Just . . . someone I know asked me. I suppose this person thought since you were in law enforcement, you'd be an expert."

His expression flashed with annoyance, then morphed to something like interest. "I could ask around."

Sheila's head spun over the weird mood switch. One of his blow-ups loomed. Several times within the past couple of days, Sheila had recognized the subtle clues of an eminent explosion. Snipped, harsh words. A tightness around his lips. His large calloused hands stretching and clenching.

Her mouth went dry. She licked her lips and forged ahead. "If you would. I'm sure this person would appreciate it."

"This *person* you keep talking about have money?"

Sheila nodded. "Yes."

"Not like I have a connection with that type of lawless deadbeat, but I can see if I might get a name and number for you to pass along. As long as no one asks where you got it. I have my career to protect."

"Of course." A bell sounded in the kitchen. "Oh . . . my rolls. I almost forgot!" She turned toward the kitchen. Glenn chuckled and mumbled something about a new boat.

Two weeks before suicide, Saturday

Abby McKenzie stood at the threshold of her second bedroom, a cramped hole that served as her computer space. The size of the rooms in the old cottage-styled house amazed her. If she put a double bed and one chest of drawers in the room, she would need a crowbar and a can of Crisco to move between the bed and door. The master bedroom wasn't much larger, but at least she could see the floor.

She had spent her childhood and adolescence in this room. Then it had provided a safe cocoon. Now, the walls threatened to close in.

Abby carried the laptop into the living room. Thank heaven Mason Dixon had installed the wireless Internet router. The only contraption tying her down was the four-year-old printer, a device requiring a direct-wired link. The dang thing chewed up paper and went through ink cartridges with a singular vengeance. The past week, one of the cartridges had failed, spilling thick black goop over the printer heads. No big loss. A good opportunity to justify a newer version, one with more capability. Good riddance to bad electronic rubbish. Even if Abby wouldn't be around to see the next one become obsolete, she could enjoy it for the time she had remaining.

Might as well relish her final days, cram in all the small pleasures. Whatever she wanted. She wouldn't buy sugar-free chocolate. She'd eat cheese. Hot bread slathered with butter. Fried everything. Maybe not wear a bra.

Abby heard Mason's double-knock and met him at the front door. "I appreciate you coming to hook up the new printer." Abby led the way to the computer room. "Suppose I could do it myself, but why take the chance of killing it straight out of the box when I have an expert living right next door."

Mason Dixon used a letter opener to snap open the box lid. "No problem, Abs."

Abby grinned at the adolescent's nickname for her. "Be sure to keep up with the time you spend. I don't consider your time a *gimme*."

"Wireless. Cool." He mumbled to himself as he thumbed through the owner's manual. Unlike many males, Mason took time to read printed directions.

Beneath his hormone-ravaged surface, Abby sensed a faint glimmer of the man Mason would become. He wasn't a high school football star or handsome in a dazzling sort of way, but sincerity and gentleness idled beneath his shy, nerdy persona. The hunky guys might take the lead straight out of the starter's box, but the steady, kind men caught up by the time the pack reached the second turn. Women weren't, for the most part, stupid. Though she had been.

Oreo walked past her in his three-legged skipping gait and trilled at Mason's feet. He picked the kitten up and settled it into his lap.

"Mason, if anything ever happened to me, would you be willing to adopt Oreo?"

He glanced her way. "Sure. He's cool."

"Your mom wouldn't be upset, would she?"

"She likes animals. As long as I pay for the vet bills, I don't think she'd freak."

Mason was a thirty-year-old in a teenager's body. If all adolescents were more like him, they wouldn't have such a bad rep. "That makes me feel better."

He extracted the combination printer, copier, fax, and scanner from its box and discarded the foam packing inserts. "You okay, Abs?"

"Sure. Just . . . one never knows what the future will hold. I wouldn't want Oreo to end up at the shelter. Not many people would want to take in a special-needs kitty."

Mason scratched the top of the tuxedo cat's head. "One less leg doesn't make him less of a cat."

"You know Mason, you are going to make some lucky woman one heck of a husband one day."

His head swung her way. "Get real."

"You want a soft drink?"

"Have any of that green tea?"

"Coming up."

Abby paused on her way to the kitchen and looked around the living room. Where would all of this stuff end up? Someone would have to go through it and glean the parts worth saving. The other junk would be carted off to the dump.

Maybe if she tried again, if she attacked a little section each day, her heir wouldn't have to deal with the same tower of possessions she had faced after her parents died. A web of weariness pressed her shoulders down. Who was she kidding? She hadn't coped with it then. Why was now any different?

Preparing for her "final destination" was like planning for a long trip. Stop the paper. Hold the mail. Leave the refrigerator void of perishables. Make sure she had her papers in order. That, she had to do for sure.

Easy sparky. Don't get too carried away. The group of four had agreed: nothing could call undue attention. Their deaths had to appear spontaneous, not carefully mapped out and financed.

A will. She didn't have one. Funeral plans? Nope.

She could go online and download a simple will. Better yet, call that attorney in Tallahassee, the woman Elvina always crowed about. It wouldn't be terribly expensive, and she would rather not run the risk of screwing up. Abby knew who her beneficiary would be.

Abby's plans stretched to the workplace. So much to be done. She would leave the front office organized: that she could do. Though she liked to think she was indispensable to Dr. Payne after so many years, Sabrina's recent extended absence had highlighted one fact: no one was irreplaceable. Some people might leave a larger ripple when they passed, but all would be forgotten. The tide would rush in. Their footprints would fill in with fresh sand.

"Here you go." Abby set a tall glass of iced green tea on a coaster beside the computer armoire.

"Thanks."

"You're most welcome." Abby hesitated. "Have you given any thought to college yet, Mason?"

His thin shoulders lifted, fell. "I'd like to attend FSU, but it's expensive. I'll end up at some junior college for a couple of years. Maybe by that time, I can save up enough to transfer. No way can my parents come up with that kind of cash. And I don't want to graduate with a boat-load of school loans."

"Don't tell me . . . computer science."

He pushed his thick glasses back on his nose. "What was your first clue?"

"A lot can happen between now and when you're ready for college. A chest of money could fall into your lap."

"Right." He plugged in the printer. It beeped, flashed lights, beeped again. "Abs, you need to lay off those drugs."

Elvina Houston pulled the Oldsmobile to the curb in front of the Reverend Thurston and Lucille Jackson's modest brick ranch-styled house. A gravel-paved circular drive looped in front of the main entrance, but Elvina seldom parked there. Vehicles came and went from the parsonage, and she had been blocked in a few times too many. Steering forward was one thing. Worming her way out of a tight spot between two cars was another.

She toyed with the idea of entering through the side access before deciding to ring the front doorbell. Only one house had she felt comfortable enough to enter without a formal invitation: the late Piddie Longman's. No matter if either woman caught the other half-naked or sitting on the toilet, neither had an obligation to phone first, nor even knock. A resounding *yoo-hoo* was sufficient warning to keep from scaring the ever-lovin' beejezus out of the other.

A diminutive black woman with a welcoming smile answered Elvina's knock. The crimp in Elvina's spirit loosened, as it always did whenever she saw Lucille Jackson's kind face. No small wonder Piddie had counted Lucille among her top-tier friends, Elvina being number one, naturally.

"Come in, come in." Lucille Jackson ushered her into the cozy parlor. Elvina hadn't quite made the cut for a kitchen-visiting friend.

At first, Elvina's association with the Reverend's petite wife had been born of the need to hang fast to any earthly link with Piddie. Over time, the loose connection had developed into friendship. Though not as intense for either woman, the tie served as a decent consolation prize.

"I've made us some of that green tea you like so much. And one of our members dropped off a few slices of red velvet cake. If you don't eat a piece, my Thurston will inhale every last bite. His cholesterol has been a little high, so I'd rather not have too much here to tempt him."

"I can always eat cake," Elvina said.

When Lucille smiled, an even row of teeth showed. If Elvina didn't simply adore the little woman, she'd envy a hole clean through her. How could someone pushing seventy have an unlined face and good white teeth? And she was tee-tiny to boot. Not an ounce of spare padding anywhere to attest to time and menopause. If not for the brush of silver across her eyebrows and temples, Lucille might pass for years younger.

Lucille returned a few minutes later with a serving tray. Elvina stood in front of a wall of photographs. She recognized a few of the people, other than Lucille and Thurston.

"Crying shame you and the Reverend only had the three boys," Elvina commented when she sat down on the pillow-strewn couch across from Lucille. "You would have done well with a houseful of children."

Lucille's expression darkened. She poured two cups of tea and handed one to Elvina. "There was one more, but she went to Heaven before we had a chance to meet. Sometimes God's plan isn't the same one we write for ourselves."

"Doesn't mean we have to like it."

Piddie had often alluded to the baby girl Lucille had miscarried, but never shared the details. If a thing was told in confidence, she would harelip Hell before giving it away. Piddie had taken so many confidences to her grave, Elvina wondered how that woman had fit into the urn.

Elvina squelched the burning need to pry. You didn't push Lucille Jackson. She might look like a delicate flower, but she could dig in her heels. Elvina had witnessed the preacher's wife stand down a drug-pushing adolescent boy three times her size. One scorching stare from Lucille, and he had high-tailed it out of the church playground like he had been chased off by one of the horsemen from the Apocalypse. The power of a black woman's conviction, especially one backed by the Almighty, was nothing to sneeze at.

Elvina took a bite of cake. The layers were moist, and the icing a perfect blend of sweetened cream cheese and chopped pecans. It was going to take everything she had not to wolf it down and lick the plate. "Absolutely scrumptious."

Lucille nodded. "It is, isn't it? I sneaked a little sliver earlier. The lady who made it also does a sinful coconut layered cake. Needless to say, I live for the church dinners when I know she's bringing dessert."

"Y'all holding the fall festival again this year?"

"The planning committee is working out the details now. We'd like to be able to fund another stained glass window for the sanctuary."

"I can bring a pot of chicken 'n' dumplin's. I know mine will never measure up to Piddie's, but they're passable. I can follow her recipe to the letter, and they still won't taste quite the same."

"I'll let Yolanda know. She's heading up the food committee. I'm certain she'll call you soon with a date. We're planning around FSU and FAMU football games, and all kinds of special events. Everything seems to happen at the same time, once you hit mid-September."

"And it's really a blur after Thanksgiving."

Lucille took a sip of tea and regarded Elvina. "Are you going to tell me what's bothering you?"

"How would you know I'm unsettled just by a two-minute phone conversation?"

Lucille's small shoulders rose and fell. "Comes with the job, I suppose."

Elvina wiped the red velvet crumbs from her lips and set the empty plate down on the coffee table. From its position in the entrance foyer, a maple grandfather clock chimed. "I've had the most churned-up feeling, Lucille. I can't put my finger on it exactly."

"Might be the change in seasons. Affects many people that way. We see a great amount of depression around the holidays, especially closer to Christmas."

Elvina bit on her lower lip. "My depression isn't seasonal. It's the kind that feels at home any time of year. Besides the doctor has my medication regulated. I hardly ever sink that low anymore."

"I know you miss Piddie. I miss her too." Lucille waited a moment. "But that's not why you're here, is it?"

"No. Something else is chewing on me." Elvina listened to the comforting rhythm of the heirloom timepiece. Time bustling past, one tick-tock at a time. "I bumped into Choo-choo Ivey a couple of days back."

"She's such a sweetheart."

"You know she lost that little dog of hers?"

Lucille moved her head from one side to the other. "I hadn't heard. She must be terribly sad. The loss of a pet often makes people feel as bad as losing a family member. Which really, they are."

"That's what has my puzzler sore," Elvina said. "I saw her the day after she had Prissy cremated and she was torn all to pieces. I didn't even think she liked that little dog. Can't say I blamed her. It had the nastiest disposition and had gotten bad about peeing all over her house, though to hear Choo-choo tell it, Prissy had learned to confine it to one rug. The last couple of times I visited, the smell made me gag."

Lucille's nose crinkled. "Dear!"

"Then I saw her up at the Triple C yesterday when she came in for a color and cut. It was like she'd won the lottery. She had a skip to her step, and Mandy said she even double-tipped. If you know Choo-choo, you'd know that ain't like her. She'll squeeze a dime until it spits out change."

"People have reasons for their actions, Elvina. It's not necessarily a cause for concern."

Elvina's brows knit together. "You believe people get happier right before they die?"

"I've seen it happen. Why?"

"At my age, I attend more funerals than birthday parties. I never know when I see one of my older acquaintances, whether it will be the last time or not. They can be so full of life and happy, then the next moment, bam!"

"None of us have a stamped ticket with a guaranteed departure date. No matter if we're young or old."

"True enough. Still, I can't help but wonder if Choo-choo might be having some sort of last minute . . . what would you call it? . . . burst of grace."

One of Lucille's white eyebrows tilted up. "Maybe she has a new male friend."

Elvina froze, stunned into momentary silence. "That's it, Lucille. That *has* to be it." Elvina's eyes narrowed. "That little dickens. Here she has a new love interest and hasn't breathed so much as a word to me. Wait until I get ahold of that woman."

Lucille laughed. "Heaven help her. I'd hate to get on your bad side, Elvina Houston."

Two weeks before suicide, Sunday

Choo-choo Ivey closed her eyes and images of Charlie's face flickered past. Charlie at twenty-two: his red-tinged hair combed straight back, Irish eyes sparkling with mischief. Charlie at thirty-nine: sun-kissed and freckled, holding the bow rope of a small fishing boat. Charlie at forty-seven: still muscular and fit, his T-shirt off and looped around the waist of his faded shorts, mowing the lawn in the July heat. Charlie, sixty: hair thinning on the top, still boyishly handsome in his Sunday best. Charlie at the end: face and body ravaged by disease and pain, reaching out to grasp her hand.

Finally, the Charlie of her recent dreams: youthful, joyous, waiting for her and bouncing from one foot to the other, wondering why she was taking an eternity to arrive. Prissy sat at his feet, restored to her puppyhood, her stubby cotton ball tail wiggling a beat. Choo-choo actually looked forward to seeing the little dog again.

I will see Charlie soon! The thought repeated in her mind like a meditation mantra. How much longer—only a matter of days. She no longer prayed for death to tap her while she slept; she had snatched the Reaper's scythe.

A niggling voice inside asked, "What about Jacqueline?"

Choo-choo shoed the voice away. Three months. It had been *three* months since she had spoken with her daughter. Choo-choo had lost count of the numerous voice mail messages she had left beyond the beep, and the hand-written letters. A couple of times, Jacqueline had bothered to contact her, but always at a time when Choo-choo was away from home, as if her daughter gleaned enough information from her missives to know when to call. "Hi, Mother. I'm fine. Sounds like you are too. Later . . ."

What could make a daughter so loathe her mother? Choo-choo raked her memory for clues and came up empty. She had not been the queen of school cupcake bakes and didn't sew fancy smocked dresses, but she had faithfully attended parent/teacher meetings with Charlie and sat through every kind of sporting event imaginable. That had to count for something.

Choo-choo poured a tall glass of tea and talked to Charlie. "I know I wasn't the touchy-feely, nurturing type. You filled the role of boo-boo kisser and Band-Aid vendor. You pitched softballs in the back yard and dried tears. You gave her that mandatory 'birds and the bees' talk."

When Charlie became gravely ill, Choo-choo's latent nurse tendencies surfaced. She had fed, bathed, comforted, medicated, and monitored. Finally, she understood why others displayed altruistic behavior. It felt good, and at least she could do *some*thing. Too late for her relationship with Jacqueline, selfless love had altered Choo-choo's life.

She broke off a piece of dry toast and chewed. How could she leave behind some fashion of farewell without prompting guilt and remorse? A letter, a recorded message?

Choo-choo settled on the former. She grabbed the small notepad next to the phone. She scribbled and scratched out words, entire paragraphs. Started and stopped. Drank tea. Wrote some more. But words seemed inadequate to bridge across the years of estrangement and silence. The remainder of her estate after the hit man's payoff—house, car, stocks, bonds, and certificates of deposit—could fill in where words failed.

Choo-choo pushed the notepad aside and dug the slip of paper from her purse. How Sheila Bruner—timid little Sheila—had managed to obtain the assassin's contact number was beyond belief. As instructed, Choo-choo dialed, waited for a generic greeting, and left her home number and first name. Within the half-hour, the phone rang and a deep male voice gave instructions.

Choo-choo scribbled on the notepad beneath her feeble letter to Jacqueline. "Got it."

She heard the disconnect click, then dead air.

A couple of hours later, Choo-choo stood inside of the Mid-view Truck Stop café near Tallahassee. Eleven a.m. sharp. Choo-choo's pulse thrummed. Charlie would've loved this. He had been a big fan of crime and thriller novels. The whole thing seemed so deliciously James Bond-ish.

She scanned the line of booths and spotted the woman—the Yellow Dress lady, left side, 5th table from the buffet bar. Five, her lucky number. A good omen.

Time to dust off her latent actor capabilities. Choo-choo cleared her throat.

"Just one this afternoon?" A server clad in gingham asked.

Choo-choo ripped her gaze from Yellow Dress long enough to reply, "No. I'm meeting my great niece and there she is." She tucked her clutch beneath one arm and scuttled toward the fifth booth. "Yoo-hoo! Sandy!"

Yellow Dress spotted her and slid from the booth. They embraced like long-lost sisters separated at birth. Choo-choo pushed back, held Yellow Dress at arm's length. "Look at you. You haven't changed a bit in five years."

A couple of women cast bored glances their way, otherwise no one took note of an old lady and a twenty-something female throwing a reunion in a truck stop diner.

Intriguing. Would the assassin be female then? Choo-choo appreciated the idea of women in traditionally male roles, but this? Or was the mysterious woman in yellow his wife? Did hit men even have wives? Surely they did, or at least girlfriends. A hit man was still a man. Maybe this "Sandy" didn't fully grasp the nature of her mate's line of work.

They sat down, maintaining a running banter. They ordered brunch: the Country Slammer for Yellow Dress Sandy and a biscuit for Choo-choo, two coffees. No way Choo-choo could choke down even a bite, but she'd try. For appearances.

Until the food arrived, they caught up on fictitious old times. Yellow Dress Sandy blathered on and on about her parents, how she'd started back to college for her master's, about sick relatives.

Goodness, she was a pro. Choo-choo played along, asking about the latest baby—"Leticia, right?"

They spoke in code, like the man had instructed on the phone. Four of us. The date, time, location. A figure, agreed upon. Even what to wear. All in a storyline any eavesdropping busybody wouldn't suspect.

The pretend drama scrambled Choo-choo's stomach. Lord, don't let me get the runs. No telling about truck stop bathrooms. Choo-choo fiddled with the paper napkin in her lap, twisting it into a sweaty baton.

"Oh, I almost forgot." Yellow Dress Sandy slipped a piece of paper from her purse and slid it across the table. "Our new address and phone number."

Choo-choo forced her hand to lift, take the paper. Bank routing numbers. The olden days of briefcases packed with unmarked bills had caved to the new digital age. Too bad. It could've added so much noir to this little play. She nipped a few buttered bites of biscuit.

"Wish you'd eat more, Auntie. I worry so about your health." Yellow Dress Sandy wolfed down the Country Slammer breakfast. Mopped egg yolks with wheat toast.

Chapter Nine

One week before suicide
Tuesday

Loiscell Pickering hoisted a bulging bag of clothing and added it to a growing tower of boxes bound for charity donation. Why hadn't she done this years ago? The pants—in the "old Loiscell" pre-cancer sizes—could wrap around her body one and a half times with material to spare. Ruby red pumps—when had she worn those? Christmas, Valentine's Day, Wizard of Oz costume party?

After she completed the closet purge, the carpet showed through the few pairs of stacked shoes. How long it had been since the closet floor had seen daylight was anyone's guess.

Loiscell moved on to the hall linen closet, pitching sets of sheets, towels, plastic-wrapped comforters, and stacks of tablecloths. The heirloom pieces—an ecru lace coverlet of her grandmother's and a couple of hand-embroidered holiday table runners—missed the grab and toss. By midmorning, she stopped for a cup of cocoa and a handful of peanuts. Everything had started to look like junk. No need to get carried away.

Her son Lance wasn't sentimental. With the exception of a few of his father's old hand tools, Lance wouldn't care what she chose to leave behind. Lisa, his polar opposite, would covet all of it down to the last paper clip. By cleaning out at least a little, Loiscell was doing her daughter a huge favor. Otherwise, Lisa and the twins wouldn't be able to find a pathway between rooms. The times Loiscell had traveled to Atlanta, she had hidden her shock at the amount of stuff Lisa had accumulated. Her daughter had taken the pack-rat gene supplied by her mother and multiplied it tenfold.

Loiscell smiled. Gangly, athletic, belated flower child Lance. Last time she saw him, his meager possessions had included two bicycles—one off-road and one city cruiser—outdoor gear, minimal clothing, one set of sheets, a pillow, blanket, and a few toiletries. If his hair was an inch or two longer, Lance would have appeared well-suited for life in the sixties, a joint dangling from one hand, with a dreamy-eyed, willowy female in the passenger seat of his dirt-pocked Volkswagen van. Yet being a new-age hippie, Lance shunned animal fat, alcohol, chemicals, and drugs.

What money Loiscell possessed—a small savings account and a few certificates of deposit—would help her children. Lisa could finance the twins' college education and assist Rachel and Rick to start their lives free of so much debt. After the income from the children's books started to flow, Lisa might take time to travel, write, and enjoy life. She might find time to date.

To Lance, the cash would seem an encumbrance. He might even push it off on his sister. Loiscell hoped he would use it to visit some exotic place, to ride his bike through a shadowy, medieval forest, or camp in the jungle with the call of Howler monkeys for a lullaby.

Loiscell reminisced as she sorted through years of closet flotsam. Lance's worn pair of soccer shoes. Lisa's bagged high school cap and gown with the colored honor tassels still looped around the yoke. Old term papers, notebooks, and containers of snapshots. Loiscell boxed the mementoes and labeled them with a black permanent marker. The items belonged to her children's past; best for each to decide what snippets to discard or carry forward.

How would her death affect her children? Loiscell sat back for a moment.

Cosmic Lance would view his mother's death as part of The Big Plan. At some point, he might take a moment at the base of a waterfall or atop a red rock cliff to remember his mom and allow the universe to envelope her spirit.

Lisa would fold into herself, scrunching up like a garden slug sprinkled with salt. Loiscell recalled the way Lisa had handled both her daddy's death, then her own failed marriage. Crying, then cocooning. Finally throwing herself into a cavalcade of busyness. At least Lisa had the twins, her profession, and the upcoming book release to help her move forward.

"Can't be helped," Loiscell muttered. She pitched a lumpy stuffed Easter bunny over her shoulder to the trash pile. No way she'd leave that mangy thing for her daughter to cart back to Atlanta. It was a health hazard.

Time to "get real," as her grandchildren put it. She was going to die soon, one way or the other. She had cheated cancer twice. What were the odds? One near-future path led to chemotherapy and radiation—a drawn-out suffering—to steal a little more time. The other, to a swift, well-planned exit. Prolonged pain had a way of wearing down even the most stalwart, positive patient.

She moved to the den, stacking outdated magazines into the recycle bin. How might she comfort Lisa and Lance? She couldn't talk with them in advance or even send an email. Too much of a chance of becoming morose and sentimental. Lisa would drop everything and drive home.

A letter. Loiscell would write each of her children and grandchildren a long missive. Tell them how proud she was. How she admired Lance's free spirit, Lisa's fortitude, Rachel and Rick's youthful humor and potential. Before the Big Event, she would slip the letters into the mail. By the time they arrived, tucked between bills and credit card offers, Loiscell would be free.

One week before suicide, Thursday

Abby McKenzie stared at the insurance pending roster until the numbers blurred on the monitor display. For almost two weeks, Ben had delivered Dr. Payne's office mail during the mid-morning mad-house when she was at her busiest. He left the usual stack of magazines, bills, flyers, and payment envelopes with a nod and a simple "good morning." She had tried to gain his attention in yoga class, but he came in late, sat at the back of the room, and left before they could speak.

Except Ben hadn't come at all today. Maybe he'd just open the door and throw their mail into a waiting room chair. Avoid any chance of seeing her.

Hurting someone as gentle as Ben Calhoun was right up there with slapping baby bunnies or snatching an all-day sucker from a toddler. Ben didn't deserve it, and Abby was a total witch.

Face it, sweetheart. A decent relationship with a male is a no-go for you. The thought depressed her so thoroughly she found it hard to breathe. Soon it would be a moot point. If reincarnation was the truth behind it all, perhaps she'd be able to come back and make a fresh go of things. Next time around, she would have the perfect father, fall in love, marry, have children, and grow happy and fat with the man of her heart's choice. All this, given the chance she didn't come back as a cockroach to repay the suicide karma mortgage.

Abby took bites of double meat/double cheese pizza chased with sweet tea while she thumbed through a mound of insurance correspondence. The heck with scrimping with PB&Js and diet cola. The staff had cleared out for lunch, and the waiting room was blissfully quiet.

Abby sliced open a thick white envelope. "You are flipping kidding me." Though the day's insurance claims were submitted electronically, she often received written communication asking the most asinine questions. For the fifth time in less than two months, the same company had written for additional information. "What more do you want? A testament from the President? I've already sent you two copies of the x-ray, a letter from Dr. Payne, and everything short of a plea from God."

Abby snapped. She scribbled notes and drew arrows in bright red marker across the letter, taped another x-ray envelope in the middle, folded the paper until it was less than four inches square, stapled it a half dozen times, then stuffed it into a stamped return envelope and shoved it in the outgoing mail. "There you go! Pleasure doing business with you."

Maybe they'd disburse funds this time. Sometimes it paid to go a little nuts.

Abby had just taken a huge cheesy bite when she heard the click of the front door. She slugged a huge gulp of tea to unglue the pizza spackled to her teeth.

"Good morning." Ben handed a stack of mail through the opened window and retrieved the outgoing correspondence.

"Actually," Abby glanced down at her watch, surreptitiously licking the tomato sauce from one corner of her lips, "it's afternoon."

"Abby, I—"

"I'm sorry, Ben. I really am."

He fiddled with the clasp on his messenger bag. "I overstepped."

Abby shook her head. "You didn't. All you asked for was a cup of coffee. I . . ."

Ben held up a hand. "No need to explain."

"Do you think we could be friends, Ben?"

When he smiled, the fine lines around his eyes crinkled, but his expression remained defeated and sad. "I thought we were."

Chapter Ten

Two days before suicide
Saturday

Glenn Bruner checked the rearview mirror twice before slowing and pulling into a sandy road barely wide enough to accommodate a vehicle. Scrub oak branches reached like tentacles and grabbed the truck's flanks and undercarriage.

At a small clearing, Glenn parked, looked at his watch, and switched off the ignition. The pick-up's engine sputtered blue exhaust, coughed twice, and died. Might as well relax. He reclined the seat. Sometimes he missed a good smoke. He had given up the habit a few years back. Besides, smoking would be hazardous to his health. Imagine that, a hit man worried about dying of lung cancer. That there was funny.

The rumble of a motor and the crack of underbrush called Glenn to attention. He flipped the lever and the seat snapped upright. A dusty dark blue Chevy Blazer pulled alongside the pick-up. When Glenn opened his driver's side door, the rusty hinges squealed like pigs at a slaughter.

"Where'd you find that piece of crap?" Clay asked when Glenn slid into the Chevy's passenger seat.

"Belongs to one of my poker buddies, his hunting truck. We swapped for the afternoon. I didn't recognize where you were telling me to go, and some of these dirt roads are narrow as all get out. No way I'd bring my truck down here. Surprised you brought yours. Sides are probably scratched to hell and back."

"Doesn't matter. Not mine." Clay offered a thin, humorless smile.

"Remind me to never let you borrow my truck."

Clay shook his head and his eyes flicked up then back down. He stared at Glenn for a long moment before he spoke. "I'm concerned." He swiveled his head, squinting into the sun's glare. "Small town like Chattahoochee. You're bound to know most everyone. I'm not altogether comfortable with that fact."

Glenn's hands curled into fists. "I'd gun down my own grandma if that's what it took. Who am I going to whack?"

"Did you just say *whack*?" Clay turned to face him with one eyebrow lifted. "Never mind. Of course you did," he added before Glenn could respond. "There will be four targets."

"Four?"

"That a problem?"

Glenn grinned. "Four times the payola, way I see it."

"Four . . . women."

Lordy, that called for a drink. Glenn wished he'd brought his bigger flask. "Now why would four gals want to off themselves, you reckon."

"Isn't required that you know that, any more than a pilot has to know the end destination of every passenger onboard." Clay paused. "We provide a simple service for a simple, yet exorbitant, fee."

Glenn glowed inside. Clay had said *we* . . . We! "Reckon, if those folks want out bad enough to pay for it, then I'm the man to make their dreams come true."

"You might have a promising future in this business." Clay narrowed his eyes to appraising slits. "You can dead-center the practice dummies, but can you manage a perfect kill shot on a live subject?"

"You got me a semiautomatic revolver. Heck, I could aim one of them in my sleep." Glenn rubbed his palms together. "I'm raring to get started."

"Easy there, girly-boy." The toothpick rolled from one corner of Clay's mouth to the other. Menace boiled off him in waves. "First we'll go over the plan until you can see it in your sleep. Follow it to the letter. No adlibbing. Understand?"

"When do I get my money?" Glenn wiggled.

Clay turned the key and the Chevy's engine responded. "Not until I have confirmation of your success. Don't fret. You'll get your due." He motioned toward the other vehicle. "Get back in that rattletrap and follow me. You and I have some time to put in at the firing range."

Glenn gestured to the pig-trail. "On this road?"

"Little-known side entrance. No one sees us come or go. No questions."

Sheila Bruner scooped the cooked potato from the halved skins, careful not to pierce the outsides, then mashed and whipped the white chunks to a creamy texture with butter, sour cream, and shredded sharp cheddar. The trick was to achieve the perfect ratio. Though she had made Glenn's favorite twice-baked potatoes many times, she didn't "eye" the seasonings, but used measuring spoons for the garlic, salt, chopped chives and parsley. No worries about lumps or about competing with her mother-in-law's masterful cooking. Stuffed twice-baked potatoes were Sheila's own "special" recipe—copied from some woman's magazine, then tweaked.

Sheila chewed on her lower lip until she tasted blood. Yoga class once a week with a cup of tea at Bill's afterwards was one thing, dinner out in Tallahassee was another. It wouldn't cost in terms of gasoline. She and Loiscell planned to ride over with Choo-choo. It seemed right that they should do the whole thing together, but Abby had some last minute important errand. The final result would be the same: good meal, scrumptious dessert, and The End.

She released her damaged lip and hummed an old spiritual, spooning the potato mixture into the hollowed skins and adding roofs of shredded cheese and chives. When she popped them into the oven—cozy in their baking dish—intense heat blasted her face and she wondered about Hell. Maybe it wasn't so bad. They'd have a lot of things to clean in Hell. Perhaps, she could scrub her way up to a cooler level.

The closer to "SSC-Day," as the women had named it, the more Sheila prayed for forgiveness. She asked for release from earthly pain, a break from Glenn's abuse. With so little time to go, she marveled at the lack of new bruises on her body. A miracle in itself. God was already listening.

Now, the last hurdle. She could leave without Glenn's permission, but the chances of his tracking her down were too high. Two Angus beefsteaks marinated in the refrigerator, and the stuffed potatoes baked. A crisp tossed salad waited in a sealed bowl. Add homemade buttermilk dressing, thick slices of toasted garlic bread, and maybe Glenn would be agreeable.

They ate in silence, accompanied by the click of silverware. Sheila tried to judge his mood. He'd been somewhere in the deep woods. She could pick out that scent better than cologne.

The aroma of the grilled beef—usually appealing—caused Sheila's stomach to lurch. "Glenn . . . ?"

119

Her husband speared a thick bloody chunk of meat and crammed it into his mouth. "What?" he asked around a mouthful of half-chewed food.

"My yoga friends are planning to ride over to Tallahassee for dinner day after tomorrow. I would like to go." She ducked her head. "That is, if you're okay with it." She watched him from the corner of her eyes.

Conflict painted his features: anger followed by something else. She sent up a silent plea: Please, please let him say yes.

"Your piece of crap car won't make it over there. No way you're taking my truck."

Sheila leaned forward, meeting his stare. "No problem there. A couple of us are riding over together." She added before he could reply, "and I'll have everything made for your poker night, ahead of time."

Glenn frowned, twisted his lips to one side. "Eating out costs money. I don't bust my hump every day so you can waste it with your biddy friends."

"I can have a salad and iced water. I won't spend much."

"Okay. But you eat, you come straight home. Clear?" The sheen of beef fat glistened around his mouth. Glenn returned his full attention to the meal.

It took a moment for her to grasp. "Yes. Perfectly clear."

Chapter Eleven

Suicide Day
Monday

Abby McKenzie moved at a crawl. A cliché popped to mind: You'd be late for your own funeral.

If she didn't feel so rotten, she'd laugh. All morning, she had felt rundown and a little nauseated. Fear, had to be. Who wouldn't be apprehensive, knowing this evening's meal would be her last?

The menu she had printed from the Bella Bella website protruded from her purse, unfolded and refolded so many times, some of the lines were illegible. Should she pick rigatoni, spinach lasagna, baked ziti with extra meat sauce and gobs of melted mozzarella? And bread. She could eat an entire mini-loaf of crusty Italian bread. No, wait. The appetizer Loiscell suggested was bubble bread—hot thick pizza-like crust with fresh spices and melted cheeses. Best not to overdo and leave no room for dessert. Dessert. Cheesecake? Chocolate Sin Cake? Abby pursed her lips. Tiramisu! Might as well go with the whole Italian theme. Or heck, order one of each.

What if Italian food was all wrong? Wasn't the traditional last meal of death row inmates steak and the trimmings? Abby shook her head. Always a chance of getting a tough cut of meat, one with more fat and gristle than substance.

Best to stick with Italian. Dependable. Comforting. Cheesy.

As time neared for Abby to leave the house, a deep pain lodged in her lower back along with the uncomfortable flush of a fever.

"Great. I'm coming down with something."

She pressed precise creases in a pair of black pants and a white shirt: the outfit dictated by Choo-choo's instructions. Good thing she wouldn't be around to stress about the shirt. Bloodstains on white cotton were impossible to remove.

Abby chose limited accessories. One ring. A watch. A small black clutch bag. Sensible flats.

Before she left, Abby walked through the small house, pausing in each room. She filled an automatic feeder and water dispenser in the kitchen. Oreo circled her feet with his bouncy three-legged hobble and she picked him up for one last nuzzle. "You'll be fine until Mason Dixon takes over."

As soon as word spread of the tragedy in Tallahassee—she envisioned the *Tallahassee Democrat*'s headline—Mason would use her spare hidden key, let himself in, and rescue the little cat. She put Oreo down next to the food bowl and stroked his fur, then wiped her cheeks. Quit with the tears. No time for regrets.

By the time she merged onto Thomasville Road from Interstate 10 in Tallahassee, her stomach pitched and rolled. Could the mayonnaise in her tuna sandwich have been spoiled? Should've gone with plain turkey and cheese. No matter. She could do this.

One final stop by the attorney's office to pick up the prepared legal packet, and she could drive across town to meet the Yoga Rat Pack. Someone would find the documents in the car later. Most important, the will. Her attorney Claire served as her executor. All would go smoothly. No problem.

The important errand had provided the perfect excuse for taking the day off. Hey, she never took time off. She didn't call in sick even when she was half-dead. Christine could just suck it up and cover Abby's position. Good practice for her.

"You should have a designated health care surrogate and living will, Abby," the attorney had insisted when Abby called about getting her legal affairs in order. "If you're unable to speak for yourself, someone you don't know will make the call. You could end up on life support, hooked up to a ventilator, even if your brain is not functioning. Think about it. Is that what you want?"

Good things to have. Abby conceded. In case the bullet didn't meet its mark. Surely not a problem with a professional assassin, but who knew? People didn't seem to have sound work ethics these days.

A fresh wave of abdominal cramps struck as she unlocked her car later, outside of the attorney's office. Her mouth watered: the precursor to violet retching. She managed to make it to the edge of the parking lot, and vomited into the shrubs. Once, twice, three times until nothing resulted beyond acid and bile.

Back in the car, she speed-dialed Loiscell. Of the three, Loiscell was the only one with a cell phone. Amazing. After four rings, the voicemail announcement sounded. Abby pitched the phone into her purse. Might as well drive to the restaurant and ask for a postponement. How absurd, rescheduling the Suicide Supper Club until she felt well enough to enjoy her final meal.

At the Centerville Road intersection, Abby made a quick decision and veered into the left-turn lane. The cramping—almost unbearable now—matched the intensity of the rising fever. She pulled into the emergency entrance for Capital Medical Center and whipped into the first available parking spot.

The exit from her car elicited another round of violent dry heaves. She couldn't stand upright, only scuttle crab-like toward the double automatic glass doors. The waiting area held a handful of people. Too early for the alcohol-prompted bar fight injuries and late enough to clear most of the morning's maladies.

Abby stumbled to the reception desk. "Help me, please."

Glenn Bruner had not eaten the lunch Sheila packed. Time oozed by. His stomach burned and growled. His skin itched all over, as if he was covered in prickly heat. He pulled up his shirt and checked. No rash. Just his excitement causing the creepy-crawlies.

He checked his watch. Five p.m. Finally.

Glenn couldn't clock out fast enough. The daylight hours had decreased with the impending fall season. It would be solid dark by the time he took up position in the restaurant's side parking lot.

Oh yeah. Gotta call up my poker buddies soon as I step in the door and tell 'em I ain't feeling too hot. Catch y'all next week. Beer's on me. So many dang details.

It took every smidgeon of control not to break the speed limit as he negotiated the few miles across Victory Bridge and into Chattahoochee. Glenn reviewed Clay's instructions. The man knew his stuff. One day, Glenn would be able to plan as well. One day, he could walk into the prison and give 'em his resignation. Tell them to kiss his lily-white butt. Then again, maybe he would keep the state position as a front. Plenty of money in his new business, but with health insurance and enough of an income not to alert Uncle Sam. The cash, he would hide. Live too far beyond his obvious means, and Uncle Damn would come sniffing around. He could keep the extra money for fishing tournament fees and man-toys. Anything he wanted. Gravy on the potatoes.

If only he didn't have to share it.

Glenn huffed. Sheila might have to go missing and he amused himself thinking of ways it could happen. He would be devastated, of course. People would feel so sorry for him. Bring him casseroles and invite him over for meals. He could hire some woman to come in, to cook, clean, and wash clothes. Better than finding a replacement wife. Sex could be hired out too. With the kind of cash the new business supplied, he could afford the best. Maybe more than one at a time. That thought thrilled him as much as the new boat. Almost.

He pulled into his driveway and cut the engine. His senses sharpened. He luxuriated in the final minutes leading up to his first hit. Like licking the batter bowl before the cake was even in the oven. Delicious. Glenn's lips twitched at the corners. His day of reckoning. The day he started on the pathway of a new and stellar career.

And what better excuse to have his wife out of the way than with her clutch of hens? Not that he would have to answer to her for his absence. He didn't have to tell her squat. But why take any chances? He could get ready for his outing without Sheila buzzing around him like an annoying housefly.

As soon as he changed from his uniform, Glenn packed a tattered dirty backpack with supplies. Worn clothes. A light overcoat two sizes too large. The handgun, fitted with a silencer—cleaned and polished of any fingerprints. A pair of gloves. A sweat-stained baseball cap.

Clay's voice played in an endless loop inside his head like the words of a song he loved and knew by heart. The plan was so brilliant, so seamless. A blind hog could carry it off.

How would he feel afterwards? Giddy. Pumped with adrenaline, better than the rush of bagging a twelve-point buck. Hearing the sirens, but taking his sweet time. Let those idiots swarm the area.

The professional assassin's final statements rang in Glenn's head like a mantra. "The most important thing is that you stay calm and *think*. If you can do that, this business will reward you beyond your wildest dreams."

Choo-choo Ivey pulled the Lincoln to the curb. "Look at this! Front door parking. It's like someone reserved our spot."

The small Italian eatery occupied a building facing Fifth Avenue. A set of concrete steps led to the glass door entrance. Wrought iron

124

tables lined a narrow porch, perfect for outdoor dining when the heat and humidity didn't drive patrons inside.

Loiscell smiled. "Don't know that I've been by here, when this space was open. Usually, I have to park on the side or clean down the road."

"Meant to be," Sheila said in a quiet voice.

Choo-choo glanced around. "I don't see Abby's car anywhere."

"Probably caught in traffic." Loiscell grabbed her purse. "Let's go on in and get a table. I have a feeling this place gets busy as soon as people are off work."

When the three walked into Bella Bella, the blended fragrance of basil, oregano, garlic, and simmering red sauce trilled their senses. The intimate restaurant held a half-dozen tables, covered with vintage linen printed tablecloths topped with glass. Each held a spray of fresh flowers and a small oil lamp. Original paintings dotted the walls.

"This place is delightful," Choo-choo said. "I can't believe I've never been here."

Loiscell motioned to a table next to one of the windows. "I come for lunch every now and then whenever I'm over for a doctor's appointment. They have the best tomato basil soup I've ever tasted. Everything is scrumptious."

A young woman appeared. "Three for dinner?" The server ushered the group to the table and handed out menus.

Choo-choo sat down and snapped the cloth napkin into her lap. "Supposed to be one more."

The server left and brought back four tall glasses of iced water. "May I bring you something to else to drink?"

"We should get a bottle of wine, don't you think, ladies?" Choo-choo asked.

Loiscell nodded. "Sounds good."

"Count me in," Sheila said.

"Bring an extra glass, please. I know Abby will want one," Choo-choo requested. "Your house merlot will do nicely." The server scuttled off.

Loiscell glanced at her watch. "It's not like her to be late. I hope that car of hers didn't break down."

Sheila sipped her iced water. "Maybe she decided not to come."

Choo-choo and Loiscell stared at her a moment before Choo-choo spoke. "She wouldn't do that. And if she did, she would have at least called. Abby's very dependable."

Loiscell dug in her purse and checked the cell phone. "No voicemail. Besides it's only a quarter after. It's not like she's hours late." She punched a button on the side. "I think I have this thing on vibrate. I can never tell."

"You could always let callers leave a message and call them back tomorrow," Sheila said.

The absurdity of the comment struck them all at once, and they dissolved into a shared fit of near-hysterical laughter.

The server arrived and doled out wine glasses, uncorked the merlot, and poured. "Sounds like you ladies are having fun."

Choo-choo swiped the moisture from the corners of her eyes. "We're just getting warmed up."

Loiscell took a sip. "Should we go ahead and at least order an appetizer? I'm starving. We can save Abby a bite. I've been dreaming about their bubble bread for days."

Sheila agreed. "I didn't have much breakfast or lunch. Too excited to eat."

Choo-choo studied the menu. "Go ahead and bring us some of that hot artichoke dip along with the bubble bread."

"Two appetizers?" Sheila's eyebrows shot up.

Choo-choo shrugged. "You only live once."

Loiscell cackled. The server scribbled on her order pad.

"I think we should break one of our agreements," Sheila said after the server left. She tasted her wine, winced, and swallowed.

"What do you mean?" Loiscell asked.

"I think we should tell why we want to do . . ." Sheila leaned forward. ". . . this."

Choo-choo and Loiscell exchanged glances.

"Maybe we should wait on Abby," Choo-choo said.

"I don't mind saying. I'll tell Abby when she gets here. It might make me feel lighter to get it off my chest. Then I can enjoy my bubble bread." Loiscell fortified herself with a gulp of wine. "My cancer is back."

Choo-choo reached over and rested a hand over Loiscell's. "Oh honey. Why didn't you tell us earlier?"

"I don't know." Loiscell shook her head. "I really don't know."

Sheila asked, "How long have you known? How——?"

"Found a lump. Went to the oncologist. Had a biopsy. Malignant." Loiscell glanced first at Sheila, then at Choo-choo. "I can't do it again. Feeling nauseated all the time. Being so tired I can barely blink. Losing

126

my hair. Wondering. Hoping and coping. I don't have the courage to carry me through it again. I just don't. Plus I know Lisa will come running. I can't put her through it, either. She has kids, a life of her own."

Choo-choo dabbed the corner of her lips. "I certainly understand, Loiscell. I was with Charlie during the . . . final days." She turned her attention to Sheila. "And you? What could possibly be so wrong with your life? You always seem so busy and organized."

Sheila studied the napkin in her lap and bit the edge of her bottom lip. "My husband . . . he . . ." She closed her eyes and took a shaky breath. "Glenn is . . . "

Loiscell rested a hand on her friend's shoulder. "Go ahead, Sheila. Say it."

"My husband hurts me." Sheila looked up. "Over and over. He doesn't mean to, and sometimes he can be so sweet. Lately, it's gotten much worse."

"That bastard." Loiscell's lips drew into an angry thin line.

"Why didn't you report him, Sheila?" Choo-choo asked.

Sheila's eyes flicked around like nervous prey. "I couldn't do that."

"There are places for women," Choo-choo said. "You could stay with one of us."

"You don't understand. Glenn would find me. He would either kill me, or us, or bring me back. And then it would only get worse. No, this is my only way."

Loiscell glanced at the gathering dusk through the front window. The muffled sound of rush hour traffic was barely discernible over the bistro's low jazz music. "I don't think we should try to talk each other out of anything, or judge."

Choo-choo nodded. "You are absolutely right."

Sheila motioned to Choo-choo. "What about you?"

"I am old, ladies. Old and tired. I keep praying to fall asleep and drift off, but it hasn't happened. Given a few more years, or months, I could end up unable to care for myself and get shuffled off to some long-term care home. Either my mind or my body will slip, or both. I miss Charlie every second of every day, and now, believe it or not, I miss that darn little dog, too." Choo-choo paused. "My daughter hardly ever calls, and rarely visits. Other than yoga, my Hospice work, and you all, I have nothing to look forward to. I feel like I'm taking up space. And the Hospice work . . . it used to fulfill me. I've found myself actually a little peeved that everyone else is getting to leave, and here I sit."

The server appeared with two platters. Aromatic steam rose from both. The group broke huddle and sat back to allow room for the food and plates.

"Enough of all of that, now," Loiscell said. "We need to enjoy this . . . last meal. Abby's going to miss out. What the heck is keeping her?" She took a bite of bubble bread and moaned. "Oh my gosh. This is to die for."

Choo-choo dipped a toast point into the gooey artichoke dip. Strings of melted cheese stretched from the edges. "Good choice of words, dear."

Abby McKenzie groaned. For the past twenty minutes, everyone short of dead Elvis had stopped by the curtained emergency room cubicle to ask questions.

Your insurance cards and picture I.D.? Do you have a living will? A medical health surrogate? Next of kin? Allergies? Past surgeries? Describe your symptoms. When did they start? Are you in pain? She was surprised they didn't ask for her favorite color or if she preferred lime or orange gelatin.

A representative of the admissions department stopped to secure a co-payment, offering the comforting assurance that her insurance company had been contacted and supported her visit. Abby scribbled her signature on consent forms between moans.

"Believe it or not, I have my living will and the medical power of attorney thingy in my car, if you have someone who would be willing to go out and get them. I don't think I can walk." The bizarre, blind synchronicity of life slapped Abby full in the face.

Now, the latest in the line-up of concerned health care workers— the emergency room physician—breezed in, his lab coat laundry-commercial white and creased. The nurse passed along the vital stats: elevated temperature, elevated blood pressure, severe discomfort in the lower back and abdomen with nausea and vomiting. Abby struggled to remain focused on the doctor's litany of questions.

"Any history of colon cancer in your family?"

A wave of pain caused her to squeeze her eyelids shut. She breathed through her mouth in small puffs until it subsided. "My father had some sort of growths removed, but they weren't cancerous. He's deceased. My mom too. But not from that."

"Have you had a recent colonoscopy?"

"I think my doctor wants to do one this year, or is it next year? Seems to come with getting older. They want to do all these tests on you. I've done those disgusting little stool sample cards, though. Never had any problems."

He pressed on her belly in spots, noting her reaction. "I'm scheduling a contrast CT scan, Miss McKenzie. We need to see what is causing your pain." He entered information into a computer on a rolling cart, talking to the nurse as he typed. From the list of medical abbreviations, Abby judged she was in for more than one test.

"Want to translate all that, please?" Abby asked after the doctor left.

The attending nurse smiled. She appeared to be about Abby's age, with a calm efficient manner. Abby relaxed a little. "He ordered an ECG—electrocardiogram—to check your heart, full blood panel, and the CAT scan. Each test will tell him what to rule out, since many conditions mirror the same symptoms. You'll have to drink the contrast liquid before the scan. But don't worry. They mix it in with a sports drink to make it palatable."

Abby moaned. "If I can hold it down. Every time I have one of those pains, I feel like I'm going to heave all over again."

"I'm going to start an IV. He has pain meds ordered, and something to help ease the nausea. That should help."

Abby's mind raced. "I need to sign something—a form?—so you will give out information to certain people. I work in a dental office, and I know all about all that HIPPA privacy crap. I need to let you know who to talk to, you know, if I'm out of it."

"I'll put their names into the computer," the nurse replied.

"Loiscell Pickering. Sheila Bruner. Choo-choo Ivey." Abby frowned, trying to bring faces and names to mind. Why list her best friends? They might even not be alive by now. Her spirit tanked. "Might as well add Elvina Houston, oh and Dr. Payne."

The nurse tapped keys. "Before I start this IV and give medications, is there anyone you need for me to contact?"

Abby's thoughts swam through the muck. "I can do it. My cell is in my purse." She moved her head from side to side, searching. "Where is my purse? I had it when that lady from your financial office came by."

The nurse pulled a white plastic bag from beneath the gurney. "In here."

Who to call? Who to call? Abby selected a number from the address book and punched send. A voicemail picked up after five rings.

"Loiscell? Abby. Listen, it might be too late to let you guys know. I'm obviously *not* at the restaurant. I'm at Capital Regional Hospital in the ER."

What the heck was she doing? Were they supposed to call the whole dang thing off and come hang out with her? What if it was all over? An intense mix of loss and sadness washed over Abby, as if the Titanic had left port without her on board. "Um . . . anyway. That's where I'll be. I don't know for how long."

Feverish sweat iced her skin. Her stomach rolled again. Times like this, she cursed being single with no living relatives. Who would care? Still it seemed important to let someone know. The pain medication made her sluggish and the contact number roster wavered in and out of focus. She squinted and punched one from the list.

Again, a voicemail answered: "Hello, this is Elvina Houston. If you reached this, then by all means leave me a message. It's not that I can't be bothered answering you; I'm a busy woman. I will call you back as soon as I can. And be aware. I have that caller ID thing, so I'll know if you don't leave me a message. I could spit nails when folks call and hang up."

When Glenn stepped into the Lake Ella Publix in Tallahassee, he marveled at the way no one paid much attention to him. Nobody stopped to say howdy and shake his hand. Not one person asked inane questions about Sheila or if he was going to attend some church function, or any of the dull life details he couldn't imagine anyone needed to know.

In the capital city, Glenn was just another man on his way somewhere, a man who stopped by the grocery store for beer. With half the student population doing the same thing, he was in the majority. Not like Chattahoochee, where someone would see him and report back to the church elders. Most of the time, he drove half-way to Marianna to buy booze just to give the nosey old bags like Elvina Houston less to talk about.

Maybe after a few of Clay's jobs, he would move to Tallahassee. Some swanky neighborhood with a yard big enough the neighbors couldn't look out their windows and track his every move. More bars over this way too. Bars full of college coeds who would overlook his spare tire and age if he dressed fancy and threw enough cash around. If he wanted to keep up the front of upstanding correctional officer, he could transfer to that institution off Capital Circle.

A Mercedes. He'd buy one for a second vehicle. Pearl black with tinted windows. No, a Hummer. It was macho and money all rolled into one gas-guzzling package.

He picked up two cases of Budweiser and walked to the front to a cash-only lane. Stupid woman in front of him had more than ten items.

Glenn's thoughts ran wild. The fancy car and new house wouldn't fit in with his plan to remain low-key. A prison guard could never afford such luxuries. What did other career assassins do? Move to some island to escape the IRS stink-eye? The Caribbean might be nice. He could always make trips back into the states to hunt. Hell, with the kind of money he was going to have, he could fly anywhere in the world. And deep sea fishing! He'd buy a huge saltwater boat and go for the big ones.

"Sir?"

Glenn snapped back to reality. The Publix cashier waited.

"Oh, sorry." Glenn handed over a couple of bills, accepted the change, and grabbed the beer satchels and threw them back into the buggy. "You have a good day, you hear?"

He forced himself to amble back to the truck. The beer, he deposited behind the seat. The buggy, he shoved into a nearby cart corral. Would be nice if he could use it for one of his props instead of the cheap wire shopping cart Clay had provided, but the grocery store's version had an anti-theft gizmo to lock up the wheels past a designated area. Boy, nobody trusted nobody these days.

The side parking lot was empty, except for one woman carrying a loaded plastic hamper. He waited until she disappeared into the Laundromat. Glenn pitched the backpack into the folding wire cart and strolled toward the edge of the pavement with purpose. He slipped behind the dry-cleaners at the end of a small strip of stores and tried to navigate the cart through the underbrush. Briars and low bushes snagged the oversized wheels.

After several attempts to pull the cart behind him, he gave up and continued with only the backpack until he assured himself no one could see him through the thicket. He peeled off his T-shirt and exchanged it for a hole-pocked men's cotton shirt several sizes too large. It stank to high heaven, also part of the plan. For several days, he had wiped every disgusting thing he could think of on the shirt. The most odorous: a catfish blood bait that smelled like the north end of a southbound mule. A whiff would send anyone who dared to get too close scurrying away with his or her nostrils pinched.

Next, a seedy long duster. Might be a trifle too warm for an overcoat, but Glenn thought it a nice touch. He pulled out a nappy black wig and slipped it over his head, then covered the top with a sweat and dirt-ringed ball cap. Clay would be proud of the way he had come up with the idea of the wig all by himself. In the get-up, Glenn looked as if he hadn't had a haircut in years. A beard would've been a nice addition if he'd had time to develop one. Last, he pulled on a pair of stained gloves.

The whipped topping on the disguise sloshed in a bent flask in the jacket's side pocket: home-brewed white lightning, compliments of one of his work buddies. Clay hadn't suggested that either. Glenn patted himself over the additional dramatic touch. He would be just another smelly, homeless drunk. Plus the fortification of a few swigs would help steady his nerves and his aim.

Glenn tipped his head back and took a long draw of the booze. The fire burned down his throat into his stomach, and he realized he hadn't eaten since mid-morning. No time to take care of that now. He'd have all the time in the world to drive through a fast food joint after the job was finished.

Just a guy eating fries and a double cheeseburger, and heading home with his beer. Just a guy who had plugged four women, eating fries and a double cheeseburger and heading home with his beer. How normal and manly could you get?

Glenn took a second slug of the home brew. He folded his T-shirt into a zippered plastic freezer bag—hey, no way he'd put his good shirt in with all that raunchy smell—then he shoved it into the bottom of the pack for later, when he'd turn into Just Normal Glenn again.

Time to get this show on the road.

He retraced his steps, rescued the wire cart, and peered from the edge of the woods until he was sure no one watched. Finding a few extra pieces of trash to put in the cart along with the backpack took a minute. He cut through the alley behind a strip of stores at the shopping center's south side and stepped onto the sidewalk along North Monroe Street. Exhaust fumes from the tail end of rush hour traffic mingled with scents from the Mexican restaurant across from Lake Ella.

Glenn warmed to his role. He kept his head down and muttered to himself. A few times, he stopped to pick up some piece of paper or aluminum can to add to the cart. A lone pedestrian passed him as he made his way toward Fifth Avenue, and she made brief eye contact before giving him wide berth. No one else seemed to notice him, or care. He might as well have been invisible.

He should'a been a freakin' movie star. Easy gig.

When he reached the intersection of Fifth and North Monroe, he paused. Best to go one more street down, in case. He picked up his pace. The next side street was deserted and poorly lit. Perfect. Two blocks after he turned, he doubled back to the right and hid the cart in a small parking lot behind a row of offices.

Glenn looked around. All of the worker bees had flown back to the hive for the night. No security lighting. That Clay knew his business.

From the backpack, he extracted the handgun with its silencer. He took a long swig of hooch before slipping from the shadows and following the curb to within a few feet of the Italian restaurant. Two cars occupied the parking spots in front of the eatery: a white Lincoln Towncar and one of those electric/gas combo sub-compacts he could have fit into the bed of his pick-up. One streetlight illuminated a small patch of pavement: the site of his debut.

The side parking lot dipped sharply away from the road. Glenn huddled in the restaurant's alley, positioning his body for an unobstructed view. While he waited, he sipped from the near-empty flask.

Three warmed plates arrived: vegetarian lasagna for Sheila, eggplant parmesan for Loiscell, and baked ziti with meat sauce for Choo-choo. "Would you like more bread?" the server asked.

Choo-choo swept her hand through the air. "Bring it on. And another bottle of vino!"

"At this rate, we're going to be stinking drunk." Sheila giggled and stifled a belch.

Choo-choo downed the last sip from her glass. "Not like any of us have to worry about being the designated driver." She laughed so hard, the couple at the next table stopped to stare. "Plus we'll be half-way to embalmed."

Sheila hiccupped. "Goodness, Choo-choo."

Loiscell dug into the hot eggplant dish. "I wonder what happened to Abby."

"She chickened out. That's what." Choo-choo blew on a forkful of ziti and crammed it into her mouth.

Sheila's lids fluttered over her bloodshot eyes. "I think I'm a little tipsy. I keep hearing that one song from *The Nutcracker* and it's not even Christmas."

Loiscell jumped as if she had been poked with a cattle prod. "My cell! That's my someone-has-left-a-message ringtone."

Choo-choo frowned. "I thought you had that dang thing shut off."

"Nope. I turned down the ringer." Loiscell jabbed buttons. As she listened, her expression morphed into a blend of fear and shock. "It's Abby. She's in the hospital!"

The other two stopped their forks in mid-air.

"What the—" Choo-choo started.

"Something bad has happened to Abby." Loiscell snapped the phone closed. "All she said is that she's in the ER."

"We have to go to her." Sheila waved for the server.

Choo-choo threw a wad of cash on the table. "That ought to more than take care of the bill and tip. C'mon!"

"Wait!" Sheila said after they had filed outside. The group stood beneath the lone streetlight next to the Towncar. "Which hospital?"

"Capital Regional. That's the one on the other side of town," Loiscell answered.

"Had to be that one." Choo-choo fumbled in her purse for the keys. "I know my way blind to Tallahassee General. Aren't there some new roads they've cut through? And us here in the dark, stupid and half-drunk, trying to find our way."

Chapter Twelve

The suicide

Glenn Bruner jerked awake and peered through the shadows. He wiped spittle from his chin with his coat sleeve. Was that sound the restaurant door? He blinked twice to clear his vision and glanced at the illuminated dial of his wristwatch. Almost an hour had elapsed since he had taken up position beneath the live oak in the darkened parking lot. How had he dozed off? The lost sleep from the past week, had to be it. Good thing his other senses were so sharp, or he might have slept straight through. He shuddered, thinking of Clay's reaction.

For a moment, he held the image of the sparkly bass boat in his mind's eye. He expanded the vision, and hooked it to the back of a brand-spanking new pick-up. Perfect match. When the sun hit right, spangles of refracted light shone from the glitter chips in the paint.

Only time and four bullets separated Glenn from his dreams. Clay had assured him the money was already there, resting in an offshore account. By tomorrow, Glenn would have his share. What a difference a few hours could make in a man's life.

He took three deep breaths and stifled a sour-tasting belch. The start of a hangover threatened. His vision blurred. No matter. At this distance, he could surely fire dead drunk and still hit his mark. On more than one occasion, he had nailed a buck when he was so sloshed he could barely stand.

Some women stood in the pool of yellow light. Glenn blinked, squinted, and counted. One. Two. Three. A white-haired old woman and two others. One with her back to him looked vaguely familiar. Clay had warned him of that possibility. Where the hell was the fourth one? He hung back in the deep shadow of the building. His fingers caressed the gun in his coat pocket. The anticipation, at once thrilling and agonizing.

Another woman joined the group. Glenn panted. He counted again. Four times the payola, buddy boy.

Bingo. Party time.

As he stepped forward, he eased the weapon from the pocket, released the safety, and held it close to his body. For a moment, Glenn stood, relishing the heady sense of power. The white-haired woman noticed him one second too late. Her mouth hung open. Like that mounted largemouth bass in his living room. He raised the gun, took aim, and fired.

The first shot spun one of the women around. She flailed and fell. The others' faces mirrored shock, then horror at the pool of blood forming beneath the woman's body. The shortest of the three screamed. Glenn fired again. The screaming stopped.

That woman, the screamer. Sheila. Glenn reeled backwards, stumbling, falling. The last two shots sailed high, one ricocheting off the streetlight pole.

A sharp, white-hot pain pierced through his head when he hit the asphalt. Then darkness.

Choo-choo Ivey stared for a moment—seemed like much more. Struck dumb. Her mind, not comprehending the scene unfolding around her. Who was screaming? There had been shots. And that iron stench of discharged body fluids, faint at first, then blooming up and up. Separate scents: one a trifle fruity like overripe apples, the other the smell of wet rust.

Loiscell's voice filtered through. "Ambulance! . . . shooting! . . . two people!" The words ran together, jumbled into nonsense.

People shouted, ran toward them. Diners who had witnessed the scene through the long windows poured outside. One of the owners and two young male servers banged from the bistro's front door. The three men gestured wildly and ran toward the crumpled man who had fired the shots. One kicked the handgun from the downed man's hand, then stood over him, menacing. Another spoke into a cell phone. All around them, people jabbered to each other and to whoever listened on the other end of their cell phones.

"Let me have your sweater!" Loiscell snagged at her sleeve. Choo-choo slipped it from her arms, handed it over.

"Hang in there, Sheila. Honey, help is on the way." Loiscell's voice sounded absurdly calm. As if she comforted a child with a skinned knee. Sheila moaned. Didn't open her eyes. Dark blood seeped through

136

Choo-choo's favorite cream sweater—the perfect weight for a summer evening. Loiscell pressed down. "Get that little blanket you keep in the back of your car. I think the other lady's worse off."

Choo-choo snapped from the inertia. Blanket. In the trunk. She grappled with the catch on her purse and located her keys. She hit the key fob button; the trunk popped open. She found the Hello Kitty blanket.

Another man hunkered over the second prostrate lady. He sobbed and said Lucinda, Lucinda, Lucinda. The woman didn't respond. Choo-choo stepped over and crouched down. What to do? Stop the bleeding. How long before those ambulances arrived? A pool of liquid spread from the woman's midsection and flowered outward. Sobbing Man turned to her. "My wife . . ." Choo-choo couldn't understand the rest of his words.

The crowd surrounded them now, circled as if in protection. Voices talking at once, women crying. One lady filmed the action with her cell phone camera. Four men now flanked the shooter. He moved his head and moaned. Where were the police!

Choo-choo used the balled-up blanket to help Sobbing Man apply pressure. Hello Kitty turned from hot pink to deep red. "Help's on the way, Mister. Hang on."

Sirens whined nearby. Hurry, please hurry. People should move out of the way. Let them through! My friend has been shot! Back up people. They need air. This isn't a circus.

The blood on Choo-choo's hands stung and puckered as it dried along the edges. She was going to throw up. Deep breaths. You've seen worse than this, Choo-choo, done worse than this. Her head swung to watch the men corralling the shooter. Two police cars screeched to a halt—City of Tallahassee logos swirled down their flanks. A female officer jumped from one, a male from the other. Both held revolvers in ready position. The female took the lead, calling out, "Where is the gun? Step away from the gun!" She motioned the bistro servers to move aside, and removed the shooter's gun to her squad car.

Chain of evidence. Secure the scene. Choo-choo thought of all the cop shows she loved to watch. And here it was in full color and sound.

The male officer stationed himself with the downed shooter. The female talked into the mic mounted on her shoulder as she jogged over to where the two victims lay. She assessed the situation, added, "three down. One gunshot to the gut. One gunshot to the shoulder. Shooter immobilized." The rest, a series of code-talk for the EMS vehicles in route or waiting nearby for clearance from the officers on scene.

Two more squad cars arrived. Tallahassee Police and Leon County deputies. Doors opened, slammed. Barked commands. Step back, people! Blue and white light strobes streaked the darkness.

Emergency vehicles arrived in quick succession. First, a fire engine. Its red lights joined the blue lights, ricocheting off buildings, windows, and peoples' frozen faces. Loiscell and Choo-choo stood back when the paramedics swooped in. Sobbing Man had to be pulled from his wife. Medical chatter passed back and forth as the first responders triaged. Two ambulances arrived, additional paramedics joined in. More lights streaked the night.

Paramedics wheeled the other victim into the first waiting ambulance. Sobbing Man spoke with an officer. This one, clearly the commander in charge, stopped long enough to nod a couple of times before pointing to the passenger side of the EMS vehicle. The ambulance doors banged shut. Sobbing Man climbed inside the cab with the driver, and the ambulance pulled away, its sirens screaming. A patrol car pulled out and followed.

Choo-choo looked from the paramedics securing Sheila to a gurney, to the crowd of officers with the handcuffed shooter. He sat up. Something black fell from his head. An officer picked it up with a gloved hand, held it out as if it was vile. Beside her, Loiscell watched the scene, then swore beneath her breath and turned to face Choo-choo.

"I'm going on this ambulance with Sheila," Loiscell said in a low voice. "Anybody asks, I'm her sister."

Choo-choo blinked. Frowned at Loiscell.

"Soon as they let you leave, go to Capital Medical, check on Abby. If you can't drive, sweet-talk one of these officers. We can get your car later. Can you do that?" When Choo-choo failed to reply, Loiscell grabbed her upper arm and gave it a firm shake. "Can you *do* that?"

Choo-choo nodded.

"Remember," Loiscell whispered into Choo-choo's ear. "I'm Sheila's sister."

Loiscell stepped over to the same official that Sobbing Man had spoken with a few moments before. Around them, other law enforcement officers corralled the crowd. One rolled out a yellow police tape boundary. The rippling line of spectators became an audience. Controlled chaos.

Choo-choo couldn't hear the exchange over the babble, only see Loiscell's adamant expression, see one finger jab toward the gurney. The officer led Loiscell to the second ambulance and she slid into the front passenger side. With Sheila inside and the doors closed, it pulled away—lights and sirens—with a TPD squad car close behind.

God. This was all her fault. She had set this up, paid for it! Her dear friend. That poor, innocent other woman. The weight of it all settled over her shoulders. It was supposed to be one bullet, one perfect aim through each heart. Boom and then down. A graceful freefall, not this violent, jerking slam. The movie special effects showed these kinds of scenes through molasses air. Bullets spooling past, allowing the intended target ample time to flash raw emotions—shock, realization, panic—before the projectile crept through pliant flesh, bone, organs. The body spinning, yielding to gravity, a pirouette. A ghost image rising from the spent carcass like curling paint, hovering and regarding the Earth shell with compassion and prayer hands.

Choo-choo listened until the sirens turned into a faint whine before she turned once more to the shooter and his law enforcement escorts. He stood, stumbled. They herded him to an awaiting squad car. The group paused for a moment in a pool of streetlight. Choo-choo saw his face, long enough.

The man, the shooter: Glenn Bruner.

She staggered a couple of steps back to lean against the side of the Lincoln. A handsome, dark-haired TPD officer—one with a baby face, young enough to be her grandson if she only had one—supported her arm. Questions, and more questions. When would they end?

Puddles from the earlier afternoon summer shower pooled by the curb. A thin line of red had joined the gathering runoff. Choo-choo forced herself to inhale.

She glanced up at the evening sky. A few dim stars, nothing as impressive as in the country. Bats skittered through the air. The scent of garlic and oregano wafted from her shirt.

Chapter Thirteen

The suicide
One hour after

Elvina Houston pushed the accelerator hard and the Oldsmobile shot forward from the side parking lot of the Triple C Day Spa and Salon, sending a spray of rocks in its wake. Sedating endorphins moved aside for a jolt of adrenaline. So much for the afterglow from Stephanie's expert massage. When she paused at a stop sign, Elvina pressed an icon on the cell phone's keypad and listened again to the voicemail messages. Three were of no consequence. Normal town babble. The last two made her heart race: one from Abby McKenzie and one from Loiscell Pickering. All Hades had broken loose over in Tallahassee, from the sound of things.

"I'm out of touch for an hour, and the holy white shit hits the fan!" she said aloud, then admonished herself for cursing. But sometimes, doo-doo or crap didn't cut the mustard.

That would teach her to take a moment to herself. Being the head of the little-ole-lady hotline required constant vigilance, like being President of the U. S. of A. She needed an administrative assistant, someone to monitor the cell phone when she needed to sleep, eat, pee, or get a massage. Even the Good Lord Almighty took Sunday to rest.

Her mind raced. What to do first? By the house to throw plenty of dry food and water down for Buster. Grab some of the reserve cash hidden in the sewing basket. Throw a change of underwear, tooth-brush, and her medications in a bag.

Elvina turned into her driveway and killed the engine. What was she thinking? She could no more drive to Tallahassee this time of night than she could pedal to the moon. Chattahoochee streets were one thing for failing vision; the capital city traffic was another. She hit the icon for the address book and tabbed down. Time to call for rein-forcements.

Less than a half-hour later, Ben Calhoun manned the wheel of Elvina's gas-guzzling boat of a car. He turned onto the entrance ramp for Interstate 10.

"Go ahead and give her the juice, Ben. She's had a tune-up on her V-8 and she'll flat-out move when she needs to. We've got two folks in dire straits, and now's no time to worry about the speed limit. If one of those highway patrol fellers pulls us over, let me do the talking. I've been stopped a handful of times, and I've yet to drive off with a tick-et."

"If you say so, Miz Houston."

"For heaven's sake, call me Elvina. Mrs. Houston was my mother-in-law."

Ben nodded. The faint coral glow from the dash lights painted his features. He wasn't half bad-looking.

"What's going on?" Ben asked. The speedometer registered ninety.

Elvina shrugged. "Heck if I know. The first call was from Abby. Didn't even sound like herself. Said she was in the hospital off Capital Circle. Second one was from Loiscell. She was all kind of hysterical. I could barely make out what she was talking about, or yelling about, I should say. Something about a shooting, and Sheila and some other woman on the way to Tallahassee General in ambulances. She screeched something about Choo-choo and Glenn Bruner I couldn't make heads or tails of. If I didn't know better, I'd say Loiscell was a little tipsy. That aside, it sounded like a big flaming mess."

"Which hospital should I go to, first?"

Elvina tapped her chin. "Would've been more convenient if they'd both landed in one or the other." She held the smartphone with one hand and jabbed the digital keyboard with the other. "Wish everyone would join this century and text, for heaven's sake. You should see that phone of Loiscell's. I'm surprised it doesn't have a crank." She paused. "Loiscell? This is Elvina."

High-pitched keening echoed across the car. Elvina held the phone away from her ear a couple of inches. Waited for a pause.

"Take a deep breath. There. Now. Calm down long enough to give me some information. I have Ben Calhoun with me. We're flying the highway."

The conversation lasted a couple of minutes, then Elvina stored the cell phone into its pouch on the side of her purse. "I said to myself that all hell had broken loose. Nix that. The Devil himself has rose up and tromped through in a fire-snorting gallop."

"So, TGH or Capital Regional?" Ben asked again.

"Loiscell sounds like she's near to falling apart. She's at TGH with Sheila. She's been shot."

"Loiscell has been shot?"

"No, no. Sheila's the one who's been shot. Loiscell is there with her. Try to keep up, Ben." Elvina took a breath to steady her frayed nerves. The effects of the massage were long gone. "Choo-choo is on her way to see about Abby at Capital Regional."

Ben glanced away from the road, his worried expression highlighted by the dim light from the dash gauges.

"Let's go see if we can keep Loiscell from ending up in the psych-unit first, then we can dash over and see what's up with Abby."

Ben clasped the steering wheel so hard, his knuckles turned white. "Why don't I drop you off at Tallahassee General, and I'll run on over to the other hospital? You have my cell number. We can touch base as soon as either of us knows anything."

Elvina reached over and patted his shoulder. "That's a wonderful idea, Ben. I knew you were the one to call with all of this. You're so steady and calm."

Ben sighed. "People seem to think because a man doesn't fall apart or emote uncontrollably, that he doesn't feel fear, dread or . . . love."

Elvina studied Ben's profile. The word *love* hung in the silence between them, a loaded sentiment suspended on a gossamer thread.

So I have this hole in my colon." Abby McKenzie's statement slurred from the effects of the medication dulling the deep pain in her abdomen.

"Yes. That is what the tests revealed." The emergency room physician's expression remained a mask of professional distance. "Could be a number of causes. Colorectal cancer. A weak spot in the colon. An ulcerated diverticulum."

Abby searched her memory for the term. Years of reviewing patients' medical histories helped with a basic familiarity of anatomical lingo. Still, doctors needed to come with some kind of translation manual. "Diverticulitis. Isn't that some kind of condition where you have to avoid eating certain things?"

"There are various schools of thought on the relationship between diet and this condition." The doctor pulled up a chair and sat down.

"Let me explain; a diverticulum is a pouch-like herniation of the muscular wall of the colon. Sometimes, one or more may become inflamed and cause cramping and bleeding. Other times, one might become ulcerated and rupture, causing fecal matter to be expelled into the abdominal cavity."

"Not good."

"Of course, colorectal cancer can mirror some of the same symptoms."

Abby closed her eyes and the word *cancer* echoed in her head; the mere mention could send a person into a dark place. Cancer lurked everywhere, and took no prisoners. All ages. All walks of life. Rich or poor. Cancer: the equal opportunity disease. Abby opened her eyes and fought to blend the twin images of the doctor back into one person. "You're a breath of fresh air, doc."

"Either way, you require immediate treatment. Our on-call surgeon is on his way in."

"Surgery? Can't I rest in bed for a few days and eat chicken soup or something? Give the hole a chance to heal over?"

"Unfortunately, no. You are becoming increasingly septic. The longer we wait, the graver your condition will become."

A fresh wave of discomfort hit, in spite of the pain medication. "Anything you have to do to stop this is okay by me."

The curtain parted behind the doctor and the nurse stuck in her head. "One of your family members is here, Miss McKenzie."

Family . . . *What* family? "Who is it?"

The nurse consulted a small notepad. "Choo-choo Ivey. Would you like for her to come on back?"

Relief rushed in, better than any drug. "Yes, please."

The doctor rose. "You'll be in good hands with Dr. Gunter. As soon as the surgical team is assembled, we'll be taking you back. Dr. Gunter will stop in to meet you first and explain the procedure."

The sight of Choo-choo Ivey's face peering around the edge of the cubicle's curtains brought tears to Abby's eyes. "Oh, thank God. Choo-choo!"

The old woman rushed to the bedside, leaned down for a gentle hug, and pulled the chair close to the gurney. The scent of garlic and wine boiled off Choo-choo and accosted Abby's nose. Her stomach gave only a slight lurch, a marked improvement over earlier.

"Abby, what in the world has happened?"

"I have a hole in my colon, of all things. I'm having emergency surgery." Abby fought the sedating effects of the anti-nausea and pain medications. "Sheila? Loiscell?"

Choo-choo started to speak, then hesitated. "They aren't here just yet, dear. Don't worry. I won't leave you."

Abby reached over and managed to squeeze Choo-choo's hand. "I'm so glad you're here, and not—"

Choo-choo held a finger to her lips. "Hush now. Let's not speak of unpleasant things. We have to get you through this."

Behind them, a scrub-attired man appeared. "Abigail McKenzie?"

Abby nodded. She had been called by her real first name more in the past hour than in the past ten years.

He extended a hand. "Dr. Gunter. I am your surgeon." His grip, strong and warm. Between that and the compassionate expression he wore, Abby took an instant liking to him. He was not old, but old enough. Abby guessed mid to late thirties.

"I guess that makes me your patient." Abby silently chastised herself. Drugs never had a good effect on her ability to sound intelligent.

The surgeon glanced to Choo-choo, and then back to Abby. "I need to go over your procedure."

Abby lifted one heavy hand and tried to motion in Choo-choo's direction. "It's okay to talk in front of her. Pretty sure I won't remember a thing later. She can fill me in."

"Very good then." He smiled again. On certain people, all that smiling might appear solicitous, but his features took to it as if the expression was a frequent guest.

"I'll perform a resection of part of your lower colon, the sigmoid colon, about four or five inches. I'll send tissue samples to the lab for evaluation. Then, I will take one end and bring it to the surface to form a stoma. You will have a colostomy bag when you awaken. I have to do it this way in order to allow the infection to subside. If I did it now—given the amount of contamination—the site would not heal."

The little moisture Abby had in her mouth dried to dust. "A co . . . colostomy?"

"You will have this for at least six to eight weeks. Afterwards, I can go back in and reconnect the bowel."

"*Two* surgeries?" The air left the cubicle.

Dr. Gunter nodded. "It is very good you came in when you did. Given a little more time, the infection could have compromised the colon so that you would have had a permanent colostomy." His next words stopped Abby cold. "Or you would have become so septic, you might have died."

"Sweet Jesus," Choo-choo muttered.

Still nursing what remained of her alcohol and adrenalin high, Loiscell Pickering paced the surgical waiting room at Tallahassee General. At the late hour, only a handful of people shared the elongated room. An overhead television set on CNN offered no balm. Anyone would get depressed watching the unfolding world situation. A second digital screen scrolled limited information about surgical patients. She pulled a slip of paper from her pants pocket and read Sheila's tracking number for the twentieth time in less than an hour. The readout had not changed. Sheila was still in surgery, and it had been going on two hours.

"Loiscell, you have to sit down," Elvina said. "You are wearing me out."

Loiscell stopped long enough to frown down at Elvina. "I can't sit. I'm about to jump out of my skin. How can you stay so calm?"

"Practice. When you're my age, you've spent hour upon hour in rooms like this one. It won't do any of us any good if you collapse. No news is good news. Sheila's been in there for a long while. That means they're taking care of her."

"I suppose." Loiscell shot a look at the woman sitting behind the information desk. "I'm going to ask that Pink Lady volunteer."

Elvina huffed. "Might as well save your breath. That one there has been in this very spot since Moses parted the Red Sea. I know she was the same one from when Jake Witherspoon had his emergency surgery a few years back. She runs this waiting room with an iron hand."

"Won't hurt to try."

"Go ahead on, then. But don't get your feathers ruffled if she doesn't give you more than the basic information. You'll come away with as much knowledge as you went in with." Elvina lowered her voice. "These days, I sense conspiracies lurking around every corner. No telling who knows what, and the FBI and CIA are probably behind it all. Those Pink Ladies are pawns in a much bigger game."

Loiscell waved Elvina's comment aside and walked over to the woman in the hot pink jacket. Loiscell hated to outright lie about anything, but what other choice did she have? Sheila Bruner had no next of kin to speak for her. The new HIPPA privacy rules be damned! She had to pose as a relative in order to get any information at all. Besides, she had been up to her wrist in Sheila's blood. If that didn't count for something, nothing would. Even a fake sister rated higher than a rat husband who'd just tried to kill you. God only knew what she was going to do about the lies she'd told that investigator. She had downright lied to the police! Good Lord.

"Excuse me. How will I know when my . . . um . . . *sister* makes it out of the OR?"

"The status bar will tell you when the patient is moved from surgery to the recovery area." The volunteer offered a trained compassionate smile and pointed to the overhead digital monitor. "Her doctor will come out and talk to you."

When Loiscell walked past to resume her pacing, Elvina's brows flickered. "Told you so."

Loiscell reviewed the incredible scenario, still beyond comprehension. There had to be some mistake. Surely, Glenn Bruner wasn't the professional hired by Choo-choo Ivey. No way. They had simply gotten mixed up with that butthole's desire to hurt his wife. But why trail her to Tallahassee? Seemed like a lot of trouble to go through. Glenn was a rabid hunter. Sheila was always complaining about trying to find ways to fix the pounds of venison packed in their freezer. Wouldn't it have been far less conspicuous to shoot Sheila and dump her body somewhere in the woods? Unless another hunter walked up on the body, Glenn would be home free. No telling how many bones rested in shallow graves—or not—along the dirt roads in Gadsden County.

Plus, Loiscell had never figured Glenn bright enough to plan anything short of a boozy card game. She glanced at her hands. Though she had washed them five times, the aura of blood and violence clung to her skin. She hadn't had time to think, only react. What did one do with a gunshot wound? They didn't cover that in basic CPR classes. Her limited knowledge came from watching hours of hospital-themed television dramas. Stop the bleeding. Call for help. Don't move the victim.

Choo-choo's sweater was ruined. Even if the dark crimson stain washed out, who would want to wear a garment that had been drenched in a friend's blood? If it had saved Sheila from hemorrhaging to death before the paramedics arrived, the sacrifice was worth it.

The irony wasn't lost on Loiscell. If things had gone as planned, each member of the Suicide Supper Club would be laid up on a cold

146

slab with a neat bullet hole, and deader than a doornail. When it came right down to it, Loiscell's first reaction had been to do anything in her power to cheat death.

Her thoughts flailed around like a gigged frog; the leftover wine buzz didn't help. What about that other woman, the poor lady who had stopped to offer directions? She had remained unconscious in spite of the wail of emergency sirens, unlike Sheila, who had opened her eyes once. That ambulance had pulled away first, taking her to an ER, but which one? Had to be here. This hospital had the trauma center.

Loiscell steered around some lady's bag of knitting supplies as she paced. Must be some way to get details. She shot the stink-eye at the Pink Lady. Trying to pull information from her would be like smuggling cheesecake past a yo-yo dieter. Loiscell paused and studied the others in the waiting area before walking over to stand in front of Elvina. "Do you remember seeing a man in here earlier? Or in the ER?"

"Plenty of men coming and going."

"About average height, darkish hair . . . " Loiscell's brow furrowed. "He had a mustache, I think."

"Not to berate you at such a trying time, Loiscell dear. But now is not the appropriate time or place to troll for a man."

Loiscell stomped her foot. "Oh, for the love of Pete, Elvina. I'm not cruising men!"

"Well I beg your pardon then."

"That other lady—the one I told you Glenn shot—*her* husband. I'd like to find out if she's okay."

Elvina narrowed her eyes. "Come to think of it, there was this one fellow. Pink Lady summoned him a while back. Believe it was when you were in the restroom. He looked like he'd been run over by a dump truck. Reckon that was him?"

"Might have been. Gosh, I feel like such a rat. I could've gone over to him and at least offered support, or something. We were both up to our wrists in blood. Side by side. You'd think I would have at least said something to him."

Elvina reached up and patted her on the arm. "I don't think he would hold it against you. Not like you had ever met him, or his wife, before this evening. I'm sure there was a world of confusion—what with police and ambulances crawling all over and you having to give your statement to that investigator that followed you here. I'm sure we can find out something about her later. I'll phone up my friends at the police department."

"In Chattahoochee? How you figure they'll know anything?"

Elvina caressed the small pouch on the outside of her handbag where her trusty cell phone rested. "They've heard. Trust me."

"But this is Leon County."

"So it is. They all share information. And believe you me, they'll be talking more in the next few hours about Glenn Bruner. I'll speak with J.T., Melody's beau. If it can be found out, J.T. can do it. Mandy cuts his hair—what little there is left of it—and we hear all kinds of law stuff like you wouldn't believe."

By the time Loiscell made another round of the waiting area, the read-out had changed. Sheila had been moved to recovery. Loiscell exhaled and caught a whiff of her own breath, and man, did her mouth taste horrible. A little of the tension in her body released like a tire with a slow leak. Thank you, God. Sheila's still alive!

Loiscell flipped open her cell phone and dialed. "Sheila made it through surgery. She's in recovery. No details yet. What's up over there?"

"Abby went back about twenty minutes ago," Ben Wither's calm voice answered. "The doctor told Choo-choo the surgery would last about an hour and a half."

"Yes, but will they tell either of you anything? This privacy stuff is a real bear to work around."

Ben voice's lowered. "Choo-choo told them she's Abby's aunt."

"Amazing, how all of us are related all of a sudden. I'll bet they get a lot of that." Loiscell cast a quick glance toward the Pink-Lady volunteer to make sure she wasn't watching before she continued. No telling if the woman could read lips. For sure, Elvina's paranoia germ was contagious. "I'm Sheila's long-lost sister."

"Wouldn't be a problem here, even if Choo-choo wasn't claiming to be family. Turns out, I'm down as Abby's medical power of attorney. They showed me a copy of the legal paper."

Loiscell paused. "Well now. Ain't that something?"

Chapter Fourteen

One day after suicide
Tuesday

Sheila Bruner tried to reign in her anesthesia-muddled mind. A single, nonsensical thought bobbed into her mind: she had never learned to do a cartwheel.

As a child, she could skip, jump rope double-time, somersault, hopscotch, and run. But every time she tried to cartwheel, her legs refused to fly gracefully into the air, and she landed in a crumpled-up mess. Finally, her auntie forbade her to try, as all Sheila succeeded in doing was flipping her dress up and showing her underpanties to the world. Not very lady-like.

The first time Sheila had worn a pair of Bermuda shorts, cut above the bend of the knees, she had flown out of the house and sailed into what should have been a perfect cartwheel. No dress or petticoats in the way. Nothing to stop her from achieving perfection. A week later, the multi-colored bruise on her left buttock still mocked her in the mirror.

As a teenager, Sheila had discovered basketball. She could pass and dribble. She could run fast enough to cover the court. Best of all, the game required no cartwheels or any other form of flashy gymnastics. The perfect sport. If only she hadn't fallen into the trap of love. She might have gone to college and played for Florida State. So much of her life could be summed up with *if only*.

Sheila blinked to clear her vision and squinted, taking in the details of her surroundings. Nurses. Monitors. Other people on gurneys in various stages of wakefulness. Where was she? Seemed like a post-surgical holding pen in a hospital. Which one, she hadn't a clue since her eyes couldn't focus well enough to read the logo on the nurses' nametags.

Four words rang in her memory: The Suicide Supper Club.

Sheila squeezed her eyes shut to stanch the flow of hot tears. The shots ringing through the dark. The pain. Now here. She had survived and her friends were dead. No other explanation. She couldn't even die correctly.

Glenn was going to be furious when he found out she was laid up in a hospital. He had tormented her on the handful of occasions when a cold or the flu took her from her duties. Though she hadn't ended up in the hospital following the miscarriages in her early twenties, she vividly recalled how he had reacted to the three days she had spent at Tallahassee General after the hysterectomy. No one to cook his meals. No one to make sure the house remained perfect. No one to throw down and rape. Yes, rape; call it what it was.

Even after she came home, Glenn continued to rant about his sorry plight and stupid excuse for a wife. Holding her belly, Sheila had inched around, carrying the soiled laundry to the washer piece by piece, vacuuming in measured squares. A meal that normally took a half-hour to prepare took much longer, since she had to stop often and collapse into the kitchen chair. The only respite from her wifely duties had been the freedom from his rough sexual abuse. The red-edged incision scar repulsed Glenn, and he didn't touch her for over six months.

Given her husband's recent rages, a stay in the hospital would send him far over the edge. She would be forced to hear it, and now, have no friends to share the burden. Sheila would go back to that house, that life, that undiluted hell.

"Oh, good. You're awake. Your sister is in the waiting area." The nurse's face faded in and out of focus. "As soon as we get you to your room upstairs, I'm sure she'll be right in."

Sister? Things weren't making sense. Did she have a sister? Not last time she checked. At least, the nurse didn't say *husband*. A few hours of rest before she had to face Glenn would be a small gift from God.

Sheila attempted to move her left arm, but a confusion of bandages held it firm. When she glanced down, the corner of a surgical dressing showed beneath the sheet. What kind of a hit man had Choo-choo hired? The idiot had missed anything vital by a country mile.

The next time Sheila opened her eyes, she lay between pristine white sheets in a private room.

"Hi, sugar," A soft voice said.

Sheila squinted. "Loiscell?"

A warm hand grasped hers. "That's right."

"Loiscell, you're here! You're alive! How . . . ? Choo-choo . . . Where's Choo-choo? And Abby?"

"Of course I'm here. Now, don't go getting yourself all upset. You need to remain calm."

A second woman stepped up behind Loiscell. Sheila frowned as she tried to get her vision to cooperate. "Miz Houston?"

Elvina smiled. "It's okay, dear. We're not going to leave you. Don't you worry about one little thing, you hear?"

"But . . ."

Loiscell gave Sheila's hand a gentle squeeze. "We'll talk about everything in great detail as soon as you're a little clearer in your mind. For now, you are safe and we're here."

Elvina motioned to the remote for a patient-controlled analgesia unit. "You should press that little black button when you feel any pain. The nurse said so. Don't scrimp on that morphine. There's no need—no need at all—for you to hurt."

Sheila opened her mouth to speak. It was all too confusing and tiresome. She squeezed the PCA button. Within seconds, a comfortable warm flush washed over her, dissolving worry and that nagging throb in her shoulder.

"She'll sleep now," Elvina said in a low voice.

"I'm going to ask for a cot. I don't want her to be alone tonight."

Elvina nodded. "It's always good to have an advocate when you're in the hospital. The nurses can't be here every second."

Elvina pulled out a notepad and pen. "If you'll tell me what I can get for you, and give me a house key, I can bring some clothes and toiletries back over here first thing in the morning." She glanced toward the bed. "And if you don't think she'll pitch a fit, I can go into her house and bring a few things too."

Loiscell handed over her own house keys, and dug in Sheila's small clutch for the other set. "As her sister, I'm giving you permission."

Glenn Bruner woke with the mother of all hangovers. He opened his eyes to thin slits, moaned at the barrage of fluorescent light, then snapped them shut. Something clung to the back of his skull. When he fumbled with one hand to the spot, his trembling fingers encountered some sort of padded bandage. Must've been a heck of a fight.

Impossible. He wasn't a mean drunk, except when it came to dealing with Sheila. Left to his beer or whiskey, he fancied himself an easy-going guy. Must've been a sucker punch to have ended up on the back of his head. What kind of yellow-bellied coward resorted to hitting a guy from behind?

He opened his eyes again and looked around the room. He was lying on a single cot in some sort of a holding cell. What the hell? Those crazy prison guard buddies of his, this was their doing. The goons had gotten him drunk, dragged him into the unit, and slapped his passed-out self onto an unoccupied cot. Very funny. He would've laughed aloud, but he wouldn't give them the satisfaction of knowing they had pulled a good one. He'd deal with them, each and every conniving one. Paybacks were rich, and he'd make sure the revenge was quick and satisfying.

But this room looked nothing like the ones at the correctional institution where he spent forty hours a week. Glenn had never seen this place. And when he looked down, he didn't recognize his clothing. Those fools had even gone to the trouble to dress him in a standard prison-issue jumpsuit. Had to give them points for thoroughness. Must've been one hell of a party. Were there any loose women there? Maybe he had gotten lucky.

Never—not once—in his drinking history had Glenn experienced total blackouts. Within minutes, his alcohol-soaked brain could call up most of the sordid details. He knew who required apologies, where his truck was parked, and what combination of spirits he could hold responsible for his pounding temples and the burning riot in the pit of his stomach.

Now he searched for snippets of this last exploit.

Flashes of the previous evening paraded by. Parking the truck, shopping in Publix, and slipping into the woods. And drinking rotgut hooch. Beyond that, the small pieces registered in a jerky timeline. Women, shots flying wild, screaming.

Then falling, pain, and blackness. The back seat of a police cruiser, smelling of piss and vomit. The acrid scent of a hospital. Medical mumbo-jumbo. Struggling against people who strapped him down and shoved him into some sort of machine.

Toddling, later, into a low block building, his hands cuffed behind him. The room: White. White walls. White linoleum floors. Being clamped to a rail while his personal items were recorded and placed into an envelope.

By then, the fight had seeped out of him. He had taken note of a bright blue pad hanging on the adjacent wall, a place to cushion a prisoner if he happened to get rowdy and the officers had to use force to slam him into submission.

The longer his mind grappled, the clearer the details became.

There had been a strip search in a separate barren room. He was allowed to use the toilet. Then, on to a holding room with glass walls and two rows of plastic chairs. The faces of other arrestees swam in and out of focus, a flotsam of deadbeats caught up in the criminal justice system.

He had slipped into a hunched-over sleep. A correctional officer shook him awake and led him to a machine where his fingerprints were scanned and recorded digitally. He managed to stand upright long enough for his full frontal and side booking pictures. An officer handed over a garish orange jumpsuit. At least it smelled better than his clothes. Finally, he was herded into a narrow room where he fell onto a cot. The last thing he recalled was the metallic clang of a secured lock.

One purple-Jesus hell of a night, buddy boy.

Glenn squeezed his eyelids shut as tight as possible. If he could just fall back into blessed oblivion, maybe he would wake up in his own bed, bellow at Sheila to get his coffee and breakfast going, and stagger to the bathroom to pee and maybe vomit.

He opened his eyes for a brief moment and fought the cloak of claustrophobia threatening to stifle his breathing. The white cell walls, still there. Here he was on the wrong side of authority. He was not the one with the badge, gun, or keys. He wasn't the one shoving a man's face into a blue-cushioned wall.

This time, he had really screwed the pooch.

Abby McKenzie's eyes traced several long loops of white plastic-sleeved wire and clear tubing extending from her body. Twin monitors on either side of the spongy bed chirped and whirred like contented yard chickens.

Her lips felt like she hadn't touched moisture in days. As much as she wanted to lift the white sheet to check out whatever lay beneath, Abby couldn't muster the energy. Any pain? She sent the inquiry out to her body. Possibly, it answered. Not enough to warrant drama. Kudos for pain meds.

Faces swam into memory. A young, dark-haired RN starting an IV. People hovering, anxious expressions. A surgeon called in. People telling her they would take good care of her. Had Choo-choo been there? If she could just stay awake for a few minutes, she could get a grip.

She slipped from consciousness.

When she awoke, her body ached as if she had been hit by a truck. Not just a pick-up, either. Something major. Something heavy. A semi-tractor truck. Maybe even one of those double-trailer models people blamed for ruining Florida's roads.

Funny thing about pain medications and her body: what made most people pass out cold turned Abby into a babbling wild woman. She would sleep for a while after depressing the button, only to awaken, ready to chat up any poor medical person who ventured into her intensive care room. Whether it was a nurse, doctor, or someone from housekeeping, it didn't matter. Tell me about your life. How's your mama and them? How do you feel about our current president? Do you like sushi?

Abby could imagine her nurse huddled behind the centralized monitor desk, pondering ways to slip in for the mandatory check without having to answer forty-eleven questions. The staff was probably surprised Abby didn't have some kind of long shepherd's hook to drag unsuspecting passers-by into her room.

She consulted the plate-sized wall clock beside the mounted television. Two-oh-five. Was it morning or afternoon? The room had no windows, and she had lost track of time. Her mid-section throbbed. Abby pressed the PCA button and drifted off into a hazy half-sleep.

When she opened her eyes again, she glanced first to the clock: four forty-seven. At this rate, it was going to be a long night, or day. She could turn on the television and figure it out based on the programs, but noise and flickering lights made her nauseated. The last thing she wanted to do after major abdominal surgery was vomit.

"Hi, sunshine," A familiar voice said.

She twisted her head to the right. The motion caused the room to tilt in an uncomfortable way.

Choo-choo Ivey sat nearby in a taupe, upholstered chair.

"How long have you been there? Was I asleep?"

The older woman rose and stood by the bed. "I've been here off and on since you went back for surgery. I did take a little break for a bite of lunch."

"Is it morning, afternoon, night? What?"

"Early afternoon," Choo-choo answered.

Abby touched the area around her abdomen. "Feels like I'm about twenty-four months pregnant." She lifted the sheet and cotton gown. A bandage spanned most of her midsection, with a strange looking contraption held fast to her skin on the left side.

"You have a pretty long incision, from what the doctor told us," Choo-choo said. "The other thing—the one that looks kind of like a clear plastic baggie with a long clip at one end—that's your colostomy bag."

Abby tried to wrap her mind around the changes. "Something is stuck to my inner thigh."

"That'd be your catheter tubing. You'll have that in for a couple of days. A bit of a bother, once you get to feeling a little better. But it keeps you from having to get up to the bathroom every time you have to pass urine. With as much fluid as they flooded you with during the surgery, you'll be doing a lot of that as your body throws off the excess."

Abby plucked at one of a series of white, opaque wires snaking from her gown. "And these?"

"Monitors that go to little patches on your skin. For your heart." Choo-choo slid one of her hands beneath Abby's and lifted. "The little clip on your index finger is to measure your blood oxygen level. They'll have someone in here from the respiratory therapists' group soon, I'm certain. You have to do breathing exercises to make sure you don't develop pneumonia. You can build up fluid on your lungs pretty easily when you're not up moving around. Which, by the way, they will have you doing tomorrow."

"Feels like every part of me has something attached," Abby said.

Choo-choo smiled. "That's because there is. You have these wraparound things that pump up and release to keep you from forming blood clots in your legs. You have an IV in both hands, normal saline and a couple of different kinds of antibiotics, looks like. With the catheter and monitor cables, the drain coming from your incision, the automatic blood pressure cuff, and your pain pump . . . needless to say, you couldn't escape easily."

"How do you know so much, Choo-choo?"

"Some of it, from when my husband was in the hospital. Other stuff, from my hospice work. I've seen about every contraption medical science makes." She leaned closer. "Try to remember to refer to me as Auntie Choo-choo, dear."

"Right. Forgot we're supposed to be related." Abby smiled. "Where's everyone else? Sheila? Loiscell?"

Choo-choo pursed her lips. Nodded once, as if she had reached an important decision. "Last night, Sheila was shot. She's okay. I've talked to Loiscell, who's over at the other hospital with her. Elvina's there too, so they can take turns staying with her."

"Shot! So it *did* happen." Abby tried to rise up, but the combination of morphine and the lingering aftereffects of anesthesia sent the room into a tailspin.

Choo-choo pushed gently on Abby's shoulders. "I shouldn't have said a word. I'm a silly old woman sometimes. I'll tell you about it, but you have to promise to try to stay calm."

Abby moved her head up and down once.

"After we got your message last night, we were on our way over here. Glenn Bruner stepped out from beside the little eatery where we had gathered for our . . . dinner. He shot Sheila, and unfortunately, some poor woman who had stopped to give us good directions to the hospital from Fifth Avenue. I know how to get to Tallahassee General blindfolded. That's where Charlie was always taken. But this hospital is another story."

"Was—" Abby frowned. "So that wasn't the hired—?"

"No. No." Choo-choo glanced at the fancy equipment, all beeps and clicks. She lowered her voice. "At least, I don't think it was."

"Somewhere, the real one is still out there?"

Choo-choo's gaze flicked around the room. "I suppose so."

The sliding glass partition opened, and Ben Calhoun stepped in. "Well, look who's back with us." He walked over and stood by the bedside, a loopy grin on his face. A flood of mushy emotions washed over Abby. Love, lust, hope. What was up with all that?

Abby glanced from Ben to Choo-choo and back. "How'd you find out I was in here?"

"Elvina Houston. Who else?" He chuckled under his breath. "She's already alerted every prayer circle this side of the Mason/Dixon line, plus a handful on the Internet."

Choo-choo said, "Elvina called Ben and asked him to drive over with her last night after she talked to Loiscell. Besides, Ben needed to be here, since you made him your medical power of attorney." Choo-choo's left eyebrow arched.

"Oh, that," Abby said. "My attorney suggested it. I can explain . . ."

Ben held a finger to his lips. "Shhh. It's okay, Abby. Rest. We don't have to go into all of that right now. Later, there'll be plenty of time."

Time. Abby's spirit felt as sore as her body. *Do we have that luxury?*

Abby fought to keep her eyes open, but the gentle cadence of Choo-choo and Ben's muted conversation—familiar and comforting—lulled her into a dreamless sleep.

Glenn Bruner finished lunch: boiled potatoes, shriveled green peas, a hard roll, and a slab of overcooked chicken. Even Sheila on her worst days could beat jailhouse cooking. Still, it helped somewhat to settle his queasy stomach. Now if he could force his brain to work on a way he could get out of this quagmire.

The offer for one phone call stood. Who could he dial? Not his wife. Was she dead or alive? Dead, she was no good to him. Alive, she might be of some use, if she would even come after he had tried to gun her down. He couldn't call his boss at the correctional institution. Glenn swore under his breath. The boys were going to have a freaking field day over this one.

For a white-hot second, he considered phoning Clay. Right. Like Clay would come running to help out someone who had mucked up a job. He'd snuff Glenn with his bare hands.

Glenn knew his rights. Legal council would be provided. He'd surely lose his job, and with no job and bills coming out the butt and a five-hundred a month plus truck payment, Glenn could kiss the notion of a fancy lawyer goodbye.

His truck! Was it still parked by Publix? By now, they had no doubt located it and hauled it off to some impound lot. If the wrecker had scratched the paint, he would sue.

Right. He'd sue. With what, charm and good looks?

Glenn raked his fingers through his sweat-stiff hair. The situation couldn't possibly get any worse. The clang of metal against metal jarred his sore head. A guard slid the door aside. "Get up, Bruner. You have visitors."

Bless her stupid little heart. Sheila was alive after all. He could sweet-talk her, down on his knees if he had to, and she'd find a way to post bail. Get him out of this shit-hole. The officer led the way to a cramped room, barren except for a table and four chairs. Glenn sat as ordered.

The door opened. Two men in dark suits walked in, closed the door, and stood on the opposite side of the table. Even before they flashed badges, Glenn knew who they were: Feds. They all had that same look. Chiseled jaws, blanched complexions, and expressions like they hadn't gotten drunk or laid in a month of Sundays. Glenn would place even odds that a dark-hued Crown Vic with tinted windows stood outside.

The men introduced themselves. Agents Wickler and Hurst. Wickler: the older one with a slight paunch and a fatherly manner. Hurst: mid-thirties, obstacle-course-trim body, with his shoulders poked back like a bandy rooster itching for a cockfight. These two—whatever their mission—would no doubt act out the age-old, good cop/bad cop routine. Big surprise there. Glenn fought back the mocking smirk threatening the corners of his lips. It was one thing to joke with a Fed when you were on the same side of the bars, quite another to piss them off when you weren't.

"Well, son." Agent Wickler leaned down and rested his hands on the table in front of Glenn. "You've gotten yourself in a bit of a mess, haven't you?"

Yep. The old guy's going to play the good cop. Glenn nodded. Best to keep his mouth shut. The less said, the better.

Agent Hurst huffed. How long would this young buck allow his partner to kid-glove before getting all up in Glenn's face?

The senior agent slipped his hand into his jacket, withdrew a short stack of photographs, and flipped them onto the table facing him. Glenn's eyes reacted before he had a chance to swipe his expression to bored contempt.

Wickler didn't miss a beat. "Okay. So you know him."

Glenn shrugged. "Am I supposed to?"

"Figured you might."

"Might not, too."

The second agent stood with his hands fisted at his sides. Tiny muscles worked around his temples. Any other time, Glenn would've told him not to clench his teeth so hard. Bad for the joints. He ought to know. Most mornings, Glenn's jaws were so blasted sore from grinding, he was amazed he had any teeth left.

The older agent continued, "You see, Glenn. We got a call first thing this morning. Seems you said a few things last night to your arresting officer. About how you weren't some poor beleaguered husband who finally snapped and shot his wife. About how it wasn't your fault. How you had some help."

Glenn's pulse stammered. He could've said most anything. His mouth ran like a bad case of diarrhea whenever he had a few.

Agent Wickler pulled out a chair. Sat down. Tugged his tie until it loosened a little. Crossed one leg and rested the ankle over the other knee. The old let's-all-settle-down-and-talk-like-good-buddies move.

"You kept telling the arresting officer to 'call Clay.' Said this Clay fellow set up the whole deal." The senior agent paused. "Any of this sounding familiar?"

Glenn cleared his throat. "I don't recall."

The agent pointed to one of the pictures. A military identification photo. Several years had passed since, but the identity of the soldier was unmistakable.

"He's had so many aliases, his real name is all but useless. He was Special Ops. Only for the past few years, he's had a new chosen profession. He moves around. Finds others to work beneath him. Banks the cash in some offshore account. Disappears again to resurface in another place with another face."

Agent Hurst finally spoke. "Used to do all the work himself. Now he finds some witless, no-hope, dead-end loser to do it for him." His nostrils flared. The young agent took obvious pleasure in this part of his job.

The senior agent held up a hand to calm his partner. "We'd like to round him up, Glenn. Why catch the mouse when you can have the cat?" Wickler flashed a smile.

Where the hell did Feds get their brand of humor? Was it something they taught in Special Agent Stand-up Class? Sign these two goons up for a mic at improv night.

Hurst took a couple of steps toward the table. The menace in his body language, unmistakable. If the three were in some back alley, this dude would chain Glenn to a fence and beat the living daylights out of him. And enjoy it immensely. Whoever Clay was, the Feds wanted him bad.

Glenn pushed back in his chair. "What's in it for me?"

"You help us get Clay, and we'll have a talk with the State's Attorney," Wickler said.

"No time served?" Glenn waited.

"Can't say. Maybe. Maybe not. Either way, it will be much more favorable for you if you cooperate."

Agent Hurst leaned over and put his face so close, Glenn could smell the half-chewed mint on his breath. "You shot two women."

"Two?" Glenn frowned. "Are they—?"

"Dead?" When Agent Hurst smiled, the effect was as far from enchanting as a bull gator in mating season. "Can't say. Maybe. Maybe not. I don't seem to *recall*."

A prickle of cold sweat popped out above Glenn's brow. Florida had the death penalty. If one of the women was belly up on some morgue slab, his future would dim to a pinprick.

Something niggled at him. Why the hell had Sheila hired a hit on herself? That cost money, *his* money! This whole mess was her fault. If it wasn't for having to support her lazy ass, he'd already have that boat and he would've never gotten mixed up with Clay. Sheila would pay for this, *if* she was alive, *if* she bailed him out. With *his* money.

He'd figure a way to handle Sheila, but what about that other woman? Crap in a crocodile cradle. He glanced down at the photographs of the man he knew as Clay. If he cooperated with the Feds, he would make an instant enemy: one, Glenn was sure, who wouldn't use a judge and a jury of his peers.

Time. He had to buy time to consider the consequences from all sides. He licked his cracked lips. Time, and a drink. His insides quivered like a small engine's twitchy idle.

Glenn looked Agent Hurst in the eyes. Any sign of weakness at this point would not be cool. He said the only words he knew that held power. "I want an attorney."

Chapter Fifteen

Two days after suicide
Wednesday

When Sheila Bruner opened her eyes, the first thing she saw was Elvina Houston sitting in the lounge chair next to the bed with a computer in her lap and a cell phone balanced on the armrest.

"Elvina?" Sheila started at the unfamiliar rasp of her own voice.

"Well, mornin' glory!" Elvina tapped a couple of keys and snapped the lid closed. "I was working on my blog: *Essentials from Elvina.* I got one of those wireless cards where you can get on the Internet anywhere you are. A miracle of modern technology. Too bad my dear departed friend Piddie didn't learn to use all of this before she passed. She would've gotten such a kick out of how you can find out anything with the click of a few keys." She ran her hands over the laptop's sleek crimson cover. "I can check email and surf the net with my phone, but I do better on the computer for my blog. Hope I didn't disturb you."

"No." Sheila's gaze roamed around the private room. "May I have some water, please? My throat—"

"Surely, sugar. I'll go round up one of those little Styrofoam pitchers. By now, they won't mind you having something to drink. You hungry? Bet you'll get breakfast shortly. They usually want you to start eating as soon as you're able. Builds up your strength."

Sheila's mind grappled with the stream of prattle.

"That, and heaven as my witness, they'll have you trotting up and down the halls with your rolling pole later today. Not like you feel like doing a marathon, but you'll have to walk a little. Prevents the blood from pooling in your legs. I've found this to be God's gospel truth: if you keep them happy—peeing, pooping, walking, and eating—they'll let you go home."

Sheila shifted positions to alleviate a cramp in her lower back. Her stomach roiled from the sting of the incision, then at the thought of returning home.

"My cat. He's bound to be hungry by now. Elvina, could you . . .?"

Elvina raised a hand. "All been taken care of, sugar. Your little buddy Doreen at the vet's office uptown called me right after she heard the news. I met her over there when I went to pick up a few of your things, and we looked high and low. Finally she stepped outside and discovered his little house. He's mighty sweet. Came right to us. Doreen took him home with her. Hope that's okay."

"Good thing Glenn was at work," Sheila said. "He doesn't know I have Buttercup. He's not one much for cats . . . any animals for that matter."

Elvina pursed her lips. "Never could understand a person who didn't like pets."

Sheila winced. "I'm kind of queasy."

"That's the aftermath of that stuff they use to put you to sleep. It'll wear off." Elvina slid the laptop onto the rolling bedside table and stood. "Now let me go get you that water. I've already scoped out where they keep the cups and ice. Those poor nurses are worked plumb to death."

Elvina bustled from the room. In a few minutes, she returned with a full pitcher of ice water, cups, bendy straws, plastic spoons, napkins, and a cup of lime gelatin.

"Lady at the main desk said they serve breakfast in about an hour. I managed to scavenge up some Jell-O. Your nurse said you could eat and drink, slowly at first until you get used to the notion. They're changing shifts right now, so a new one will be by to check and prod you soon." Elvina studied the control panel for a moment before hitting the correct button to elevate the head of the bed. She stuffed a second pillow behind Sheila's back.

"Good thing it's not my right shoulder that's hurt. I can't even scribble with my left hand." Sheila lifted the cup and tried to aim the end of the straw in the correct direction.

Elvina helped her to guide it to her lips. "Here. Now, that's better. You're still pretty weak. Sip a little at a time. Last thing you want is to drink too much too fast and upchuck."

The effort used what little energy Sheila had. She lowered her head onto the pillow with a sigh. "Best water I've ever tasted."

"When you're up to it, I'll spoon you some Jell-O. Jell-O's not my favorite, as a rule. But I became quite fond of it in rehab after I broke my ankle last year. Ate so much of this lime flavor, I'm surprised I didn't come out looking like an alien."

"Maybe I'll have some in a little bit." Sheila closed her eyes. It would be so easy to give into the painkiller fog and forget about the whole royal mess. Any second, Glenn would burst into the room and she'd have to hear his take on things. By the time he bossed the nurses around, she'd be doing good to get them in the room if she was on death's doorstep. "Do you know what happened last night, Elvina? Or was it even last night?"

Elvina rooted out a spot on the bed and perched. "What do you remember, shug?"

"The three of us were standing outside of the restaurant trying to decide the best way to get to Abby." Her eyes flew open. "Abby! How's Abby?"

Elvina touched Sheila's hand. "She's doing just fine. I had a voicemail message from Ben. They've moved her to Intensive Care for a bit. She had some kind of bowel thing. They had to take a piece out, but it sounds like she cruised through surgery without a blip."

Any other time, Sheila would have asked for precise details so she could appoint the proper level of concern and make plans on how to lend a hand. Not that she wasn't worried about her friend. She was. She didn't have the vigor to stretch her compassion much past the confines of her own skin.

"Good. Glad she's okay." Sheila turned her head. "Could you hand me the phone and dial my house? I need to talk to Glenn. Or have you called him?"

Elvina blinked, hesitated. "You're going to find out, so I might as well be the news-bearer, and there's no gentle way to put this. Glenn was the one who shot you, Sheila."

"Wha—?"

"He was drunker than Cootie Brown, from what I heard, and that's all that saved you and that other woman from dying."

"Other woman?" Sheila blinked to clear the spots swimming in front of her eyes.

"Glenn fired a bunch of times. Hit you and some bystander. She's in ICU. I managed to find that out. She got shot in the stomach, so her injuries are more severe than yours. I caught up with her husband late last night. He was trying to rest in the little waiting room off the Intensive Care Unit. Bless his heart, he looked like he'd been beaten up in a back alley."

"Is she going to . . . make it?" Sheila's mouth felt as if a thick wad of gauze had soaked up every smidgeon of moisture. She closed her eyes. Too much.

"The husband said she was in serious, but stable, condition." Elvina busied her hands straightening the sheets and bedcover. "I've added her to the prayer lists on all of my online forums, and at the churches in Chattahoochee. Along with you and Abby, of course."

Sheila took a deep breath to steady her quivering insides. "What if she dies, Elvina?"

For the first time in as long as she could recall, Loiscell Pickering had a decent night's sleep. Not because of any prescription sleep aids. Not because of complete peace of mind. Rather, exhaustion so absolute, it splayed her into submission. For the first few moments of wakefulness, she curled beneath the cool smooth sheets, unwilling to break the spell. Then the doorbell sounded.

She glanced at the bedside digital clock radio. "Oh no! It's past nine!"

The covers flew in two directions. She fumbled for a light house-coat, but she couldn't find one of her bandanas. Whoever it was would have to get over the fact her hair looked like rusty steel wool.

Loiscell's voice left her when she opened the door.

"Mom?"

Loiscell cleared her throat. "Lisa?"

Her daughter pushed through the front door and grabbed Loiscell in a fierce hug. "I got your letter. And I've called and called! Why haven't you been answering your phone? I've been worried sick!"

Crap. The letters.

No use to deny anything. It had all been put to ink. The cancer. The plea for forgiveness. The insistent urging for both Lisa and Lance to continue with successful lives without her.

"I was going to drive, but I was so frantic, I caught the first flight out and snatched a rental car in Tally." Lisa shoved a rolling suitcase out of the way, then dashed for the bathroom. "I left messages for Lance on his cell," she called out. "He's biking the Rockies, from what

I was able to find out. No telling when he'll be in a spot with enough reception to check his voicemail."

"That's your brother," Loiscell said in a loud enough voice to carry down the hall. "He'd bike the moon if he could flag a shuttle."

Loiscell heard the trickle, the flush. Her daughter walked back into the living room, fastening the button on her pants. "Got any coffee? I could use a cup. That airline stuff is rotten."

"I'll start a fresh pot. The one I programmed to come on at six has been sitting there for three hours now. I seem to have overslept a bit."

Lisa's expression darkened. "I don't like that. You hardly ever sleep in."

Loiscell raked a hand through her hair. With no make-up and horror-flick hair, she must look like death-not-warmed. "I feel okay, myself. I've been sitting with a friend in the hospital. Actually, two friends." She glanced toward the wall-mounted phone. "Which reminds me. I need to make a quick call to Elvina Houston. I'm supposed to be over at TGH this morning."

Lisa settled onto one of the kitchen chairs. "I could drive you."

"Elvina's quite resourceful. She has a stand-by list of people as long as God's arm. I'll ask her to call on someone else. Besides, by the time I get showered and drive over, the morning will be mostly over."

"Why do I have the feeling that more is going on than just your . . . cancer?"

Loiscell rubbed the tight spot between her daughter's shoulders: a loving gesture that never failed to relax Lisa. "Tell me about you. What's happening with your book? I'm so excited about you becoming a published author, I can barely stand it."

Lisa grasped her mother's hands and turned to fix her with a stern stare. "We'll have plenty of time to talk about me later. This is about you, Mom. Not me. Not my job. Not my writing. Not Lance. Not the twins."

Tears formed at the corners of Loiscell's eyes. "I'm glad you're here."

Lisa jumped up and enfolded her mother in her arms. Her daughter had that same fresh linen scent she favored. No heavy perfume, just clean. They swayed back and forth in the same fashion Loiscell had rock-and-hugged Lisa as a child.

Loiscell pushed back from the embrace. "I'll put on that coffee and call Elvina. I have a couple of Joe Fletcher's sweet potato biscuits I can warm up. He has that little bakery uptown, you know. We can sit and have a nice, long talk."

Nothing had prepared Glenn Bruner for the amount of thinking he would have to do, locked in a cell alone without the benefit of a beer. Instead of mixing Glenn with the general inmate population, the powers in charge had isolated him. Because of his law enforcement background? Who knew. At least meals came at regular intervals, though he'd eaten better slop at a greasy spoon diner.

"Bruner, you have a visitor." A guard unlocked the cell door and motioned with one hand.

Glenn stood and ambled from the cell. No use giving the corrections officer any lip. It would shine a bad light on himself.

Again, he was led into a cramped room. This one, without the partial wall of one-way mirrored glass. A small-stature man entered, an expensive oxblood-colored leather briefcase in hand. Glenn checked the cut of his suit. The man was no public defender. His thinning hair was slicked from one side to the other in one of the worst comb-overs Glenn had ever seen. And no snarky attitude like the federal agents who had graced him with their presence earlier in the day.

What kind of vehicle would this fellow drive? Glenn enjoyed the game, matching a person to a make and model. The man was no law enforcement type. No dark Crown Vic with darkened windows for him. Judging from the set of the thin shoulders and the flashy wrist-watch, Glenn guessed a late model S-Class Mercedes. Better yet, some low-slung, over-priced foreign convertible. That comb-over would fly back like a flag stunned straight by a stiff breeze.

"Mr. Bruner. I'm Martin Washington. I have been retained as your council." The man didn't extend a hand, only nodded and slapped the briefcase onto the metal table.

Where had Sheila found this clown? And where had she gotten the money? One good thing: the arrival of the attorney assured him that his wife wasn't stone-cold dead. Tried to snuff the woman and she still loved him. Atta girl. Glenn released the breath he hadn't realized he'd been holding. "Guess you've met Sheila, then. How is my wife, anyway?"

The attorney flipped open the briefcase. "Your wife is in the hospital, from what I can surmise."

Glenn pulled out the plastic chair and sat down.

The lawyer unbuttoned his jacket, a practiced move so slick it looked like sleight of hand. "I've not met your wife. Neither have I met the other young woman involved in the alleged incident."

Glenn frowned. "Who hired you, then?"

Martin Washington's mouth twisted on either end. The result was an imitation smile, one that didn't make it to the rest of his features. "Let's just say . . . a mutual friend. One who wishes to remain anonymous."

Glenn crossed his arms over his chest. "None of my friends have that kind of cash."

The attorney settled into the chair opposite of Glenn. "I'm certain if you give it a little thought, you know someone who has a vested interest in the progression and outcome of your case."

A claw of ice wrapped around Glenn's heart and squeezed. "I see."

"As your council, I advise you to carefully consider the consequences of your actions in regards to your cooperation with the authorities."

Glenn narrowed his eyes. "You a real lawyer, or just someone sent here to threaten me?"

Martin Washington offered a second tight-lipped smile. "I assure you, I am quite qualified to settle your charges. Taking into account, of course, the best results for all involved."

No reason to act coy with this guy. Clearly, he knew the details. Dancing around the issues would take more oomph than Glenn could muster. Oh God, he needed a drink. "If I decide to take the Feds up on their kind offer, what then?"

Something black and oily flickered across the attorney's face, swiftly replaced by a bland expression. "Prison can either be an experience one can master, or one that provides insurmountable, and often fatal, obstacles."

Glenn huffed. "Who said I was guaranteed of serving time? I give 'em what they want, and they take care of me. Heard of the witness protection program, buddy?"

The attorney extracted a neat pile of papers from the briefcase. "If you make unfortunate errors in judgment, Glenn—" He paused. "I may call you Glenn?" Then after Glenn nodded, continued, "there will be no place to offer complete solace. Safety is an illusion."

A childhood memory flashed into Glenn's mind. He and one of his buddies had gone against parental warnings and tramped into the swampy low land near a remote river landing. The recent torrential spring rains had left the soil boggy, and the two boys reveled in the muck. At one point, Glenn's feet sank into a patch of unstable ground. The more he pulled and struggled, the more his body lowered until he was locked into place up to his groin. A water snake slithered by, stopping to taste Glenn's fear with a flick of its forked tongue before disappearing into the cypress knees and splashing into the river.

Glenn recalled the suffocating panic. How his throat constricted and his heart rate increased so that he heard the fluttering thuds echo in his ears. Left to his own, he might have stayed there, stuck for all eternity. His buddy had managed to find a long branch to extend across the bog, and Glenn used it to pull himself over to grab onto a cypress knee. His clothing was torn and muddy. He'd face his mother's wrath later. But he was out of the swamp, whole and alive.

Now Glenn couldn't tell who was extending the branch.

"I look like a skunk ape," Abby McKenzie said. "I don't think my hair has ever been this filthy."

Ben rummaged in a backpack and pulled out a plastic bottle. "I'm here to save the day, my friend."

"Is that something to drink, or are you going to dip me like a mangy dog?"

Ben smiled. "I knew you wouldn't be able to wash your hair, so I asked Mandy at the Triple C if she had some kind of dry shampoo. She suggested this astringent instead. Said to apply it to the scalp and it would absorb some of the oil. I figured I could use a washcloth and help you wipe it on. It's alcohol-based, so it'll evaporate fast. That way, you won't have wet hair."

Abby jabbed the bed switches to raise the head of the bed. "Bring it on. It's worth a try. Choo-choo helped me get a bath last night. But this hair is driving me insane."

Ben saturated a cloth and massaged Abby's scalp, working toward the end of one hank of hair. His fingers, gentle and strong at once. Abby closed her eyes and gave herself over to his touch. Somewhere beyond the bandages, other parts went tingly.

"I'm going to owe you big for this," she said. "You, and everyone else who has been so amazing to me throughout this whole thing."

"No debt between friends, Abs."

The easy familiarity between her and Ben had none of the prickly sensations she associated with male/female interactions. Abby didn't even mind that he had picked up the nickname Mason Dixon used for her. "You'd make a great nurse. Where'd you learn to be so good at all of this?"

Even through the painkiller fog, Abby realized the stupidity of her question. She reached up and grasped Ben's wrist. "I'm sorry, Ben. I didn't mean . . ."

"No harm, no foul." His hands didn't miss a stroke. "I did have lots of practice."

"I can't even begin to imagine what you went through." She listened to his breathing—even and slow.

"It was a difficult time, with my wife. And remember, I'm a father too. My son has never had to go through anything as traumatic as cancer, but I've experienced my fair share of spilled body fluids and otherwise."

His fingers caressed her scalp. Abby leaned into his touch. "Tell me what's been happening over in the Hooch."

She heard him inhale and exhale. When Ben spoke again, the aura of sadness had been replaced with his usual calm humor. "Let's see . . . Your office is managing without you at the helm, barely. Sabrina is propped up at the front desk when she's not with a patient. She's easing back into her job. Said to tell you they finally got a payment from some insurance claim you'd been waiting on. Said you'd know what she was talking about. That it was clearly a miracle."

Abby grinned. All those staples and red marks had worked! At least she'd gotten that one right. She should author an office management manual.

"Dr. Payne's wife comes in a couple of hours a day to help out," Ben continued. "She's a little . . . umm . . . stuffy."

"Mrs. Payne is not unfriendly. I think it's because she's not from the Deep South, and a little more reserved than people are accustomed to."

"Right." Ben laughed. "If you don't know a person's life history, darkest secrets, and favorite color by the time you've spoken ten minutes, something is amiss."

"Elvina Houston says that the Bible tells her to love her neighbors. And she has to know all about their lives to do that. Kind of a divine permission to meddle. She got that philosophy from her late friend Piddie."

Ben chuckled, poured more liquid onto the cloth. The sound of his laughter helped her more than drugs.

"What else . . . ," he said. "Joy and the yoga class miss you and Sheila terribly. Loiscell's managed to go, but Choo-choo's been too tired to make it. I've missed once, but I find the movements help me stay a little calmer, so I try to go. I feel guilty, though—what with you and Sheila in the hospital."

"Don't. It's only right you have a little down time. I'll be back to class as soon as I heal enough. Might not make it there before the second surgery, but for sure after my insides are reconnected. I've been doing a few of the shoulder and neck movements, and the breathing thing we do in class. Beats blowing in that little plastic contraption the respiratory therapists are so keen about."

"Deep breathing's important. Keeps you from getting pneumonia."

"I know. I know." Abby pushed out an exaggerated sigh. "Joy called me the first day after surgery. Can't even begin to tell you what we said. I was pretty doped up. It was sweet of her. She has such a mellow voice. Now, what else?"

"Mason Dixon's taken it upon himself to oversee Oreo's care and feeding. Nice kid."

Abby felt a pang of guilt, but couldn't bring herself to share her prearrangement for the kitten's care, or the reason why. One day. Maybe.

Ben talked as he worked each strand of hair through the damp cloth. "Joe Fletcher added this fantastic new Chocolate Dream Cake to his menu. Can you have sweets? If so, I can bring you a piece."

"I think it's okay, as long as there aren't any nuts. The dietitian is supposed to come by sometime today and review my list. I've been thrilled to have the Jell-O." Abby stuck out her tongue. "Cake doesn't even sound appealing right now, believe it or not. And I love Joe's baking. About the only thing I've wanted since they've allowed me to eat has been bland stuff, like mashed potatoes and cream of wheat."

The sliding door opened behind them and a woman stepped inside. "Hi, I'm Janice, the Ostomy Care Nurse. Is this a good time for us to talk?"

"You want me to leave, Abs?" Ben asked.

Panic seized Abby. She needed Ben. The realization stunned her and scared her spitless at the same time. "Would you stick around? My memory isn't too hot right now. And if there's something important I have to know later . . ."

Ben's face softened. He fastened the top onto the astringent bottle. "Sure. Glad to."

"I'm going to *show* you how to care for your stoma, how to empty and change the ostomy bag. Since your surgeon had to leave your incision open to drain, so close to the stoma, it will take a bit of extra care until the wound fills in and heals." The nurse's gaze shifted from Abby to Ben.

"Okay with me, if it's okay with Abby."

Abby winced. Kind of a creepy thing to ask the man to do. He'd been in the room when the nurses cleaned and packed the wound, but this was taking it to a new level.

"I've seen and done just about everything. When my wife—well, let's say it won't be an issue." He offered Abby a warm smile. "You might need a little help the first few times you do this. But if you'd rather it be Loiscell or Choo-choo, tell me. You might prefer a female. I'm good with whatever you decide. Really."

Abby flipped the sheet down to reveal her abdomen while still keeping her private parts covered. "I've got to learn how to deal. The sooner, the better. Hand me a pair of those rubber gloves and let's do this."

Chapter Sixteen

Three days after suicide
Thursday

In Sheila Bruner's dream, the FSU women's basketball uniform fit perfectly. The material: shiny white with garnet and gold trim. Sheila looked up. Sue Semrau motioned for her. She was going in! As soon as she hit the court, a teammate passed the ball, and Sheila zoomed down the court. No one could stop her. Her feet worked in rhythm with her hands. Two more steps. She charged forward for the perfect lay-up.

A rap sounded at her hospital room door. Sheila jerked awake and the dream faded. No court. No FSU basketball team. No smiling coach. No cheering fans.

Probably Loiscell and her daughter coming back after lunch. Bless her heart, the poor woman shouldn't even be over at Tallahassee General again. Sheila had tried to talk her out of coming. Sheila could get up and walk to the bathroom unassisted, as long as she used one foot to jumpstart the rolling pole over the bathroom threshold.

Sure, time passed faster with someone to talk with, but Sheila didn't mind being alone. When a person had shared so many years of bad company, solitary time was a gift. It gave her pause to listen to the small inner voice she thought long dead. That voice told her, "your husband tried to kill you, your husband tried to kill you." Part of her still didn't believe it. Stupid, since she had worried about it nearly every moment of every day for years.

"Come in," she called out when the knock sounded again.

Instead of Loiscell and Lisa, a man with close-cropped silver hair walked in, a large bouquet of flowers held in one hand. "Sheila Bruner?"

"Yes."

"These are for you." He stood and stared at her, as if he was trying to absorb every detail of her face.

The man's eyes: cold. The way he held himself: military erect. A coiled spring. A rattlesnake.

"Um . . . put them down on the little shelf there, if you please."

The man took two measured steps and slid the arrangement into place. When he looked back her way, Sheila fought the urge to leap from the hospital bed and move as fast as she could manage. Anything to get as far away, as fast as possible.

Don't be silly. Not every man is out to get you. Her breathing calmed a little with the self-talk. The least you can do is be cordial. "Usually the Pink Ladies bring flowers and cards."

The man smiled. The expression was far from pleasant. "We make an exception for special patients."

The door behind him swung open, and Loiscell and her daughter entered. "We just had the most wonderful lunch! I wish you could've—" Loiscell stopped when she spotted the man. "Oh, I'm sorry. Didn't know you had a visitor."

Sheila swallowed. Her throat felt as dry as it had after surgery. "He's delivering flowers."

The man nodded first to Sheila, then in the general direction of the two women, taking particular note of Loiscell. He walked past and closed the door behind him.

"He was a little odd," Loiscell said. "Didn't seem quite like the flowery type."

Lisa tsked. "Like, you have to be a certain type to work for a florist, Mom?"

"That's not what I meant. He looked . . ." Loiscell brushed the notion aside with one hand. "Never mind me."

Sheila motioned to the shelf where the elegant bouquet stood. "Would you see who sent them?"

Lisa slipped the small white envelope from its plastic prong holder and handed it over. Sheila's lips moved as she read the insert. "This is weird." Sheila handed the card to Loiscell.

"May your fondest wishes come true," Loiscell read aloud. "What the heck is that supposed to mean? And it's not signed." She turned the card over twice, as if she expected a reasonable answer to appear.

Lisa plopped down onto one of the vinyl upholstered chairs. "Maybe you have a secret admirer, Sheila."

Elvina Houston entered the modern lobby of Capital Medical Center and paused to admire the interior design. Everywhere she looked, the wood, tile, and floors reflected the ambient light. At least at its entrance, Capital Medical resembled an architect's grand office complex more than a hospital. After all the years of visiting sick friends, anything to take one's mind off suffering and disease was an improvement in Elvina's view. Being sick was bad enough without depressing surroundings. Even the air smelled fresh, not covered up with some mountain-spring, dewdrop air spray.

In the center of the cavernous room, a smiling information person sat behind a large glossy circular counter. No Pink Lady here.

She stepped from the third floor elevators into a pleasant atrium and continued past the nurses' station with a nod to one of the ladies behind a computer screen. Elvina stopped dead in her tracks. A robotic automatic floor cleaner/polisher eased forward. It was the most remarkable piece of equipment, and she loved to confuse it. She glanced over her shoulder to make sure no one watched, then stepped directly into its path. It beeped, twice. Stopped. Lowered itself. A slight whirring noise and a few clicks sounded as it contemplated its next move. Then it elevated a couple of inches, turned forty-five degrees, moved forward a couple of feet, stopped again to straighten out, lowered itself, and proceeded with its buffing duties, missing Elvina altogether.

"You're downright amazing, is what you are," Elvina said as it whisked past. She tapped on the door to room 315 and entered after she heard Abby's muffled answer. "Good afternoon, sunshine!"

Abby muted the wall-mounted television. "I'm so glad you're here. I couldn't stand one more second of CNN. News is so depressing. I watched *The Young and the Restless*. But the other soaps, I don't keep up with."

"I brought you a big stack of magazines and my Kindle loaded with books. I know how it is, once you start feeling a little better."

Abby punched the switches to elevate the head of the bed. "Need to take a walk. Would you mind going with me?"

Elvina set the tote bag on a chair. "Of course I don't mind. The sooner you look like you can get around, the sooner you can go home."

Elvina helped Abby slip on her house shoes and robe, careful not to dislodge the I.V. She checked to make sure the surgical drain was secured to the gown, then unplugged the IV pump from the wall socket and hung the cord over the top of the rolling pole.

"I feel less like an octopus since they took all of those monitor wires off. I don't have to wear that oxygen clip on my finger like in the ICU. I should be getting this drain out tomorrow. Then all I'll have left is the IV. Not that I was mistreated in ICU, but it's much quieter here on the floor. Trying to rest in that intensive care unit was like trying to sleep in the middle of a band concert."

"Most of those patients are out of it, or in a coma. You were an exception. You were pretty hopped up on that morphine." Elvina smiled. "Your color's improved. You were stone gray last time I was up here."

"I *felt* gray." Abby tugged at her gown's shoulder. "One size fits all. It keeps slipping down like I'm trying to be sexy or something."

"Don't you love hospital gowns?" Elvina commented. "Like my dear friend Piddie used to say, 'they can be a bit air-ish in the rear.' "

A knock sounded at the door. Abby paused, her hand on the pole for support. "They just did rounds and took vital signs. What now?"

A man stepped inside, a huge vase of fresh cut flowers in hand. His gaze slid from Elvina to Abby. "Abby McKenzie?"

"Yes."

"These are for you. Where shall I put them?"

Abby motioned to the cabinet beside the bed. "Over there's fine, thank you."

The man stood for a moment, taking a long look at the two of them. He offered a creepy half-smile, set down the arrangement. He tipped his head. "Good day, ladies."

"That was strange," Elvina said after he left. "Over at TGH, the Pink Lady volunteers deliver the flowers. Don't know how they do things here. That fellow didn't have any kind of logo on his shirt, like he was from a florist shop."

"Dunno. The other arrangements came when I was doped up. Honestly, Cleopatra could've delivered them." Abby shrugged. "Those might be from my office. Sabrina called earlier and said they were sending some."

"Or from Ben Calhoun." Elvina winked.

Abby stepped over and slipped the florist's envelope from its holder. Her brows crimped. "It says 'may your fondest wishes come true.' "

"No name?"

Abby checked the backside of the card, then the envelope. "Nope."

Choo-choo Ivey stood behind her screened front door and blinked a couple of times to assure her eyes weren't fooling her.

"Mother?"

Jacqueline Ivey stood on the porch, her shoulders squared. Her daughter had gained a few inches around the waist, and her hair was severe, almost masculine. Her face: stern with few frown lines.

"My word. Well, come on in." Choo-choo glanced over her daughter's shoulder. A young woman stood behind Jacqueline, a nervous smile worrying her lips.

They stepped inside. Jacqueline motioned toward her companion. "This is Tee."

The young woman extended a hand: small, quivery like a trapped sparrow. "Pleased to meet you, Mrs. Ivey."

Back in the olden days, someone would've said Tee looked wormy, like she needed to eat some good, solid meals. With a few pounds on her frame, and a good stylist to calm down that mass of wild blonde curls, Tee could be almost attractive. Maybe a little make-up. She was too pale.

"Please, do call me Choo-choo." She glanced back to her daughter, her mind still trying to fold itself around the fact Jacqueline was actually standing here, in her living room. And it wasn't a major holiday.

"Jack, do you want me to get the suitcase?" Tee asked.

"Not yet." Jacqueline's gaze lingered on her mother for a moment before she stepped inside.

"I'm pleased as punch to see you, Jackie. But I wish you had called ahead." Choo-choo looked from her daughter to Tee. "The guest room linens are clean, but I like to give them a good washing, freshen them up, before anyone sleeps on them."

"It's okay, Mother." Jackie Ivey glanced around the room. "Where's Prissy?"

"Oh. I haven't spoken with you since . . . Prissy passed, Jackie. I left several messages on your phone. Asked you to call."

"I've been busy."

Choo-choo swallowed past the lump of hurt squeezing her chest. "Where are my party manners? You girls come on in the kitchen and I'll find something for you to eat and drink. You must be hungry after such a long trip. I can't imagine what time you had to get up, to fly all the way across the country from Oregon." Choo-choo turned and walked toward the kitchen. Was Jackie still a vegan or a vagan, or whatever they called themselves?

"I have some cheese and crackers." Choo-choo winced. "But you don't eat dairy, or do you? Oh dear. I haven't had much time to go to the store. A couple of my dearest friends are in the hospital. I've eaten out the past few days."

"Cheese and crackers will be fine." Jackie sat down at the kitchen table. "What'd you do with the other chairs, Mother?"

"They're stored. Took up so much room, and after your father . . ." Choo-choo pulled a plastic-wrapped hunk of aged cheddar from the refrigerator. No family to sit in them, but why would her daughter concern herself with that? "You two sit. I can bring in another from the dining room."

Tee eased onto the chair opposite Jackie.

"I have sweet tea or coffee," Choo-choo said. "I think the milk is good. It's two percent."

Tee offered a meek smile. "I'd love some coffee."

"Water for me," Jackie said.

Choo-choo slid a plate filled with slices of cheese and Ritz crackers onto the table. She tried for a light tone. "What brings you two to this side of the country?"

"Seriously." Her daughter's eyes narrowed. "Are you kidding me?"

Tee reached over and rested her hand over Jackie's. "Jack . . . please."

Jackie breathed in and out. "We're here because of your letter."

Choo-choo blinked. Letter? She closed her eyes for a moment. "I had forgotten about that."

Jackie's eyebrows shot up. "For-got-ten? You write me this five-page epistle, and you forget? What, do you have dementia now?"

"Don't be fresh, Jackie. I may be a little rattled at times. I have a lot on my mind at the moment." She set a glass of iced water in front of her daughter, then turned to bring two coffee mugs to the table. "Cream is in the little pitcher. Sugar's in the one with the lid. I have artificial sweeteners if you prefer."

"Thank you, this is fine. I drink mine black," Tee said.

Tee looked a little scrawny, but at least she had manners. Her blue eyes were kind. Choo-choo took an instant liking to the young woman who was the polar opposite of her daughter.

"Back to the letter." Jackie snatched a cracker from the plate and bit down.

"Have some cheese. 'Everything goes better on a Ritz'. " Choo-choo chuckled at her own quip.

Tee smiled. Jackie did not.

Choo-choo took a deep breath. Her heart stuttered. "I wrote that letter to try to clear the stale air between us, Jackie. I wanted to go to my grave knowing my daughter didn't despise the very ground I walk upon."

Jackie's eyes flicked toward Tee. "Tee was the one who talked me into coming here. She said we should talk."

"I have you to thank then." Choo-choo brushed the young woman's shoulder.

Tee wrapped her hands around her cup. "I'm glad we're here. I've never visited the South."

"I'll make it a point to show you around our corner of it, then."

Tee stood. "I'm a little tired. Would you mind if I rested for a bit?"

"Of course not. The guest bedroom is the first door on the left as you go down the hall. Make yourself to home. The bathroom is directly across the way."

"She'll be sleeping in my room," Jackie stated.

"Well, okay. If you'd like. You take the guest room then, Jackie. Both have good mattresses. Suppose it doesn't really matter much—"

"No, Mother. Tee and I will both sleep in my old room. She's my wife."

Elvina Houston often felt sorry for God, when she wasn't aggravated at Him.

What would it feel like, being there at the top with no one to talk to and no one to complain to but yourself? Not to mention that every living soul on the planet—regardless of what religion he or she attested to—was busy either pleading for your help or cussing you. After Piddie died, Elvina chatted with God on occasion, but she had lost the one person who had shared her innermost secrets, the one friend who understood the blue spells that could send her to bed for several days in a row.

The Oldsmobile practically steered itself onto Wire Road. When she spied the little Morningside A.M.E. church, Elvina smiled. Just knowing Lucille Jackson was somewhere close-by made her instantly feel better.

Elvina talked to Piddie's spirit every day when she visited Piddie's memorial garden, and that one-sided conversation offered a smidgeon of solace. But a hole still gaped in her spirit, large enough to drive a tractor-trailer through. Lucille Jackson provided a balm.

Elvina edged the Delta 88 into a parking slot next to the parsonage and killed the engine. When she didn't receive an answer to the knock on the Jackson's front door, she walked the short distance to the Morningside A.M.E. sanctuary and entered through the unlocked wooden doors. She spotted Lucille sitting at the piano, a pad and pen next to her on the bench.

"Am I interrupting?" Elvina called out.

Lucille glanced up and her face lit with a smile. "Oh, not at all. Come on in."

"You plinking away on that piano, are you?" Elvina set her purse down on the front pew.

"Join me." Lucille gathered some papers and patted a spot next to her on the bench. "Chiquetta's going to sing this Sunday, and I'm choosing the hymns to go along with the Reverend's sermon."

"You know I'll be polishing my usual spot on the front pew. Still don't know how that woman's voice doesn't crack the stained glass. She's got an amazing set of pipes on her."

Lucille uh-huhed agreement. "Glad you stopped by. I planned to call you later on to check on Abby and Sheila. Thurston and I are visiting the Tallahassee hospitals later in the week."

"I just left from over there. Sheila might be able to come home soon. Abby's a different story. It'll be a few more days for her. Though the way she's been coming along, her doctor could let her out early."

Lucille clasped her hands together. "Praise be! Prayers are answered!"

Elvina took a deep breath. The simple, old sanctuary's aura of peace settled around her. "You ever think that sometimes things get stirred up and trip all over each other trying to happen at once?"

"Like death coming in threes?"

Elvina nodded.

"It's a nice morning with a touch of the promise of fall." Lucille closed the hymnal. "I just put on a pot of coffee down in the community room. Why don't we grab a couple of cups and sit in the peace garden?"

Perfect, coffee and Lucille Jackson's take on things.

A few minutes later, the two descended the concrete steps leading from the rear of the community room, to a small enclave of camellia bushes and flowering perennials. A rock fountain bubbled beside a cluster of wrought iron chairs.

"I'm glad y'all put in this little sitting area." Elvina took a cushion from Lucille, positioned it on one chair, and settled in.

"When the weather permits, Thurston offers private council out here. People tend to open up when they're not confined inside a building." Lucille patted her cushion into place. "The benches are hard as a rock, though. I always have to bring along a pillow and make sure to take it back inside afterwards. This heat and humidity mildews everything. But summer will pass. Bad and good seasons come and they go." She took a sip of coffee. "Now, where were we?"

"Life happening at once."

"Ah . . ."

Elvina held up a hand, counting with her fingers as she spoke. "First there was Abby, then Sheila. Though those two things happened so close, it's hard to say which came first. Then Loiscell's daughter Lisa shows up from Atlanta, and they've been busy talking and so-on. Turns out, Loiscell has cancer again, bless her heart. Now I hear from Choo-choo that her long-lost daughter and her friend have flown in from across the country, and they're having a big—if you'll excuse my reference—come-to-Jesus meeting."

Lucille chuckled.

"And there's Glenn Bruner in the Leon County Jailhouse." Elvina slipped in a breath. "Plus someone sent these mysterious flowers to Abby and Sheila."

"Still having that unsettled feeling you told me about?"

When Elvina bobbed her head, the sprayed-stiff mound of curls on top trembled. "It's even stronger now. Thought maybe it would fade after what all happened in Tallahassee."

"I do believe God taps us on the shoulder from time to time, sends messages to us. We're wise to heed them."

Elvina frowned. "Cold as the feeling I've been having on the back of my neck, I'm not so sure the Almighty's the editor of *this* newsletter."

Hours passed and the fog in Glenn Bruner's brain cleared to a few murky pools of low-lying mist. The things he would miss if he had to stay locked behind bars waded through his mind. Fishing on Saturdays. Home fries at Bill's Homeplace Restaurant. The start of NASCAR season, chased with a couple of ice-cold brewskies. Hunting season.

Damn, he was going to miss hunting season! The crisp early mornings with the scent of the woods, a flask of Jack Daniels Black keeping him warm. The solitude of a deer stand: the other place besides a fishing boat where he felt a sense of peace.

"If I have to spend weeks, months, years, with these four walls closing in around me, I'll go freakin' nuts," he mumbled. His hands shook with the lingering effects of alcohol withdrawal. Sweat beaded on his forehead and upper lip.

The guard paused in front of his cell. What now? Suddenly, he was Mr. Popularity. Even the officers noted how often he had been called to one of the cement-block meeting rooms.

The wormy attorney had been by twice, each time reinforcing less-than-subtle threats: all the nasty little things Glenn would encounter if he cooperated with the State. The Feds had been sniffing around too.

Something bigger than one hired gun and Glenn's get-rich plans was behind it all. Had to be. No one would put out this much full-on effort for one man. Not since high school football days—before the play that had busted his leg and his future—had Glenn felt so powerful.

He had something they all wanted. If he could just get one of them to show his cards, Glenn would know whether to fold or raise the ante. If he could trap them all in a room and watch them try to out-bid each other, that would be helpful. Let's Make a Jailbird Deal, the new reality TV game show.

"C'mon, Bruner. Your prom dates are here." The guard offered a crooked half-smile.

"Good thing I got on my tux," Glenn said.

The guard chuckled. Clearly, the man knew Glenn wasn't one of the usual redneck deadbeats. Got to show those real inmates who's boss, don't give them any slack. This guy probably got in a good punch or two when he could. Way it should be. All that sensitivity training was a load of crap.

The guard escorted Glenn to the bare walls room, the one without the sheet of one-way glass. Great. The slimy attorney again. The Feds favored the arena with the viewing gallery. Watchers on the other side probably made popcorn and settled in like they were tuned into the Super Bowl.

The correctional officer motioned for Glenn to be seated and left the room, closing the heavy door behind him. In a few minutes, Agents Wickler and Hurst swept in. Glenn twitched. This couldn't be good.

"Time for another round of Good Cop/ Bad Cop?" he asked before he had a chance to consider the consequences.

Hurst—the younger one, the firebrand—took a step forward. His nostrils flared.

The senior agent held up one hand and stopped him. "Why don't you go get us a cup of coffee?" Wickler pulled out his wallet and threw a twenty to his partner. "Go down to that little coffee shop on Tennessee. I can't take the swill they make here." Then to Glenn, "Or would you prefer a soft drink?"

Glenn leaned back in the chair and crossed his arms over his chest. Room service? This was getting more interesting by the moment. "Coffee's fine. I like it white and sweet, like my women."

Agent Hurst's eyes skewered a hole through him. No doubt, the young rooster disliked being a go-fer when he'd rather stay in the close room and intimidate Glenn. Or better yet, pummel him to a bloody mush. He snarled and snatched up the cash.

When the door closed behind Agent Hurst, Agent Wickler pulled out a chair and sat down. He loosened his tie. "You all right, son?"

Glenn started to offer a smart-ass reply, then reconsidered. "Getting by."

"I asked the other agent to leave on purpose," he said, "so you and I could speak in private."

Glenn arched one eyebrow.

"I'll get straight to it, since he'll be back shortly. It's not only the man you know as Clay that we're interested in."

Glenn waited.

"Julius Herndon—Clay to you—does use his recruits to make easy money. True. We'd be interested in finding him for the wake of death he's left behind. He's ruined a lot of lives, and not just the ones whose contracts were successfully fulfilled." Agent Wickler tapped his finger on the table. "These local boys would like to strangle him on account of having to deal with his last lady friend. Julius took off in her Blazer and cleaned out every bit of her spare cash before he left. Found the vehicle in Georgia, wiped clean of prints. Think that woman would take care of him for us if she could lay her hands on him. But hey, he cut her some slack. She's still breathing."

The agent settled back in his chair, all comfortable like he was talking football with a good buddy. "Julius has offered quite a challenge to us over the past few years. I'd like to see him brought in for the amount of aggravation he's caused me." He took a deep breath and blew it out. "But he isn't working alone. And he's more than a hired assassin. Much, much more. He's one of many in an international network, operating out of Central America. The group's implicated in just about everything. You name it—political assassinations, guns, drugs, human slave trade, laundering money for international terrorists. Many are ex-military, like your friend."

"He's not *my friend.*"

"I stand corrected. Former business associate, if you will . . ."

Glenn dipped his head.

"We've managed to place a few undercover agents inside the operation, but we'd like to get someone like you—someone they see as owing them allegiance—into position."

Glenn took his time answering, glancing around the room, tapping a staccato rhythm with one foot. "What's in it for me?"

"Not being dead, for one thing." Agent Wickler leaned forward on his elbows. "You're not a criminal. You let the idea of all that money override your good sense. I'd like to believe you didn't plan to murder your wife, only to provide a service for a good fee. All of us have something we work for. Me, I like rare coins."

Where the hell was this going? "Coins?"

"Everyone has a hobby." The agent paused. "I gather, by the way that little boat of yours is kept up, one of yours is bass fishing. I do a little saltwater fishing myself."

"I prefer fresh."

"You hunt too. So do I. Mostly ducks."

In spite of himself, Glenn warmed to the older man. Did Wickler have a son? What would it be like, to have a father who might choose his boy over a bottle?

Agent Wickler continued, "You may not have made the smartest move by hooking up with the likes of Julius Herndon, but you didn't really think things through."

The agent leaned back in his chair again. "Let's reason this thing out, shall we? If you take a dive for this man, you end up serving time. You piss off the Attorney General. Lots of years will be stolen from your life. When you get out, you start over. By then, I'm sure that fancy truck of yours will be long gone back to the creditors. Same with your house. Your wife, *if* she's alive, since you *did* try to kill her, will divorce you. You won't be able to get any kind of job that makes diddlysquat.

"Or you decide to work with the State. You get a reduced sentence. Julius's—Clay's—people see to it that you never make it out, except in a body bag." The agent pulled a quarter from his coat pocket, flipped it into the air, then slammed his hand across it as soon as it hit the table. "Either way, you're seven shades of screwed."

"And the Federal government is all concerned about my welfare." Glenn stared at the hand with its captive coin. Heads or tails? "Touching."

"I'd hate to see you end up in the place you're heading." Without revealing the tossed coin, Agent Wickler slid it into his hand and back into his pocket.

Glenn fought to swallow around the lump forming in his throat. He'd give it to the man, he was good at playing the strum-the-heart-strings game. And he'd make one hell of a poker player.

Wickler continued, "Here's my proposal. We *allow* Julius's people to grab you from our custody. We have plants within their organization. We can iron out the details.

"You work for them. Keep your eyes and ears open. Learn as much as you can. Then at the right moment, we'll extract you. Give you a new identity, a new home. Somewhere nice, with good fishing. You can start a new life."

Glenn stared, incredulous. "I'm no trained agent. What makes you think I can do this? And what makes you think these people will buy it?"

"They will buy it because they understand one age-old, simple fact: the most dangerous man is one with nothing left to lose. If they think they're rescuing you, you will be in their debt. They will own you. Why would they doubt your loyalty when, in their view, you have no other choice?"

Agent Wickler glanced at the wall clock, then at the door. "Of course, you could play me and turn coat as soon as your feet hit foreign soil. I'm taking a risk here. But I'm banking on the fact that underneath it all, you're a patriotic American boy who will step up to the plate. For your sake, son, I hope I'm not wrong."

The senior agent stood up and reached a hand to rest on Glenn's shoulder. "All you have to do when Agent Hurst comes back is tell me you want to speak to your council. I will know then, that you're with me." He stepped back when the door latch clicked.

Agent Hurst walked into the room clutching three Styrofoam to-go cups. His eyes shone with anticipation, jonesing for a fight.

A slow smile teased Glenn's lips. He took special pleasure in ruining the rooster's fun. Though he directed his words to the senior agent, Glenn's gaze rested on Hurst. "I don't think we have anything to talk about. I want my attorney."

Chapter Seventeen

Four days after suicide
Friday

Elvina Houston steered the Delta 88 into her special parking spot and switched off the ignition. The Witherspoon mansion never failed to impress her. Not like some of its modern competitors.

Ostentatious houses reminded Elvina Houston of toads. They squatted on their lots, overpowering the shrubbery, intimidating the trees. Far from making her drool with envy, the overdone houses made Elvina laugh. Chattahoochee didn't have the lion's share of the toad-houses—not like certain neighborhoods in Tallahassee.

The Witherspoon Mansion was no toad-house made of perfect brick. The home graced its rolling lawn and provided a tasteful statement instead of a rude interruption. Elvina knew the mansion from the days of the paint-by-numbers club and its charter members: Betsy Witherspoon, Sissy Pridgeon, Piddie Longman, and herself. Now all of the women were deceased, save for Elvina. And some days she didn't feel so good, herself.

As soon as she stepped from her car and toward the stately old home, Elvina's spirit lifted. Like so many of the older women who walked through its portal, the home had seen more than a few decades. After Betsy Witherspoon died, the house had changed hands to her only offspring, but the debts from Betsy's extravagance made it impossible for Jake to retain ownership.

When Holston Lewis finally purchased the mansion from a south Florida couple who never so much as set foot in town, the Greek Revival-style house looked like a down-on-her-luck dowager. With a lot of elbow grease, a few tubs of spackle, pots of paint, and a generous amount of love, the house had resumed its rightful place as the town's crown jewel. The perfect throne for the head of the little-ole-lady hotline.

When she walked into the back door—the one used by staff, for deliveries, and by patrons familiar enough to come through the less-impressive entrance—Elvina felt the old house fold around her. Some days, she sensed the spirits of her deceased friends looking over her shoulders as she measured out coffee and wandered the lower level in search of plants that needed attention. In the quiet moments before Mandy, Wanda, or Melody came in, the house spoke to her in a low language: creaks and clicks that might startle a less stalwart person. Elvina listened, sure that each sound echoed those long-silenced voices.

Soon the phone would ring. Someone with a hair emergency. Someone who had pulled a back muscle scraping the leaves from the gutters. Someone in terrible need of a nail fill. Elvina sat at the massive mahogany reception desk with a hot cup of coffee cradled in her hands.

Snippets of thought bumped into each other. Something about the series of events surrounding Choo-choo Ivey and her yoga minions disturbed Elvina's waking moments, and had started to creep into her dreams. It reminded her of an annoying arithmetic word problem: one where a train leaves from Town A at 2:30 and from Town B at 4:15, heading toward each other. If one was going so fast and the other so fast, then when would they crash? She despised word problems. Too many variables.

Elvina woke the computer and typed in her password. The day's schedule appeared, neat and orderly. The way she liked things. Since Elvina tended to think in a straight line, the abstract gathering of seem-ingly unrelated facts annoyed her. Given the correct equation, she would solve the problem. But how in Hades did she figure out the formula on this one?

Piddie had often told Elvina that she could "beat a dead horse until it turned into a wall hanging." If something festered in the backside of her brain, Elvina had no choice but to keep worrying it until it came to a head.

As soon as Ben Calhoun stepped into Abby's hospital room, he heard crying coming from the bathroom. He dropped his duffle bag and tapped on the door.

"Abs? Abs? You . . . okay in there?" He heard a muffled answer, but couldn't make out the words. "Do you need me to get your nurse?"

"No!"

That one, he got. Should he go in? He shoved his keys in his pants pocket. The toilet flushed. He heard shuffling, the clang of the rolling IV pole, and the door swung open. When she saw him, Abby burst into tears, huge gulping sobs, her shoulders shaking up and down.

"Abs, what . . . ? Here, let's get you back into bed." He rocked the rolling pole over the low tiled threshold. One wheel stuck; he cussed it and jiggled it over the hump. Then he slipped his arm carefully around Abby's waist and led her, still crying, to the bed.

"I'm so messed up," Abby managed between bursts of emotion. "So messed up."

He pushed past his hesitation and gathered Abby into his arms, cooing comfort, swaying gently. She clung to him and cried harder. If that was even possible.

Someone tapped at the door. A nurse walked in, took in the scene, and mouthed, "I'll come back."

Ben nodded.

For what seemed like forever, Abby cried. Then, as if someone had flipped a switch, she stopped and pushed back. Snot streamed from both nostrils and her red eyes had already started to puff around the edges.

"Here, Abs." Ben handed over a couple of tissues from the bedside table. Abby blew her nose twice and wiped her eyes.

"I'm sorry."

"No need to apologize."

She took a shaky breath, puffed it out. "It all just kind of hit me."

"Wanna talk about it?" Ben didn't leave his position on the side of her bed, only pulled back a little. His wife had always needed to talk after the bad spells, until she couldn't communicate at all. Listening was the best and often only thing he could do.

"I'm so messed up, Ben."

"You said that before." He offered a slight smile. "Going through extensive surgery, the pain, the days in a hospital room—those things can sideline even the bravest person."

Abby shook her head. "It's not just that. I'm not proud of some of the things I've done."

"Nobody's perfect."

"I don't deserve you, Ben. I probably never will."

Words gathered in his mind, aching to get out. His timing often sucked. "Besides my mom and granny, I've only cared deeply for two women in my life, Abs. My wife was one." He stopped. He had her full attention now. She wasn't even sniffling anymore. Here goes nothing. "You're the other."

Her gaze fell to her folded hands. "I don't know how to do this, Ben. I'm damaged goods."

"What? A few extra seams here and there? A nice little decorator bag for a few weeks?" He grinned. "Not like I'm Brad Pitt."

Abby's lips quivered, then lifted at the corners. "I was married once." She coughed, cleared her throat. Ben poured a glass of ice water and handed it over.

Here it came: the past love and life talk. At some point, every man and woman had it. He'd tell her about his stuff too, at some point. Get that out of their way.

"His name was William Harvey Hansel. Stupid, stupid, stupid. That any woman should get married straight out of high school. Just stupid."

Ben held Abby's hand.

"Will was charming and dashing, even at that age. Perfectly outfitted. Always precise with the right thing to say. Good with special touches. And I was just plain old Abby McKenzie." She took a deep breath. "Will's family moved in from up north when I was in my junior year. He was so exotic with that Wisconsin accent. I had landed the prize. First time in my life. I got what those cheerleaders and silly Buffy-type girls longed for.

"I was a virgin when we got married. Will slept with me that first night, and a few times afterwards. Then he found convenient excuses not to. Weeks stretched into months, and we did little more than hug." Abby stopped. "I can't believe I'm telling you all this."

Ben squeezed her hand. "I'm right here. Tell me as much, or as little as you wish."

She raked her free hand through her hair. "Other than the physical part, the marriage was as perfect as the magazines and romance movies promised. Until I came home early from a college class in Marianna and found my perfect husband in bed with his . . . male lover."

What could he say to that? "Oh."

"It's not that I'm all against Will's lifestyle. I'm not. It's just . . . Why can't people be who they *are* instead of trying to be who they're *not*?"

Ben noted the way Abby held her free hand, fisted, the knuckles white. "Times were different then. Not to defend him. Cheating on your spouse is never okay, no matter who you cheat with."

The small muscles at Abby's temples pulsed. She jerked her hand from his grasp and pounded both fists on the bed. "Why, why can't people be what they're supposed to be? Tearing up families! Hurting everyone around them? All those years and years of lies! If I can't believe in *him*, how can I ever believe . . . in anyone?"

Ben was no expert on women, heck what man was? But he could read people, had always been able to. This wasn't about a brief doomed marriage. "Abs . . .?" He touched her hand, a gentle brush. "Tell me. Please. If you can."

She squeezed her eyes together. Let out a deep shuddering breath. "That man, the one in bed with my husband, was . . . was . . . my father."

Abby opened her eyes and looked past him, into space. "We all went back to McKenzie-normal. His parents moved out of town shortly after our divorce. I got curious a while back and found Will on the Internet. He lives in San Francisco, a highly successful designer. Goes by the title W. Harvey." She stopped for a beat, continued. "My father never said a word to me about it, never said anything to anyone, as far as I know."

When Abby looked at him, Ben saw the pain etched across her features. She reached for him and he held her. Abby's body seemed to curl up, to shrink, as if he cradled the young girl instead of the grown woman. Her head pressed against his chest, reminding Ben of the way his own son had done, listening to the comforting thrum of his daddy's heart. Ben rocked her, side to side.

Finally, she pushed back and studied his face. "That's me. Screwed up me. Guess that's why I can't get past hello." Tears pooled in her eyes again. "But I want to. I really, really want to."

Ben reached over and brushed a stray slip of hair from her temple. He caressed her cheek, still damp from tears. Leaned over and kissed both of them, pulled back. Abby's eyes showed a mixture of hope and fear.

Ben cupped her chin. Moved in slowly and pressed his lips to hers. Tender. Easy. Warmth flowed from him to her in waves. He pulled back. Later, the kiss could be longer, deeper.

"I think you and I have gotten a little past hello, Abs."

"Aren't you pleased as punch? You get to go home today!" Loiscell Pickering plumped the pillow behind Sheila's head and stood back to study her friend's expression. "Only, you don't look pleased."

"I'm happy to be leaving here. They've been wonderful to me. It's . . ." Sheila's eyes watered. "I don't know if I can set foot back in that house."

"Choo-choo and I discussed that very thing this morning. We made a plan. Her daughter and friend are visiting from the West Coast, so she wasn't able to come over today. You're going home with me."

"Loiscell, I don't—"

"I'll not hear any guff out of you, young lady. I have plenty of room. While my daughter Lisa was here, she helped me set the guest room in order. It had gotten a little out of hand, what with me being such a—"

"Pack rat," Sheila supplied.

Loiscell lifted one eyebrow and let it fall. "True. I am that. Everything I couldn't bear to throw away had ended up in there. It was cleansing to shuffle most of it off to charity. Now I have all the room in the world, and I'll be happy for your company." Even more amazing, that Lisa couldn't drag anything back to Atlanta with her, since she'd flown down.

Loiscell gathered a stack of get-well cards and stuffed them into a zippered pouch in Sheila's overnight case. "If you'll tell me what clothes you want, I'll get whatever you need. We've already moved your little cat to my back porch."

"Buttercup?"

"So that's his name? I've been calling him *Little Yeller.* I tried letting him sleep inside, but he wasn't happy there. He can come and go from my porch, and still has a safe place to get in out of the weather."

Sheila's eyes misted over. "He's really very sweet. Glenn would never abide an animal, so I kept him outside."

"Not much your husband *would* abide, it seems." Loiscell bit back a torrent of harsh criticism. No need to belabor the facts.

Sheila picked at the cuticle on her right thumb until a pearl of blood appeared. "There's something I need to do before I leave the hospital. Would you walk with me?"

"Sure, hon. Moving around is good for you. But we can get out and patrol the streets when we get back to the Hooch. You might want to conserve your strength today. The trip home will wear you out." Loiscell dug in her purse and handed Sheila a bandage strip. "Best to

191

cover that cuticle. No matter how much they clean, there're all kinds of evil bugs in a hospital. Last thing you need is to get a Staph infection."

"Please, Loiscell." Sheila grimaced with the effort to rise. "There's someone I need to see . . . here." She wrapped the bandage strip around her finger.

"No harm in that I suppose. Long as we keep it brief."

The two women made their way down to the opposite end of the hall where Sheila stopped in front of the door leading to another private room.

"Someone from back home in here?" Loiscell rummaged through her memory. Surely, Elvina would have told her if one of their other friends had been hospitalized.

Sheila shook her head. "No, just a lady I need to speak with before I leave."

A soft voice answered Sheila's knock. When they entered the room, a bedridden woman flipped the television volume down. "Yes?"

Sheila nodded to Loiscell, then crossed to the chair beside the bed. "I know you might not remember me. I'm one of the ladies you stopped to help in front of the restaurant."

The woman's eyebrows knit together. "I'm afraid I don't recall much from . . . that night. It was almost dark, and then . . . ."

"I met your husband in the hall last night when I took one of my walks. Forgive me for bothering you, but I need to—"

Loiscell's hand rested on Sheila's good shoulder. Sheila took a deep breath. "I've spent my whole life pretending. Pretending to have a perfect marriage. Pretending that nothing hurt me. I'm finished with all of that." Sheila paused. "I can't take back what has been done to you, to both of us."

"What—"

"I don't even know your first name." Sheila repositioned her wounded shoulder.

"Lucinda . . . Lucinda Myers."

"That's pretty." Sheila's expression turned wistful. "Lucinda sounds like the name of a sweet little girl in ruffles and lace. I like it."

The woman glanced from Sheila to Loiscell, her eyebrows raised.

"I know this all seems odd to you, Miz Lucinda . . . " Loiscell stopped speaking when Sheila held up her hand.

"Please, Loiscell. I've been letting someone else speak for me for a long time. Way too long." Sheila's features softened. "Lucinda—I hope you don't mind me calling you by your first name—I'm here to tell you

192

how very sorry I am that you got hurt. And how very blessed I feel that you are alive."

"Thanks, but—"

"I can't turn back time and take any of this away. If I could, I would. I would do so many things differently." Sheila closed her eyes and took a deep breath. "I am so deeply sorry."

From where she stood, Loiscell noticed the slight tremor of her friend's hands.

"I'm Sheila Bruner. My husband was the one with the gun."

Elvina Houston laced up her walking shoes and put down a snack for her cat. By the end of her long day, the stream of worry had prompted another of her common ailments: insomnia. "I'll be back, Buster." No need to take one more drug, even if it helped her achieve sleep.

Elvina made her way through the neighborhoods, hugging the curb with a small flashlight hanging from a clip on her belt—for the spots not illuminated by streetlights. The darkness revealed more than the light of day. She caught snippets of a heated argument, saw the lights of those who shared her nocturnal affliction. At one house, she spotted the vehicle of someone's clandestine lover partially hidden behind a tall hedge.

After years of nightly roaming, Elvina knew exactly who lived where, what kind of car or truck they drove, and if they kept their dogs inside after dark.

A police cruiser drew up alongside and slowed. Elvina waved. It picked up its pace and turned at the next intersection.

Elvina checked the time on her nightglow watch. She slipped her smartphone from its clip-on holster and stepped from the sidewalk into the deep shadow of a magnolia tree. She hit the message recorder app.

"Friday. Eleven forty-five p.m. Older model sedan, dark color. Choo-choo Ivey's house." She polished the fingerprints from the face of the amazing piece of equipment before slipping it back into its case. Gone were the days when she had to carry a notepad and pen. This phone had it all. If she could get close enough to that car to snap a digital photo of the tag number, she could have one of her contacts at the police station run a trace. Odd, how the little white license plate light wasn't shining. Wasn't that illegal or something?

This car—the same one she'd seen the two previous evenings, around the same time—was conspicuous because it was trying not to be. A few late-shift workers routinely shared the neighborhood streets with Elvina. Most were going above the posted speed limit, anxious to get home to a soft bed and sleep, and not particularly worried about pedestrians or law enforcement. On the weekends, it was the hormonal teenagers, out beyond curfew and showing off with their screeching tires and acceleration.

The sedan crept along below the limit, coming to full stops at the intersections, even using turn signals. And most intriguing, slowing as it neared and passed certain addresses.

One thing about this little town, the streets had a thousand eyes. But none as watchful as Elvina's.

Chapter Eighteen

Two weeks after suicide
Monday

Abby McKenzie paused at the threshold of her home. Its perfume—vanilla wafting from an essential oil diffuser and a vague blend of older smells—filled her nose. Houses possessed personalities, reflections of their people: light, dark, cluttered, spare, cozy, or airy. The moment she entered a home, Abby could tell a lot about the human inhabitants. Did they make you feel as if you could plop down on the couch with your shoes off? Or did they hold you at arm's length—cold and detached?

Each of her friend's houses held signature scents. Choo-choo Ivey's home smelled of brewed coffee and cinnamon, and before Prissy went to dog heaven, a lingering undercurrent of dog urine. Loiscell's house spoke of flowers and all manner of growing things with a hint of earthy incense. The one time Abby had visited Sheila's home, an over-powering mixture of lemon-scented bleach and disinfectants had hit her full in the face.

Abby inhaled. Her house's scent held veiled layers of the family: her father's Aqua Velva aftershave, her mother's Channel No. 5, the ghosts of fried chicken, sautéed onions, and warm sugar cookies. Now it was hers—regardless of the clutter—and it reached out in welcome. Her eyes stung.

"You okay, Abs?" Ben held the door open, juggling her carryall and a bag of groceries.

"Yeah. Fine. A little winded."

"It'll take you a while to get your energy back. Don't feel like you need to run a marathon."

"With a ten-inch bandaged open wound and a colostomy bag, I doubt I could run anywhere." Abby made it to the recliner and lowered herself with a groan.

Ben dropped the armload onto the couch and tucked a quilted throw around her legs. "Rest. I'll make you a little something for supper."

"God only knows what. That list is restrictive. No fiber. No fresh fruit or vegetables. No nothing!"

Ben patted her on the shoulder. "Best to focus on what you can have, rather than what you can't."

"I have to eat white bread. White bread! I hate white bread! I can't remember the last time I've had white bread! I never, *ever* eat white bread."

Ben smiled. "Love ya, Abs. But if you say white bread one more time, I may have to strangle you."

Abby's inner petulant child took over. "I don't have most of the stuff on that dietitian's list. I don't even remember what's in the cupboards."

Ben picked up the grocery bag. "That's why I stopped by the store before I rescued you from the hospital. I bought white rice, chicken, broths, all kinds of soups, canned fruits, and I grabbed a loaf of fresh Italian bread. It's not nearly as mushy as a commercial white loaf."

"You're cooking for me?"

"Tonight, I am. By tomorrow, Elvina will have the ladies of the hotline in here in a steady flow of dishes. Don't worry. I gave her a copy of the diet restrictions to pass along to the neighborhood cooks. Keep in mind, this is only until your surgeon reconnects you. After that, you'll be able to get back to eating what you want."

Petulant child sulked back to her corner. "Guess I should hush. It's only for seven weeks. But after that, I'm having a salad the size of the Rock of Gibraltar with everything in it."

"Atta girl. Tonight, you'll be treated to my famous chicken and rice. Then, there's dessert—"

"Tell me it's not Jell-O."

He laughed. "Nope. I wouldn't do that to you. Something a bit more appetizing. Chocolate pudding parfaits."

"I would kill for a slab of fresh strawberry shortcake."

Ben walked toward the kitchen, calling back over his shoulder, "rain check on the strawberries, unless it's strawberry Jell-O."

She watched his rump. Looking good in those jeans. "You are cruel, Ben Calhoun!"

A tap sounded at the front door and Mason Dixon poked his head inside. "Cool, you're home."

"C'mon in."

The boy stepped inside, a wiggling black and white kitten cuddled in his arms. "I brought Oreo over. Figured you'd want to see him. Or would you rather I keep him at my house?"

Abby held out her hands. "Hand him here." She cuddled the kitten to her face and nuzzled the velvety patch behind his ears. "I have missed you, little one."

Mason pushed his glasses up on his nose. "I updated the virus protection on your laptop, updated your browser. Ran a scan too. It's ready to roll."

"I can't thank you enough, Mason, for all you've done." Abby sniffled, wiped tears onto her sleeve. Had to be the lingering effects of the surgery. She wanted to either cry or laugh, sometimes at once. And then there was that mushy, lusty feeling whenever Ben was around. She shook off the emotional flush. "Was Oreo a bother?"

"He stayed in my room most of the time." Mason reached over and scratched between the kitten's ears. "He likes to sleep next to my desktop monitor while I do my homework. My dog even got used to having him around."

"I'm sure we can work something out where Oreo can visit. I may need a little help taking care of him for a while. I can't lift anything, so cleaning the litter box will be out of my range. I'm doing good to put on my own shoes, much less bend over very far."

Mason's expression brightened. "I can stop by before I go to school and after too, if you'd like. Feed him. Do the litter box thing. Whatever."

A rap sounded on the front door. Choo-choo Ivey entered with a quilted casserole carrier suspended from her arm.

"Choo-choo! Great to see you."

"I know Ben's cooking tonight, but this is a little breakfast thing. It's got eggs and milk and white bread and cheddar cheese. I cut back on the cheese, though. Figured you shouldn't have too much, on account of cheese might bind you up. And one thing you don't want is that, so close after your surgery." Choo-choo tapped the carrier. "It's supposed to sit overnight in the refrigerator, then you bake it. The bread soaks up the eggs and milk, and it comes out all hot and gooey. I used to make it on special occasions for brunch when Charlie was alive. It was one of his favorites."

"It has to beat the cold, hard scrambled eggs I had in the hospital," Abby said.

"They don't season things to my liking." Choo-choo waved a hand through the air. "Food tastes better when you're at home."

"True."

Choo-choo nodded toward Mason. "Good to see you again, young man. It was fine of you to take on the care of Abby's cat while she was laid up."

"Yes 'um."

Abby smiled at Mason, then glanced back to Choo-choo. "Elvina told me your daughter was home. Bet that was a surprise."

"She and her lady-friend left yesterday early. For the first time in as long as I can remember, I was sad to see Jacqueline leave."

"It went well?"

Choo-choo shrugged. "Hard to make up for years of not saying much of nothing, but we made a dent. She and Tee—that's her lady-friend—plan on coming back home for Thanksgiving! Not only that, but Jackie said it's okay if I make a turkey, though it has to be organic. Suppose I'll have to drive over to Tallahassee to find that. What is an organic turkey, you reckon? One that wears only a hundred percent cotton?"

Abby laughed, holding her bandaged stomach.

"No chemicals added," Mason said. "And the food they're fed too . . . no additives."

"Glad you cleared that up for me." Choo-choo favored him with a nod. "Anyway, they'll come in for the holidays, and maybe we can take up where we left off. Jackie's got her issues, and I've got mine. Don't think we'll ever be thick as thieves, but it's a start."

"I remember you saying how much you wanted to connect with her before you—"

"—left this world?" Choo-choo supplied. "I suppose my most important wish has come true." She fixed Abby with a knowing look. "Glad I stuck around."

"Glad we all did."

"I'll be here first thing in the morning to put this in to cook, and to relieve Ben. He's the one staying the night."

When Abby started to protest, Choo-choo held up a stop-hand. "Won't do you any good whatsoever to carry on. We got it all figured

198

out so we can look after you and Sheila 'til you both get back on your feet."

Abby sighed. "Too bad you can't corral us in one spot."

"Not such a bad idea." Choo-choo tapped a manicured nail on her lips. "If you don't mind having a house guest, we could move Sheila over here. For obvious reasons, she doesn't much want to go back to that house."

"I have two bedrooms, if she can see past the clutter. Besides, I doubt I'll be sleeping in a bed for a while. Imagine I'll be parked right here in this recliner. The incision pulls too much when I try to lay flat."

Choo-choo nodded once. "Decided then. That'll take a load off Elvina. She's been running around like a chicken with its head cut off, trying to get the food brigade moving in two directions at once."

"I'm going to owe you all big time when this is said and done."

"No debt between friends. And keep in mind, Elvina Houston lives for navigating a good drama." Choo-choo glanced toward the kitchen. "If you and Mason will excuse me, I'll go store this casserole in the refrigerator and make sure Ben is finding his way around your kitchen."

Two weeks after suicide, Wednesday

The transport people—three grim-faced guards—arrived and told Glenn Bruner to don a Kevlar vest beneath his prison garb. What the hell? They formed a joyless procession from his narrow cell, down a hallway, through a set of heavy doors. He stepped outside.

The lead guard motioned toward a prison van. Glenn's pulse picked up. Something hit him in the back, battering-ram hard. He crumpled to his knees, fell forward and planted his face in the gravel. Dizzy, trying to catch his breath, figure this out. What crazy sumbitch would shoot him here, with law enforcement people raging like fire ants? A madhouse of excited conversation flowed around him.

Hands pawed at him, flipped him over, tossed him onto a gurney, and shoved it into the maws of an ambulance. Where the hell had that come from, and how had it gotten here so fast? The ride from the Leon County Jail to Tallahassee General Hospital—if that was where they were headed—should have been a short one, but the ambulance kept rolling and the sirens silenced after a few minutes. For the next half-hour, Glenn lay on the gurney—dazed but unharmed because of the vest. No one said a word, and he got the distinct impression he shouldn't either. Something huge was going down.

Following a series of stops and sharp turns, the emergency vehicle halted. Glenn was snatched up and herded into the back of an unmarked transport van, the ambulance left behind. The journey continued. Time passed. More turns and twists. Then the doors rolled open. Glenn didn't recognize the area—a small rural airstrip lined with rows of pines. The same two grim-faced men who had posed as paramedics unlocked his restraints and shoved him into a cement block bathroom with a stack of civilian clothing and a pair of worn leather boots.

The remainder of the trip, he spent in the company of a series of silent pilots. Middle of nowhere airstrips. Refuel. Move on. A couple of times, Glenn dozed off. One of the men offered a limp sandwich and bottled water. Since he didn't know when he would eat again, Glenn took it. So much for airline cuisine and courteous service.

Abby McKenzie jumped when the loud knock sounded at the front door. Oreo dove for the protection of the underside of the couch.

"That can't be your wound care nurse this early, can it?" Sheila asked. "Thought she came around noon."

Abby set her half-full mug on the table beside the recliner. "It has to be Elvina or Choo-choo. No one else would show up here much before nine in the morning, or face Elvina's wrath."

Sheila opened the door. Two men in dark suits stood on the porch. The older one spoke. "Excuse me, Ma'am. We're looking for Mrs. Sheila Bruner. We were told she might be at this address."

Sheila's hand fluttered to her throat. "That's me. I'm Sheila."

As if on cue, both men flipped open identification badges and shoved them toward her. "May we speak with you, Mrs. Bruner?"

Sheila glanced back toward Abby, then nodded toward the men. She held open the screened door and motioned the two inside where they took seats on the couch.

"What we need to say might be best in private," the older man said.

Sheila shook her head. "You can talk in front of Abby. She's a dear friend."

Abby sat up as straight as the recliner and her incision would allow. "What's going on?"

The older man spoke again. "I'm Agent Wickler. This is Agent Hurst. FBI."

Abby and Sheila exchanged nervous glances.

"Mrs. Bruner, I'm afraid I have bad news about your husband, Glenn Bruner."

Sheila leaned forward. "Yes?"

"Unfortunately, your husband was shot this morning. Despite the efforts of emergency personnel, his injuries proved fatal. I am very sorry for your loss."

Sheila's face drained of color.

Abby managed to speak. "Shot? What the—"

The younger agent talked next. "From what we can tell so far, Ma'am, it was a professional hit."

"Hit?" Sheila's expression flickered between fear and bewilderment. "But he's in jail. Isn't he? I mean, he was—"

"Your husband complained of a severe headache. Because of his recent injury, he was being transferred to TGH for a CT scan and further examination." The older agent cleared his throat. "Your husband's body will be held at the Leon County Morgue until a release is authorized."

"I was going to go over there. I was. Maybe, even later today." Sheila gripped her hands together so snugly, the knuckles paled beneath the stretched skin. "I couldn't before now. I just got out of the hospital, and then, there's Abby . . ." She closed her eyes. "I was waiting until I knew what to say . . . I . . . I didn't know what to say to my husband. Do you understand?"

The agents looked at each other, then back to Sheila.

Sheila stood. "I should go to him."

Agent Wickler rose and reached for Sheila's trembling hand. "Mrs. Bruner, there is no graceful way to say this. Your husband's face was terribly disfigured. You might not want to . . . It might be best to wait until your funeral director can— "

"We need to know who we need to contact, for the arrangements, Mrs. Bruner," Agent Hurst said. His expression showed no emotion, no compassion.

Sheila stumbled backward and sat down. She stared, her eyes unfocused.

Abby said, "Everyone around here uses Mr. Burns at Memorial Gardens. I'm sure, if you call him. . . ." She reached for the phone directory on the table beside her recliner. "I can find the number."

"No need. I'll locate the business." Agent Wickler rested a hand on Sheila's thin shoulder. "We'll take care of everything, Mrs. Bruner."

To Abby, the senior agent said, "You might want to avoid watching the news for a couple of days. That's one reason we felt it imperative to come. I'll have the city police patrol the house."

"You think—?" Abby frowned. Her eyes flicked in Sheila's direction.

Agent Hurst gave a curt nod. "The media will crawl all over this. I'm shocked they didn't beat us over here. You can bet they're on the way."

The senior agent handed Abby a plain white business card with block style printing. "I'll be in contact as soon as the coroner releases the body. Please, call if you need anything."

The two men let themselves out. A million and one questions swam in Abby's mind. The FBI? Why were they involved? A tornado of hot mess, that's what this was turning into. "Sheila?"

Sheila rocked back and forth, her arms wrapped around her midsection. A low, monotone hum sounded from deep in her throat.

Choo-choo Ivey took her coffee to the back porch swing. Though summer had yet to relinquish its chokehold, the last couple of mornings had brought a tease of cooler, drier air. The leaves up north were already turning, but in the Florida Panhandle, only a few of the dogwood trees had picked up the hint.

She anticipated the fall and especially enjoyed the winter. The chill made her joints ache, but she could live with that minor annoyance. When Charlie was alive, cooler weather had meant long mornings spent cuddling. The man radiated heat. He had never once complained when Choo-choo stuck her ice-cold feet under his.

A cardinal sat on the wooden fence and sang his clipped song. Soon, Choo-choo could dig out the fluffy thick sweaters, bulky socks, scarves, and gloves from the storage bins beneath her bed. The down comforter could unfurl from its plastic storage bag too.

Her head hurt from all the self-analysis she'd done lately. In her youth and through the busy middle years, Choo-choo had seldom taken time to ponder her actions. If she felt peaceful, good. If she felt bad, it would pass. No reason to look for boogers behind every bush. No need to let a daughter get you flustered either.

Maybe working with the Hospice patients had forced her to slow down. When she sat with someone who counted the time in days, hours, then minutes, she listened to the murmur of her own life's unanswered questions. Could she have been a better mother? Why had her compassion waited until so late in life to surface?

Jackie's visit had stirred the sludge from the bottom of the pond. At first, Choo-choo blamed her daughter's lifestyle on their estrangement. Easy answer: Jackie was a lesbian, and therefore had pushed Choo-choo away out of fear of rejection. But didn't her daughter know? Choo-choo loved her, always would.

Choo-choo frowned, shook her head. But it was more than that. The problems went much deeper. All the times Choo-choo had held the infant without feeling a connection. The times she had brushed the little girl aside whenever she rushed toward her mother with open arms. The times she had ignored the troubled teenager.

After three days, she and Jackie had carved a few inroads. But where would they go from here?

Choo-choo took a sip of coffee, watched a second male cardinal arrive. The two fought for dominance of the birdfeeder. Was everything on this earth a struggle? Charlie hovered just above her shoulder; she often sensed his spirit, but more often lately. Over and over during the conversations with Jackie, Choo-choo had heard Charlie's words in her mind: "Judge not, Choo-choo. Judge not."

Jackie had talked. Ranted. Shared. Cried. And her mother listened. Finally, really listened.

Choo-choo lifted her gaze upward. "Thank God you were there to shield her from my indifference, Charlie." It had not been enough to cloth, bathe, feed, and provide shelter. Every child deserved to feel cherished. Every child deserved to feel good enough in their parents' eyes.

In spite of Choo-choo's shortcomings, Jackie Ivey had evolved into a secure and good-hearted woman. Once Jackie lowered her defenses, Choo-choo witnessed a keen sense of humor, thoughtfulness, and empathy: the same traits that had made Charlie Ivey such a golden man.

Inside, the phone trilled. Choo-choo huffed. What good was a portable headset if she kept forgetting to carry the stupid thing with her? And who was calling her so early, anyway? Surely not Elvina. They had an agreement about not phoning first thing in the morning, unless the gossip was so hot it couldn't cool down before delivery. She bustled in and caught it on the fourth ring.

"Mother?"

Choo-choo glanced at the kitchen clock. "Jackie? What's wrong?"

"Oh, did I wake you? You always get up so early, I figured—"

"I've been up a couple of hours, but it has to be what, four a.m. there?"

"I couldn't sleep. I have to talk to you about something."

Jackie calling to talk? Was she ill or . . . dying? Oh, heavens no. Not now, when they had finally reached a square of common ground. Choo-choo settled into a kitchen chair.

"Mother, are you there?"

"Yes dear."

"Tee and I were discussing Thanksgiving."

Oh that was it. "You're not coming."

"Maybe . . . no . . . I mean . . ."

This new, odd Jacqueline took Choo-choo off-guard.

"We would—*I* would—like for you to consider coming out to Portland for the holidays."

"Oh?"

Jackie's voice picked up its pace and took on the tone of a delighted child. "I'll take care of the reservations. If you'd be willing to make the flight. I'll make sure someone assists you between gates in Atlanta, and Tee and I will pick you up at the airport."

"Well, I . . ."

"And you can stay until after New Years'. It's only a little over a month. I can show you around, you can see our house."

Jackie wasn't just asking her into her house, she was inviting her into her life. Choo-choo felt warmth around her heart. Usually she might attribute it to acid reflux, only she hadn't eaten breakfast yet, and this glow felt gentler.

"I've always wanted to visit that part of the West Coast." And besides, this way she wouldn't have to run all over Tallahassee searching for that free-spirit, organic turkey.

"G-g-great! Okay, so I'll check with the airlines and call you back as soon as I have details. Hey, I'll even spring for first class. And you have to get a cell phone. Even one of those short-term ones without the contract. I'd like for you to be able to reach me. Okay?"

"All right, dear."

"Gotta run. Love you, Mom!"

Choo-choo barely managed to squeak out the words, "Love you too, Jackie." She clicked the disconnect button and set down the phone as if it was fine china, and very fragile.

"She called me *Mom*." Choo-choo looked up. "Hear that, Charlie? Our daughter called me mom!"

The phone rang and she jumped. Oh, no. Jackie's changed her mind.

When she answered, Choo-choo heard Loiscell's voice, strained and breathy. "Something awful has happened. You best get on over here to Abby's house as soon as you get dressed."

"What in the world?"

"I'd rather not say over the phone."

Choo-choo ran her hand through her unkempt hair. "I haven't even had my bath."

"Just come."

Two weeks after suicide, Thursday

Glenn Bruner looked from the window of the small prop plane to nothing but miles of tropical forest. No use asking the idiot pilot questions. The man knew only a few words in English. The rest of their limited communication had been accomplished with gestures and grunts.

With no small talk to pass the time, Glenn had room to think about how things had gone down. Good thing, too. Took his mind off his sore midsection. Kevlar vest aside, his chest still felt like he'd been stomped by a bull moose.

The man known as Glenn Bruner was no more; that fact appealed to him. These things happened. Most people knew a fraction of what went on behind the scenes. Still, how the Feds had staged his disappearance had been impressive. Too bad he couldn't be in Chattahoochee to witness his own funeral. Would Sheila cry? He really didn't give a rip. And who, or what, would they put in the coffin? Rocks? Some stiff, homeless sap stand-in? Or would they send some random ashes to Sheila? That would make more sense. No lingering evidence.

Excitement trilled his body like thundering acid rock. How many men had the chance to taste true adventure? No more eight-to-five bullshit. No more lame life. He could be anyone he chose, take any name he fancied, and have a different woman every night.

Would he be the good guy or the bad guy? Now that he was out from under the clutches of the authorities, the choice was his. Crime was a lucrative business. He could have a fleet of boats, a new truck every year, and hot and cold running women. His services from this point forward would go to the highest bidder.

A change in the pitch of the engines alerted Glenn. The plane descended and landed on a dirt strip, a slash between the dense tree canopies. The pilot motioned for Glenn to deplane, threw a couple of wooden shipping crates from the cargo hold, and gestured for Glenn to move aside before he crawled back into the cockpit. The plane taxied away and took off, leaving Glenn alone with the sounds of strange birds and wildlife.

He sat down on one of the crates. Just yesterday, he had been cooped up in a narrow cell. Glenn looked around. What the pluperfect hell was he supposed to do now? Squat here in the midst of some god-forsaken jungle and wait for the mosquitoes to feast? Did any of the bigger critters eat people?

A motor noise broke through the riotous jungle sounds. A Jeep appeared at the edge of the clearing and sped in his direction. It halted feet from him, kicking up a wake of dust. The driver—a massive muscular black man dressed in crisp khaki shorts and a T-shirt—stared at Glenn from behind dark sunglasses. He jerked his arm from Glenn to the crates. What the hell? Glenn frowned, but loaded the two crates into the back of the vehicle. Dude was huge and Glenn was too damned road-weary to pick a fight. Later he'd make sure to explain the proper way to treat the new boss from the U. S. of A.

Glenn vaulted into the passenger seat and grabbed onto the steel roll bar with one hand and the underside of the seat with the other. The Jeep jostled over a rutted trail worse than any pig trail leading into his old hunting camp. A runaway tractor ride with a drunken redneck would have been smoother. A couple of times, all four tires left the ground. Vines lashed at the vehicle's metal flanks, making a screeching noise like rabid caged monkeys. Finally, the driver slowed. They entered a planted field of some sort: row upon row as far as he could see. The trail widened and became less treacherous as the Jeep navigated the periphery of the acreage. A compound of white block buildings came into view. Guards with automatic weapons patrolled the front gate. The Jeep passed through unchallenged.

The driver pulled to the front of the main structure and killed the engine. "Go in."

Yep. He'd have to teach this boy some down-home Dixie manners. For sure.

The whole thing seemed like one of those spy movies. Hardly real. Glenn stepped onto the wooden porch. Two overhead fans turned in lazy, ineffective circles. The air hung thick. Sweat beads multiplied on Glenn's upper lip and moisture trickled between his shoulder blades. Crazy hot, worse than he'd experienced in ten hellish Southern summers.

Inside the building, a single window unit air conditioner struggled.

"Welcome, Mr. Bruner." A tall man with a faint accent—British?—stepped from behind a carved mahogany desk. He didn't extend his hand. "Drink?" He motioned to a crystal decanter of amber liquid and two glasses on one end of the desk.

Glenn licked his cracked lips. About time someone started to treat him like a guest.

A second glass container—this one with a lid—rested next to the decanter. Something gray and bloated bobbed in the clear liquid. Glenn stared. Couldn't help himself. The two shriveled graying objects looked vaguely familiar.

"Like my little keepsake?" The man poured, handed Glenn a glass. "Those private parts belong to the last associate who defied my orders." The man raised his own glass with a slight dip of his head toward Glenn. "Here's to a long and fruitful relationship, eh?"

The man waited for a beat before he spoke again. "One way or the other . . ." He shifted his gaze from Glenn to the floating orbs and back. "You are mine."

When the man smiled, Glenn couldn't help but notice his cold, vacant eyes. Glenn's hand trembled. He lifted the drink to his lips and took it all in with one slug.

Chapter Nineteen

Four weeks after suicide
Monday

Abby peeked out from a slit in the blinds. No reporters lurking by the curb in hopes of a hot scoop. Thank God for Elvina Houston. The woman was part saint, part high school hall monitor in charge of bathroom passes. And nobody got past her. People still dropped by Abby's house with food offerings, but the cards and flowers had stopped arriving. Chattahoochee settled back into reasonable normalcy.

Elvina stepped into Abby's living room with the last of her warmed-over coffee. "You need anything else, dear?"

Abby held one hand to her stomach. "I'm full, Elvina. Those soft-scrambled eggs were perfect."

Elvina glanced toward the back of the house. "I worry about that poor, poor girl. She has barely touched a bite since the funeral. And she's not big as a minute to start with." Elvina lowered her voice. "It's bad enough what all went down, even worse to have her husband so mangled, she couldn't even view his body."

Abby agreed. "Even with her injured shoulder, the only thing that seems to make Sheila content is cleaning. My house has never been so spotless, or so organized. The grout in the bathroom is white again. And she's helped me get rid of all kinds of stuff I had shoved back in the closets. I won't be surprised if she moves onto Daddy's workshop next. That will keep her busy for days."

"Her way of grieving, I suppose." Elvina checked her watch. "I have to get on up to the Triple C. You sure you two have what you need until Loiscell gets here?"

"We'll be fine. I can move around pretty good now. Choo-choo's down the road, and Ben will be coming by as soon as he's off work."

"You two are thick as thieves now aren't you?" Elvina smiled. "Won't be long, I expect, 'til we hear wedding bells."

"He asked, but . . ." Abby's cheeks flushed. Before everything happened, the thought of marriage would have clamped down her breathing. Now, the certainty of pledging her life to Ben wrapped around her like a hand-sewn quilt. Not too heavy, not too light. And comforting. "No time soon. I haven't had the chance to meet his son. Plus I still have another surgery to get past."

"I can't believe you've planned that for the week before Thanksgiving. You won't be able to eat a decent meal."

Abby snorted. "Not like I could enjoy any of it now. Most of my favorites are off-limits. I'll be home before the holiday. That's all that matters. By then, I may be able to have a slice of turkey and some mashed potatoes." Abby considered adding "I would *kill* for a salad," but anything referring to death, even in jest, gave her the shivers.

Elvina untied the apron and draped it over one arm. "At least you'll be pretty far along with your healing by Christmas. I'd hate you to miss out on the entire end of the year festivities."

"To be whole again will be enough for me." Abby glanced at her abdomen. "Don't get me wrong, having this colostomy wasn't the end of the world. It's keeping me alive. If I had to live with it, I could. The equipment is so exact, I'm barely aware of it. Still I'll be glad to be rid of it. It's time intensive, taking care of the skin around the stoma and keeping it all clean. I will never take my anus for granted again!"

Elvina tilted her head. "I guess I never gave mine much thought."

Abby jabbed a finger into the air. "Well you should. Everyone should. Matter of fact, I think there ought to be some kind of national appreciate-your-anus day, or something."

"Sounds like the kind of craziness Piddie Longman would've come up with." Elvina's expression softened with the mention of her friend. "I can imagine the T-shirt logos."

Abby held her stomach and giggled. "Like . . . *have you hugged your anus today?*"

When the laughter dwindled to a few sniffles, Elvina said, "I don't recall the last time I laughed hard like that. Makes my insides feel ten years younger."

"Mine too. Though the incision still doesn't like the work-out." Abby nodded her head once. "I've decided. I'm going to do everything in my power to return to work by the first of the year. Get my life back to normal."

Elvina frowned. "Good intentions never hurt, but you shouldn't rush yourself, sugar. Even after your new incisions heal, there's still a lot that's mending inside. Dr. Payne's wife and Sabrina are doing a passable job of keeping the front desk running. I hear a little grumbling around town, nothing serious."

"I can only watch so much *Ellen* and *Food Network*. The walls are beginning to close in around me." For the first time in as long as she could recall, Abby appreciated her small and ordinary life. "I *need* to get back."

Sheila Bruner sniffled through the entire yoga class. Not on account of her wounded shoulder. Joy took special care to point out the movements Sheila should either alter or avoid. All of the tamped down emotions—fear, anger, frustration, guilt—enveloped her like the black coroner's body bag she imagined wrapped around her husband. She had not viewed Glenn's body. Was warned against it. "Everything has been taken care of, Mrs. Bruner," the federal officers had assured her. Reality trickled in as the drama unfolded—the visitation, the expressions of sympathy, the memorial ceremony, and the tears that burned her eyes, yet never flowed. And the way people looked at her with their unanswered questions.

Surrounding her, Sheila's friends formed a close circle. Choo-choo on her hot pink mat to the left. Loiscell in that deep purple bandana to her right. Ben in the row behind her. Beside him, Abby sat on a cushioned folding chair, doing the rhythmic breathing and a few upper body stretches as her incisions allowed.

The choreographed movements and controlled breath work brought the simmering miasma of emotions bubbling up from Sheila's core until it reached her heart. Intense heat blossomed where cold detachment had been since the FBI agents' visit. In reality, for much longer.

The energy seared and foamed. Sheila trembled with the effort to stuff it back down. Where it lived, had always lived.

What hours of prayer had failed to unleash, the yoga movements accomplished. By the time Joy's soothing voice led the final meditation, tears lined Sheila's cheeks. She couldn't make them stop.

"You okay, hon?" Loiscell reached out to touch Sheila's shoulder. "You didn't overdo it, did you? This might not be such a good idea."

"I'm fine," Sheila managed to mumble. She rolled the mat, jammed it and the meditation pillow into a duffle, and dashed for the double doors.

Choo-choo stood with her hands on her hips. "What's going on, you reckon?"

Abby watched the door close in Sheila's wake. "I'm worried about her. She's barely said two words since Glenn's funeral. She's seemed so . . . like she's going through the motions." Ben helped Abby to stand and folded the chair.

"I think we need to go to your house and be with her," Loiscell said. "Maybe she'll open up if we're there for support."

"She rode here with me," Loiscell said. "Unless she's waiting in the car, she's taken off on foot." She grabbed her mat and cushion and hurried from the room.

"I'll drive you home, Abs," Ben said. "Then I'll go on to my house. Sounds like this might be one of those girls-only things."

Choo-choo hesitated before she collected her yoga props. "I'm coming, too."

The four members of the Suicide Supper Club gathered in Abby McKenzie's living room. Oreo watched from his perch on a nearby chair.

Sheila cried: great, heaving sobs that shook her thin body. Loiscell hugged her from one side. Choo-choo sat on the other. Abby rested in the recliner across from the three with a box of tissues in her hands.

"It's okay, sugar." Choo-choo rubbed her palm up and down Sheila's back. "Let it all out."

"It's all my fault," Sheila managed between gasps for air. "If I had left Glenn years ago, this never would've happened. He'd still be alive. That woman in Tallahassee wouldn't be hurt."

"If. If. If," Choo-choo said. "If a frog had longer legs in the front, he wouldn't hit his butt when he hopped. There's more than enough guilt to go around, if you want to start pointing fingers."

Abby joined in, "I'm still not convinced Glenn wasn't involved with whoever we hired to . . . you know . . . to—"

"Kill us all?" Loiscell added. "Me neither, Abby. I'm not one to chalk it up to pure coincidence."

Sheila blew her nose. For the moment, the tears had stopped. "You're asking me to believe my husband actually signed up to kill people?"

Loiscell said, "I hate to speak evil of the dead, but Glenn was far from a saint, Sheila. If someone waved a big enough wad of cash in front of him, sure, he might have taken it."

Sheila's shoulders drooped. "That makes it even worse. That he might kill for hire."

"It's the only thing that makes sense, especially now. I mean, why would the FBI be involved? And who shot Glenn?" Loiscell said. "It's all so twisted."

Abby wiped the moisture from her eyes. "I still can't get over how close I came to not being here, how close we *all* came. What were we thinking?"

Choo-choo blew out a breath. "We weren't. That's the problem. I'm going to blame it on the awful summer heat."

The other three stared at Choo-choo. Abby's mouth hung open.

"You all know how this has been the most crushing summer in years. Weeks and weeks of over a hundred degrees and the air so thick you could slice it with a butcher knife. Makes folks do uncommon things." Choo-choo warmed to her theory. "Why, you hear on the news every winter, how some Northerner cooped up too long because of all that cold and ice, goes all crazy and hauls off and kills himself and a houseful." She stamped one foot for emphasis. "I'd match our gosh-awful summers to their winters anytime."

No one spoke for a beat until Loiscell said, "Hon, I do believe that's the most outlandish rationalization I have ever heard."

They joined in nervous twitter, then the mood soured.

Loiscell wrung the tissue in her hands. "If Glenn was the one, and he didn't do such a hot-shot job . . ." She glanced to each of the others in turn. "The one who gave him the orders is still out there. Waiting."

Sheila's crying started anew. "I don't really want to die."

Tears burned Choo-choo's eyes. "If things had gone according to plan, I wouldn't have had the chance to make things right with Jackie. God knows, I miss Charlie something fierce, even miss that silly little dog much as I hate to admit it, but . . ."

Abby snuffled. "And Ben and I . . ."

Loiscell hung her head. The outpouring of emotion overwhelmed her. "I have to start chemo and radiation again. Heaven knows, I don't want to. But Lisa will be with me."

212

Abby handed Loiscell a tissue. "We'll be there for you too."

All four women cried. When one started to calm, another started afresh. If the old cliché about "grief shared being grief halved" held true, the four women of the Suicide Supper Club would've reduced their bond of sorrow down to dust within a few moments.

Elvina Houston spotted Choo-choo and Loiscell's cars parked by the curb in front of Abby McKenzie's house. Those gals liked to get together after yoga, but they usually did their gathering up at Bill's. The front porch and living room lights were on. Had something happened with either Abby or Sheila? Sheila was having a bad patch of things, what with that husband of hers shooting her and that other woman, and ending up in jail, then getting himself killed on top of it. Elvina stopped walking and scanned the area. There didn't seem to be much action around the place; Elvina figured everything was okay. She walked past, not one to barge in uninvited. At the next block, she circled around. That's when she spotted it, that mystery car, parked a block over, in front of a vacant lot. Her hackles raised up something fierce.

As soon as she got sight of Abby's house again, she spied a shadowy figure creeping up the back stairs. Ben Calhoun? No, Ben would come in through the front. And he surely wouldn't creep.

The figure—clearly a male—groped above the back door jam. Abby kept a spare key hidden there. Elvina and the casserole committee members had used it to let themselves in. She hunkered down next to a line of shrubs and watched him unlock the door and disappear inside. Not right.

Elvina crossed the back yard, careful to keep to the shadows. She tiptoed up the steps, through the door, and inched inside. Her heart skipped. A man in black lurked in the dark dining area, watching the living room. Abby, Loiscell, Sheila, and Choo-choo sat in a cluster, crying and carrying on like someone had just shot Elvis. Words of warning formed in her mind. Before they reached her lips, Elvina saw the gun. Lord help!

The little black and white cat on Abby's lap lifted his head. His pupils widened and his ears flattened back. He rumbled low.

Elvina took a couple of steps back into the kitchen and grabbed the first thing she could find. No time to reconsider. She slipped up behind the man in black, reared back, and knocked the fool out of him.

Whack! The sound broke through the melody of women weeping: a strange noise like a metal paddle hitting an overripe melon.

The man in black managed to squeeze off one reflexive shot before he fell to the floor like a sack of concrete. The bullet went wild, shattering a hole in the sheetrock behind the couch. Didn't make much of a noise, a muffled pop. Everything happened in a scramble. Someone screamed. Sheila dove to the floor. Oreo hissed and shot from the room as fast as his three legs could run.

Everyone spoke at once. Choo-choo held one hand over her heart. Loiscell jumped up, arms gesturing in crazed arcs. Abby grappled for the phone. Elvina stood over the vanquished intruder with the heavy iron frying pan in her hands. Her hands shook.

Two men rushed into the room from the back of the house. Before Elvina could take fresh aim with the skillet, the older of the two called out, "FBI!"

The skillet dropped from Elvina's grasp and clanged on the wooden floor. Sheila grabbed Loiscell. Choo-choo's mouth hung open. Abby's eyes flicked from the crumpled man to the two agents.

The older of the two federal agents held out his hands. His voice came out soothing and even. "Ladies. Ladies. Let's all take a deep breath and calm down. Talk this out."

That voice reminded Elvina of the handsome black man who did the insurance commercials. The kind of tone that would make you buy anything and think you'd gotten one heck of a deal.

The man-heap moaned once, low. The younger agent—the one with the severe hair and stern expression—crouched down and slid two fingers to a point on the fallen man's throat. Nothing on the young agent's clothing was without a precise crease. He glanced toward his superior and nodded.

"I'll need for all five of you to sit, to remain seated," the older man said. "Miss McKenzie, put down that phone."

Without taking her eyes from the agent, Abby moved the cell phone to the table by her recliner. Elvina walked into the living room and took a seat on the couch.

The senior agent offered a thin smile. "Thank you." He swept his gaze across the group. Four women perched on the couch, at the edge of their seats. One sat in the lounger. "Agent Hurst and I will remand this man into custody." He paused, fixed his attention on each woman in turn, an intense look. "Remain in the house. Do not try to phone

214

out or contact anyone." His eyes bore down on Elvina. "Mrs. Houston, no text messaging, no emailing."

Five heads bobbed ascent. Elvina remained silent. The young agent slid a white packet from one pocket, snapped and held it beneath the prostrate man's nose. The man shuddered; his eyelids flickered and opened. He moaned again. Agent Hurst shoved him into a prone position, pinned his hands together, and secured them with a thin plastic strip.

The senior agent joined his partner and they pulled the bound man to his feet. The man's head bobbed back and forth. Then they shuffled him through the dark dining room and out the back way.

The door snicked shut. Elvina jumped up and scuttled to the side window and parted the blinds. "They're shoving him into the back of a car."

"Police car?" Abby asked. Oreo peeked around the hall corner, meowed, then three-legged back into the living room and scrabbled into Abby's lap.

Elvina glanced over her shoulder. "Dark sedan. Probably a Crown Vic. Feds always drive Crown Vics."

Choo-choo cleared her throat. Tried to speak twice before the words finally came out. "You watch too many cop shows."

Elvina didn't turn around. "I know what I'm talking about. Those Feds keep Ford in business. Why do you think that company did so well when the rest of the automakers were floundering? The U. S. of A. government, that's why. Whoa!" She released the blind slat and bustled back toward the couch. "One of 'em's coming back in."

"Which one?" Choo-choo asked.

"The handsome fella with the gray at the temples," Elvina said.

"Wickler," Abby supplied. "His name is Wickler."

Loiscell scrunched closer to Sheila and Choo-choo to make more room for Elvina. Agent Wickler entered. Amazing, how he stepped so light for a large man. Guess they covered that in Fed training.

The agent glanced around, spotted a spare dining room chair, and moved it into a position facing the women. "Ladies, this has been quite interesting for all of you, for all of *us*." Sweat stains ringed his shirt at the neck and armpits. "My partner is keeping our guest—" he said *guest* with invisible air quotes "—company. Time is crucial, so I'll cut off the gristle and fat and get to the meat."

He undid the top button of the pale blue oxford shirt and massaged the back of his neck. "Been a long couple of days. I know you want to phone your friends, run up a flag, call the papers, write a book . . ." His eyes slid to Elvina, "or a blog post." His pleasant expression faded; the cozy get-to-know-y'all party was clearly over. "That will not be allowed."

Elvina snorted in spite of herself. What did he mean she couldn't tell it all? This wasn't about Jan Silverman's bunion removal or some back-room love affair. It was only the most exciting thing to happen in this town since Jake Witherspoon's abduction and assault back in the late '90s, and this government fellow was ordering her not to crow?

Agent Whitaker continued, "This is far beyond what I have the leisure or clearance to explain. Suffice it to say, there will be grave consequences if any of you," he speared them with his glare, "break confidence. National security issues, the protection of everything you hold dear, everything good and American, depends on your coopera- tion."

Elvina's lips twitched. Laying it on a little thick there, Mr. Fed.

"We know everything about you." One corner of his lips lifted. "*Every*thing. The actions you all took are punishable, could drag you down, through the courts, attorney fees, public knowledge of your little . . . arrangement."

Arrangement? Elvina narrowed her eyes and turned toward her friends.

"From this point, you will not discuss or acknowledge the events leading up to and including this evening. With any one, at any time." He paused. Breathed. The mantle clock chimed. The Visit Florida silk pillow toppled from her end of the couch and Elvina nearly jumped out of her skin.

Any other night, neighbors might still be moving around outside. Enjoying their yards, sipping beers. But the stubborn heat clung to its power and ran any sane person into artificial air. Any other night, one person would know something had gone south at Abby McKenzie's house. That person was sitting right here, in the middle of this circus. And she couldn't bark to another single soul.

Agent Wickler stood, returned the chair to its former position. He faced them. "Good night, ladies. May you not have the misfortune to see me again."

His steps made little noise. The back door closed behind him. A car door slammed; an engine started. A beam of light swished through the blinds. The motor noise faded until only the cicadas and the call of a lone owl fouled the quiet.

"Well now. Ain't that some shit." Elvina pivoted to focus on the others. "I'm in this thing up to my neck. Might as well spit it out. All of it."

Four weeks after suicide, Tuesday

Elvina Houston lowered her rump onto her bench seat beside the Piddie Longman Memorial Garden. Three squirrels appeared, eagerly watching her movements.

"All right. All right." She dug in the pocket of her skirt and pulled out a double handful of peanuts. "Here."

The rodents grappled for the scattered nuts. Two more joined the fray.

"Good thing y'all can't share the secrets I tell out here, or I'd have to ask you to leave." Elvina brushed the peanut husk dust from her hands.

"Piddie, I'm glad I have you to turn to. I've got a weight on me that I can't even share with Lucille. Looks like it's something I'll have to take to my grave." She paused. "Reckon I'm more like you than ever now, with no-tells to carry with me to the Great Beyond.

"I surely wish you were here. I feel more alone right now than I ever have." The crunching of peanut hulls punctuated Elvina's words.

"I was a hero last night. Me. Little ole me. And the sad thing is, I can't even take credit for it, on account of four people ending up in a mess of trouble with the U. S. government."

One of the squirrels nibbled and watched her from the end of the bench.

Elvina breathed out, deflating like a pricked balloon. "They told me all of it, Piddie. Still can't quite wrap my mind around it."

Another squirrel hopped onto the bench beside Elvina. She held out a peanut and it took it from her fingers.

"Honestly Piddie, when it comes right down to it, I don't know how I'd handle the fame of being a hero, because I'm not one, not really. I don't reckon anyone could stand by and watch someone cold-blood murder four people. Now those folks over at Bella Bella, the way they came out and took charge—they were the true heroes. For sure."

Elvina pulled the remainder of the peanuts from her pockets and threw them onto the bench.

" I . . . I didn't have the slightest clue that four women—one of which is a pretty close friend—felt so down and out that they had planned to get themselves killed. I don't feel even a little sorry for that Glenn Bruner. He was an ass. Got himself mixed up in something he couldn't pull clear of, and it cost him his life."

She dug in her pocket for a handkerchief. Wiped her eyes. Then directed her attention to the small garden where her best friend's ashes blended with the rich soil.

"Like you always said: If you dance with the Devil, don't be surprised when you end up with hot feet."

Chapter Twenty

Nine months after suicide
Monday

Abby McKenzie crawled onto a flat rock and assumed a lotus meditation position. She absently patted the spot where the colostomy bag had once been attached, still grateful at seven months beyond the second surgery not to feel anything but a five-inch raised scar.

No one had prepared her for the strange depression and sense of detachment that followed physical trauma. After the pain of reconnection and the slow process as her bowel adapted, Abby believed she was past the worst. Then, her attitude crashed and every day became a gray expanse. Ben stood by, offering support and steady love, and more important, allowing her time to totally experience each dark moment.

Three months out, a strange unfocused anger broke the surface. Everything and anything annoyed her. She lashed out, punched pillows, and screamed in the shower. When Abby scraped aside her deep-seated mistrust of all men, the Daddy Issues came bubbling up. She met them full-on with a counselor who urged her to "get to the core."

Remember, Abby. All of it. The times your father held you when you were sick. The times he cheered you on. The times he believed in you. The times he broke your heart.

The only way out was through. Abby kept moving until the weighty darkness eased a little. And her father became just another flawed person, doing the best he could. Her daddy.

Abby took a deep breath and closed her eyes. For a moment, her thoughts drifted to the time in the Intensive Care Unit, her body criss-crossed with monitor wires, IV tubing, and fluid-filled drains.

She opened her eyes to a better reality. Zion National Park's red rock cliffs soared around her. The air: clean, sweet, and dry. The sound of water trickling down the ferns suspended from the overhead grotto soothed her spirit. She smiled and closed her eyes again.

"Perfect!" Sheila held a digital camera at arm's length and aimed. "Now look all chilled out and peaceful."

Not a hard assignment. Abby focused on her breathing and allowed her shoulders to relax. She rested her upturned hands on her knees.

"Great! Got it!" Sheila slipped the slim digital camera into a small belt pouch and joined Abby. "I want you to take one of me too. Only, not here. Maybe tomorrow when we reach the top of Bright Angel Trail." She lowered herself to the rock beside Abby. "I just wish Loiscell could be up here with us."

"She's shopping like it's nobody's business, trying to find the perfect piece of Native American jewelry to take back for Elvina."

"We owe Elvina our lives. I pitched in for her gift."

Abby nodded. "Me too. Not like we could ever repay her. And Loiscell's content to hang out with Lance. It's great of him to take time to be here with us, helping plan the hikes and show us the best spots in Zion. I'm sure he'll work around his mom's limitations. She still doesn't have a lot of energy."

Sheila's gaze roamed across the red rock canyon. "Never thought I'd see something as beautiful as this. I'm glad we planned this trip."

"Yeah." Abby nodded, smiling. "I haven't had much time to spend with y'all since I returned to work—except for yoga."

Sheila reached over and gave Abby's hand a squeeze. "I'm so sad about Choo-choo. She should be here with us. I still can't believe she's . . . gone."

"She's here in spirit." Abby shifted her weight to relieve the cramp in her leg. One day she might be able to hold the lotus position, but for now, her feet went numb and prickly after a couple of minutes.

Sheila brushed red trail dust from the top of her new hot pink and purple hiking boots. "Who would've ever thought she'd pick up and move across the country like that? Elvina is still devastated."

"Choo-choo wanted to be close to her daughter. I mean—other than us, what did she have in Chattahoochee? Her husband was gone, her dog. Just her in that house with memories. The last email I got from her sounded upbeat. She's made new friends in the retirement condo, spends a lot of time with Jackie and Tee, and actually owns a computer *and* a cell phone. Imagine that."

Sheila toyed with a small beetle that had scaled her shoe. "I still miss her terribly."

"So we save up and take our next trip out to Portland. I haven't ever been to the Pacific coast. Heck, I haven't seen much of any place other than north Florida. Before I got sick, I hadn't taken more than two days off in a row since my parents died."

The two friends sat in compatible silence for a few moments before Sheila spoke. "You and Ben, that whole thing is so wonderful."

Abby looked down at the modest engagement ring circling her finger. "Yeah, he is all that."

"Suppose I'll be losing my roommate soon." Sheila glanced over and winked.

"No rush. Ben and I want to take our time getting to know each other better. Though, we had a pretty intense crash course with my surgeries."

"No doubts then?"

"I can't imagine my life without him."

Abby would tell Ben everything about the Suicide Supper Club. It was time; she agreed with her counselor. No more hiding behind that last wall of fear. Ben had seen the insides of her guts; what could possibly compare? Symbolic, really.

Sheila removed the beetle and placed it on a fern. "One day, maybe I can find that kind of love."

"Anything and everything is possible," Abby said. "You can live at my house as long as you want, or need to. You know that. Ben and I both own homes. We can always rent mine, or his, to you after we're married. It'll work out."

"That won't be necessary, Abs. I've made a few decisions." Sheila raised her arms to encompass the rock cliffs, then brought them back down and wrapped herself in a hug. "Being out here in all of this amazing glory has helped. I'm going to renovate our—*my*—house."

Sheila's features softened. "I've never had a place of my own. I went straight from my aunt's house—she raised me after my parents were killed in that wreck—to Glenn's. The house is paid off, on account of the mortgage insurance. And I have a little of Glenn's life insurance and 401K money left after paying off the credit cards and buying my little Honda. Of course, that truck and boat are history. Good riddance." She brushed her hands together. "I'll repaint my house, inside and out." She splayed her fingers in the air. "Bold, modern colors. New furniture, refinish the wood floors. And I'll set up one bedroom for Buttercup. My cat has lived too long as a hobo."

"I thought the house reminded you—"

"It does. It *did*." Sheila frowned. "I've lived a lot of my life there, and some of the time was happy. Most wasn't. But a house is only a shell you make into anything you want."

Abby high-fived her friend. "Atta girl! That counselor you've been seeing seems to be helping you get your stuff together." She motioned to Sheila's colorful hiking ensemble, so bright and wacky, Abby almost had to squint to look at it. "Heck, even your wardrobe's different. I haven't seen you in one of those Stepford-wife dresses in months."

"Packed them up and gave them to the women's refuge house in Tallahassee. I have a long way to go still . . . I've even had this crazy idea of how I can make a living."

"I'm all ears."

Sheila's eyes sparkled. "You know how I like to clean and organize?"

Abby laughed. "You're kidding, right? All of the labels on the canned goods in the pantry are facing forward, and I can see the floor in Daddy's shop."

"My point. I want to start a cleaning and organizing service. Not like a weekly maid business. I'll go in and help people clear out their clutter, get things more manageable. Like I did at your house. The whole idea makes me quiver."

"Love you to death, Sheila, but you are one strange bird."

"You ready for what I'm going to call my business?"

Abby waved one hand through the air. "You're on a roll. Don't stop now."

"The De-Clutter Diva." Sheila beamed.

Abby's eyebrows shot up. "The logo possibilities are floating through my mind. *Let the Diva De-clutter Your Dive.*"

"Catchy." Sheila tilted her head, considering. "I already have a couple of potential clients. One is Lucinda Myers."

"That woman Glenn shot? Get out!"

"We've kind of become friends. Strange, I know. I visited her in the hospital, then we started talking over the phone." Sheila paused, pointing to where two deer had stepped from a thicket of woods. In the national park where no hunter's gun held them in its sights, the animals appeared unalarmed by the presence of humans.

222

Sheila slipped the camera from its pouch and snapped a couple of pictures. "Can't believe they're so calm."

"It's almost like they're paid park employees." Abby glanced at her watch and pantomimed. "C'mon, Harold. Fluff your tail and get a move on. We're supposed to be down by the river at eight sharp! They're unloading two busloads of tourists from Michigan."

They laughed. The deer stopped grazing long enough to take note of them, then continued to nibble without concern.

Sheila's eyes glistened. "I believe in divine intervention, and that good can come from bad. Do you?"

"After what we've all been through? Yes, I'd say I give it credence."

"Lucinda and her husband were out to dinner that evening, discussing separation and possibly divorce. But after they had to go through everything . . ." Sheila smiled. "Lucinda told me they have found their way back to each other. They're not perfect, but they're at least trying."

Abby twirled the engagement ring around on her finger. A good fit—not too loose but not binding. Ben, with his crooked smile that sent a warm glow from her heart to parts in the nether-lands. Steady Ben. Old-fashioned Ben. They hadn't become intimate yet. Imagine that.

From easy friendship founded in drama and trial, to gentle affection, to devotion based on respect. Wasn't that giddy teenage lust based on the first guy who looked her way and winked. Technically, she'd be a virgin on their wedding night. Six fumbling times in her late teens didn't count as a love affair, nor a marriage. This coupling would be new. She hoped it would prove permanent, with plenty of time to explore and be explored. Sounded so romantic, two lovers paddling into the crimson sunset with a host of angels singing the chorus.

And her hair. Even that had improved. The short, layered cut with a different part—thanks to Mandy and professional hair products— looked half decent most of the time. Like Mandy said, "a woman can never have enough quality hair spray."

Her hair. Her life. Seemed as if she had a clue. She'd been a realist for so long, such blind optimism was an awkward stretch. Hopeful yet guarded, she might achieve.

Sheila's voice came out childlike, musical. "And Choo-choo is working things out with Jackie. Loiscell's getting stronger every day after her chemo and radiation. And you are—"

If Sheila could manage a bit of optimism, by God, so could she. Abby's gaze rested on a spot where the morning light created a crystalline halo across the canyon walls.

"Me? I'm good."

THE END

If you enjoyed this book, the author would appreciate the time you take to leave a review on the book's webpage on Amazon.
She thanks you, hon!

Want to read more from Rhett DeVane? These titles also available online from Amazon.

Other titles in the Southern fiction series:

The Madhatter's Guide to Chocolate
Up the Devil's Belly
Mama's Comfort Food
Cathead Crazy

Coauthored novels:

Accidental Ambition (with Senator Robert W. McKnight)
Evenings on Dark Island (with Larry Rock)

Middle Grade Fiction:

Elsbeth and Sim

To learn more about Rhett and her writing, visit her website and blog:

Rhett's website: www.rhettdevane.com
Rhett's crazy Southern blog: www.southernhat-titude.blogspot.com

A note from the author

I've always felt that stories come from some higher source—provided for me to write, or not. When the idea for this book arrived, I balked. A novel about a group suicide—are you kidding me? I'm part writer, part comedian. Suicide is serious, and I tend toward adding in a touch of comedy. How insulting would humor be for those family members that have had a loved one take this irreversible step!

But the muses wouldn't let me be. I started this novel many times, only to push it aside for other projects. Until it wouldn't allow that. Nope, they said, you're going to sit down at that fancy laptop and crank this one out, whether you like the subject matter or not. Either that or we'll move along to a writer that deserves our time.

Turns out, I should've listened from the start. Far from an endorsement of suicide, the story of these four very different, yet equally desperate women illustrates the endless possibilities of life. Plus, it showed me how full of dark humor and folly we humans can be.

If only one person on that cliff-edge reads this and entertains a way out other than death, this novel serves its ultimate purpose.

My best to all of my readers,

Rhett DeVane

About the Author

Rhett DeVane is a true Southerner, born and raised in the muggy, bug-infested forests of the Florida panhandle. For the past thirty-plus years, Rhett has made her home in Tallahassee, located in Florida's Big Bend area, where she splits her workdays between her two professions: dental hygienist and novelist.

Rhett is the author of four published mainstream humorous fiction novels set in her hometown of Chattahoochee, a place with "two stoplights and a mental institution on the main drag": *The Madhatter's Guide to Chocolate, Up the Devil's Belly, Mama's Comfort Food,* and *Cathead Crazy.* She is coauthor of two novels: *Evenings on Dark Island* with Larry Rock and *Accidental Ambition* with Robert W. McKnight. Also, Rhett has released the first in a series of middle grade fiction books, *Elsbeth and Sim.*

"One of the best things," Rhett says, "is sharing my brand of Southern crazy with others. When I write, and especially when I step in front of a mic, the stand-up comedian that idles inside me snatches the wheel. I never know where that kook will take me."

Rhett donates a portion of her book royalties. "It is important—no, vital—that I use what life has provided, to help others. Even small amounts over time add up. I may be a tiny ripple in a big pond, but that ripple can still make a difference."

Rhett writes to stay balanced. The way this world is today, it's a must. "Humor lifts me. I think it lifts others. As long as I am on this side of the dirt, I will find a way to laugh, and to share that with people."

Recipes from the SSC Ladies

It has been my custom to scatter a few Southern recipes through my novels. I figured this one might be a bit too serious in nature for such frivolity.

Then some of my faithful readers groused. So I thought about what the characters might say on the subject.

They spoke right up, told me they wouldn't mind sharing a favorite recipe, "not a'tall." Said food was what might make life worth living, especially after what they went through. "You see," they told me, "we Southern folk use food as a balm for most anything."

So I caved. Oh, and while I was at it, I included one of my own.

Rhett DeVane

Abby's Easy as Apple Pie

I don't cook. Well, sometimes if I have to. But this recipe is super easy and makes me look good.

1 stick of butter (room temperature soft)
I cup sugar
¾ cup self-rising flour
8 ounce Velveeta cheese, slightly melted
2 cans Whitehouse sliced apples

Cream together first four ingredients. Butter a small oblong casserole dish and spread apples over the bottom. Cover with the flour/sugar/butter/cheese mixture.
Bake in preheated 375° oven for 30 minutes.
Serve warm with ice cream or whipped topping.

Choo-choo's Grape Salad

This is one of my favorite salads. Easy, easy! Especially delightful in the summer, served cold. Use as a side dish or light dessert.

1 lb. seedless green grapes, washed and allowed to dry
1 lb. seedless red grapes, washed and allowed to dry
3/4 cup white sugar or equivalent amount of Splenda or Stevia Extract sweetener
8 ounces sour cream
8 ounces of softened cream cheese
1 Tbsp. vanilla

Cream together sugar, sour cream, cream cheese, and vanilla until smooth. Add grapes and toss with spoon until all grapes are coated.

Topping:

¾ cup brown sugar
1 cup chopped nuts

Toss sugar and nuts together until blended. Sprinkle over the top of grape mixture.
Chill overnight. Serve cold.

Note: I often use plain Greek yogurt for ½ of the sour cream. I use sugar substitutes for both the white and brown sugar.

Loiscell's Tomato Pie

When I was undergoing chemotherapy, my stomach couldn't abide spice or acidity. I got so tired of chicken and rice! As soon as I could, I whipped up my tomato pie and ate nearly all of it by myself. This is a good way to use those homegrown tomatoes and the sweet Vidalia onions we have down here, but it's still good with most kinds of tomatoes and a good, sweet onion.

1, 9-inch pie shell
½ yellow or white onion, chopped
3-4 tomatoes, cut in half horizontally, squeezed a little to remove excess juice, then roughly chopped to yield about 3 cups
¼ cup sliced basil (about 8 leaves)
2 cups grated cheese (I use sharp cheddar and Monterey Jack)
¾ cup mayonnaise
1 tsp. Tabasco sauce (or more to taste)
Salt and fresh ground black pepper

Preheat oven to 350°.
Cook pie shell for 8-10 minutes or longer until slightly golden. Remove from oven.
Squeeze as much moisture from chopped tomatoes, using either paper towels, or a potato ricer.
Sprinkle bottom of the precooked pie shell with the chopped onion. Spread the tomatoes over the onion, then sprinkle the sliced basil over the tomatoes.
In a bowl, mix together cheese, mayo, Tabasco, a pinch of salt, and a little black pepper. This will be a gooey mixture. Spread the cheese mixture over the tomatoes.
Bake until browned and bubbly, anywhere from 25 to 40 minutes.

Sheila's Banana Nut Muffins

I take these everywhere. Really good with coffee for a quick breakfast. This is a wonderful way to use those overripe bananas instead of throwing them out. I even peel and freeze the bananas and use them later, too. No use to waste!

1 ½ cups all-purpose flour
1 cup chopped nuts (optional)
½ cup toasted wheat germ
½ cup brown sugar
1 Tbsp. baking powder
1 tsp. cinnamon
½ tsp. salt
¼ tsp. ground nutmeg
2 ripe bananas, mashed
¾ cup milk
5 Tbsps. melted butter
1 egg
cinnamon sugar (optional)

Preheat oven to 400°. Fit 12 muffin cups with paper liners, then spray with cooking spray.
Mix flour, nuts, wheat germ, brown sugar, baking powder, cinnamon, salt, and nutmeg in a large bowl. Stir in bananas, milk, butter, and egg. Mix until blended.
Using an ice cream scoop, fill muffin cups evenly with batter. Sprinkle with cinnamon sugar if desired.
Bake muffins until a toothpick inserted into centers comes out clean, about 20-22 minutes.
Cool for 1 minute, then remove from the muffin pan and cool on a wire rack. Serve with butter or honey-sweetened cream cheese.

Rhett's Easy Pasta Salad

The last thing I want to do when I'm busy writing or editing is slave in the kitchen. I can whip this up in no time!

3-4 cups cooked pasta—rotini, small shells, or macaroni
1 can diced stewed tomatoes, drained of excess fluid
1 cup crumbled feta cheese
1 can artichoke hearts, drained and roughly chopped
1-2 Tbsp. extra virgin olive oil

Cook pasta in salted water. Drain. Splash with the olive oil and toss.
In a large bowl, mix together the tomatoes, feta, artichoke hearts.
Add pasta and toss.
Chill.

Sometimes, I add in 1 cup of cooked, diced chicken or canned chickpeas.

Book Club Discussion Points

1. The intense Southern summer plays into the drama of these four women's lives, providing a pressure cooker for their misery. What external factors have altered your life in such drastic fashion, and how?

2. One person's reason for suicide might seem trivial compared to another's. In your opinion, which woman proved the strongest case for such a measure?

3. Sheila comments that "good can come from bad." How did this play out for those involved in the Suicide Supper Club? Have you experienced this manner of twisty fate?

4. What about Glenn Bruner? Based on his past, how do you think his new life will work out for him? What caused him to take such a convoluted path?

5. Last, a loaded question. How do you feel about suicide? Is there any scenario where you feel it is justified?

Made in the USA
Charleston, SC
28 February 2014